Pilate's Daug

Fiona Veitch Smith

For Gill and the Kalk Bay writers' line

Table of Contents

Chapter 1 – Lake Tiberias, 28 AD

The moon shimmered over the lake, spotlighting the boat as it glided towards the shore. The guard watched it skirt the jagged rocks, its pilot expertly funnelling it into the safe channel that only a local could know was there at high tide. The guard yawned. Only fishermen and soldiers were up at this time of night. Still, he needed to keep his eyes open. The captain of the guard had told them at muster that some very important guests were coming to the palace – visitors from Rome – and that the king was anxious there would be no trouble.

The guests had arrived earlier that evening. He caught a glimpse of them as he was finishing his supper in the guard house. An aristocratic Roman family: a man in his forties, athletic in build with muscles that had slackened with age; a former soldier perhaps. His wife was a typical middle-aged Roman beauty: dyed blonde hair pinned high, and the painted face of a girl half her age. The guard doubted she would have been much younger than his own mother if she were alive – YHWH give her peace – but the privilege of wealth helped disguise it. Then there was the daughter. The guard couldn't get a good look at her as she was ushered into the palace by a bevy of serving women the moment her precious Roman foot touched the Galilean soil. He spat into the dust at his feet and churned the spittle into a little pool of mud.

The guard did not yet know their names. He would find out in the morning after his shift finished and he had breakfast. His stomach grumbled at the thought. There were still three hours to go before he could satisfy his hunger. Suddenly, the whiff of grilled fish teased his nostrils. He looked down the hill from his post at the gate and saw that the little fishing boat had landed and the fisherman had lit a small fire on the beach.

He shouldn't be that close to the palace, thought the guard, and decided to investigate. He roused his colleague who was taking a clandestine nap. "Stand watch, I'm just going to check something out." His colleague grunted and half roused himself. *Lazy Idumean*, thought the guard. It didn't really matter though. It would only take him a moment to usher the fisherman on. His hand moved to the hilt of his sword. He doubted he'd need it; the man was just a fisherman.

The Idumean was snoring again. The guard kicked him. "Wake up!"

"All right, all right," grunted the Idumean, shaking off sleep. "Stinking Jew," he muttered to himself.

The Jewish guard heard but chose to ignore him. He had a job to do: move the fisherman on and confiscate some of his catch for the trouble.

It was just a few hundred cubits down to the shoreline.

"Shalom, brother."

There was no answer. The fisherman's back was turned and he was bowed over the fire. The guard tried again: "You can't stop here. This is the property of the Herodians." Even as he said it, he realised how ironic that sounded with one Jew speaking to another. But perhaps this man wasn't Jewish. The area around Galilee had as many gentiles as Jews. He put his hand to his sword. "I'm speaking to you. You need to move on. Now!"

Suddenly the man spun round and the guard saw a glint of metal in the moonlight. He ducked and the knife sliced the air a hair's breadth from his scalp. The guard drew his sword and called out to his colleague on the hill. The fisherman lunged at him again and the guard parried, knocking the knife out of his assailant's hand. He kicked him in the gut and the man fell to all-fours. The guard pressed his sword-point between the man's eyes then gasped. "Matthias!"

"Shalom, brother. I have a message for you from Barabbas." The man called Matthias put his finger on the side of the blade about to pierce his forehead and tapped a rhythm.

"You all right down there?" came a voice from the hill.

The guard grunted then lowered his sword as he called up to his colleague. "Yes. I'll be up in a moment."

"Filthy Idumean," said the fisherman.

The guard smiled.

Chapter 2 – A Broken Vase

The lines were as finely drawn as Claudia had ever seen. She traced the red figures on the black background with her fingernail, outlining the form of the young lovers as they embraced. She circled the pedestal to follow the story as it unfolded on the three-hundred-year-old vase. It was a tale she knew well: the heroine was Antigone, the daughter of Oedipus and his mother Jocasta, to whom he had made love before knowing her true identity. Now Antigone was finally tasting love with Haemon, the son of Creon, who had taken the throne after her father.

Claudia stroked Haemon's back with her knuckle; the fine cracks in the glazed clay lightly grazing her skin. She wondered what it would be like if the Theban prince came to life and wrapped his arms around her, instead of Antigone. Or perhaps some god could turn her to clay and she could join the lovers in their tableau… whom would he choose? Should she intrude or should she instead become Antigone? Her tongue ran across her sun-chapped lips, softening her mouth for an imaginary kiss. She closed her eyes, tilted her head and waited for the kiss to fall…

The patter of footsteps and murmur of voices told Claudia she was not the only person awake in the palace. She looked over her shoulder, embarrassed in case she had been seen. *Be careful what you wish for*, she chided herself. Claudia knew Antigone and Haemon's tale would end tragically. Her finger followed the story from red figure to red figure until she finally cupped her palm around the grieving Haemon, clutching the lifeless body of his lover, buried alive in an underground tomb. He had arrived too late to save her. Claudia wished she could redraw the figures, or rewrite the play. But she could not. Their tragedy would remain for as long as poets wrote poetry and potters shaped clay.

The red figure vase was spot-lit by a beam of moonlight coming through the library window and illuminated from below by the glowing embers in a fireplace. The vase was the centrepiece in a spectacular collection of rare, valuable scrolls and objets d'art, famed across the Empire. She had slipped into the room barefoot and in her nightshift, unable to sleep in the unfamiliar bed despite being exhausted from the long journey from Tyre. The ship from Ostea had been forced to port before reaching Caesarea due to an unseasonable summer storm and she and her parents were breaking their journey to Jerusalem by staying a few days at the Palace of Tiberias, the official residence of Herod Antipas, tetrarch of Galilee.

She heard a door creek open and shut on the balustrade outside the library and the guttural "Shaloms" of the palace guard as they changed shift. She stepped out of the moonlight into a shadow in case one of the guards saw her through the window. But as she did, the sleeve of her nightshift caught a protruding handle of the vase – the vase that was over three hundred years old and worth, she was sure, more than her father would earn as governor of Judea in a whole year – and it fell to the floor with a bone-shattering crash.

Instantly, the door of the library opened and a slave girl, fully dressed, rushed in. Claudia leapt behind a chest of scrolls, hoping she hadn't been seen. She peeked over the chest and saw the girl hurry over to the shattered vase and poke at the debris with her sandal. Her eyes, as bright as a cat's in the moonlight, scanned the shadows and then stared intently at the chest where Claudia was hiding. "Who is there?" she asked in accented Greek and then repeated the question in Aramaic. Claudia held her breath, sure that her pounding heart would be heard.

The girl, still looking in the direction of the chest, sighed then lowered herself to her knees and began picking up the pieces.

"What have you done!" A male voice from the doorway. Claudia raised herself to see who it was, fearing it would be the owner of the priceless vase she had just destroyed. But it wasn't. It was a palace guard in full uniform, his bronze breastplate almost the same colour as the slave girl's eyes.

"The vase is broken," said the slave, matter-of-factly.

"And someone will pay." The guard stepped into the room, his military sandals slapping on the mosaic floor. Claudia thought for a moment that he was going to strike the girl, but he was only lifting his arm to undo his chin strap. Curly black hair sprung out like wool on a spring lamb and Claudia wondered what it would be like to twist her fingers into it. The guard shook his head and the curls loosened and fell to his shoulders. "Oh Nebela, what have you done this time?"

"I did not do it."

"But you will be blamed."

"I know."

The guard knelt down and started to help the girl pick up the pieces and place them in his helmet.

"Perhaps we can put another vase in its place. The storeroom is filled with artefacts the king's father collected and others he's received as tribute."

"And bribes."

"Yes, and bribes. This is just one of many. I've seen them: just like this with red figures on a black background."

"Do they tell the same story?"

"No, but you will only know if you look closely. Perhaps the king will forget which vase was on display. He changes them occasionally. He may not even notice…"

The guard looked down at the slave girl, expecting some gratitude for his help, Claudia assumed, but it was not forthcoming. The girl got up and fetched a broom and pan from the fireplace and swept up the finer pieces.

"Do you want me to get another vase before sun-up?"

"Thank you, Judah, but it will not help. It will be spotted and I will be punished. The king has had slaves skinned alive for less than this."

Claudia could take no more. She stood up and stepped forward into the moonlight. The guard leapt up, hand to sword-hilt. "Who are you?"

"I am Claudia Lucretia Pilate. Daughter of the new governor of Judea: Pontius Pilate. We are guests of King Herod Antipas and Queen Salome. And it was I who broke the vase."

"My lady!" The guard bowed and lowered his eyes. Claudia became suddenly aware of her sheer nightshift, clinging to every curve of her body, no doubt partially transparent with the moon shining through it. She wished she had taken the trouble to wear a cloak, but she hadn't expected to meet anyone on her pre-dawn excursion, let alone a handsome young guard. And – oh yes – a slave. She noticed the girl had not risen.

"Girl, what is your name?"

"Nebela, my lady."

"Nebela, you will not have to be skinned alive; though I doubt the king would go to that extreme. I'll confess in the morning. It will be an embarrassment for my father, and no doubt I'll be punished, but King Herod will not lay a finger on me, of that I'm sure."

"You are very kind, my lady." The guard's eyes were still lowered. "Isn't she, Nebela?"

Nebela raised her eyes – which on closer inspection were more amber than bronze – and looked directly at the Roman girl. "Yes, my lady, you are very kind."

Was that a smirk? Claudia wondered. But it was gone as quickly as it came, to be replaced by the generic dead-pan expression of any slave, in any home, in any part of the Empire.

"Clean this up," she commanded; unnecessarily she realised, but at least it gave her a line on which to exit. And as she left the guard and the slave girl still kneeling on the library floor, she wondered if they too were lovers.

Chapter 3 – The Hunt

Judah ben Hillel didn't enjoy being on horseback. He had never ridden as a child and had only learnt the most cursory elements of horsemanship in order to secure his appointment as a palace guard. The beast between his legs seemed to sense his nerves and kept jerking its head to left or right and pawing at the ground, forcing him to keep the reins constantly taut and to clench his thighs and buttocks as if he needed to relieve himself. Fortunately his incompetence in the saddle was overlooked by his military superiors as he made up for his lack of equestrian skill with an above-average ability in hand-to-hand combat. If Judah was ever called to fight in a formal, pitched battle, it would be as an infantryman.

However, in the nine months he had spent at the Palace of Tiberias, there had been no hint that the army of Herod Antipas was about to be called upon to defend the borders of the realm. To the north, the vassal states of Syro-Phoenicia and Asia Minor were well under Rome's thumb, while to the south, beyond Roman-run Judea, there was Idumea, birthplace of Herod Antipas' father, Herod Agrippa, as well as Arabia and Egypt: all were as submissive as kitchen mongrels at scrap time. To the east, Antipas' brother Philip – tetrarch of the Decapolis – provided a buffer from the potentially threatening Seleucids and Parthians, but these days the Eastern tribes appeared more interested in maintaining their trade routes than expanding their territory.

Apart from the occasional foray of Zealot raiding parties into the region – and the conflict of interest that always brought him – Judah had to admit that life in Galilee was a pretty cushy posting. The spa town of Tiberias provided baths, taverns and theatres. The guards were encouraged to relax as much as possible on their days off and many of them had girlfriends in the town. The Jewish guards were allowed to take off the Sabbath as well as all of the seasonal festivals. Antipas was a Jewish convert – although his lifestyle might not suggest it – and he was keen to keep his Jewish and gentile staff and subjects equally happy. Judah, a far stricter Jew than his master, did not approve of the lax standards of observance at the palace but was grateful to be allowed to attend the synagogue and follow his own ritual observance without harassment. And so he did. He hoped one day for a posting to Jerusalem – that most holy of cities and the jewel in YHWH's crown – but for now this is where he had been instructed to stay.

Today, Judah was part of a detachment of a dozen Herodian guards riding on the left flank of the royal hunting party. Their Roman counterparts – a dozen to match – were riding on the right. Together they formed a protective phalanx around the party of aristocrats. Judah's captain had given them strict instructions to polish their breastplates until they could see their faces in them. The plumes on their helmets were combed and trimmed and their leather kilts buffed to a sheen. Their swords, of course, were sharpened to a razor edge, sharp enough to shave the hair off a hog's backside.

The Romans were equally resplendent, but, Judah noted smugly, looking a little travel-weary after their ride from Tyre yesterday. Today they were again accompanying the Roman governor and his family, just as Judah and his companions were accompanying the Herods.

The hunting party had left just after the midday meal, giving Judah time to catch a few hours sleep after his night shift. He would have had more time if he had not been distracted by the goings-on in the library just before dawn. He cast a glance at the Roman girl – Claudia Lucretia Pilate, she had called herself – and wondered if she had indeed been punished as she said she would be. Her face was unblemished, so if her father had struck her, it didn't show. She had confessed, though, he was sure of that: Nebela had come to tell him about it before he mounted for the hunting party. Apparently the king had just laughed it off saying he valued the friendship of his Roman guests far more than an old Greek pot. Both Judah and Nebela knew he would not have felt the same if a slave had indeed broken it. And although they might not have been skinned alive – Antipas was not as brutal as his notoriously bloodthirsty father – they would certainly have been whipped within an inch of their lives. Judah was grateful that Claudia had spared Nebela, even if the Babylonian girl did not seem to appreciate it.

There was nothing romantic going on between Judah and Nebela – heaven forbid he should consort with a gentile – but he had a soft spot for the girl and had on more than one occasion helped her out of trouble. She had not been born a slave, apparently, and she found it difficult to bite her tongue and know her place. Judah knew exactly how she felt, being compelled to kow-tow to a self-appointed royal dynasty that was not really Jewish at all. Judah shook his head, forcing the thoughts from his mind. He could not afford to be distracted. He had a job to do, and if that meant feigning allegiance to a puppet king for the greater good of the Kingdom then so be it.

The horse pulled again to the right, sniffing out the fresh water of the lake. It was chancing its luck. It had been amply fed and watered before the hunt and would be again afterwards. Life at the Palace of Tiberias was a cushy posting for the horses too. Judah looked across at the quiet bay mare ridden by the Pilate girl. From what he'd seen of her temperament a few hours before he was surprised that she had accepted such a placid mount. Perhaps she was tired too. He stifled a yawn.

The Roman girl had surprised him. She was not what he had expected. Yes, she was beautiful, with her chestnut hair and blue, almost violet eyes, but he had guessed that much when he saw her step out of the carriage. Up close though, she was breath-taking. Judah cast another furtive look in her direction. She was wearing a sage green riding cloak, which unlike her sheer nightshift, modestly covered what Judah had earlier seen of a ripe young body. Judah flushed and again shook his head to rid himself of such distracting thoughts. A hood covered much of her hair, but a stray tendril caught the breeze and plastered itself against her cheek. She flicked it away impatiently. She looked distracted; those remarkable eyes – the colour of the sky before a summer storm – were fixed on a distant horizon. Judah doubted she was looking for the wild boar the rest of the party was pursuing.

Suddenly, the hounds bayed; they had caught the scent. King Herod, as squat as a toad on his long-suffering mount, let out a cheer and hailed the party forward. All but Claudia spurred their horses into a gallop. But none of the guards or the royal party seemed to notice she had been left behind. Judah, whose horse was galloping along with the rest of them, called over to his captain: "Sir! The girl! The Roman!"

The captain looked back and grimaced. "Damn!"

"I can get her sir," Judah shouted above the clatter of hooves and baying of hounds.

"Do it," ordered the captain before digging in his heels and surging forward with the rest of the pack.

With more muscle and willpower than horsemanship Judah forced his horse to slow and turn, then galloped back to where Claudia and the bay were clopping quietly along. However, he was not able to stop his mount in time and they nearly ran into the more placid pair. His horse swerved violently at the last moment, throwing him out of the saddle. It then reared up, hooves flailing the air. The terrified bay reared up too, throwing a startled Claudia to the ground like a sack of potatoes.

She lay still for a moment and Judah feared she had been knocked unconscious – or worse. But before he could reach her, she groaned and stirred and looked up at him, hovering over her.

"What in Hades' name do you think you're doing?"

"I'm sorry, my lady. You were being left behind."

"I wanted to be left behind!" She ignored his hand and clambered to her feet, dusting herself off. Her sandal caught on a protruding root and she stumbled. He reached out his hand to steady her. She whipped around and impaled him with her violet eyes. He immediately let go of her elbow.

But then, she looked at him, curiously, and her eyes and voice softened. "It's you. From the library."

"Yes, my lady. Are you hurt?"

"What's your name, soldier?"

"Judah ben Hillel. Are you hurt, my lady?"

"Judah ben Hillel." She mouthed the words as if tasting an exotic delicacy. Then she laughed and her face lit up like the sun emerging after a short, sharp storm. "Well, Judah ben Hillel, I think I'm fine. At least I'm in better shape than the vase." Then she grabbed her mare's reins and leapt into the saddle with a most unladylike bound.

"Are you coming or not?"

Flustered, Judah scrabbled for his own horse's reins and tried to mimic her leap. But his horse, unsurprisingly, conspired to humiliate him and stepped aside at the last moment. Claudia laughed again and reached out to hold his horse steady. Red-faced, he finally managed to mount the beast and together he and Claudia rode to catch up with the hunting party; but this time, she set the pace.

*

A Dream of Procula Pilate

What's that? Over there: down that alley? A procession? A hunt? It matters not. He means nothing to me. The one who does, where is she? I still feel her, filling my belly, stretching my flesh. I'm going to burst if she doesn't leave me. I will lose myself if she does. But I still feel her, screaming her way out into the world. Flesh of my flesh, bone of my bone. We are one. The hunt has moved on. I'm running in the opposite direction. I've forgotten my sandals. The cobbles are cutting me; curses on these Jewish stones. Why can't they smooth them off like they do in Rome?

Chapter 4 – The Pilates

"But I want to go with you to Jerusalem." Claudia pouted at her mother who in turn raised her eyebrows in mock rebuke. Claudia, who could never be angry for long, softened her mouth into an ironic smile. "I'm being punished, aren't I? For the vase."

"Of course you're not being punished. Although perhaps you deserve to be. What were you thinking, parading around the palace in your nightshift?"

"I couldn't sleep."

"Neither could I, but I still managed to maintain my decorum."

"I would expect nothing less of a Claudian."

"Don't mock me, girl."

"I'm not, mother. Sorry." Claudia smiled winsomely at her mother until she was sure she had been forgiven, then turned her attention to the job at hand: trying to coax her hair into a semblance of a style. However, she was still perturbed about not being allowed to go to Jerusalem with her parents, and huffed and puffed as her hair would not obey her.

"Here, let me help you."

The girl relaxed under her mother's touch. Procula Claudiana piled and pinned her daughter's tresses into a style favoured by the Empress-apparent Livia, but it was perhaps a little too old for the seventeen-year-old seated in front of the cedarwood dresser. Claudia scowled mockingly at her again; Procula sighed and tried another style.

"What are you so upset about anyway? Jerusalem is full of priests and bearded old scholars. We just need to go there for a few days then we'll meet you in Caesarea. We've asked Herod to arrange an escort for you."

Claudia nodded her approval at her mother's renewed efforts with her hair. "I would simply like the freedom to choose for myself."

"Freedom? A decent girl doesn't have any freedom! You've spent too much time reading that Plato."

"It's not Plato who teaches about freedom. And a woman as intelligent as you would know that." Claudia raised her eyebrows and smiled at her mother's feigned ignorance.

But Procula's soft brown eyes narrowed. "Don't let anyone worthwhile hear you talking like that, Claudia. There's nothing more off-putting for a man than a woman who knows more about philosophy than he does."

Claudia huffed again. The last thing she wanted was to be drawn into a discussion about suitors.

"How's that?" Procula held up a mirror for her daughter to admire her handiwork.

"Lovely." Claudia pushed back a tendril of chestnut hair that had already broken free from its restraint.

Procula patted her own honey blonde tresses which, as usual, were immaculately styled. "Well thank you, Claudia. I always knew that I was a woman of many talents. If your father's finances don't pick up soon I could always become a hairdresser."

"Now mother, don't start that again. Father says that he's sure the budget will increase next year. And as soon as he starts making connections with some of the better class of Jews –"

"Is there such a thing, my dear?" said a deep, masculine voice.

The two women, startled, turned to see the object of their conversation enter the chamber unannounced. He looked young for his forty years; sixteen years in the army had seen to that. But his muscles that had first thrilled his wife had begun to soften. His cropped chestnut hair was greying at the temples but his violet eyes, so like his daughter's, were still bright and full of humour.

Claudia Lucretia rose and bowed slightly to her father and lord. Procula Claudiana, his wife, nodded her head to the man she loved even though his bloodline was so far beneath hers.

Pilate took his wife's hands and kissed them, one at a time, "I just heard something very interesting."

"Palace gossip?"

"I'd like to think of it as a bit of inside information. Apparently, it was not our daughter who broke the vase after all."

Claudia stiffened.

"Who was it, Pontius?"

"A slave, apparently. The Babylonian one called Nebela. Is this true, Claudia?"

Claudia shook her head, not in the least surprised that the palace gossip had got it wrong, but concerned, nonetheless that the slave – or perhaps the young guard – might get the blame after all.

"No, father, it is not. I did break the vase. But the slave was going to get the blame for it and I didn't think that was fair."

"Well, what can I say? That was very kind of you Claudia."

"Thank you, father."

Pilate stroked her cheek. "But don't forget your place, my dear. You are a Roman aristocrat. It has certain privileges and those less fortunate than you may interpret your kindness as weakness."

"Yes dear, don't become too familiar with the slaves. It's not our business how the Herods treat them."

"But they might have skinned her alive! Have you seen the way they treat their slaves, here?"

"It's natural to their race, my dear," said her father. "But let them not hear us say that. They have been very gracious in allowing you to stay here while your mother and I go on to Jerusalem."

Claudia opened her mouth to object, but closed it again as her father held up a warning finger. He turned then to his wife who was rubbing her temples.

"Headache?"

"No, no. I just had a disturbing dream last night."

"Again? Perhaps you should speak to an augur about it. Or, maybe we can find a soothsayer when we arrive in Caesarea."

"Perhaps."

"Are you up to meeting with the Herods? I can give your apologies…"

"No. It's all right. We need to be diplomatic."

"That we do," agreed Pilate ruefully, and ushered his family to their next appointment.

Chapter 5 – The Herods

The Herods were waiting for the Pilates in the white marble reception chamber at the Palace of Tiberias: the king's summer residence on the shores of Lake Galilee. Tiberias had been built in honour of the current ruler of the world: Tiberius Julius Caesar, the son-in-law of Octavian known as Augustus, who had been Antipas' father's best friend. At least, that's what the old man told his sons before he went mad. Nonetheless, Herod Antipas was proud of his palace and dreamed of the day that Tiberius himself might visit. But for now he would have to make do with the emperor's representative.

"I see you inherited your father's flair for architecture," observed Pilate.

"Thank you." Antipas bowed slightly, indicating that the Roman should join him on the couch. "It's a modest little place but I hope you and your family feel right at home."

"Oh, far from modest, Antipas. If this masterpiece is anything to go by, the palace at Caesarea should be spectacular." The two men chinked goblets and drank. Immediately a slave offered to replenish them. Pilate indicated his should be tempered with a little water.

"A fabulous hunt, what? We should have the hog later for supper."

"Don't your subjects mind you eating pork?" asked Pilate, who had been surprised that the object of the hunt earlier in the day had been a wild boar.

Herod tutted. "Not so much here in Galilee. I wouldn't do it in Jerusalem, mind. They're a bit more sensitive there, as you will soon find out. Stay away from the pigs. That's my advice!" He chuckled to himself, no doubt enjoying an image of Pilate shocking the Jews with a hog's head on his plate.

"And in Caesarea?"

"Much the same as here. A more diverse population. You, of course, are Roman so you can do what you please."

Pilate wondered if that was the best approach when dealing with the Jewish population. He was in two minds about being assertive or placating, but didn't want to discuss it any further with Antipas. He changed the subject. "The ladies seem to be getting on well…"

Procula Claudiana, tastefully dressed in a peach-coloured silk gown, was in close conversation with a spectacular Eastern beauty: Herodias, Antipas' second – or was it third? – wife. All Pilate remembered was that Herod had divorced a Jordanian princess to make room for her, and that had nearly led to a war. *Reckless*, thought Pilate, *totally reckless*. It wouldn't have been allowed to happen on *his* watch.

"They do indeed," agreed Antipas. "But let's discuss your trip to Jerusalem –"

"If you're going to discuss politics," Queen Herodias chipped in, her voice as imperious as the palace's décor, "I think we ladies should retire to the salon."

Procula and Salome, Herodias' sixteen-year-old daughter, nodded in agreement. Claudia, however, looked as if she was about to object. Procula shot her a warning look.

The king waved them away. "A very good idea. We don't want to bore the ladies, now do we, Pontius?"

Claudia looked at her father beseechingly. He tried to keep a smile off his face. "Most certainly not, Antipas, most certainly not." Then he winked at his daughter as she trudged off after the other women.

*

The ladies left the chamber, accompanied by two serving girls and a palace guard: the one called Judah who had apparently helped Claudia after her fall earlier in the day. Thankfully she was unharmed. Procula despaired of her daughter's boyish recklessness; it would not aid her in her quest for a husband.

Herodias led the way down a white marble corridor lined with statuettes of Roman gods and paved with intricate mosaics. From the main thoroughfare, Procula caught glimpses of rooms cluttered with chests and couches of Persian and oriental origin.

"You have blended East and West in a most unique way," observed Procula, cringing as they entered a particularly garish salon.

"You're too kind, but unfortunately, I can't take all the credit for it. My husband receives tribute from his home country of Idumea as well as the lands to the east every year. Although I tell him that a Roman house should be more minimalist, he never listens. We have only been married for a few years, so there is still time for me to change him."

Procula, aware of Herodias' previous marriage to Antipas' pleasant but idle brother Philip I, just smiled. "I'm sure it was quite a culture shock after living in Rome for so long with your first husband."

"Quite. But being the wife of a king has many advantages. My previous husband was merely a civil servant. The best he could do, I suppose, after his father disinherited him."

Procula chose to ignore the civil servant insult and instead mulled over what she could remember of Herodias' scandalous history, hoping to find a suitable retort to deliver at the appropriate moment. There was plenty material to choose from. Herodias was a child bride, married to the weakest son of mad King Herod Agrippa as payment for some regional alliance or other. Procula thought she might also have been a cousin of Philip I (one of two brothers by the same name), or granddaughter of his father by another marriage, was it? Oh, it was all too complicated to remember. But there was something about a bloody family purge when Herod tried to kill all his children and then Philip fleeing to Rome to escape it.

After that, it was well documented, and Procula had read all about it in her preparations for becoming the wife of the Governor of Judea. According to the records, two years after Philip and Herodias fled to Rome, the old king died and Caesar Augustus divided Palestine between three of the surviving sons: Phillip II ruled the northern kingdom Decapolis and Damascus; Archelaus took Judea, Samaria and Idumea, and Antipas was granted Galilee and Perea. Herodias' husband, Philip I, received nothing. By then a teenager with social ambitions, Herodias turned her attention to flirting with her brother-in-law Archelaus, ruler of Judea. But then her paramour fell out of favour with Rome and was replaced by a line of governors, of whom Procula's husband, the honourable Pontius Pilate, was the latest.

She wondered how Pontius was doing with the dreadful Antipas: what Herodias had seen in him on a physical level, she could not fathom. From what she could remember of Philip I, having met him once or twice at her parents' house in Rome, he was a good-looking man who had aged well. On the surface one could not see why Herodias had dumped him.

But one only had to spend a short time with the woman to realise that she was a creature of ambition.

Undaunted in her quest to be queen, rumour had it that Herodias lured brother-in-law Antipas into her bed while he was visiting them in Rome. At Herodias' insistence, Antipas then divorced his first wife to make room for her. Then approaching forty, and having been married to Philip for nearly thirty years, Herodias divorced him, married Antipas and relocated her then thirteen-year-old daughter and herself to Galilee. Salome, now sixteen, was Herodias and Philip's only child, born when they had given up hope of ever having children. Philip doted on her – an unexpected gift, he called her – but it was not enough to save the marriage. Procula felt sorry for Philip and the child from whom he was now separated, thanking the gods that she and Pontius had so far been able to provide a stable home for Claudia Lucretia.

*

The two girls were in animated conversation. Well, at least one of them was.

"So where has the Empress-apparent been seen lately?" asked Salome.

Claudia stifled a yawn. "The circus, I suppose. And the theatre."

"Did you see her?" Salome was sucking up the gossip like a leech on a festering boil; her almond-shaped eyes wide with vicarious passion.

"Yes."

"Where? *Where?*"

"Oh, I don't know. A performance of Sophocles, I think. She came in halfway through the first act. It was most ill-timed of her."

"Ill-timed? She's the Empress-apparent, girl! She can do what she likes. Did she leave early too?"

"Unfortunately, yes. Moments before Oedipus was to realise he had married his mother and killed his father."

Salome tossed her beautiful head like a wild mare. "Well, I don't blame her. All that boring family drama! Only dullards go to the theatre. I prefer the circus. I once saw…" she then went on to list a host of who's who in imperial circles.

Claudia doubted she'd seen half of them, but let her prattle on. Over the girl's shoulder she saw the guard – Judah was it? – standing to attention; his face impassive. It was a beautiful face, Claudia thought. His tawny skin set off his eyes like nuggets of coal. They were framed by dark brows, arching inwards towards a strong Semitic nose. Although he wore a helmet, Claudia could see a suggestion of black curls at the nape of his neck. He was clean-shaven, unlike many Jews; Claudia supposed it was because Antipas liked to model his soldiers on the Roman army. But there was a shadow of stubble along his strong jaw. She indulged herself for a while, wondering what it would be like to run her hand over it, but Salome's droning voice kept her from slipping too far into the fantasy.

Claudia sighed and wondered if the guard was listening to all this tittle-tattle. She raised an eyebrow and caught his eye. His lips twitched. Was that almost a smile? Claudia had to restrain herself from smiling back and focused in again on Salome's monologue...

"Then of course, there's the amphitheatre. I remember when Tiberius and Julia..."

Bored of all the social chit-chat but knowing her parents were depending on her to be diplomatic with the Herodian girl, Claudia changed the subject: "I believe your grandfather built the palace we are going to live in at Caesarea."

Salome's eyes lit up again and she gestured like an actor at the mime. "Not just the palace, the whole town! There was nothing there except rugged coastline before he arrived; now it's one of the most spectacular man-made harbours in the Mediterranean! He also built the new Temple in Jerusalem. Have you seen it yet?"

"No, not yet. My parents are going on to Jerusalem without me."

"Not surprising with those Jews all a-froth about one of their stupid festivals."

"But I thought *you* were Jewish?" observed Claudia, innocently.

The darker girl flushed and narrowed her sultry eyes: "I'm not a *Jew*! I'm Idumean; and a Roman citizen!"

Claudia thought she saw Judah tense; but she couldn't be sure. Nonetheless, she felt for a moment that they were allies, both offended by this ridiculous imposter: she by her efforts to be more Roman than the Romans, and he by her claim to be princess of the Jews while not being Jewish at all.

Claudia smiled mischievously. She couldn't help it. She could not abide social snobbery; she'd had enough of it between her mother's and father's families back in Rome and the temptation to put this pompous princess in her place was too much: "Ah, a Roman citizen. Your family must be *terribly* wealthy to afford that. It's only the best families, like the Claudians, who are born into it, you know."

"We didn't *buy* it, it was granted to my grandfather, Herod the Great, by Julius Caesar himself for conquering almost all the East on Rome's behalf! Now what have the Pilates done to compare to that? In a hundred years, the name Pontius Pilate will be lost in history!"

Claudia, with one eye on Judah, was about to retort when her mother interrupted: "What are you girls talking about history for?" I hope your daughter isn't like mine, Herodias, spoiling herself on intellectual pursuits instead of helping me to find a husband for her."

"No, this is the first time I've heard her talk this way," answered Herodias. "Now stop it, Salome, before your stepfather hears you. You know you don't have the mind to grasp such things."

Salome glared, but lowered her eyes.

Claudia felt suddenly ashamed for deliberately trying to humiliate the girl. "I'm sure that's not true, Queen Herodias, Salome has a very fine mind, I can tell."

Procula stifled a smile at the look of shock on Herodias' face, but realised, for the sake of diplomacy, that she needed to put her daughter in her place. "That's enough, Claudia Lucretia. Apologise to our hostess at once."

The two girls looked at each other for a moment, wondering if they were just temporary allies or future friends. Salome, weighing the two options, seemed to decide on the former: "Yes, I think you should apologise."

Glaring, Claudia rose to her feet, tossed a brusque "I'm sorry" to the queen, and stormed out of the room, blushing fiercely as she passed the Jewish guard.

"You'd better get her married quickly, my dear, before she takes herself off the market," observed the queen before selecting a truffle from a jewel-encrusted platter and not bothering to offer one to her guest.

Procula bristled. "Oh, I'm sure there'll be someone who appreciates her. She *is* a Claudian, after all."

Chapter 6 – A Walk by the Lake

Claudia curled her toes into the sand as cool water tantalised her ankles. She looked out over the lake: as smooth as glass and streaked with the colours of sunset. In the distance she saw some fishing boats silhouetted against the horizon with the backdrop of the town of Tiberias filling the skyline. To her left was the well-trodden path to a series of hot springs, with the snowy peak of Mount Harmon brooding above them. Behind her the Palace of Tiberias cast its shadow; she was hemmed in by civilisation; it was stifling.

But if she turned her head to the right, she could glimpse the wilds of Galilee leading off into the hinterland and imagine for a moment that she was free to go wherever she pleased. A ribbon of beach twirled its way along, skirting the grass, shrubs and trees; home to deer and wild pigs. An Ibis, startled by something or other, took to flight, and in its turn startled an Egyptian goose and her young who had been idling on the lake. The mother flapped and squawked her indignation at the Ibis before re-gathering her flustered offspring. Claudia smiled. She looked over at the slave, Nebela, hoping to share the moment, but the Babylonian girl's face was impassive. Her eyes stared beyond the horizon of Tiberias to some unknown place – perhaps the land of her birth – dreaming too, Claudia imagined, of what it might be like to be free.

Nebela was carrying Claudia's sandals during the evening stroll – no doubt reluctantly. Claudia had expected some kind of gratitude for saving her in the vase incident, but the thanks had never come. The girl was polite, but Claudia could tell it was only surface deep. It shouldn't really matter, she was only a slave, but Claudia felt sleighted. Truth be told, she was starved of friendship in this land so far away from home, and had hoped for some connection with somebody: even if it was just a slave. Salome was no longer an option. After the incident in the salon there had been at best a steely politeness between them; they would both be relieved when Claudia finally left to go to Caesarea. Claudia hoped there might be someone there she could confide in; someone she could call a friend.

And that person had to be of a similar station. It would simply not do for the daughter of the Governor of Judea to be touting for friendship with slave girls and palace guards. Judah, as usual, was hovering in the background, scouring the shoreline for signs of danger to his charge. Claudia sighed. Since the day of the hunt there had been no further interaction between them. She had been embarrassed by being put in her place in front of him and had avoided his gaze for the next few days. But when the embarrassment had finally worn off and she had sought to connect with him again, he appeared to have withdrawn from her. Or was it her imagination that there had been any connection there at all? It was impossible. She was a Roman aristocrat, he a Jewish guard. And as he continued to ignore her, Claudia realised that he knew his place even if she didn't.

Yes, she was ready to go to Caesarea; whatever little fantasies had started to brew were no doubt down to her being out of sorts after her long journey from Rome. It was time to leave this place. To her left she could hear the chattering of bathers as they sauntered from one hot spring to another. The renowned therapeutic qualities of the mineral springs attracted visitors from around the Empire. The wealthy paid good money to be allowed a place in the formal bathing houses erected over the spas, rubbing shoulders with aristocrats, generals and successful merchants.

Claudia's father, she knew, had been loath to leave the spa town to attend to his civic duties in Jerusalem. Like any other Roman, Pilate was obsessive about hygiene and spent a good few hours every day at the public baths. Not blessed by the naturally heated pools of Tiberias, baths elsewhere in the Empire made do with underground hypocaust heating: an engineering miracle that made cleanliness, if not godliness, accessible to even the lowliest citizens of the known world. Some masters even allowed their better-bred slaves to bathe alongside them, although that was not something Pilate approved of.

Claudia had bathed an hour ago. For her it was simply functional and she would have far preferred to swim in the open air – perhaps right here in the lake. Claudia felt the cool of the water slap against her ankles and fantasised for a while what it might be like to throw off her gown and swim across the lake. She wondered if the guard would think she had gone mad and try to rescue her. She smiled at the thought.

But no, decorum would not allow such a thing, and Claudia knew her bathing must be confined to the formal bath houses. So she had quickly moved from one heated room to another, allowing Nebela to oil and scrape her before plunging into the largest, temperate pool in the complex. On the way in she hadn't lingered in the exercise courts where scantily clad bathers worked up a sweat, and on the way out she bypassed the patio where patrons were enjoying a post-bath drink.

In fact, the overheated environment of the bath house had given her quite a headache, so she had decided to take in some fresh air at the lake. There were few people around, as most of the better-heeled citizens were either still bathing or preparing for the banquet to be held at the palace in Claudia's honour that night. It was not deserted, though, as fishermen from the villages hugging the forty-mile round shoreline plied their trade at this fruitful hour, coaxing the lake's inhabitants into their nets.

Claudia paddled a little further into the water, hitching up her lilac tunic to reveal gently swelling calves. A group of fishermen approached from the right, nets in hand, but were stopped by the guard. He said something to them in Aramaic. They muttered, then, disgruntled, turned back the way they had come. The group stopped about a stadion from the young Roman woman who had invaded their waters. One of them stripped off his outer garments and waded into the lake. He had a circular net, a *sagene*, draped over his shoulder. Then, like a discus thrower at the Olympiad, he spun around, building up speed, tossing the net over the darkening waters. By this time the other fishermen had joined him, but Claudia saw only him.

His white loincloth contrasted starkly with his sun-bronzed body, and though tall and lean, he had a well-muscled frame. As the older men closed in on the net, drawing it closed with tethers, the young fisherman stepped back to allow his elders to complete the catch. His long black hair had fallen free of its thong, and as he tossed it aside, he turned his face towards Claudia. Their eyes met, just for a moment, then he turned away to help his colleagues haul their harvest to shore.

Transfixed, Claudia didn't hear Judah approach her from the left. She jolted sharply as he spoke in simple Greek: "It is getting late, my lady. My lord Herod has sent word that you should return to the palace and prepare for the banquet."

Claudia was embarrassed. What had he thought of her staring so unashamedly at the young fisherman? Was he jealous? Or simply disapproving of her uncouth behaviour? Claudia sneaked a glance at him, but his face gave nothing away. Claudia was suddenly and inexplicably angry with him. She glared and then gathered up her skirt, waded into shore, and without looking back, headed straight for the palace.

Chapter 7 – The Banquet

King Herod Antipas had announced there would be a banquet to bid farewell to the Pilate girl, when he received a message that her father wanted her sent to Caesarea under armed guard as soon as possible.

There had been trouble in Jerusalem. Antipas wasn't surprised, but he was pleased. Pilate had a lot to learn about the Jews and it would pay him to listen to the tetrarch of Galilee in future. He had tried to tell him as much when the governor had mentioned his plan to march into the Jewish holy city carrying standards bearing Emperor Tiberius' image. But the Roman would not listen. *Perhaps he will now*, thought Antipas pleasantly as he listened to the breathless report of the Jerusalem debacle from his trusted servant, Alexandros, whom he had sent along to keep an eye on his new friends.

Pilate had swept into Jerusalem at the head of a cohort of four-hundred-and-eighty men, decked in full ceremonial gear and carrying the imperial image of Tiberius. Although common practice for an army to carry the standards before them, it was an unwritten law that this would never be done in Jerusalem. In fact, the holy capital of the Jews was the only city in the empire where the image of Tiberius was not displayed for public adoration: on military standards or public buildings. Pilate's predecessors considered the price they would have to pay if they offended the monotheistic sensibilities of the Jews and decided that discretion was the better part of valour.

But Pilate could not afford to be discreet and needed to stamp his authority on his subjects as soon as possible. He would never have been given this governorship if it hadn't been for the good graces of Tiberius who was a distant relative of Procula, as well as the influence of Lucius Aelius Sejanus, chief legate of the elite Praetorian Guard. It was a fabulous story and Herod had nearly choked on his wild boar when he first heard it.

Pilate, so the story went, was fortunate enough to have rescued the high ranking official from a rampaging bull while he was holidaying at the Villa Pilatus on the Black Sea. Sejanus was picnicking in a field bordering the Pilate property with a boy famed for playing female roles in the Roman theatre. It seemed that the lad's smooth cheeks and slim figure had attracted the attention not only of theatre directors but the husky Legate of the Guard too. Pilate, riding past and spotting his neighbour's bull charging at the blissfully occupied Legate, had done no more than rear his horse and shout abuse at the beast, but it was sufficient to distract the animal and allow Sejanus and his young friend time to leap over a nearby wall.

Sejanus, grateful to be alive and keen to keep his dalliance a secret (although the young actor had told a friend who had told a friend who had told Antipas), offered to have Pilate appointed to the next governorship that became available. The gods decided this was Judea.

The night that Pilate arrived in Jerusalem he headed straight for the fortress of Antonia and instructed the soldiers to erect the standards on the outer walls, so that the first thing the Jews would see on waking would be the divine Tiberius. It was, and all Hades erupted with wailing and crying in the streets and gaggles of priests tearing their clothes and throwing themselves at the gate of the fortress.

The howling went on for two days until Pilate and his wife could bear it no longer. Pilate refused an audience with the Jewish ruling council, the Sanhedrin, as its leader, Caiphas, the only member with whom Pilate had so far had any contact, was out of town. Not knowing anyone in the council chamber would have put the governor at a disadvantage, and Pontius Pilate did not like to be at a disadvantage. So he and Procula left Jerusalem under the cover of darkness and travelled the sixty miles to their new home at Caesarea. Pilate left strict instructions that the standards were not to be removed. "They'll get over it," he said to his wife as the howls began to fade in the Judean night. "Caiphas will understand. He knows how the world really works. We'll come back then, once they've accepted that Tiberius is greater than their god."

"Is that what he said?" asked Herod of the messenger who had told his tale with the finesse of a Greek actor.

"Yes, my lord," laughed Alexandros. "But he didn't account for the Jews following him to Caesarea."

"They followed him to Caesarea?" echoed Herod incredulously.

"Yes, my lord, a few hundred of them; including half the Sanhedrin."

"It just gets better! Pour yourself some wine, Alexandros. And top mine up too."

"Thank you, my lord. Hmm, a good vintage. Now where was I? Oh yes… the Jews in Caesarea. Well, they stood outside the palace for five days, imploring Pilate to remove the standards from the holy city."

Herod chuckled. "I bet that went down well. What exactly did they say?"

"Please, sir," mimicked Alexandros with a disgruntled whine, "remove the standards. They offend us, they offend our ancestors and they offend our God."

This time Herod guffawed. "Marvellous! Marvellous! What did Pilate say?"

Alexandros took a sip of his wine before continuing, "He said that to remove them would be to offend Tiberius and that Yahweh may be the god of the Jews, but Tiberius was the god of the world."

"The god of the world! Brilliant! I would have loved to have seen the look on their faces. What happened next?"

"Well, it really egged them on."

"I bet it did."

"But not to riot. They hosted a silent demonstration at the stadium."

"Ahhhh. Clever. How did Pilate react?"

"Well, initially with force. He sent in his troops to surround them and ordered them to draw their swords."

"And then?"

"Well then…" Alexandros sipped his wine, eking out the very last drop of dramatic suspense.

Herod was on the edge of his seat.

"…then the Jews closed their eyes and pressed their throats against the Roman swords. They said that they were prepared to die if Pilate didn't remove the standards."

"Poor Pilate." Herod chuckled.

"Indeed, sir."

"So what did he do?"

"He ordered the soldiers to sheathe their swords and for a messenger to go to Jerusalem to remove the standards."

This time Herod laughed so loudly it brought tears to his eyes. "Oh, I haven't had so much fun in ages! Round one to the Jews!" He slapped Alexandros on the back and downed the rest of his wine. "Come,

Alexandros, you have done well. Tonight you will sit with me at the banquet!"

*

Claudia was beginning to feel ill. She had had to endure an army of servants bringing in endless courses of food: enough to feed half the population of Galilee never mind the two dozen over-fed guests who claimed to be from the finest bloodlines in Palestine. The first course consisted of ten giant lobsters, garnished with asparagus, truffles and mushrooms, carried aloft on trays of silver. They were placed at intervals around the four banqueting tables, in easy reach of the reclining guests. The wine was already flowing and the diners tucked into the appetiser with relish.

Course after course was laid before them: carp, lamb, goat and boar – roasted whole with its tusks intact – and each dish washed down by goblets of the best vintage. Although Claudia suspected that the wine was getting cheaper as the evening progressed; not that anyone would notice though, particularly the diners who had to purge themselves over the balcony after each successive course.

Claudia had eaten her fill after the lobster and would have been happy to go to bed but it would not have been politic to do so. And she knew that her parents were depending on her to keep relations with the Herods on a positive note while they were away.

She was sandwiched between Antipas on the right and his brother, Philip II, on the left. Philip was a surprisingly good-looking man, despite approaching middle age, and was, initially, a rather charming dinner companion. They had shared a bit of small talk earlier in the evening and Philip proved to be as well-read and appreciative of the arts as Claudia. But it had not lasted long. As soon as Salome arrived – fashionably late and revealingly clad – Philip turned his full attention on his niece, leaning in to her every word in a way that left Claudia feeling decidedly uncomfortable. So that left her with Antipas. A man who clearly enjoyed his food, he took up more than his fair share on the dining couch and Claudia had to keep shifting her position to avoid his fat rolls sagging against her person. Each time it happened, she cast a furtive look to see if the guard Judah had noticed. But as usual, his face remained impassive. Claudia sighed. It was going to be a long night.

*

After the last of the boar was licked from his lips, Herod Antipas tapped his goblet to bring the guests to attention. They ignored him. He tapped a little louder: they ignored him again. Finally he drew a dagger and hurled it with all his might into the middle of the opposite table, missing a slave by the breadth of a boar's whisker. The slave stifled a scream and quickly withdrew to a safer distance. All eyes turned to the quivering dagger impaling what was left of a suckling lamb, then to their host who was equally aquiver. There was silence.

"Now that I have your attention," said Herod, slowly bringing his breathing under control, "I suggest that we have some entertainment before we enjoy dessert."

"What kind of entertainment, brother?" asked Philip.

"Well, seeing that it is Claudia Lucretia's last evening with us, I propose that *she* entertain us." A murmur of agreement spread around the tables as the guests looked at Claudia with one eye and the dagger with the other.

"What say you Claudia? Will you do us the honour of performance?"

"If you wish, Lord Herod."

"Oh, I wish. And I'm sure my brother does too."

"Yes," Philip smiled, "I think a performance from the lady would round the evening off very nicely."

"Very well, then." Claudia ignored the dagger-like stares from Salome and took Philip's proffered hand. He helped her over the couch and she was aware of him watching her as she walked to the centre of the banqueting hall. It made her feel even more ill than she already did.

She was wearing a gold gown that shimmered in the light of a thousand candles. The bodice was fashionably cut to enhance the shape of her bosom without revealing too much; the skirt lightly caressed her thighs before cascading to the floor like a golden waterfall. Precious jewels twinkled in her softly flowing chestnut hair held aloft by a delicate tiara, while her violet eyes shone below her finely-shaped brows.

The musicians were poised waiting for her to begin, wondering if she would start her dance slowly and seductively or launch full speed into her routine. The lyre player caught her eye with the unspoken question: "What shall we play?" But Claudia ignored him and turned to face her audience.

"I shall recite a scene from *Antigone*, a tragedy by the Greek playwright Sophocles."

"A *recital*?" asked Antipas.

His brother stifled a laugh. "Ah, the subject of the vase which you – which was – broken in the library."

"Yes. It's by way of apology. Do you have any objections?"

"Well..." Herod began, but was interrupted by his wife, whispering something in his ear. "No, no, if a recital is all you have, then I suppose you can go ahead. What is it about, this *Antigone*?"

Philip laughed again. "It was your vase, brother."

"I have many vases – *brother* –"

The two men sized each other up.

Herodias quickly sat up. "Come, come. Let us not have any of that. Claudia, the floor is yours, my dear."

"Thank you, my lady. I would tell you of the story of a young woman, the daughter of the late king of Thebes, Oedipus."

"The one who killed his father and married his mother," Philip explained to his brother in exaggerated tones.

"Yes, that's right. Then when he found out he killed himself in shame," Claudia continued.

"A little extreme, don't you think?" asked Herodias.

Claudia didn't answer but continued her tale. "The new king is Creon, Oedipus' brother and Antigone's uncle. Her brother has been killed fighting against the new king, and his body has been exposed. Creon has issued a royal decree that anyone who buries the corpse will be put to death; but Antigone goes ahead and does it anyway, prepared to face execution for the honour of her brother. When it's discovered that it is she who has disobeyed the king, every one, including her betrothed, Haemon, the son of Creon, beg the king to recant."

"Well, does he?" asked Antipas.

"No, he's too proud."

Herod winked at his guests. "No my dear, he is a *king*. A king cannot go back on his word or everyone will think he is weak."

"Perhaps; but Creon loses everything anyway. He locks Antigone alive in a tomb and his son Haemon tries to rescue her. But it's too late. I'll let Sophocles' messenger continue the tale..."

"Well, let's hope he's quicker than you are," drawled Salome, downing another goblet of wine.

Claudia ignored her, adopting the stance of a classical orator and in a confident voice proclaimed: *"The king was shattered. We took his orders, went and searched, and there in the deepest dark recesses of the tomb we found her – hanged by the neck in a fine linen noose, strangled in her veils. And the boy, his arms flung around her waist, clinging to her, wailing for his bride, dead and down below, for his father's crimes and the bed of his marriage blighted by misfortune.*

When Creon saw him, he gave a deep sob, he ran in, shouting, crying out to him: "Oh, my child – what have you done? What seized you, what insanity? What disaster drove you mad? Come out, my son! I beg you on my knees!"

But the boy gave him a wild burning glance, spat in his face, not a word in reply, he drew his sword – his father rushed out, running as Haemon lunged and missed!

And then, doomed, desperate with himself, suddenly leaning his full weight on the blade, he buried it in his body, halfway to the hilt. And still in his senses, pouring his arms around her, he embraced the girl and breathing hard, released a quick rush of blood, bright red on her cheek glistening white. And there he lies, body enfolding body... he has won his bride at last, poor boy, not here but in the houses of the dead. Creon shows the world that of all the ills afflicting men the worst is lack of judgement."

Claudia stood silent. All eyes were on her, including those of Judah the guard. Was that a smile of approval or did she just imagine it? Claudia flushed. The guests waited for their host to lead the applause. But instead he just belched. "Well, that was interesting. Now it's Salome's turn. What are you going to do for us, step-daughter?"

Salome stood up triumphantly. "I shall dance, of course." And then, with a sideways look at her uncle Philip. "What else should a woman do?"

*

A Dream of Procula Pilate

I must forget about the pain in my feet. There are more important things to think about. My child is in trouble. Why won't she come to me? Why must I chase her through these Jerusalem streets? Have I not been a good mother? Have I not loved her as I have loved my very soul? But she has gone. No, she hasn't – she's still here, running around in the same maze that I'm trapped in. I can still hear the sounds of the hunt, cutting through the night like a sacrificial knife. Who is it they are looking for? Whose blood are they trying to shed? Ah yes, now I remember, it is the one who has caused all the trouble. It is the one who has caused my child to run from the mother who gave her birth.

Chapter 8 – The Road to Caesarea

Claudia was relieved to be going home; even though it was a home she had never seen. By all accounts Caesarea was a beautiful place and the palace that would be the Pilate's private residence was famed throughout the Empire. But the main reason she was happy to be leaving was to put as much distance between her and the awful Herod family as possible.

She had never been so humiliated in her life. After her recitation, that little harlot Salome had not even waited for her to take a seat before launching into the most provocative dance Claudia had ever seen. Dressed more like a concubine from a Carthaginian harem than a princess, the girl had flaunted her breasts and flashed her loins to nearly every man in the room. And the men, her two uncles included, were all but drooling in anticipation of bedding her.

But what disgusted Claudia more than anything else, was the demeanour of the queen. Rather than being shocked at her daughter's lascivious behaviour, Herodias sat by proudly as Salome put into practice every feminine wile she had ever taught her. Claudia, not being able to take any more, had retired to bed, not even bothering to say goodnight. But it didn't matter: no one would have noticed if the bookish girl was in the room or not.

Judah the guard had escorted her. She had tried to dismiss him but he had been adamant that he accompany her. They walked to her chamber in silence. At the door, he opened it and stepped aside to let her pass. As she did he cleared his throat, as if to say something. She stopped and looked up at him. His coal-dark eyes, usually so impassive, were filled with something Claudia had never seen before. She couldn't put it into words. What was it? Compassion? Admiration?

"Did *you* like my recital Judah?"

He cleared his throat again. "I did my lady. It was very – very –"

"Intellectual?"

"No, my lady, it was brave. It was very brave." And then he turned on his heel and was gone, leaving Claudia to enter her bedchamber alone.

The next morning she bade farewell to the hung-over Antipas and Herodias who had reluctantly roused themselves to see her off. Salome and Uncle Philip were conspicuous by their absence. The only thing that had taken Claudia by surprise was the gift that Antipas had given her: the slave girl, Nebela.

"You can use her for as long as your family is in Judea," explained Herod; then he waved to the centurion to start the journey to Caesarea. Claudia and Nebela were helped into a litter and the troop of thirty Roman cavalry and six Herodian guards clip-clopped their way out of the courtyard.

Claudia flushed when she recognised one of them. It was Judah. But his face was once again impassive as, on his commander's instructions, he stretched down from his horse to pull the curtains around the litter. Claudia reached out her hand to stop him and their fingers brushed for an instant before he quickly withdrew. She gripped the thick velvet. "Leave the drapes open. I want to see the countryside."

He nodded his assent.

*

As Nebela seated herself opposite her new mistress, she caught a glimpse of her mother weeping near the kitchen door. She raised her hand to say goodbye. Her mother raised hers too.

"Well, Nebela, we're off. Are you excited to be going to a new home?"

"Yes, my lady," lied the Babylonian, hoping the Roman girl would not expect to enter into a conversation. Fortunately she was distracted by the drapes so Nebela was free to pursue her own thoughts.

Nebela wondered if she would ever see her mother again. Perhaps if Claudia Lucretia visited the Herods she could go with her. Nebela was saddened but not surprised at her sudden dislocation: it was after all the lot of slaves; although she had not been born into bondage. Ten years earlier, a debt collector had dragged her and her mother away from her hapless father: an unsuccessful businessman who had defaulted on a loan. The mother and child were sold to the Roman governor of Syria who in turn sent them to Galilee as a coronation present for Herod Antipas. Nebela did not remember much of her father, other than the shiny coins he would leave under her pillow for good fortune. But he should have left the divining of fate to his wife.

Zandra was a fortune-teller. She was a woman who had no qualms in separating a man from his last denarius in order to tell him that his fortune would soon turn for the better, and if he came back to her next month she would tell him just how. "People won't pay if they know they are going to get bad news," Zandra told her daughter as she plucked a fowl for the Herods' table.

"But don't you think people would prefer to know the truth?" asked Nebela.

"Why? They will find it out soon enough."

If Nebela didn't know any better, she would have believed that her mother was a hack; but she wasn't. She had predicted the death of Solomon, the Jewish stable boy, and not by horses' hooves either. Even Nebela could have predicted that, the way he crawled under the straw for a nap unnoticed by the groom who led the horses back into their stalls. No, Zandra had said that he would choke on an almond – three weeks before it happened – and he did.

"Why didn't you warn him, mother?"

"Why? His destiny could not be undone."

Nebela had wanted to know what *her* destiny was as she took leave of her mother. "You will find out soon enough, my child." But then, just as her daughter was about leave, Zandra grabbed her arm and whispered: "The Roman girl: stay close to her; your destiny is yoked to hers."

Nebela looked at her new mistress sitting next to her in the carriage, lost in her own thoughts. What joint destiny could they possibly have?

*

Claudia was not thinking about her new slave or their joint destiny. She was thinking of the young fisherman from the night before. She remembered his rippling muscles reflected in the water and wondered if under his breastplate and tunic Judah looked just like him. She knew that she would have to get over this little infatuation with the Jewish guard. No doubt as soon as she was safely delivered to Caesarea he would turn around and return to Galilee. This journey was the last she would ever see of him. Her father would never approve of a match between her and a Jew.

No, her parents already had their eye on a potential suitor: Tribune Marcus Gaius Sejanus, nephew of the Emperor's favourite, Lucius Aelius Sejanus, commander of the Praetorian Guard. Marcus Gaius had conveniently been posted to Judea a few months before her father had received the governorship, and was in charge of the garrison at Caesarea. They had met a few times in Rome and once, if she remembered correctly, when she was a child in Pontus. Oh, he was good looking enough, Claudia had to admit, and powerfully built; but he never had anything intelligent to say! Yes, Marcus was gallant but dull, and Claudia knew she would be bored before the passion of their wedding bed was spent.

The litter lurched suddenly as the path took a steep turn. Judah reached out his hand and steadied it, but he did not meet her eyes. Was it because Nebela was in the litter with her? Was her first instinct correct? That he and the Babylonian were lovers? Claudia's heart sank. Surely it couldn't be true! She looked at the dark-haired beauty beside her. She could not blame him if he was attracted to her, but oh, she could not bear it if he were. She watched, intently, to see if there was any communication at all between them. A furtive glance? A secret code? But no, there was nothing. Claudia chided herself on her petty jealousy. For Jove's sake, so what if they were lovers? At least they would have a chance to be together.

The cavalcade was moving into rocky country. Up until now they had been travelling through the gentle valley between Tiberias and Cana. With the small town of Nazareth to their right they began the ascent of the hilly region that separated Galilee from Judea. Soon the fertile valleys were left behind as the horses picked their way through the scattered scrub of a narrow mountain gorge.

Claudia thought she saw some movement on the cliff above them. Knowing that the area was famed for bandits, she mentioned it to Judah as he rode beside them.

"It is only a goat, my lady."

"Are you sure?"

"Yes."

But then another soldier shouted: "Take cover! It's an avalanche!"

Then all hell broke loose.

Rocks rained down on the cavalcade from the cliffs above. The leading group of horses and riders were crushed under a deluge of boulders and uprooted trees. With the death cries of their companions in their ears, the surviving horses bolted back down the gorge only to be impaled on the spears of a dozen or so bandits who blocked their path. Six horses fell, blocking the escape of the others. The surviving riders reined in their charges, turned sharply and headed back up the gorge.

Claudia leapt from the litter, shouting for Nebela to follow her. But before she could gather her skirts she was bowled over, out of the path of rampaging hooves. Judah had his arms around her and lifted her bodily onto a nearby boulder then jumped up beside her. There was no sign of Nebela.

With one arm around her, Judah drew his sword from its scabbard and pulled her into a crevice, partially masked by shrubs. Together they watched as dozens of sand-cloaked men descended on the surviving cavalry. The soldiers by now had alighted and were trying to regroup in a cluster of rocks. The sandmen swarmed.

The advancing bandits were met with Roman iron and three or four of their number cut down. The battle raged with the trained military men holding their own, but soon the superior numbers of the bandits began to tell. After a while the only sign of Roman life were the surviving horses pawing the ground.

Claudia spotted Nebela crawling from under the carriage and running down the gorge.

"Get the girl!" cried one of the bandits, pointing his bloodied sword.

"It's just the slave. Where's the Roman?" answered another.

The bandits were facing the other way and Claudia realised she and Judah hadn't yet been spotted in their make-shift hideaway. But it wouldn't be long. "Quick, we must get out of here before they see us," she whispered, slipping out of the crevice and starting to clamber up the hillside.

But Judah grabbed her ankle and dragged her back down. She started to protest but he straddled her and put his hand over her mouth.

"Do you have her, Judah?" someone shouted from below.

"Yes, I have her." His eyes bored into hers.

She wrestled her mouth free and managed to speak one word: "You!"

He pointed his sword to her throat.

Ignoring the blade, she spat at him. He wiped away the saliva and bludgeoned her with the hilt of his sword.

Chapter 9 – The Zealot Camp

High up on the cliffs above the gorge a group of sand-cloaked men huddled around a camp fire. Guards were posted at four points and on a clear night would be able to spot a rescue party from at least a league away. But the night was already clouding over and the men knew they would have to rely on their ears as well as their eyes until morning when they would make good their escape. The horses were tired and needed to rest, as did a half dozen of their number who had been injured in the skirmish. All of the Romans and Herodians had died. The zealot leader, Barabbas, had calculated that it would take at least until mid-morning for the Roman garrison at Caesarea to realise something was wrong, so he decided they should wait until the pre-dawn light before moving on. Until then the men at the fire whispered so as not to mask the sound of an attack.

Two men sat apart from the main group: an older man in his fifties, powerfully built and battle scarred with a grey-streaked beard plaited with slivers of cloth torn from his victims' tunics; and a younger man in his early twenties, with long curly black hair, rippling muscles and eyes too pretty to belong to a boy.

"What do you think we should do with her, Barabbas?"

The older man cleared his throat and grunted.

"Do you think she will be more valuable to us alive?"

"Why?"

"We can tell her father that if he doesn't withdraw his army she will die."

Barabbas lowered his voice so it would not carry to the captive. "The entire Roman army will not pull out of Israel for the life of one girl, Matthias. Pilate is a heathen pig but he's not stupid."

Matthias looked across the camp to where the girl was being held. It was quite a turnaround from the previous day. She, a Roman aristocrat brazenly appraising him from the beach; he, a young fisherman, plying his trade to mask his real purpose: delivering a message to Barabbas' inside man at Herod's palace.

"But we are going to kill her?"

"Eventually. I think we should keep her alive until she can be of some use to us." Barabbas ran his thumb down his blade, cocked his head to one side, then picked up a stone and started sharpening his sword with rhythmic strokes. "We won't be able to win the war with her, but perhaps a battle or two."

Barabbas looked up and his eyes bored into the younger man. Matthias wondered if he could see the uncertainty in him; the fear. Barabbas did not tolerate fear. Nor did he tolerate insubordination. He hand-picked men who would follow his orders without question; men, who like him, believed no price was too high to pay to free Beloved Israel from Roman oppression.

Barabbas finally released Matthias from his interrogative stare, turning his attention back to the blade and stone, re-establishing his rhythm. "You ask too many questions, Matthias. Go and see if Judah needs any help with her."

*

Judah ben Hillel watched from across the camp as Barabbas and Matthias huddled together. He wondered what they were talking about. He didn't trust Matthias. He'd heard it said that Matthias had suggested to Barabbas that all his time at Herod's palace had turned him soft. That he'd begun to sympathise with the sell-out Jews who worked for the Idumean upstart; that he'd made friends with gentiles and ate wild boar with Roman pigs.

Judah was disappointed he had not been allowed to take part in the battle in the gorge; it would have proved he was willing to spill Roman blood with the best of them. But Judah knew better than to question his leader. Jesus Barabbas was a man with a plan, and if fulfilling that plan meant that Judah had to become a palace guard of the despised Herods and nursemaid to a Roman girl, then so be it. It was all taking them one step closer to their dream: a free Israel, like in the days of Judas Maccabeus.

It was the stories of Israel's heyday under the great Judas and his brothers that had attracted the young Judah to sit around Barabbas' campfire. Orphaned as a young teen because of a Roman platoon's refusal to help his abused mother, Judah found solace in the heroic tales of the group of Israelites who drove the invading Seleucids from the holy land. The Maccabees would not have allowed the Romans the power of life and death over his mother. The Maccabees would not have stood for the blasphemy of the Herods. The Maccabees would not have negotiated with Pilate after he set up a craven image of the emperor in the Holy City.

No, they were so filled with righteous anger when the Greek king Antiochus Epiphanes defiled the Temple by sacrificing a pig on the altar that they set up a kingdom that had not been seen since the days of Solomon and David. Ah, but that was nearly two hundred years ago, and the descendants of the Maccabees did not have the anointing of their noble fathers, and the likes of the Herods ruled God's land on behalf of the Romans. Romans like Claudia Lucretia Pilate.

The girl stirred beside him. It was the first movement he had seen since he knocked her unconscious. He was relieved that he hadn't killed her. He'd hit her far harder than he'd intended and he regretted it. She wasn't bad as far as Romans went. He hadn't forgotten her kindness to Nebela and she had shown some dignity on the night of the Herod banquet. She stirred again.

"Are you awake?" He shook her gently by the shoulder.

"Yes, where – where am I?"

"You're with friends of mine." He helped her into a sitting position. "Does your head hurt?" he reached out to change the wad of cloth he'd used to staunch the bleeding welt.

"Yes, it does." Claudia dabbed at the wound above her left eyebrow and pulled out strands of hair. She flinched then tried to focus on her immediate surroundings. "What happened?"

"Don't you remember?" He shouldn't have hit her so hard. Why had he hit her so hard?

She shook her head.

He should test her faculties. "What's your name?"

"Claudia Lucretia Pilate. What's yours?"

"Judah ben Hillel."

Claudia looked at him intently. "Have we met before?" There was no fear in her eyes. Did she really not remember him?

"Do you know why you're here?"

"No!" said the girl sharply. "I don't know why I'm here, how I got here or who all these dirty..."

48

"Jews," he finished for her. "You don't know who all these dirty Jews are. Do you?"

"No," she said quietly. She looked sick. She probably needed to lie down. Judah balled up his cloak and put it under her head.

"Thank you," she whispered.

Judah's heart lurched. She seemed so fragile; so different from the proud girl who had stood up to the Herods at the banquet. He swallowed to steady his voice. He needed to focus; to remember why they were there in the first place. Perhaps Matthias was right. Perhaps he had gone soft. He forced himself to remember his mother lying in a pool of blood until his heart hardened again. "Don't thank me," he said gruffly. "We have to keep you in one piece until your father gives us what we want."

"My father? What can he do for you?"

"He can take his gods and go back to Rome."

"But why would he do that? The Emperor himself told him to come here."

"And YHWH himself has told him to go!"

"Maybe you should abduct the Emperor's daughter; you may have better fortune with her."

"The Emperor doesn't have a daughter. Or didn't you think a dirty Jew like me would know what goes on in Rome?"

"I don't know what Jews think."

"Obviously." Judah stoked the fire. "Are you scared?"

"No."

"Well you should be. See those men over there?" He nodded towards Barabbas and Matthias. "They want to kill you."

"Why?"

"Because of your father's blasphemy."

"What blasphemy?"

"He brought an idol into Jerusalem."

"An idol? Oh, you mean the Emperor's image on the military standards."

"Yes, an idol. He should not have done that. Now we're going to make him pay."

"With what? My life?"

"If necessary."

"And will it be necessary?"

"It might."

Claudia curled her body into a tight little ball. Her breathing was shallow. Judah felt his heart lurch again. He reached out his hand to touch her shoulder, to reassure her, but stopped himself in time.

"Are you scared of me, Claudia?"

"I don't know. You saved me, didn't you?"

"You remember that?"

"I think so. You carried me onto a rock, didn't you?"

"Yes. But I wasn't saving you; I was following orders."

"But you could have killed me."

"You are no good to us dead."

Claudia's shoulders relaxed slightly and she tried to sit up again. He helped her.

"I'm thirsty. Is there any water?"

He gave her a water bag. She drank fully.

"That's enough. Where do you think you are? Rome? We don't have water flowing through the streets here."

"Well, you could have. That's one of my father's plans: to build aqueducts in Judea. That's just one of the many good things he can do for you."

"YHWH supplies our water."

"Well he hasn't done a very good job so far."

He should have slapped her: Barabbas would have. But he didn't. He didn't say anything. They sat in silence for a long time then he got up and walked over to the main camp.

*

Claudia watched her captor go. This was her chance. She looked around to see if there was any way she could escape, but before she could formulate a plan, another man sat down beside her. She was sure she had seen him before. Her memory was coming back – of Judah and this new man; it was the young fisherman from the night at the lake. So, the conspiracy ran far deeper than she had thought. This was not an opportunistic abduction by a man she was foolish enough to be attracted to, but a carefully planned kidnapping. Claudia shook her head to clear her thoughts. She knew she needed all her wits about her if she were to get out of this alive.

"Hello," she said. He didn't answer.

"Hello," she tried again, this time smiling slightly. That caught his attention and he smiled back.

"Do you speak Greek?" No answer. She tried again in her limited Aramaic. "Claudia." She said, pointing to herself. Then to him: "You?"

"Matthias," he said, smiling.

"Ah, Matthias. You help me?"

"Yes," he said, taking her outreached hand.

"You will?" This was better than she had expected. "We go?"

"Yes," he said again; then something she didn't understand. He edged closer to her, blocking her view of the rest of the camp. He took her hand and pulled her to her feet. She felt dizzy and swayed against him. He caught her and held her to his chest. Regaining her composure she pulled away from him, but he held her tightly. Then his hands moved down her back. She froze, hoping he would stop. He didn't. Holding her firmly with one arm, he allowed the other to wander at will: over her breasts, her belly, her loins. She tried to scream but his mouth came crashing down on hers. They fell to the ground, grappling. He straddled her, pinned down her arms with his knees then ripped her dress from neck to waist. One hand slapped over her mouth while the other roamed freely below.

Claudia screamed silently. She had to do something or he would have her. He pulled away for a second to grapple with his loincloth and she took her chance. She elbowed him in the crotch as hard as she could. He yowled and fell off her. She tried to crawl away but he kicked her twice in the stomach.

"No!" she screamed; this time out loud. Suddenly Matthias was being dragged away from her. It was Judah and he was shouting at the young man in Aramaic. Matthias was shouting back, gesticulating wildly at her. Eventually Matthias stormed off, leaving Judah breathing heavily beside her.

"Thank you," she said, trying to pull her torn dress together.

"I was only trying to stop a true Israelite from defiling himself with a gentile. I remember that night at the lake and so does Matthias. He was just giving you what you wanted."

"But I didn't! I didn't!" she sobbed, curling once more into a ball. "That's not what I wanted at all."

He looked at her, bleeding and dirty. Then with a sigh he reached down, wrapped his cloak around her and sat on the other side of the fire. He did not speak to her again.

Chapter 10 – Marcus Sejanus

Tribune Marcus Gaius Sejanus did not enjoy having his sleep disturbed, particularly when it meant he would have to ride like Hades to cover thirty miles before sunrise. But what could he say? The governor himself had awoken him at the second hour, according to the water clock in the courtyard.

The governor, barefoot and in his undergarments, was frantic. "Tribune, get your men together; you must ride at once!"

"What is it sir?" asked the tribune, stretching and scratching his unshaven chin.

"It's my daughter. She's been taken by bandits."

"Your daughter? Captive? How do you know this?" asked Sejanus, suddenly awake.

"A slave who was accompanying her was found near Nazareth."

"By whom?"

"One of Herod's men! Does it matter?"

"No, no, of course not." Sejanus pulled on his outer garments.

Pilate was pacing, his usually immaculate hair standing on end. "You have to find her Sejanus!"

"With Mars' help, I will, my lord."

"By all the gods you had better!"

Sejanus looked earnest as he strapped on his leather body armour and iron breastplate; decisive as he took up his sword. "What happened to the patrol? Thirty cavalry, I recall."

"Ambushed, according to the girl; all dead. But my daughter, with Juno's blessing, was taken alive. Make sure you find her that way, Sejanus."

"I will, sir. Where's the girl?"

"The slave? She's here." Pilate opened the door of the tribune's quarters and called in Nebela.

Sejanus looked her up and down. She looked exhausted: pale-faced and dishevelled. "Come," said Sejanus, "you can tell me what happened on the way." Then to Pilate: "Near Nazareth, you say?"

Pilate nodded. The tribune put his arm around Nebela and led her into the courtyard shouting orders to his men as he walked. Before the waterclock marked the third hour, one hundred mounted men followed Marcus Gaius Sejanus out of the Caesarean fortress with the Babylonian slave seated before him on his horse.

Three hours later, Sejanus and his men were looking down on Nazareth. Behind them was the range of hills that separated Galilee from Judea and before them the valley that sloped down towards the lake, twenty miles away. The tribune roused the girl who had fallen asleep against his chest. It had been a long ride doubled on his mount, but his horse was strong and the girl was light. After getting general directions, Sejanus had allowed her to drift off into a fitful sleep. He could feel her breathing even through his armour.

"Wake up, girl, we're here. Is this where it happened?"

Nebela, who was used to being called at any time of night by one or other of the Herod family, was instantly awake. She looked around her then pointed behind them.

"We've gone too far. It was back there, in the gorge. About five minutes' ride."

"Yes, of course. Those Jews would not have had the courage to confront a Roman platoon in the open. Dismount!" The men obeyed instantly.

Sejanus sent ten of them back the way they had come with orders to search for a trail from the gorge and see where it led.

Nebela, emboldened by three hours in the arms of the Roman tribune, spoke to him directly: "But sir, surely you saw the bodies. That would have told you where it happened?"

The tribune, who should have chastised her for speaking without being invited to, answered casually: "Yes, I did. But I wanted to test you. For all I know you could have led us into a trap."

"I still could," said Nebela softly.

"I know. And I won't make the same mistake as my fallen comrades: my men will not be trapped like boars in a pit. Here, eat something, the scouts will be back soon."

Nebela took the proffered bread like an equal: her fingers touching his, her head not bowed. He looked at her for a moment and smiled before withdrawing his hand, his fingers caressing her wrist as he did so. The girl wondered if she had been offered more than bread. If she had been she might have some choice in the matter: Sejanus did not own her, the Herods and, temporarily, the Pilates did. It would not be politic for him to force himself on someone else's property. So if it transpired that she had some power over the attractive man behind her, she would use it wisely. She took in his grey eyes that were looking beyond her to the gorge and wondered what it would be like for them to look upon her – and desire her. She caught a glimpse of a fringe of light brown hair under his helmet and wondered what it would be like to run her hands through it; and over his densely muscled chest that she was sure was under his leather jerkin. Zandra was not the only one with a gift. Her daughter believed she had inherited some of the second sight too, and what she saw was her own future with this man.

Or it could simply have been the longings of any eighteen-year-old girl who had been held close for the last couple of hours by a handsome man.

*

The first glimmer of dawn was rising over the land of the Decapolis in the east when the Roman scouts returned. It would be less than an hour before the pink fingers reached the hills near Nazareth, and Sejanus knew that he and his men had better hurry if they were to launch a surprise attack on the Zealot camp.

He divided his men into four groups. Twenty-five soldiers retraced the path up the gorge, picking their way through the bodies of their fallen comrades, continuing south as if returning to Caesarea with as much noise as possible. The second group of twenty-five, led by Sejanus himself, skirted the cliffs to the east, moving carefully through the dense brush that clung to the foothills. They dismounted then turned back west, scaling the steep hill and taking cover in the rocks and scrub. The third group moved into the gorge and started preparing the dead soldiers to be transported to Caesarea. The fourth group remained on the Nazarean side, out of sight of the mouth of the gorge.

As predicted, a Zealot scout spotted the main group heading back to Caesarea as well as the smaller contingent attending the dead. Not being able to believe his fortune, he scampered back to tell his comrades.

*

Judah was roused from a fitful sleep by a rough hand on his shoulder. It was Matthias. "The Romans are in the gorge! Barabbas wants you to lead a group to the mouth while he comes up behind them."

Judah sprung to his feet, checked that his sword was in its scabbard and turned towards the main camp. Suddenly he remembered Claudia.

"What about her?" He nodded to the sleeping girl.

"I'll watch her," said Matthias.

Judah frowned, eager to finally see some action, but concerned that Matthias might try to finish his business with the captive.

He wanted to ask someone else to look after her, but all but a handful of men were strapping on their swords and getting ready for battle. Barabbas was already leading his group away from the camp and shouted to Judah: "What are you waiting for? We don't have long to spring the trap?"

"I'm coming!" He drew his sword and pointed it at Matthias' throat. "Keep your hands off the girl, brother. Is that understood?"

"Just do your job and I'll do mine," Matthias replied and sat down next to Claudia.

*

Judah led his men to the mouth of the gorge, whispering instructions to them on the way. They lined up from wall to wall – five abreast and five-men deep – spears braced and ready. In a few moments the Romans would be upon them: caught in a Jewish vice, with Barabbas crushing them onto the spears. All Judah had to do was make sure that his men kept the Romans inside the gorge; which wouldn't be difficult as only three men at a time, or one horse, could pass through. At last, Roman blood would colour his sword; he wondered if it would be as red as his.

It was almost first light and Judah squinted to catch a glimpse of his Roman victims. He heard a clink of metal behind him and turned to check that his men were still standing firm. Then he saw a sight that chilled his heart: Roman armour and Roman swords, quietly sneaking up behind them. "It's a trap, brothers! Turn and fight, YHWH is with us!"

Judah's men turned and clashed swords with the Romans entering the gorge, hoping that Barabbas' men would take care of the group already inside. They did for a while, but just when it seemed that the Zealots were holding their own, twenty-five mounted soldiers galloped from the rear of the gorge and more swept down the hill on foot, descending on

Barabbas' men. Completely outnumbered, the Zealot leader fled with his remaining men up a goat track. With half his own men slain around him, Judah decided to follow. "Retreat! If YHWH is willing, we will live to fight another day!"

With bloodied sword, Judah guarded the path as seven of the surviving Zealots scampered up the hillside. He managed to hack at two Romans before he followed his men up the narrow trail. The two soldiers, not felled, tried to follow him, but their wounds and heavy armour slowed them down. They soon slipped back down, blocking the path and hampering the advance of their comrades. As the sun lit the battlefield, Judah, Barabbas and the other survivors disappeared into the mountain shadows.

*

All was going to plan and as predicted, the Jews hadn't suspected a thing. As the battle in the gorge subsided, Marcus Gaius Sejanus decided it was time to mop up the remaining Zealots in their camp. His scouts had already reliably informed him that there were only a handful of them and that Claudia Lucretia was still alive. With half his men pursuing the lily-livered Jews up one side of the gorge, he took the rest of his platoon and fell upon the enemy camp.

Sejanus personally ran through three men with his sword, while his centurion made short shrift of two more. He scanned the camp, looking for Claudia, and spotted her in the arms of a young Jew who was holding a knife to her throat. Her cheek was swollen, she was bleeding from a welt on her forehead and her dress was torn from neck to waist.

Sejanus approached the pair with drawn sword. The Jew said something incomprehensible, but the knifepoint that pierced Claudia's skin was interpretation enough. Sejanus sliced the air with a flourish, drawing the young man's attention.

"Let the lady go," he said in Greek, gesturing to the well-armed Roman soldiers who by now had subdued what was left of the Zealot band. Then, in Latin, to one of the auxiliaries who spoke Aramaic: "Tell him that if he lets her go we won't kill him. The soldier translated Sejanus' offer, and reluctantly Matthias dropped his knife. Claudia fell to her knees sobbing and Sejanus stepped forward and covered her with his cloak.

"Tie up that filthy Jew. We'll take him back to Caesarea."

"What about the others?" asked the centurion, indicating the rabble of Zealots who had survived the ambush.

"Kill them," he said softly. "But wait for the lady Claudia to leave; she has seen enough already."

By now the rest of platoon had arrived with the horses. Nebela was with them. Sejanus swept Claudia into his arms and lifted her onto his horse. He mounted behind her and without looking back at the girl he had carried for three hours, headed off to Caesarea.

*

A Dream of Procula Pilate

Bang. Bang. Bang. *I am drawn by the sound.* Bang. Bang. Bang. *I have lost my child. She is somewhere in these Jerusalem streets – perhaps I will find her, perhaps I will not, but for now she has gone. I have found something else. I cannot yet see it, but I can hear:* bang, bang, bang. *It is not the sound of iron on iron. Or iron on wood – although there is both iron and wood. It is the sound I hear when I pass the kitchens in the palace: the sound of iron, cutting through flesh and into the board below.* Bang. Bang. Bang. *It is getting closer, or am I closer to it? If I just go a little further up this street perhaps I will see it.*

Chapter 11 – The Homecoming

Bang. Bang. Bang. Procula Claudiana Pilate emerged groggily from her dream. *Bang. Bang. Bang.* Someone was knocking on her door.

"What is it?

"Wake up, my lady! They have brought your daughter home."

"They've found her? Is she well?"

"Yes, my lady. They should be coming through the gates at any moment."

Procula leapt out of bed, pulled on a robe and looked out of the window. What was she doing asleep at this time of day, anyway? She had just lain down for a moment – to ease the pain of her headache and her worry – and before she knew it... she shook her head groggily and tried to focus on the palace courtyard below: it was empty. Claudia had not arrived yet.

It was not long ago that the entire square had been filled with Jewish priests pressing their throats against Roman iron; Jewish priests who were supposed to be their allies. Now she was waiting for her daughter to be returned to her from Jewish Zealots who were categorically not their allies. No one had told her life in Judea would be so complicated; or so dangerous. If they lost Claudia to this god-forsaken posting she would never forgive Pontius for bringing them here. No career move was worth that. Nothing was worth that.

Suddenly, two-dozen cavalry cantered into the courtyard, led by Tribune Marcus Sejanus on his white stallion. He was holding a girl in front of him. Claudia was back!

*

Procula found her husband waiting for her at the bottom of the marble staircase. He had not slept all night. He drew her to him and held her close. "They've found her Procula; our daughter's safe."

"Is she...?"

"She's fine. Sejanus sent a messenger to assure me no one dishonoured her."

Procula felt a huge weight lift from her chest. "They're here; I saw them from the upstairs window."

The couple, hand in hand, hurried through the maze of halls and corridors towards the main foyer. "We shall hold a circus. For Claudia Lucretia in honour of Juno," said Pilate as they turned left then quickly right.

"An inspired idea! But let it be in a few days; Claudia will need her sleep."

"And so will you," said Pilate, noting with concern the dark rings under his wife's eyes.

"No, from now on it will be fine. The dreams foretold Claudia's disappearance. But now she's returned the dreams will go."

"Perhaps. But you should speak to a soothsayer. I'm having one brought here from Galilee."

"Who?"

"A Babylonian. The slave girl's mother as reward for her loyalty."

"All right then, I'll speak with her. But first I want to see Claudia." They had arrived at the ornate foyer. Procula headed for the door, but as she did, a slave opened it to admit Marcus Sejanus, carrying Claudia in his arms. She was fast asleep. Behind him came the slave girl Nebela, equally exhausted, but still on her feet.

*

Claudia was feeling much better. Her ordeal at the hands of the Jewish Zealots was slowly disappearing under mountains of silk, linen and damask in every imaginable hue. Her father had hired the best seamstresses in Caesarea and told his daughter that she could have as many new dresses as her heart desired.

"The indigo is beautiful. Do you think it will match my eyes, Nebela?"

"Yes, my lady. But perhaps you should wear the saffron – it will set off your eyes rather than just matching them."

"Hmm, you may be right. But saffron is the colour of brides and today is not my wedding day."

"No, but it could be soon."

"You mean Tribune Marcus Gaius Sejanus?"

"Hasn't your father chosen him as your husband?"

"That's what he thinks. But neither Marcus nor I have given our consent and until we do, there will be no match."

"Don't you find him attractive?"

"Of course he's attractive, I just don't know if I'm ready for marriage yet."

"Your father thinks you are. He can force you, can't he?"

"Of course; but I don't think he will. And besides, he can't force Marcus."

"That's good," said Nebela, before she could stop herself.

Claudia stopped delving into the pile of dresses and looked pointedly at her slave. "Yes, it is. Come, let's not waste time talking about a marriage that may or may not happen. We have a circus to attend! I'll wear the indigo."

"As you wish, my lady," said the girl whose choice of gowns and marriage partners were more limited; then she started to dress her mistress.

*

An hour later, Claudia and Nebela were ready to be escorted to the circus. Claudia would have preferred to be going to the theatre as the shows there were more to her taste, but she was still excited about attending the prestigious social event. Circuses were expensive and only held a couple of times a year in the more cash-strapped provinces, so the culturally starved residents of the region took full advantage of the festivities when they arose. Anyone who was anyone in Judea, Galilee and Samaria was invited; the Herods had declined to attend because of the Zealots who were still on the loose between Tiberias and Caesarea despite increased Roman patrols. Claudia hadn't bothered to feign disappointment when her parents told her the news.

The girls, draped in garlands, left the palace and joined the procession that was headed for the amphitheatre. Pilate had declared a holiday in honour of Juno, the Queen of Heaven, who was responsible for his daughter's safe return. The people of Caesarea – mainly Syrians, Greeks and Romans – joined in the festivities with relish. The few Jews who lived and did business in the port city either stayed at home if they were pious, or sold their goods to the festival crowds if they were not.

Caesarea, built only a generation before by Herod the Great, was one of the more ostentatiously Roman cities of the Empire. If it wasn't for his mandatory trips to Jerusalem, Pilate could almost forget that he was in Judea. Apart, that is, from the priests who had dared to follow him to his Roman retreat, complaining about the Emperor's effigy. When would the

Jews learn that it was the Emperor who brought peace and prosperity to this god-forsaken land? And it was to the Emperor, at the Temple of Augustus, as well as to Juno, that the Pilates were going to offer a sacrifice before joining the rest of Caesarea at the amphitheatre.

The Temple of Augustus was within walking distance of the governor's palace and the focal point of the white marble city. The procession of worshippers and sacrificial animals headed along the arched promenade, skirting the man-made harbour where ships from a dozen nations were anchored, all of them prospering under imperial rule.

The ships' captains raised their sales in salute to the gods, billowing white on the clear blue sea. Between the arches the Caesareans waved brightly coloured scarves and tossed flowers into the path of the governor's procession. The pure white heifer and bullock, sporting wreaths around their necks and horns, trotted along with the lightest of steps, unaware of the fate that would soon befall them. But there was no shame in their death; they were chosen as the best of their herd, honoured to shed their blood in the name of the gods.

As the gay worshippers mounted the steps of the temple, the victims, now smelling the blood of their fallen comrades, lurched in vain against their tethers. But they did not suffer long. To the accompaniment of tambourine and lyre, Pilate and the chief augur slit their throats and allowed their blood to flow freely onto the altar. First, the bullock: a perfect male to the honour of the Emperor, then the heifer, a pristine female for Juno, the wife of Jupiter and the protector of all women.

The bullock was split open and its entrails collected in a silver bowl.

"What does it look like, augur? Are the auspices good for our lord and Emperor?"

The white-robed augur looked at the guts: the shape of the kidneys, the lie of the intestine, the colour of the heart: "Yes, all praise to the gods, nothing appears amiss."

"And my daughter?" asked Pilate, moving his attention to the heifer's innards.

"Hmm."

"What is it? Will her life be short?"

"No. No. It will be long. But there is something amiss."

"What is it?" Pilate lowered his voice, turning his back on the other worshippers.

The augur followed his lead. "It's the genitals, my lord. They are enlarged."

"What does it mean?"

"As I said, your daughter will live long, but it will be in the company of women."

"Won't she get married then?" asked Pilate, smiling a little too enthusiastically at Procula who was edging forward to hear the oracle.

"I don't know. It isn't clear."

"Well then, there is no need to worry then, is there?" said Pilate, slipping some gold into the bloodied bowl.

"Not at all, my lord," whispered the augur, not hesitating to soil his hands to retrieve his reward. "All is well," he declared in his most authoritative voice. "The lady Claudia Lucretia will live a long and fruitful life!"

A cheer went up from the crowd of worshippers crammed into the temple. The music struck up again and the women, led by Procula Claudiana, danced around the altar as Pilate and the augur burnt the entrails. On a separate fire, the flesh was roasted and the Pilates and their guests would eat it after the circus at a banquet in honour of Juno.

Chapter 12 – The Circus

The festive procession emerged from the temple and wended along the promenade to the amphitheatre, north of the city. The tiered seating was a marvel of Roman engineering: the main grandstand rotated by means of a series of levers and pulleys and could face either the harbour where mock sea battles were staged, or the amphitheatre proper where chariot races were the most popular form of entertainment. There was also a troupe of gladiators who plied their bloody trade.

Today there would be a series of chariot races, some athletics for the Greeks in the crowd and a re-enactment by the gladiators of the recent Roman victory over the Zealots. Then, Pilate told his guests, there would be a special treat.

"What could it be?" asked Claudia of Marcus Sejanus who had taken a seat beside her in the governor's box.

"I don't know, lady, we'll have to wait and see," said Marcus then leaned towards her and whispered something in her ear. Claudia laughed at the sweet nothing and took one of the garlands from around her neck and gave it to Marcus. In turn, Marcus kissed her hand.

Procula Claudiana looked with approval at the attentions paid by the handsome tribune to her daughter. Claudia Lucretia seemed to be enjoying it too. Procula smiled with relief: perhaps they will be married by Saturnalia. Claudia, at seventeen, was running out of time. In a couple of years she would be too old to attract a good match, and may have to settle for an old widower on his second or third marriage. Although less financially alluring, a match with the dashing Marcus Gaius Sejanus would be far better. He was a rising star in the Roman military with successful campaigns in Africa, Mauritania and Lausitania to his credit, tipped to soon make the rank of Legate. And of course, there was his uncle, the head of the Praetorian Guard who had the ear of the Emperor and the Senate; not a connection that could easily be overlooked.

Fortunately Claudia was an only child and unlike her mother who was the fourth daughter of a family cursed with girls, she did not have to share a dowry. And then of course there was the added attraction of a possible inheritance. As a girl, it did not automatically follow that she

64

would receive her father's fortune on his death, but at his discretion she might. It was well known that Pilate doted on his daughter. Many Roman girls had to be content with their dowries, but Claudia could also look forward to the rest of the family's wealth as well. Procula smiled at Marcus. He bowed his head in return.

*

Only Marcus Gaius Sejanus knew how tenuous his position really was. He wanted to win the approval of the Pilates, but did not want them to think he was desperate. He did not advertise it, of course, but he was not completely assured of inheriting anything from his uncle. True, he was the famous commander's adopted son, but the two men no longer got on. To an outside eye, Lucius Aelius Sejanus loved the young Marcus (the child of his late younger brother) as much as he loved his own three children – but that was the problem, he loved him too well. Unlike his uncle, Marcus was not sexually attracted to men and had to flee from the clutches of his drunken elder on more than one occasion. In the sobriety of morning Lucius Aelius had sworn him to secrecy: although far from uncommon, buggery was still frowned upon in some circles, particularly the army. If it ever got out that he had been the recipient of his uncle's sexual advances it could ruin both of their careers.

Thanks to Venus, Marcus was only attracted to women, and the woman sitting beside him was certainly attractive. He had first met Claudia Lucretia while holidaying in Pontus with his uncle. She was seven years old, he sixteen, and had dared to correct his Greek pronunciation. He did not like the child one bit and was surprised when ten years later his uncle suggested a marriage. But when he met her again in Rome on the way to Judea, he revised his opinion of her. The precociousness of her childhood was gone, or at least demurely hidden, and she had become quite a beauty: slimly built with rich chestnut hair and violet eyes.

No, he could do worse than marry Claudia Lucretia Pilate and she seemed to like him well enough. It didn't matter that they did not love one another; love was incidental to marriage, and more likely to occur with a concubine who had nothing to contribute to the relationship other than her heart.

Claudia, laughing at the antics of a dancing bear in the arena below, accidentally splashed some wine onto Marcus.

"Oh, I'm sorry, Marcus! Nebela, can you clean this up?"

Nebela obeyed and with lowered eyes sopped up the spilt wine from Marcus' tunic. Marcus could smell her hair as she bent over him. He caught his breath, surprised at his reaction.

"Thank you, Nebela," said Claudia, dismissing the girl.

Marcus started up the conversation again, but was soon drowned out by the roaring crowd as the athletic matches and performing animals gave way to the more popular chariot races.

*

The afternoon sped by with Claudia and the rest of the crowd standing to their feet on more than one occasion to cheer on their favourites in the races. Some of the citizens of Caesarea would go home that night much poorer than when they arrived, but others, if the gods were kind, would have over a year's wages filling their pockets.

At sunset Pilate ordered the lighting of the torches. The horses and their drivers were given their leave and the gladiators were called in. Not all gladiatorial combats were to the death, and this one was to be a mock re-enactment of the Roman victory over the Zealots.

Although not to the death, the fighting was still fierce and bloody, with a lot more Zealot blood being spilt than Claudia remembered. Claudia turned to comment on the fact to Marcus and saw that he was gone. She wondered where he had got to.

The battle below was reaching its climax with each blow cheered by the crowd. A trapdoor opened in the centre of the arena and a young gladiator dressed as a woman appeared.

"It's the lady Claudia Lucretia!" shouted someone from the crowd.

Then, as another gladiator crept up on "her", knife in hand, another shouted: "Look out, my lady, it's the Zealot Matthias!"

Claudia felt a chill wrap around her as she realised that the gladiator was not an actor, but the real Matthias. The Zealot, armed with a dagger, a broadsword and a net was reluctantly acting out the gladiator master's version of what happened as he stalked the helpless 'woman'. He lunged at her with his knife: she screamed and ran but he caught her in his net. Every move Matthias made was greeted by boos and every time the 'actress' evaded him, there was a cheer.

Just when Claudia thought the cheers could not get any louder, a masked gladiator arose through another trapdoor to frenzied applause from the crowd.

"Matthias," he cried. "Turn around and face a real man if you dare!"
The crowd roared: "Turn around, Matthias! Turn around!"

The young fisherman did as he was bid. The powerfully built gladiator strode towards him, brandishing his sword in a fiery arc. With surprising skill, Matthias drew his sword and the two men clashed in the centre of the arena. The gladiator was clearly the stronger of the two and better trained, but Matthias was nimble and blocked and parried with confidence. Pausing to catch his breath, Matthias spotted the net, brushed off by the fleeing 'Claudia', and picked it up. As if fishing at the lake, he spun around and flung the net at the gladiator, holding onto one end. Surprised, the bigger man sliced at the net with his sword, but only managed to get the hilt entangled. With a deft flick, Matthias ripped the sword from the gladiator's hand then lurched at him with his own weapon. But the gladiator was ready for him: he ducked, turned and stabbed the charging Matthias in the solar plexus with his dagger. The gladiator thrust the blade upwards: once, twice, three times then twisted it to the right. In an incredible show of strength, the gladiator lifted the flaying Zealot off the ground and held him there as he died. Fortunately, for Matthias, it didn't take long.

Claudia was overwhelmed, partly from the memory of what really happened to her, and partly by the deafening roar of the crowd: "Se – ja – nus! Se – ja – nus!" The victorious gladiator playing Sejanus walked around the arena with his bloodied hands raised, acknowledging the applause. When he reached the governor's box, Pilate and his wife rose to their feet and applauded him too.

"For the lady Claudia Lucretia!" said the gladiator, taking off his mask. It was the real Marcus Gaius Sejanus.

"Bravo!" cried the crowd.

"Bravo!" cried Pilate. "My thanks to you for saving my daughter. And now the Zealot is dead! A curse upon Matthias and his family!"

"A curse upon Matthias!" echoed the crowd.

"Claudia, you must stand up," whispered her mother. "It's not every day a man kills someone in front of ten thousand people for your honour."

Claudia obeyed and took off her scarf and tossed it into the arena below. Marcus, smiling, picked up the blue silk with the tip of his sword and brought it to his lips. The crowd cheered again. This night would not be forgotten for a long time. They had seen everything: treachery, bravery, revenge, justice and love; a greater spectacle than this they could not have hoped for.

*

The party went on well into the night, long after the Pilates left the amphitheatre. On the way home Claudia was caught up in her own thoughts and strangely quiet throughout the banquet. It did not matter, as Pilate and Marcus spent most of the evening congratulating one another on their theatrical triumph: the governor for planning it and the tribune for executing it.

It was long after midnight before Claudia was able to retire. As soon as she was in her room she dismissed Nebela and opened a window, inhaling the fresh air. The night was ablaze with festival fires reflected in the harbour water. Joyous music bounced off the walls as drunken revellers staggered past the palace. Claudia was just about to turn to her bed when she noticed a man looking up at her from the courtyard below. He was not wearing festival clothes and he didn't seem to have the same lightness of spirit as the other partygoers. He saw Claudia looking at him and turned away, but as he did his face was lit by a pedestrian's torch. It was Judah ben Hillel.

She cried out, but not loudly. Still, there was a knock on her door.

"Yes?" Claudia answered, trying to sound calm.

Procula's face appeared in the doorway. "Is everything all right?"

"Yes, mother. Everything's well. Good night."

"Good night then; and may Venus give you dreams of the one you love!"

As her mother closed the door, Claudia turned back to the window, but Judah was gone.

Chapter 13 – The Olive Grove

The days were growing shorter now that the sun did not rise as high. The Caesarean stone reflected the autumn colours of sun, earth and leaf, turning the white city into a palette of bronze and gold. The sailors in the harbour wore serge cloaks as they trimmed their sails in the chilly evenings and the residents came in early from their sunset strolls. In the olive groves, the fruit was on the brink of turning from green to black and the workers who had already filled their baskets with half of the harvest were poised to reap the rest when the magical transformation took place.

Oil flowed from the presses: thick, warm and golden, filling a myriad jugs to overflowing. It was a good harvest and Caesarean farmers patted their pockets as merchants from all over Palestine paid them the price they asked. The merchants were smiling too, knowing that their stock would light lamps, flavour food and soothe wounds from Judea to Asia Minor.

It was liquid gold and it paid the salaries of thousands of people. Caesarea would not see an influx of casual labour like this until the spring barley harvest. The town was raking in the denarii. Some of the labourers stayed with friends and family in the city, some in low-roofed hostels provided by the farmers, and some in a temporary shanty town that sprung up on the edge of the olive groves once a year. But wherever the harvesters slept, they all came into town at some stage to buy provisions for the duration of their stay and to take home to their families when they left. The streets were full: full of Jews.

Judah did not have to disguise himself. His distinctive Hebrew features – the close-set eyes, the prominent nose, the high cheek bones, olive skin and curly black hair – blended in with the other Jews who for once outnumbered the Greeks and Syrians who lived in Caesarea all year round. The "Shaloms" rang through the streets and Jewish sounds and Jewish smells almost made Judah forget that his countrymen no longer ruled their own land.

It was the Sabbath, the seventh day of the week when Jews did no work and the rest of the world wondered why. Judah would have preferred to remain with those of his own kind, but orders from Barabbas forced him to mingle with the pagan citizens of Caesarea, trying to get as near to Pilate's palace as possible.

It was not the first time he had been there. A few days after the ambush at Nazareth he had made his way to Caesarea hoping to rescue Matthias from his captors. He had failed, unable to get past the heavily armed gladiators in the holding cells under the amphitheatre. Instead he had watched with the ten thousand as the young Jew fought the dashing tribune and unlike them, closed his eyes when he was impaled on Roman iron.

The whole episode had saddened Judah. Not because Matthias had died – the young man was hardly a friend – but because his death spoke of the death of a nation. How could his people, almost outnumbered in their own land, overthrow their oppressors? How could the Jews, who had forgotten what it was like to rule themselves, once again stand tall? How could a generation that had lost the will to fight be called to arms again? The answer was quite simple: they needed a leader who could inspire them to rise up and reclaim what was rightfully theirs. For a while, Judah had thought it was Barabbas, but plan after plan had come to nought. Barabbas was, after all, just a man, and what the people needed was a god – or at least a man sent by God – they needed the promised Messiah. But despite the ever-increasing numbers of wild men clad in skins claiming to be the one, Judah was not impressed. He feared that yet another generation would pass without YHWH's anointed one coming to save His people.

Barabbas at least was doing something, and Judah decided he would rather join him than sit around waiting for his dreams to be crushed again. So when he had been told to go again to Caesarea to try to get close to Claudia Lucretia Pilate, he obeyed. For some reason the girl had not reported him when she spotted him from her window, and Barabbas thought she might be sweet on him. Judah doubted it. He had thought there might have been something the day of the boar hunt in Galilee, but surely the fact that he had led her and her guards into a bloody trap would have quenched any feelings she had for him. And yet she had not turned him in. Why? Judah was going to find out. His instructions were to strike up a friendship with her – or even to seduce her. Barabbas theorised that a love-struck maiden might divulge information about her father's business; but if she did not, and was going to turn him in, Judah was told to kill her. He did not like his assignment, not one little bit.

For the last few days Claudia had taken a late afternoon walk in the olive grove accompanied by a guard and a female slave. Up until now he had managed to follow her unnoticed, dogging her steps from the palace, past the temple and through the streets to the outskirts of town. Today he lay in wait again. He did not have to wait long.

There she was, leaving the palace with the slave and the guard. Although it was going to get cold soon, Claudia had no cloak and her sage green dress didn't look thick enough to keep out the autumn air. But she didn't seem to notice. She was flushed and clearly agitated, striding towards the olive grove with purpose. Soon the slave and the guard were left behind; their more leisurely pace a ploy to stay out of the way of their angry mistress. This was his chance. Rushing ahead, Judah picked up an abandoned basket and began picking olives, following a path that would intersect with Claudia's in the middle of the grove.

Walking quickly, while picking the odd olive for cover, Judah soon caught up with the Roman girl. He was in the next row and could see her through the branches. She had not seen him. She was breathing heavily, scuffing the ground with her sandal.

"What's wrong, my lady. Can I help you?"

She turned, startled, and saw him through the branches. Her cheeks were red, her hair damp; her blue eyes brimming over. He was struck by how beautiful she looked in her anguish. "Are you all right?"

Startled, she peered at him through the foliage. "Who are you?"

"Don't you recognise me?" Judah stepped into the open.

She inhaled quickly, ready to scream, but instead ran. She took off, back in the direction of the palace and Judah knew he needed to catch her before she ran into the guard and the slave girl who tarried around the next bend. Claudia was athletic in build and fast but her skirts hampered her and Judah soon caught up. He lunged at her, catching her around the waist and heaved her to the ground. She started to scream; he straddled her, slapping his hand over her mouth at the same time. Then he heard the mutter of voices: a man and a woman, approaching. With his hand still over Claudia's mouth he dragged her through the trees and into a shallow drainage ditch. He lay on top of her, pressing his body as low as it would go. His face was right next to hers. Their noses touched; and if his hand had not been between them, so would their lips.

"Where's she gone?" A male voice speaking Latin: a Roman auxiliary.

"She'll be fine, Felix. She just wants somewhere to cry alone." It was Nebela. Judah smiled to himself. *That girl has the survival instinct of a viper.* He was glad she had escaped on the day of the ambush. He would not have been able to protect her if she had not.

Felix and Nebela moved on, unhurried. Eventually when their voices faded into the distance he rolled off Claudia.

"When I remove my hand, don't scream. Do you understand?" His hand grasped a dagger, hidden in his tunic.

She nodded. Her eyes looked steadily into his, surprisingly unafraid. He removed his hand. She wiped hers vigorously across her mouth and opened and closed her jaw before pursing her lips. "You again."

"I'm not going to hurt you."

"And what do you call this?" She sat up and flexed her shoulders. Her scarf had fallen from her head and her hair fell loose. It was tangled with leaves and twigs.

"You're not hurt, are you?"

She glared at him again, rallying to retort, and then humphed: "No."

"Good."

"Good? Oh, so you've been instructed to bring me back alive, have you?"

"I am not going to take you anywhere. I just – just – wanted to see you."

"You have already seen me. The night of the circus."

"And you didn't turn me in."

"I still could."

"Then I'd kill you."

"We'll see." She clambered to her knees and got up, brushing loose leaves from her skirt.

He didn't know whether to apprehend her or stay where he was. She made up his mind for him; gesturing for him to follow her deeper into the grove. "Come, they'll be back soon. They can't see us together."

"Why not? I'm just a harvester picking olives."

72

"No, you're a Jew, working on the Sabbath. Even they won't be stupid enough to believe that. Besides, Nebela knows you. Unless... was it Nebela you were trying to see?"

"It wasn't."

Claudia looked like she was going to say something, but then didn't. Her easy gait invited him to keep pace. So he did. They did not speak for a while but he was aware of her every movement; her every breath. Her head came up to his chin and a few loose strands of chestnut hair whipped his face as they caught the breeze. They were still wet from her tears.

"Why were you crying?"

"I'll answer your question if you'll answer mine?"

"And what's that?"

"Why are you here?"

"I'm here to help with the harvest."

"You're lying."

"I'm not. I really am picking olives. Not today, of course, but every other."

"So, you've given up your life of crime then?"

"I've never led a life of crime."

"What do you call kidnapping an innocent girl?"

"Politics."

"Oh! How noble!"

"I've answered your question, now you must answer mine."

"As truthfully as you did?"

"More so, if you wish."

She stopped and turned to him. There was no fear in her face; no accusation. "Have you ever been forced to do something you didn't want to do?"

"Yes," he said, thinking that the last thing he would want to do would be to kill this beautiful girl.

"Well then you'll understand why I'm so upset."

"What are you being forced to do?"

"Marry someone I don't love."

"And who's that?"

"Tribune Marcus Gaius Sejanus. Do you know him?"

"Yes," said Judah, remembering the last time he had seen the tribune with Matthias' blood running down his arm.

They continued walking. The sun was beginning to drop below the horizon and the air was suddenly chill. Claudia shivered.

Without thinking, Judah took his cloak and wrapped it around her shoulders; as if this were an ordinary walk with an ordinary girl. But then he realised his knife was now exposed. She looked at it and then him, weighing him up.

"What do you want, Judah?"

"You remember my name."

"I do. And give me one good reason I should not tell my father?"

He grasped the knife hilt.

"One good reason *other* than you will kill me if I do."

"I don't want to kill you."

"What do you want?"

He looked at her upturned face. The wound on her forehead had healed but there was still a red welt above her eyebrow. He took his finger and gently stroked it. "I want you." Then he lowered his lips to hers and kissed her.

She stiffened for a moment then relaxed. His arms reached for her and he pulled her close. She did not resist.

"My lady! Where are you?" It was the Roman guard.

Claudia pulled away from him. "I'm here! Don't come any closer; I'm relieving myself."

She looked up at Judah and smiled, mischievously. "Will we meet again?" She whispered.

His hands were on her shoulders and he pulled up her scarf and picked some stray leaves from her hair. "Next week. On the Sabbath?"

She nodded, brushed down her dress and walked through the line of trees to the other side. "Don't look at me like that, Nebela. Even a lady has to go sometime."

Judah tried not to laugh.

Chapter 14 – A Rendezvous

Where in Saturn's name was she? Claudia had called for Nebela but the girl had not come. No doubt the Babylonian was sleeping somewhere unnoticed: a linen cupboard or one of the palace's unused rooms. It was becoming quite a habit with the girl, disappearing without a word to her mistress. Perhaps she had a lover. Claudia felt an inexplicable pang of jealousy. What if Judah had lied to her? What if he *was* here to see Nebela? What if they were in cahoots? It was strange how she had managed to escape from the ambush unharmed. Why was that? Did the Zealots let her go out of sympathy or because of something else... was she working with them? Was she working with Judah? Of course not! It was ridiculous to even think it. Why would Nebela have led the Romans back to the gorge if that were the case? Dozens of Zealots were killed. No, Nebela could not have been involved. But that did not solve the problem of where she was now. And where she kept slipping off to whenever she had half a chance. But, Claudia had to admit, her slave's repeated absences were working in her favour: she had the freedom now to slip off and do what she wanted to do.

It was Saturday, the Roman day of Saturn and the Jewish day of rest. It had been a week since she had met Judah in the olive grove and arranged to meet him again. She wondered if he would turn up. With the cloak he had lent her covered by her own, she headed out towards the grove, her step brisk but not unseemingly so. It was not usual for Pilate's daughter to be walking alone, so she kept her head low, hoping not to be noticed. One or two people cast her curious glances, but the scroll of poetry under the girl's arm reassured the good citizens of Caesarea that she was just looking for a quiet place to study and that her guards must be following her discreetly to give her the privacy she desired.

Thankfully, as she approached the clearing in the olive grove where she last met the Zealot, she was completely alone. The Jews were at home, doing whatever they did on Saturdays, and the other inhabitants of the town were far too busy indulging in the colourful entertainment of the market place to waste away the day in the stillness of the grove.

There were still a few hours before sunset, so Claudia wouldn't be missed, but the evening chill had already set in and it looked like there might be some rain before the moon rose. She was grateful for the added protection of Judah's cloak, although it had raised a few eyebrows when she arrived home with it last week.

"I was cold and a labourer gave me his," she answered truthfully when her mother questioned its origin.

"In Juno's name, Claudia, you should be careful about consorting with commoners!"

"I wasn't *consorting* mother, I was simply cold and he was kind enough to give it to me."

"Well, who was he?"

"How am I to know? What would you have me do, ask his name?"

"Of course not! But do be careful, Claudia, he could have fleas!"

Claudia smiled as she remembered her mother's horror, grateful that the worst she could think of was an infestation of vermin. But Procula did have a point and Claudia gave the cloak to Nebela to be washed. This led to another complication: when the cheap cloak came back neatly folded and smelling of lavender, the slave asked her mistress what she should do with it.

"Just leave it here."

"Are you going to give it back to him?" asked Nebela.

"Of course not! I don't know who the man is."

"I could ask one of the servants to make enquiries."

"I'm sure that won't be necessary."

"But what if he needs it? You said yourself that he was just a poor labourer. It must be his only cloak and it is getting cold at night."

"Thank you, Nebela, your concern for those less fortunate than yourself is admirable but a waste of time," said Claudia coolly.

"Oh no, mistress, it is not wasting my time…"

"Well, it's wasting mine!" declared Claudia, throwing the cloak on the fire. "Now please leave!"

Nebela hastened a quick retreat. Claudia chuckled, remembering that as soon as the slave had left the chamber she lurched at the fireplace and rescued the cloak, a little singed but otherwise intact. Why had she bothered? Perhaps it was because she knew that Nebela was right: this was probably Judah's only cloak. But if she were more honest, it was so she could keep the rough cloth near her as a reminder of that kiss.

Ah, that kiss… so different from the one Marcus Gaius Sejanus had bestowed on her earlier that day after announcing that he and her father were about to enter marriage negotiations. Claudia didn't know if she was more upset by the news that the dashing tribune was finally to become her husband, or the hard, unyielding kiss. As soon as she had a chance she had fled to the olive grove, looking for somewhere private to sort through her thoughts about the unwelcome engagement. And it was there that the potential solution to her problems had presented itself.

Was she destined to marry a man whom she did not love or – she quivered in excitement at the thought – had the gods answered her prayers and shown her that she could, possibly, be united with a man whom she was attracted to? It was troubling, yes, that the gods had chosen someone as – as – *problematic* as Judah, but as Claudia knew from the works of literature she had devoured since childhood, when it came to the divinities' meddling in the affairs of the human heart, love was rarely straightforward. On the other hand, what if he was still working for Barabbas? Was she just being a fool to believe that he had come to Caesarea simply to see her? Because he was attracted to her as she was to him? That his saving her from Matthias at the Zealot camp was – just as he himself had claimed – to stop a fellow Israelite defiling himself with a gentile? But when thoughts like those took hold she forced herself to remember that kiss and the look in his eyes – the *honest* look he had given her – and she *chose* to believe him. To take the risky path of love always required a choice.

"Ah, Judah," she whispered. "What am I going to do?"

She was now at the spot where she had met him last week; when she saw him, recognised him and ran. But she was not planning on running today.

"Claudia," he stepped into the clearing. Her heart leapt. His beard was starting to grow again and she thought the dark stubble suited him more than the smooth cheeks he had when he worked for Herod. He remained silent. Claudia didn't know what to say either, so they just stood there, in awkward silence. She wanted to spar, to tease, to get back what they had before, but she didn't know where to begin. Then Claudia remembered the cloak.

"I have your cloak," she blurted out.

He took it from her, laughing, and said with mock deference: "Well, my lady, I'm honoured. I thought you would have burnt it."

"Burn it?" she answered with equal irony, "I would never do that!"

"Of course not," he mocked, fingering the singe marks as he tossed it over his shoulders.

They both laughed, relieved. He offered her his arm. "Shall we walk?"

She slipped her hand under his elbow. "I would love to."

"So how did you get away?" he asked, turning into the very deepest part of the grove where they would be safest from prying eyes.

"Oh, I just came."

"I thought Pilate's daughter would be better guarded."

"Well, I am!" She bristled at the insinuation that her father had not protected her.

"It doesn't look like it now."

"I came on my own. If I had told someone, a guard would have come with me."

"But you didn't, and now we're alone."

"Yes, we're alone."

Judah stopped. "Do you trust me?"

"I don't know yet."

"And yet you came. Why?"

"I don't know." She looked into his eyes: they were dark and probing. "I, I just had to. I had to find out."

"Find out what?"

"What it all means."

He didn't ask what she meant by that. Instead, he cupped her chin in his hand and brushed her cheek with his finger. She leant into it and sighed; not a deep sigh, but a short, breathy one, like a swimmer releasing pressure in her lungs.

She leaned her head back and looked him squarely in the eyes. They were moist and sad.

"What is it?" she asked.

He shook his head, gently, and brought his lips down on hers. She didn't pull away, she was ready: she'd been preparing herself all week. Her lips parted, equal to his, and allowed his mouth to explore hers. Then, just as she was about to reciprocate, he pulled away. She protested, physically, by pushing her body closer to his. But he took her firmly by the shoulders and pushed her to arm's length. "If my comrades knew what was happening, they would kill me. And you."

"They don't have to know. I won't tell, will you?"

"No, but I have to tell them something."

"Why?"

"They will ask me for a full report. I was sent here to find out if you will co-operate with us."

"Co-operate?" she asked, feeling slightly uneasy.

"Yes."

"How?"

"By giving us information."

"About what?"

"Your father's plans."

"My father's plans? You want me to betray my father?" Her voice rose slightly.

"Yes, well, at least I did. I was supposed to find out all I could from you. But if I couldn't then…"

"You were supposed to kill me, weren't you?"

He lowered his eyes. She sighed again, this time deeper, as every last breath that might have been used for words was forced from her body. She pulled away from him, heading in the direction of the palace.

For a moment, he stood there, perhaps contemplating the crossroads that he had come to. Then he ran after her and caught her by the shoulders.

"Well, go on then," she spat, spinning around to face him. "Kill me. You've got that dagger there somewhere; just do it; because I'm not going to betray my father!"

"You don't understand what's going on here, Claudia."

"Then tell me!"

They glared at each other, both breathing deeply. Then he took her hand and pulled her down with him. They sat side by side with their backs against a tree trunk. He continued to hold her hand. She continued to let him.

"It's like I told you when you were our captive: my people will not rest until the Romans are driven out of our land."

"Is that likely? We Romans are the most powerful people on earth."

"Kingdoms come and kingdoms go. That's what the Persians thought and the Babylonians and the Macedonians. And where are they now? It is God who allows kings to rule and God who casts them down." He used the Hebrew word YHWH, so Claudia knew he didn't mean just any god. She had been in Judea long enough to know a little about the Jews and their strange religion and had been reading some of their history.

"Then why doesn't your god, Jehovah, cast us down? He's had plenty of chances over the last hundred years or so." She realised she sounded facetious. She didn't mean to be.

"Oh but He has. With the Maccabees He gave us a taste of what He could do, and when Messiah comes ..."

"Who's Messiah?"

Judah looked away from her and up to the sky. When he looked down again his face was radiating passion. "He's the One we've all been waiting for. He's the Son of YHWH who will drive all God's enemies from this land and establish a kingdom in Israel that will last forever."

Claudia didn't know whether to be frightened or inflamed by Judah's zeal. "How do you know this?"

"The prophets foretold it. It's written in our holy scriptures. The prophet Joel..." Judah stopped and put his finger to his lips, motioning for her to keep quiet. "He's coming," he whispered.

"Who? Messiah?"

"No," said Judah, chuckling, despite himself. "A soldier on horseback. I can hear them. It is probably your Tribune Sejanus. But Messiah will be here one of these days. Some say He's already among us." He got up and pulled Claudia with him. He squeezed her hands then released her. "Go, before Sejanus sees us."

Claudia didn't know what to do. Judah had all but admitted to her that he had been sent there with instructions to kill her. And instead of running she had listened to him lay out his comrades' plans to annihilate her people. All she had to do was call out and Marcus would come running. He would find Judah and capture or kill him. She heard the jingle of a bridle. Marcus was getting closer. She squinted through the trees, trying to see him. Then she turned back to Judah. "Judah, I..." but Judah was gone.

A moment later, Sejanus' white charger entered the clearing. The tribune reared him in. "Claudia Lucretia! Where have you been? Your mother was worried about you."

"Oh," she said nonchalantly, wafting the scroll of poetry in his direction. "I just needed somewhere quiet to read."

He dismounted, not hiding his irritation. "Well, you should have taken a guard with you; it wasn't very long ago that I had to save you from a filthy Jew. We wouldn't want that to happen again, now, would we?"

"No, Marcus, we certainly would not."

"Good, then let's get back to the palace; but make sure this never happens again."

Without asking her permission, Sejanus lifted her onto the horse then mounted behind her. As they left the grove, Claudia looked back, hoping to see Judah peeking at her from his hiding place. But he never appeared. She wondered if she would ever see him again.

Chapter 15 – Nebela

She smelt of apples: her hair, her skin, her breath. He liked that smell; it comforted him, made him feel safe. It reminded him of his refuge: the orchard he would go to when he was a small boy and his uncle was best avoided. But Uncle Lucius was far away in Rome and he was here in Judea with a beautiful woman in his bed. It was the fourth time he'd had her, and each time was better than the last. Thankfully, the first time, she had been a virgin, which surprised him seeing she had come from the Herod household. Unlike the Herods, he did not force himself on women, not even slaves. He wanted his women to be willing, and this one had certainly been that.

The first time had been the night of the festival of thanksgiving to Juno. He and Pilate had walked arm in arm from the amphitheatre, reliving the evening blow by blow. The women were behind them, more subdued: Procula Claudiana, Claudia Lucretia, the slave Nebela and another woman who had joined them on the way. It was Zandra, Nebela's mother, whom some said was a soothsayer, and others a witch. Marcus didn't care either way. Zandra and Nebela were speaking quietly to one another in their Babylonian dialect, and now and then he caught them looking at him. He was amused but not surprised. Women were always attracted to him, and after his performance at the circus, who could blame them?

But his charms didn't seem to be working on Claudia Lucretia. Earlier in the day she appeared to be enjoying his company, but now she was aloof, caught up in her own thoughts. Well, she was probably tired, worn out from the memories of her abduction. He wouldn't hold it against her.

During the banquet, which he thoroughly enjoyed, he tried to catch Claudia's eye, but she left before the last course, followed soon after by Procula Claudiana, wanting, perhaps, to find out what was wrong with her daughter. He noticed too that the slave Nebela had left early as well; undoubtedly her mistress needed her.

Flushed with wine and a general sense of wellbeing, Marcus took leave of his host and headed to his quarters. His servants had prepared things just the way he liked them before going to bed: there was a fire in the grate to stave off the autumn chill, the torches subdued to a gentle glow, a hot bath drawn and laced with oil. Like most Romans he bathed at the public baths once a day, but unlike many of his countrymen, he also bathed in private before going to bed. He stepped into the room and was greeted by a servant girl who had been waiting in the shadows. But it wasn't the usual one, the timid Jewess called Judith, but the tawny Babylonian, Nebela.

"What are you doing here?" he asked, kicking off his sandals and giving her his cloak.

"I thought you might need a bath," she answered, softly.

"I do, but I have my own servants who do that."

"I know. But they can't make it tonight."

"They can't?" He was amused and allowed her to unpin his toga.

"No, they can't." Nebela unfurled the draped linen from Marcus' shoulders. She allowed it to fall heavily to the floor and stood before him, boldly eyeing his muscular chest. Then she reached out to loosen his loincloth, but he stopped her, holding her hand gently, but firmly in his.

"I'll do that."

"Whatever you wish, master."

Marcus undid his loincloth and tossed it onto the bed. He noticed that there were petals strewn on it, magnolia petals.

"You've been busy."

She didn't answer but took his hand and led him to the bath. He stepped into it, quivering with pleasure as the hot water caressed his calves, thighs, buttocks, loins and back. Nebela stood above him, fully clothed. He recognised the dress; it was an old one of Claudia's, but the bold scarlet suited the darker girl far better than her fairer mistress.

She took a silver jug and dipped it into the water, allowing her loose hair to fall onto his shoulders. It smelled of apples; he liked that smell, he always had. She poured the water between his shoulder blades, letting it trickle down his back. Then, choosing to ignore the sponge on a nearby table, she washed his skin with her bare hands, rubbing and kneading the heady musk oil into every part of his body.

He was aroused, but resisted the temptation of pulling her into the water with him. It would be better if he waited. After rinsing his hair with fresh water, Nebela held out a soft towel for him to step into. He did, standing naked in the middle of the room as the girl rubbed him dry from top to bottom. But then his patience ran out. He took the towel from her and threw it aside.

"Are you angry with me, master?"

"Of course not; but there is more I want to do."

She unpinned her dress and let it fall to the ground like a scarlet waterfall, appearing to enjoy the sensation as it cascaded over her flesh. He pulled her to him, kissed her once then carried her to the bed.

"Is it your first time?" he asked.

"Yes," she said, quietly, but without shame.

"Then I will be gentle." And he was, pausing at each stage until the girl was ready to continue, knowing that next time it would be easier for them both. And next time it was, and the time after that. But this last time was the easiest of all.

*

They lay spent in each other's arms and Marcus toyed lazily with her long black hair. Nebela lent up on one elbow and stared deeply into his eyes. She loved his eyes: a slate grey, warmed with golden flecks. She loved his light brown hair too, grown a little longer than the average Roman man, brushing his forehead just above his brows. He had let himself go, he told her, since he had come to Judea; it was like an extended holiday, and she a holiday romance. She traced the dark stubble along his square jaw until she reached his lips: not as thin as some Romans', but not as full as hers. He bit her finger playfully, shaking his head from side to side and growling like a dog. She laughed and tried to pull away. But he grabbed her hand and continued to chew, nibbling all the way up her arm.

"You will swallow me if you don't stop, Marcus!"

"I know," he laughed, not minding that she used his given name.

"But if you eat me, I will be part of you," she said, slightly more seriously.

"And what is wrong with that?" he asked, apparently not noticing the change in her tone.

Best not to push him too far too soon, she thought. "Oh nothing, absolutely nothing." Then she kissed him deeply, laying her body on top of his. When she felt him respond she thought she might risk probing a little deeper. "Do you love me, Marcus?" She pulled away slightly. Her body and the attraction it aroused in him was the only power she had and she would use it to her advantage.

Now it was his turn to sound more serious. "Of course I love you, Nebela. I think I loved you from the first time I carried you on my horse."

It's what she'd been waiting to hear! Her mother said he would never admit to loving her; that it would give her too much power over him; that he was too shrewd a man to fall into her trap. But her mother, it seemed, was wrong. Ha! She did not know everything after all. So emboldened by his confession of love she asked: "Then will you marry me?" It was a risk, she knew it, but she kept her tone light so that she could retract and say she had been joking if he did not react well.

"Oh, Nebela, I would marry you tomorrow if things were different," he answered, drawing her to him. He wanted her again, she knew that. So she resisted. It was another calculated risk.

"But why, Marcus? Why can't you marry me?"

"You know why, Nebela, I don't have to tell you. If I were not a tribune in the Emperor's army; if you were not a slave…"

"But I was not born a slave!" She smarted.

"I know, I know, but you are now."

"But you could free me!" she gushed, her tears brimming over. She was not putting this on. Her shame and anger about her enslavement had not faded since the day she and her mother were betrayed by her father.

"No, Nebela, I could not. I do not own you, the Herods do."

She pulled away from him and threw her face into the pillow, weeping. Marcus frowned. Nebela, sensing his change of mood, sat up and wiped her tears. "I'm sorry." She took his hands, knowing he would be touched by how small hers looked wrapped in his. "I'm being foolish. It's just that I love you so much. You do understand, don't you?" She looked at him, her eyes awash with tears.

"Oh, Nebela, if things were different I *would* marry you, but they're not. I hope you are not going to be difficult about this."

"Of course not." She needed to regroup quickly; she wiped away her tears.

"Good," he declared and stood up to get dressed. But as he bent down to retrieve his robe she ran her hands down his thighs.

"I must go, Nebela; I must inspect the troops."

"Right now?" She giggled outwardly. Inwardly, she was assessing the situation. She realised she needed to reassert her power over him. She stood up, wrapped her arms around him and pressed her full length against him.

He spun around and pushed her down on the bed. "Well, perhaps not *right* now."

Mission accomplished.

Chapter 16 – Rosh Hashanah

It was the first of Tishri, the first day of the Jewish New Year. In the migrant harvesters' camp the workers were gathering after their day in the olive orchard to celebrate Rosh Hashanah. A double celebration was planned for the evening, as this year the festival fell on the eve of Shabbat. It was fortuitous that it had, as each year there were debates between the Jewish labourers and the non-Jewish landowners as to which festivals they would have off work. The 'greater' festivals of Atonement, Hannukah, Passover and Tabernacles were usually given – as well as Shabbat once a week – but gentile bosses were reluctant to give more time off. It did not help that there were four different 'new years' in the Hebrew calendar, marking the beginning of the calendar year, the harvest year, the year of animal husbandry and the increase of years. Rosh Hashanah was the latter. When asked for this day off, gentile landowners would say the day had no particular religious significance and that as it was already October, the Roman New Year in January should suffice.

No religious significance? Could they not see that this was the time that YHWH, the one and only Creator God, was to be thanked for the very act of creation? That without Him – and without the Jews – there would be no world for the Roman conquerors to conquer? Any other year, Judah would have been grumbling with the rest of the Jewish labourers, but as this year Rosh Hashanah fell the day before what the Romans called 'Saturday' they could work the day and then at sunset use the time of the Shabbat meal as their new year celebration.

So as Judah offloaded his last basket of olives he heard the first of the trumpets – the shofars – being blown in celebration. His heart soared at the sound. One day a heavenly shofar would blast and Messiah himself would appear. Then when the battle to end all battles was over, the rhythm of the Hebrew year would be restored. No more kow-towing to gentiles about whether or not a Jew could worship like a Jew in his own land. No more working for a handful of shekels while the fruit and fat of the land lined foreigners' pockets with denarii.

As he headed off to wash at the unmarried men's hostel, he spotted Judith, one of the indentured servants who worked in the palace. Judah knew Judith's brother. He was one of Barabbas' men and as such she was to be trusted to keep his identity a secret. He had told her though that he was no longer working for Barabbas and as far as she knew, he was just one of the migrant labourers. It did not bother her that he no longer ran with the Zealots. In fact, she wished her brother would not. Then he could work to pay off the debt that had forced her into indentured servitude for seven years. Once a week Judith left the palace and came to the camp to spend Shabbat with her own people. She was carrying a covered kneading trough which contained the dough for unleavened bread. But she was looking agitated.

"What's wrong, Judith?"

"Ah Judah, I don't know what to do. I've left a bag of herbs outside the palace kitchens. If I go back to get them now I won't have time to cook the Shabbat meal; but I need the herbs to bake the bread!" She chewed her lip and smoothed the cloth absent-mindedly.

"I'll go for you. Why don't you get started on the rest of the food and I'll get the herbs as quickly as I can."

Judith welled up with tears at Judah's generosity. He brushed it off with: "It's the least I can do for a sister Israelite," and escaped before her gratitude spilled over any further.

Judah pulled his hood over his head as he approached the palace gardens. He knew that the new growth of beard and lack of Herodian uniform disguised him. He knew too that there was no one left alive in Caesarea – apart from Claudia, Nebela and Judith – who would recognise him. But he didn't want to take any chances.

As he neared the palace gates he adopted a hunched demeanour, drawing attention away from his battle-toned physique. When asked his business, he told the guard he had been sent there by the Jewess Judith to collect some herbs. He had deliberately timed his approach to coincide with the tail-end of the day shift. From experience he knew the guards would be tired and looking forward to their dinner.

The Roman guard searched him for any weapons and when none were found took his story at face value, let him through and pointed him in the direction of the kitchen gardens. Judah had no nefarious intentions. But if he had, he would already have breached the outer wall. True, it would be more difficult to gain access to the palace itself, but a lot could be done simply by being in the grounds. This troubled him. If Barabbas knew how lax the security at the palace really was, he would be sending men to kidnap or kill the Pilates. Ah, but he already had, Judah reminded himself. *He* was the assassin in waiting.

Judah had not had a solid night's sleep since he had met Claudia in the olive grove on the last Shabbat – nearly a week ago. He was overwhelmed with the intensity of his feelings for her. What had started out simply as an exploratory mission to see whether or not she had feelings for him and could be manipulated had turned into something much, much more. Yes, she had feelings for him. Barabbas was right. But what Judah had not anticipated was that he had feelings for her too. He had always been attracted to her – that much had been clear from the day of the boar hunt – but Judah had been taken by surprise by his own reaction to the kiss. He had not been able to stop thinking of her since. His mind – and yes – his body had wandered into scenario after scenario in which he was not a Zealot and she not the daughter of the governor of the invading infidel. He had imagined them meeting innocuously in a market place or at a well. She would be the daughter of a shepherd from Galilee, he the son of a merchant or scribe. In Judah's dreams they would meet, fall in love, tell their families – who of course would be delighted – then dowry negotiations would take place. Claudia (or Rachael as she became in his Jewish fantasy) would be honoured to receive a marriage proposal from a man of his stature. And so would her parents.

These of course were his waking dreams, when he still had control of his meanderings. His somnambulant dreams were something else and he woke from them breathless and ashamed.

But whether waking or sleeping he had come to realise one thing: he cared for this girl and could not bring himself to go through with Barabbas' plan. He could not woo her and betray her; and if she resisted his advances (which so far she had not) he could not carry out the death sentence that his master had decreed. Judah did not know what to do. He knew the fate of men who disobeyed Barabbas' orders; a refusal would sign his own death warrant. There seemed to be no way out.

Then one night, when he woke tossing and turning from a particularly vivid dream in which he had saved Claudia from Matthias and she had given herself to him fully in gratitude, he had realised the only solution was to leave Israel. He could offer his services on one of the merchant ships in Caesarea harbour. Or join a camel train going east to Parthia. He had always wanted to see what was on the other side of the Jordan. He could stay there a few years until Barabbas' wrath had expired, then return. Or perhaps Barabbas might die. He had umpteen warrants against him with rewards promised for his capture or death. It was just a matter of time before someone betrayed him and cashed in. Judah, for one mad moment had considered doing it himself, but then he had come to his senses. That was not the man he wanted to be. He would not betray Barabbas. But neither could he betray Claudia. He simply did not know what to do.

As he entered the palace gardens, he had no plan other than to retrieve Judith's herbs and return to the labourers' village. But all this changed when he saw Nebela and she saw him. She was in a courtyard with a water clock in the centre, gathering magnolia petals that had fallen from the surrounding trees. Judah spotted her and attempted to withdraw, but it was too late.

"Judah!" she stood up, dropping her apron and the petals that filled it. She looked frightened. For a moment Judah wondered why, then he remembered the last time she had seen him was when three dozen men had been butchered and he had bludgeoned a Roman girl with the hilt of his sword.

She started to run, but he intercepted her, pulling her behind some manicured shrubbery, his hand pinned firmly over her mouth.

"I'm not going to hurt you, I promise."

She writhed and squealed against his hand. She was stronger than she looked and Judah had to double his efforts to keep her still. "I promise, Nebela, I am not going to do anything. I don't want to hurt you – or Claudia. You must believe me. Please."

She stopped fighting him and stood still in his arms. He took this as a sign that she was prepared to listen. "If I let you go, will you promise not to scream?"

She nodded her head vigorously. He removed his hand.

"What the hell do you think you're doing?" she spat, as waspish as she had ever been. Judah could not help but smile. Oh, he had missed her. She had been a good friend at Herod's palace and owed him for saving her skin on more than one occasion. True, there was nothing romantic between them, but he felt for her as he would for a younger sister, or childhood friend.

"So have you come here to finish the job?"

He assumed she meant Claudia. "No, there is no job. Not that kind. I've left the Zealots. I'm working as a labourer in the olive grove. I've just come to get some herbs for Judith."

He still held her, in case she ran. She looked at him with narrowed eyes, assessing the truth of what he had just told her. Judah, like most who knew her, often wondered if she had inherited her mother's second sight. She was shrewd beyond her years and knew exactly how to make people do what she wanted them to do. Would she believe him now?

The answer was no. "You have other motives, Judah, I can tell. But I do believe you when you say you will not hurt Claudia. It was never in you in the first place. That Barabbas was a fool to believe you would."

That smarted his pride – that he was not man enough – but he let it pass.

"I thought I recognised your cloak when Claudia brought it home. What have you been up to?"

Judah blushed, despite himself. Nebela smiled, knowingly. "Ah, I was right."

"Oh nothing like that has happened!" he blurted.

"No?" she cocked her head to the side and twirled out of his grasp. She sat down on a marble bench in the cloistered alcove and patted the cold stone beside her. Judah sat down too.

"Do you love her?"

Judah swept at the gravel with the toe of his sandal, making semi-circular swathes in the pebble path.

Nebela chuckled. "So you came to catch a glimpse of her."

"No."

"No? Well, good. Because she's currently walking on the beach with Tribune Marcus Gaius Sejanus."

Was that jealousy he detected in Nebela's voice? Ah, perhaps he could turn the tables here. "And are you in love with Sejanus, Nebela?"

She turned to him with her amber eyes and he knew immediately that it was true. Incredibly there were tears there. And he didn't think she was putting it on. He took her hand and squeezed it. "You are, aren't you?"

She nodded and sniffed, getting the tears under control.

"We're a right pair, aren't we? Falling for people we can never have."

"But we can!" She grasped his hand more tightly. "You can have Claudia and I can have Marcus."

"But how?"

She stood up and turned to him, ablaze with beauty and passion. "I have a plan." She started pacing up and down in the small alcove, her feet crunching the gravel. "You must woo her, Judah. She wants to be wooed."

"You sound like Barabbas!"

"Well, he's right. But woo her to love her, not to kill her."

"But to what end? We can never be together."

"You can!"

"How?"

"I have an idea, but first you need to make her love you."

"She is going to marry Sejanus."

"Not yet. They're not even engaged. Pilate is dragging his heels in the negotiations for some reason. And I have a plan to delay it even further. I will let it be known in the labourers' village that Barabbas and his men have been seen in the mountains of Samaria. I will whisper it to Judith that I've heard it said around the palace. She will be bound to mention it to someone in the village. "

"But the mountains are exactly where they are!"

"Yes, but the mountains are a big place. I will send them to the side where your friends are not. Sejanus will rush off on his charger and not have time to finalise the engagement. And if you send word you can let your friends know the Romans are coming."

"I don't know, Nebela. It's a risk."

She stood over him, hands on hips, blocking the last of the afternoon sun. "Love is a risk, Judah. Are you man enough to take it?"

He clenched his jaw as her shadow fell over him. "Yes Nebela, I *am* a man."

*

A Dream of Procula Pilate

The banging is inside my head. Nails are being driven into my skull. I must make it stop. Only when it stops will I find my daughter again. Where should I go? What should I do? I will ask this soldier: an officer, a tribune, I think. He is talking to a girl – a slave – I cannot see her face. I ask: "Sir, where can I go to stop the banging? Who can I ask to make it go away?" He points to a hill above the city: a rubbish dump with three crosses on it. I thank him. He turns his face to me. It is Marcus Gaius Sejanus, but he does not recognise me. He does not smile. I wonder why. Am I not properly dressed? Perhaps it is my bleeding feet; it does not matter. I pass a tree with a corpse hanging from it; it is a young man, his contorted face strangely familiar. But I do not stop to stare. I climb the hill until I am at the foot of the centre-most cross. A man is nailed to it: a Jewish man. His blood drips upon my head. "What do you want, Procula?" he asks. "I want this banging to stop?" I say. "Is that all?" he asks again. "No, I want my daughter to return to me." His smile touches me without hands. "Then find me, follow me, have faith in me." "But where will I find you?" I ask, as his blood runs down my face, obscuring my vision. When the blood clears he is gone, but the question still remains.

Chapter 17 – The Soothsayer

Zandra's business was going well. Her reputation had been much enhanced since she had accurately predicted the death of the stable boy at Herod's palace – the one who choked on the almond. She was a little surprised though, as she always thought that people wouldn't pay to hear bad news; but she was thankfully wrong. She wondered what she would tell the mistress of the house when she came for her consultation. Zandra had been having strange visions about Procula Claudiana: drenched in the blood of a crucified man. She wondered if it would be prudent to tell the truth; after all, this was no ordinary client, she was the wife of the governor of Judea and related to the Claudians, one of the most powerful families in Rome.

Zandra gathered the tools of her trade: the bones, the feathers, the crucible to burn the hair of her client (or the client's enemy or the client's lover), the ritual knife and the sacred bowls. These latter two were a concession to her Roman clients who had been brought up examining the entrails of animals. Zandra was a competent businesswoman and she realised that the professional Roman augurs were her major competition, so if she could approximate their techniques, she may win a few disillusioned clients from the state religion. Zandra put no faith in the blood of animals, but if a client brought a chicken or a dove she would oblige. It did not matter; her secret knowledge came from somewhere else: from the spirits of ancient Mesopotamia who spoke to her in ways she could not explain. But what were the spirits trying to tell her of Procula Claudiana Pilate? The woman who even now was stepping into her chamber?

"Ah, there you are, Zandra, I can hardly see you through all this incense. And the lights, must they be so low?"

"Yes mistress, the spirits to which I speak do not like the light. And this incense, that is to appease the gods of Rome. But I can light a lamp if you prefer."

"No, that's all right." Procula sighed as she sunk down onto a pile of cushions. "I'm sorry Zandra, it's just that I'm not too comfortable in the dark right now."

"And why is that?" asked the soothsayer as she settled on another pile of cushions in the small, dusty room the Pilates had given her to conduct her business.

"Well, that's why I'm here. Ever since I came to Judea I've been having terrible dreams and they've been getting worse. I've come to fear the dark: it's when the dreams come to haunt me."

"Hmm, so that's what's afflicting you. I've noticed, mistress, that you are pale and have lost weight. Your husband has noticed too."

"My husband?"

"Yes, that's why he brought me from Herod's palace. Didn't he tell you that he was worried about you?"

Procula smiled gently and a slight blush caressed her wan cheek. "He told me that it was to reward Nebela for her loyalty when my daughter, Claudia Lucretia, was abducted."

"Yes, it was, and for that both my daughter and I are grateful. But it was also for you. So tell me of your dreams and I will see if I can help you."

*

Procula was in two minds about telling the soothsayer of her dreams. Back in Rome, she would have gone to her own priest, the leading authority on Mithraism, but here, Zandra, a devotee of a mysterious Mesopotamian religion, was the closest she could get to the Persian worship of Mithras; a faith that was over a thousand years old. Her husband teased her about her devotion to the 'Eastern cult' as he called it, but she found comfort in the positive message that Mithras brought to mankind: of justice and the triumph of good over evil.

Mithras, known to his worshippers as 'The Light of the World', was the symbol of truth, justice and loyalty. He was the mediator between heaven and earth and a member of a Holy Trinity. According to Persian mythology, Mithras was born of a virgin who was given the title 'Mother of God'. He was celibate and valued sexual self-control amongst his followers, and he called on them to unite against the forces of evil. He was a benevolent god (unusual in the pantheon of Persia) who sympathised with his worshippers' suffering. He promised to free them from all their pain through immortality and eternal salvation in a world to come. They would reach this world after the final day of judgement in which the dead would rise and light would finally triumph over darkness.

Three years ago, Procula Claudiana had gone through the ritual of baptism to initiate her into the faith and, when in Rome, regularly took part in a ceremony, consuming bread and wine as a symbol of Mithras' body and blood. This was an act, it was said, that Mithras participated in with his closest followers, before he ascended back to the heavens. Sundays were sacred to the god, and his birthday was celebrated once a year, twelve days after the Ides of December, on the 25th day of the month. This was convenient for Procula, as one of Pontius' favourite gods was Saturn whose birthday was also celebrated on that day during the annual Saturnalia. It was a joyous time for Roman households, even those in faraway provinces like Judea.

Although Mithras was growing in popularity, particularly with soldiers, there were few worshippers in Judea. There were no priests either, so Procula conducted her devotions privately. This, however, did not impinge upon her duties as wife of the governor, and publicly she joined her husband in honouring the pantheon of Roman gods. But for Procula, there was only one god worthy of her love, and that was Mithras. She hoped that this Babylonian might have a word from him today.

As if reading her mind, Zandra closed her eyes and said: "I feel the spirit of Mithras."

"What does he say?" asked Procula, excitedly.

"I – I – cannot quite hear…" Zandra held out her hand.

Procula was angered by the taint of materialism on so spiritual a moment, but she paid without complaint then pushed Zandra for an answer.

"He says you must tell me of your dream."

"My dream? I don't know if I'm able to put it into words. It's pictures, feelings, sounds, blood…"

"Blood?" Zandra interrupted. "The blood of a crucified man?"

"Yes! How did you know?"

"Because before you came here today, I had a vision of you covered in the blood of a crucified man." This time Procula didn't balk when Zandra opened her hand for more money.

"Then perhaps you can help me after all. Perhaps Mithras has given you an interpretation."

"I'm afraid not, mistress. Not yet, but I'm sure he will. Perhaps the next time you come…"

"Next time? No, Zandra! I can't wait. I must understand it now! I can't take it any more, I can't!" Procula rose from the cushions and started pacing up and down in the small chamber. She was not a big woman, but her presence was growing with her anger. Zandra had to do something to calm her mistress down, or she would lose favour with the Pilates.

"Sit down, mistress," she said soothingly. "I will do my best to interpret your dream. Mithras will guide us." Procula reluctantly sank back onto the cushions, but her hands kept moving, incessantly.

"Now, mistress, tell me, what are you doing in your dream?"

"I'm looking for my daughter, Claudia Lucretia. I'm searching the streets of Jerusalem. My feet are bare; they're bleeding."

"Where is your daughter?"

"I don't know. But I must find her."

"Hmm, what is stopping you?"

"I don't know… perhaps it is the banging."

"What banging?"

"I'm not sure. I think it's the sound of flesh being nailed to wood."

"Like a crucifixion?"

"Yes, just like that."

"And is there anyone else in your dream, apart from the crucified man?"

"There are three others: Tribune Marcus Gaius Sejanus, a slave girl and a man hanging from a tree."

"Hmm. Tribune Sejanus… you recognised him?"

"Yes."

"Does he say anything?"

"No, not to me; he's talking to a slave girl."

"And who is she?" asked Zandra, pointedly.

"I don't know. I couldn't see her face."

"That's a pity… Does the tribune do anything?"

"Yes, he points me to the crucified man."

"The crucified man? Does he say anything?"

"Oh yes. He tells me that to find my daughter and make the banging stop, I must find him, follow him, and have faith in him."

"Find him, follow him and have faith in him. Perhaps it is the god Mithras."

"But why would Mithras be crucified? A god should not be subject to the judgements of men."

"Yes, of course, mistress. Perhaps it is not Mithras. But he is important, this crucified man, don't you think?"

"Oh yes, he's important. He knows how to find my daughter. But I must find him first. How can I find him?"

"Well, that's easy. Tribune Marcus Gaius Sejanus will show you where to find him!"

"Of course, it's so simple! Why didn't I see it myself! Thank you, Zandra," said Procula, jumping to her feet, her cheeks filling with colour. "Marcus will give me the answers I need. Just as well he's going to marry my daughter if he knows the man who can find her if she's ever lost. This is a good omen, don't you think?"

"Well, mistress, it might be. You don't want to jump to any conclusions here. This may not have anything to do with the marriage. Perhaps they should not get married. After all, he was talking to another girl in the dream…"

"A slave, Zandra, no one but a slave! There's nothing to worry about is there?"

"Perhaps not," answered Zandra carefully, "but there is still the man hanging from the tree. That is always a bad omen. Did you recognise him?"

"No," said Procula, not wanting to contemplate a negative interpretation for her dream, so soon after being released from it. "But he was familiar. I may have seen him somewhere before."

"Then watch out for him. He will bring nothing but death."

"But Marcus will bring life!" said Procula, brightly, and skipped out of the soothsayer's chamber.

"Yes," muttered Zandra, as she packed away the unused daggers and bowls. "He will bring life, but perhaps not to your daughter."

And as if to confirm it, Nebela appeared in her mother's doorway.

Zandra's face brightened immediately. "Ah, my daughter. Your timing could not be better!"

"Mother, I need to talk to you." Nebela closed the door behind her.

"And I to you." Zandra sniffed Nebela's hair as the girl entered the room. "You have been with him."

"With whom?" asked Nebela, annoyed that she could never keep a secret from her mother. "Have your spirits been telling tales again?"

"No, it is you who has been telling tales, daughter; be careful that Claudia doesn't smell him on you too!"

"Why would Claudia smell him on me? She doesn't know him like I know him. She has never been near him; nor he her!" Nebela sank into a pile of cushions and stretched out her frame, like a feline soaking in the sun. She yawned a little and smiled at her mother.

"Do not look like that little cat; you have not yet succeeded in catching your prey."

Nebela scowled. "What do you mean? I have just come from his bed! He said that he loved me…"

"But did he say that he would marry you?"

"Well, actually he did!"

"He did?"

"Yes, he did," said Nebela, pleased that she had surprised her omniscient parent.

Zandra was pouring a cup of herbal tea from a kettle. She paused and looked pointedly at her only child. "Surely not."

"And why is that?" asked Nebela, smarting. "Don't you think I'm good enough for him?"

"No, little one, you are more than a match for him. But I doubt that he will see it the same way."

"Well, he does!" pouted Nebela, plucking at a loose thread on a cushion. "He said that he would marry me tomorrow, if I were not a slave, and he a tribune in the Emperor's army!"

Zandra smiled sadly and shook her head, causing a dark-green head scarf to fall to her shoulders. At thirty-four she looked much like her daughter, although her black hair was tinged with early grey and the trials of slavery had drained her of youth – at first glance she looked ten years older. "Ah yes, I knew it was too good to be true. If only your father had not got himself into debt, we would not be in this position now: picking up leftovers from a Roman table."

"I am not picking up anyone's leftovers, mother, particularly not Claudia's. Marcus will be mine!"

"That's my girl!" laughed Zandra. "I knew that vision of you had meant something."

"What vision?"

"Well it was a dream, actually: Procula's dream."

"Procula's dream? Of me?"

"Yes, only she doesn't know that it was you."

"What was I doing in this dream?"

"You were with Marcus."

"I was, was I? And where was Claudia?"

"Nowhere," Zandra laughed, "she was nowhere in sight!"

"And you think this means something?"

"Yes, my daughter, I do. I believe that you and Marcus will be eternally linked; I'm just not sure how."

"By marriage of course! What other way could there be?"

"I don't know, my child, I don't know. Perhaps it's marriage, perhaps not; let us pray to the gods that it is."

"Yes, mother, pray to the gods, but I think there is something we can do about it too." The cat was back.

"And what is that, little one?"

"I have a plan and I need your help. Will you help me mother?"

"That depends on the plan," said Zandra, sitting down beside her daughter. "So tell me, how do you intend to make the tribune marry you?"

"With the help of Saturn," answered her daughter, purring with delight.

Chapter 18 – Dowry Negotiations

Pilate had had a good day so far. He had risen with the sun, although the water clock in the palace courtyard (an ultra-modern device and a welcoming gift from the grovelling Herods) already marked the third hour of the morning. Pilate preferred to use the old sundial that shifted with the seasons, so the first hour of dawn was always the first hour of the day. If he was to believe the water clock, he only had six hours left to cram in all of the duties and pleasures of a Roman governor before sunset marked the end of the working day. And if the local populace took note of the water clock instead of pacing their day with the perambulation of the sun, the economy would grind to a halt. And that would never be countenanced, not under Pontius Pilate's rule. His daughter, with more modern ideas than were good for her, thought it was a good idea to get up at the same time every day, as marked by the water clock. That would mean getting up when it was dark. And what would be the use of that?

No, Pilate rose at dawn, did his private ablutions then had a light meal of bread, fruit and water. Dressed and ready before the second hour arrived, he waited for his clients in one of the minor reception halls. It was a busy morning, but not overbearingly so, thanks largely to the absence of the usual rabble of Jewish supplicants from the Sadducee class who were preparing for one of their interminable religious festivals. Even those sycophants, Pilate noted, would be preparing for the most holy of days in the Jewish calendar: the tenth day of Tishri, the so-called Day of Atonement.

Pilate chuckled as he applied himself to an assortment of administrative tasks and decisions in minor legal disputes pertaining to his non-Jewish subjects – let the god of Israel deal with the rest! He almost felt sorry for the god who would have to listen to all the whining, but at least it was giving him a break. His secretary had suggested that business should be halted in case the Jews were offended.

"Offended," said Pilate, laughing. "Why should they be offended?"

"Because it is their custom and their country."

Pilate dropped his stylus and glared at the outspoken civil servant. "No, Paulus," he said frostily, "it is the *Emperor's* country, and don't you ever forget it!"

Although angered by Paulus' comment, Pilate admitted that the man had a point: it would not be good to antagonise the Jews yet again, particularly at this festival. For the last three years of his predecessor's consulship, there had invariably been some uprising or other on or around the Day of Atonement, stirred by excessive religious fervour. Pilate had been forewarned and sent reinforcements to all the major cities in the region, particularly Jerusalem, the only city with a majority Jewish population and the seat of the newly rebuilt Temple. But, remembering the hullaballoo that accompanied his insistence on raising the Emperor's standards in the city when he first arrived, Pilate instructed the centurions to keep as low a profile as possible without appearing weak.

He had even considered sending Marcus Gaius Sejanus and his men to the holy city, but thought better of it. There had already been one attempt on his family, and what better time for a religious zealot to strike out against the Emperor's representative than now. Besides, he had some business to take care of with the young Sejanus and if he didn't get to it soon, as his wife had reminded him this morning, they might lose their last chance to link their family to the most influential man in Rome. Since Tiberius had all but retired from the capital last year to live in his holiday home on the Isle of Caprae, the prefect of the Praetorian Guard, Lucius Aelius Sejanus, was left holding the reins of power. Some would say he had already held them for a long time: a puppet master holding all the strings. It was even rumoured that he had conspired with Tiberius' daughter-in-law to kill her husband Octavian and the emperor's heir. Now Livia, the daughter-in-law, who it was further rumoured was having an affair with Sejanus, had her sights on marrying the old emperor, making herself, de facto, the empress apparent. But the old man seemed oblivious to it all and whether or not any of the stories were true, one thing was for sure: Lucius Aelius Sejanus was currently the must powerful man in Rome.

And by some quirk of the gods, his nephew Marcus Gaius Sejanus, was stationed here in Judea. On the negative side he had heard rumours of a rift between the two men. He hoped relations were not too strained though; that would make the nuptial negotiations a tad more tiresome.

Pilate looked again at the water clock and sighed. Yes, it was time to act. Whatever gust of fate had blown this most eligible of suitors over their portico should be embraced; and quickly, before the wind decided to change direction. "Paulus!" Pilate called to his secretary. "I'm going to the baths."

"But sir," said Paulus, "You still have three clients to see."

"Tell them to come back on a day when the wind is not blowing."

"But you can't do that, sir!" said the secretary, cursing his master's break from schedule that meant he would now have to refund the pocketful of sesterces he'd received for bumping the three clients to the front of the queue.

Pilate slapped his secretary on the back of the head as he swept out of his office. "Correction, Paulus. I am the Governor of Judea and I can do whatever I damn well please!"

*

Pilate arrived at the baths with two of his slaves. He could have done with one but, as his wife had reminded him, he did not want to give the impression that he could not afford a larger retinue. So one man would oil, scrape and massage him while the other was free to purchase refreshments or to deliver messages to anyone Pilate wanted to do business with. No, not business of that kind, these were respectable baths and Pilate was a respectable man. Apparently, he had been told, the smaller bath complex on the outskirts of town was the place to go for that sort of thing – frequented by soldiers, sailors and actors. But in these baths, if 'that sort of thing' happened, it was not flaunted. Pilate had been informed the first day he arrived that a discreet assignation might be arranged for later in a private chamber, if he chose, with one of the well-managed prostitutes: female or male, according to taste. The latter styled themselves as masseurs.

It was only fourteen years since the death of the great Caesar Augustus, a second cousin of his beloved Procula, and the legacy of his moral reforms could still be felt in most places in the Empire. And thank Saturn for that, thought Pilate, who, for one, was much in favour of the Augustan clean-up and knew that the old man's bones would be rattling in his ossuary if he could see what went on in Rome these days.

No, Pilate was a traditional man with traditional values, and the only business he conducted at the baths was commercial. And today was one of those days. Pilate disrobed and plunged into the coldest pool. One slave stood by ready with his towel while the other went to look for Marcus Gaius Sejanus who was no doubt in the exercise yard. Pilate had reserved one of the steam rooms so the two men could speak privately. The bath manager had not looked happy about taking one of his two rooms out of action for an hour, but could not really say no to the Governor of Judea. And that, thought Pilate, was as it should be.

*

Half an hour later, Pilate had been through the pools, been rubbed and oiled and was now waiting for Marcus in the sauna. The door opened and the tribune entered, wearing just a towel. Pilate admired his toned, muscular chest: it reminded him of himself eighteen years ago while he was enjoying life as an army tribune. But then he got married. Part of the agreement with Procula's parents was that he would leave the army and take a job closer to home. Connected as they were, they had managed to get him a post in the civil service and so he had settled down to a life of petty bureaucracy. Pilate sighed. He wouldn't be expecting the same of Marcus Gaius. And even if he were, the more powerful family usually dictated the terms of the marriage. In this case, that was not the Pilates. On parchment, at least, both he and the young man in front of him were of the equus class: a good few rungs above the masses but not high enough to breathe in the refined air of the patrician class. But both knew the tribune's Roman connections elevated him to a different echelon. Claudia Lucretia would be marrying up, everyone knew it, but Pilate would be damned if he would concede that point today.

"Ah, there you are Marcus Gaius. Enjoying the baths?"

The young man smiled wryly and sat down on the stone bench next to the governor.

"Not bad for a provincial establishment."

"Not bad, not bad. And Judea is not bad for a placement."

"For you or me, sir?"

Pilate looked at him shrewdly. Was the younger man making a point about Judea being the first rung on the ladder for a young man at the start of his military career but the last rung on a downwards ladder for a bureaucrat in the doldrums of his? Or was he simply making polite conversation? Pilate did not know, but he filed the potential sleight away for future reference.

"For both of us, Marcus... It could be Britannia!" Both men laughed and stretched out their limbs, their muscles soaking up the clammy heat, relaxing in companionable silence. "So how is security?"

"Everything's under control, sir. Most of the Jews in the city have either gone back home or to Jerusalem for the Atonement rituals at the Temple. We're not expecting any trouble for the next few days."

"And the Zealots?"

"Ah well, they're always up to something, aren't they?"

Pilate nodded his assent.

"In fact, sir, I was going to speak to you about that. I've had some information about the band of fanatics who captured your daughter."

"Are there any left?"

"Unfortunately there are, sir. Some escaped during the rescue."

"Do you know where they are?"

"We have some idea. We have an informer amongst the olive pickers in Caesarea. One of the Zealots who was trying to hide out here; but my spies spotted him."

"Indeed. And you made him talk?"

"Of course. He's now a double agent."

"Good, good."

"So I would like to take a cohort of my best men into Samaria to track them down. With your permission, of course."

"Of course," said Pilate. "When do you plan to go?"

"In a few days, when things have settled down. After Yom Kippur."

The Hebrew word for the atonement festival sounded awkward on the young Roman's lips, thought Pilate.

"Of course. You will be leaving enough men here to protect the port?"

"That goes without saying, sir."

"And how long will you be gone?"

"I'm not sure. Four to six weeks, depending."

"Quite. Well, Marcus, it's just as well we're going to have this little talk now, before you leave town.

"Oh?"

"Well, yes. It's about my daughter, Claudia Lucretia."

"How is she doing, after her ordeal?"

"Much better, thank you. In recent weeks she's begun to laugh again. I haven't seen her this happy since... well, I've never seen her this happy."

"Oh."

"And I think much of that is down to you, Marcus."

"Me?

"Come, come, don't be coy. I saw how you touted for her attention at the circus."

"That's true."

"And a little bird told me there have been some walks on the beach and perhaps a kiss…"

"Yes, well, I'm sorry about that sir."

"Nothing to be sorry about my boy. I hope…"

"You're right sir, nothing."

"Good. Then nothing has changed since the last time we spoke about this. As we previously agreed, the two of you would make a good match."

The young man shifted uncomfortably on the bench next to him. "Well, I–"

Pilate suddenly realised that something had indeed changed since the last time he and Marcus had spoken. What could it be? Another potential bride? He tensed but forced himself to speak lightly. "Is anything wrong, Marcus Gaius?"

Marcus cleared his throat and sat up straight. "Well, sir, your daughter is a beautiful and – and – *intelligent* young woman. Very… bookish."

"I'm sure it's just a phase. But that aside, you can see a future with her, can't you?"

"A future?"

"A union. Between the house of Pilate and the house of Sejanus. It's what we've already spoken of. We are of equal standing –"

"Well…"

" – and Claudia does have patrician blood. Her mother is a cousin of the emperor."

"So I believe."

"She would not be an unworthy match for you."

"Of course not, sir. It's just that I would need to discuss it with my uncle. There may now be someone else…"

Ah, Pilate's suspicions had been correct. Damn, Procula Claudiana was right; he should not have waited so long. "In Rome?"

"Palestine."

"Who? Not that trollop Salome!"

"By Juno, no! Look, I need to speak to my uncle. And to do that I will need to go to Rome."

"You could leave as soon as you come back from Samaria."

"Possibly. But I would like to be around for the harvesters leaving. Perhaps I could squeeze something in before Saturnalia... or perhaps after..."

This was not going to plan. It was getting out of Pilate's control. He could not... he would not... leave here without a commitment from Marcus to marry Claudia. Both he and Procula feared it would be her last chance.

"I don't know if you're aware, Marcus, but Claudia has a substantial dowry."

"Oh?"

"And from what I've heard your uncle, although he is well placed, politically, has been having a little difficulty with his finances."

The young man's eyes narrowed. "What have you heard?"

"Oh, just that he's had to make some substantial payments to keep certain... how should I say... certain *indiscretions* with younger family members quiet."

Pilate wasn't sure, the steam was obscuring his view, but he could have sworn that the young man had gone pale.

"None of this has got anything to do with you or your honour, of course! And we would not consider it the slightest impediment in a suitor for our daughter. However... others may not feel the same."

"So what are you offering?" Marcus' voice was direct, not defensive.

"Well, my wife has a little nest egg that she's willing to contribute. That, along with some of my own money, oh, I don't know, how does four hundred thousand sesterces sound?"

"Well, sir, I... well, that is very generous of you."

"More generous than what the other girl's family is offering?"

Marcus laughed but the sound lacked any humour. He stretched out his limbs and put his hands behind his head. "Four hundred thousand sesterces." Marcus mouthed the words like a cow chewing the cud. "Did you know that my late mother was patrician too?"

"I did not."

"She, like your noble wife, was the youngest daughter of an aristocrat. My maternal grandparents were Julians. Sadly they died in a fire before my mother was betrothed. Her dowry was supposed to have been kept in trust by her older brother, but he apparently lost it when a business deal went south. The result was she had to marry below her: into the Sejanus family. Then as you may or may not know, she died as she was giving birth to me and shortly after that, my father, Uncle Lucius' younger brother, died in a riding accident."

"And your point…"

"My point is that my mother had a lot in common with your wife. They both married down, they both had to compromise their social standing – and that of their children. They did not have a choice. But I do."

"What are you saying, Marcus?"

Marcus opened his eyes briefly, looked at Pilate, then resettled into his reposed position.

"The emperor has been ill."

"So I hear."

"And if – Juno forbid – he succumbs, Livia will be free to marry someone else."

"Livia and the emperor are not married."

"Not yet. But I'm sure you've heard the rumours. Death-bed marriages to secure the succession are not unheard of. The emperor could still be persuaded."

"Indeed. Oh surely you're not thinking of…"

"No. But my uncle might be. And if that happens…"

"Five hundred thousand. In four instalments. One at the announcement of the betrothal. A second at the wedding. A third at the birth of the first child. And the fourth…" Pilate thought for a moment, doing rapid calculations with his fingers under his towel, "and the fourth on the tenth anniversary of your wedding." Pilate tried to control his breathing and relax his shoulders. With a great deal of will power he managed to master his physique so that by the time the young man opened his eyes and looked directly at him he appeared the picture of calm.

"In that case," said Marcus, "I shall book my passage as soon as it is feasible to do so."

The bath house manager appeared in the door of the sauna. He nodded politely to Pilate: time was up. Either he had to pay for another hour or open the door to the public. As Pilate had just committed more than his and his wife's life's savings to pay for his daughter to be taken off their hands, there was only one choice to make. He nodded to the manager to open the door and allow the chattering clients in.

Chapter 19 – Jilted

Judah had been waiting for nearly an hour. It was now well past sunrise and he looked very conspicuous lurking on the edge of the olive grove without the cloak of darkness. Perhaps she had been unable to sneak past the guards while they thought she was still busy with her ablutions. Perhaps Nebela – without Claudia's knowledge – had been unable to orchestrate events to let her slip away. Nebela had asked Judah not to tell Claudia that she was helping them. He did not know why, but he had agreed.

Now they met whenever they possibly could. It was a dangerous game they were playing, they both knew it, but it was one they couldn't resist. She was intoxicating: her hair, her eyes, her smell... And she made him laugh. They shared a similar sense of humour and when they were not walking hand in hand in the depths of the olive grove, she would lean against his chest, his arm over her shoulders, and talk about everything under the sun. She was bold and forthright in offering her opinions; but that didn't bother Judah. They were qualities he found attractive, even though his father had always told him that they were to be valued in a man, not a woman. He agreed, in principle, but in practice he wasn't attracted to submissive women. After all, it had never got his mother anywhere: the softer she was, the harder his father hit her.

His brother, Jairus, had been soft too – girlish, his father called him – and he would cry and pray as their mother was beaten black and blue. "Perhaps Messiah will come and help her," he told the younger Judah. "Perhaps," thought Judah, but he wasn't going to sit back and do nothing waiting for it to happen.

As he grew older, he would stand between his mother and father, sharing the blows aimed at the quivering woman. During a particularly bloody encounter, he was knocked unconscious and awoke to find a group of Roman soldiers in the house. The neighbours, it seemed, had feared he was dead, and called the soldiers in off the street. His mother was bleating like a mountain goat, his father roaring like a desert lion. His brother, as usual, was reciting Torah.

One of the soldiers noticed he was awake. He called to his companion who was attempting to apprehend his father. "Leave the Jew alone, Titus. The boy is not dead. Let them sort it out themselves. There is no charge to be answered if the boy is alive."

"But he could kill the child tomorrow!" cried Judah's mother.

"Then call us when he does," offered the soldier and walked out of the house.

The soldiers were back the next day. Judah's mother was the victim, and this time there *was* a charge to be answered. His father was found guilty of murder and executed by the Romans in the traditional way: crucifixion. Judah didn't bother to watch him die.

The two boys were sent to live with their mother's brother in Capernaum, a priest and leader of the local synagogue. And on a fleeting visit, they met their other uncle, the black sheep of the family called Jesus Barabbas. Like Judah and his brother Jairus, Barabbas and his brother had a different way of serving their God. Uncle Hillel preached the words of Torah that spoke of freedom for the Jewish people; Barabbas attempted to put them into practice. This was a man Judah could respect, and when he was old enough he ran off to join the band of fighters who ranged the length and breadth of Israel, raging a guerrilla war on the Roman invaders and punishing any Jews suspected of collaboration.

What would Barabbas think if he knew of Judah's secret desires? That he was wooing Claudia for love not strategy? Would he consider it collaboration? Judah knew the answer to that.

"Are you not going up to Jerusalem to make your sacrifice, Judah?"

Judah whipped around, his hand instantly going to the knife in his belt. A tall, cloaked figure stepped out of the shadows, his beard braided distinctively with rags from his victims' clothes. There was a good deal more Roman red than there had been the last time Judah had seen him. "Barabbas!"

The two men embraced. Judah looked around furtively.

"Are you expecting anyone?"

"Well, I wasn't expecting you! I thought you were still in the hills."

"We are. We haven't fully regained our strength since the battle in the gorge."

Judah nodded solemnly. "How many did we lose?"

"Two dozen. Including Matthias."

Judah sighed, a wave of sadness overcoming him. "I'm sorry, Barabbas, I couldn't get to him."

"I know."

"It should never have come to that. We should never have been discovered."

"The girl should never have got away."

"The Roman?"

"No, the Babylonian. You should have killed her Judah. In the carriage."

"I know, Barabbas."

"Why didn't you?"

"She had done nothing wrong. I thought she would be happy to be freed. I never thought she would go back to her masters."

"Like a dog to its vomit."

"Yes."

"Then it is time to kill the dog."

Judah sucked in air sharply. "You want me to kill Nebela?"

Barabbas laughed. "You are a romantic, Judah. You have a soft spot for the ladies."

Judah remembered his mother, cowering in the corner from his father's blows.

"I don't like hurting women. Men who hit women are cowards."

"But what if that woman could hurt you? Could hurt us? Could hurt the cause? She has already done it once. If she sees you in Caesarea…"

"I have been careful not to be seen near the palace."

"Ah, but that's the problem; I need you to go near the palace. I have a job for you to do there: Pilate has some documents that I want you to bring to me. I have someone inside the palace but he needs to pass them to someone else. No one else knows you, other than the slave girl and the Roman."

"Exactly, they both could recognise me. It's better if I stay away."

One of Barabbas' plaits was coming loose. He retied it, his thick, dirty fingers surprisingly nimble. The fabric was pink silk, Judah noted: from the dress of an aristocratic woman, perhaps?

Barabbas tied off the ribbon and fixed his gaze on his nephew. "So you haven't managed to woo her then? Despite all the times you've met?"

Judah's eyes narrowed. So, Barabbas' spies had been following him. He should have been more careful. What should he say now? He waited a moment too long to answer.

"Then you must kill her. That was always the plan."

Judah tried to keep his voice calm. He could not have Barabbas suspecting what was really going on. "The plan was to hold her hostage to get some concessions out of Pilate for her release. Then when that failed, the new plan was to get close to her to see if she could be influenced."

Barabbas tossed back his head and laughed. A new scar ran down his face from his right eye to his jaw: a souvenir of the battle in the gorge.

"No, lad; that second part was your plan. I always knew it would fail."

"But it isn't; it's working! I'm getting close to her. She's confiding in me. I know for instance that Sejanus is taking a cohort into the hills tomorrow."

Barabbas' eyes narrowed. "Into Samaria?"

"Yes. I was going to slip away this morning to tell you. I was just waiting here to say goodbye to the girl."

Barabbas sighed and leaned against the trunk of an olive tree. "She can't be trusted, Judah. She needs to be removed."

"Please! Just give me until the Roman Saturnalia."

Barabbas dug into the bark of the tree with his dagger. "And what do you hope to gain?"

"Influence. Pilate dotes on his daughter."

"But what influence could you have with her?"

"I could get her to understand our position."

"You're a dreamer, Judah, you always were. Even if you do seduce her..." Barabbas cast a sideways glance at Judah, "...or have you already?"

Judah shook his head firmly. "No, her virtue remains intact."

"Either way, all you'll do is enrage Pilate further against us." Barabbas stopped suddenly and pulled the knife out of the bark. He ran his finger along the blade. "Unless...unless... if he found out his daughter was consorting with a Jew it would enrage him beyond reason. It might force him to act without forward planning. It might... but let's not get ahead of ourselves." Barabbas laughed and patted the young man on the shoulder. "I'm not sure you'll succeed, Judah, but I'll do as you suggest. I'll give you to Saturnalia. But if you cannot seduce her by then, you must do as I ask. Agreed?"

"Agreed."

Barabbas got up and pulled the cloak over his head. "If Sejanus is launching an attack I must go and warn the brothers. Shalom, nephew. Until Saturnalia."

"Shalom." Judah watched as the older man disappeared back into the olive grove. Judah pulled his cloak closely around him and turned to go back to the harvesters' village. Claudia obviously wasn't coming. In the last few weeks she had managed to get up an hour before sunrise and come to him; she had done so half a dozen times since that kiss. Ah, the kiss... as he walked he remembered Claudia's soft lips parting under his. But his reverie was interrupted by the clink of bridles and the stomping of hooves.

"Out of the way, Jew!"

A cohort of soldiers on horseback was trotting past the olive grove. Judah scuttled to the side of the road and watched as the cavalcade passed. There were some luggage wagons and a covered carriage. Someone wealthy was travelling out of town. Judah wondered who it was. Through the window of the carriage he glimpsed a familiar tress of chestnut hair. As the carriage drew level he saw Claudia, her mother and father in animated conversation. The family were leaving Caesarea, and to judge by the luggage and the subsequent train of carriages holding domestic staff – including Nebela – they were going for an extended period. Why had she not told him? Why had Nebela not either?

Judah was so shocked he forgot to grovel and abase himself like an ordinary farmhand would do. The captain of the guard thrust his sword tip towards him.

"Step back, Jew."

Claudia, alerted by the commotion, turned to look. Her jaw dropped in shock before she had a chance to compose her aristocratic features.

"What is it, dear?" asked Procula.

Judah held Claudia's eyes. The captain noticed and kicked Judah in the groin. He fell to the ground, groaning. The rest of the soldiers clopped past, laughing.

Claudia cried out and reached her hand towards him.

"What in Mithras' name are you doing?" demanded Procula.

Claudia withdrew her hand and bit her lip. "Nothing, mother." She fell back on her cushions and the carriage trundled on along, leaving Judah on the side of the road and Claudia offering a silent prayer for his safety.

Chapter 20 – The Road to Jerusalem

"For the umpteenth time, Claudia, we are going to Jerusalem because your father has business to attend to and he didn't want to leave you in Caesarea unprotected."

"I wouldn't have been unprotected. There are soldiers there."

"There were soldiers there when you were abducted the last time. If it becomes known that the guard is split between you and your father, it would be too much of a temptation for those Jewish Zealots to resist. Your father and I aren't prepared to take the risk. Isn't that right, Pontius?"

"What's that, dear?" Pilate roused himself from his thoughts to look at his wife and daughter, the two most precious things in his world.

"We have brought Claudia Lucretia with us to keep her safe, haven't we?"

"Quite right. There's no telling when those Zealots will try their luck again. Even if Marcus does manage to rout them out of Samaria, they could pop up again like warts on a pig's backside."

"Pontius!"

"Sorry, dear."

He turned to his daughter. "I thought you'd enjoy the change of scenery, Claudia. Jerusalem is quite beautiful in its own way – different from Caesarea, of course, more Jewish – but not without its charms. The Temple alone will be worth the visit."

"Will I be allowed to go there? I thought it was only for Jews." Claudia looked mildly interested, despite her attempts to maintain the scowl she'd adopted since leaving Caesarea that morning.

"Some of it is, the inner courts, but the outer courts allow non-Jews: gentiles, they call us. Once we've settled in to our new quarters I'll ask Caiphas to arrange a tour."

Claudia looked at him quizzically.

"Joseph Caiphas, the Chief Priest. A decent chap; easy to work with. He was in the job when Valerius Gratus was here before me. Don't let it be heard outside this carriage, but my job would be a lot harder to do without him." Pilate tapped the side of his nose. "He knows that keeping the peace will be mutually beneficial to both Rome and Judea. Not an easy job in a nation full of religious fanatics."

Suddenly the carriage came to a stop. Pilate looked out of the window to see what had caused the halt and grasped the hilt of his dagger. They were on the Roman road, summiting a hill, a few miles north-east of Jerusalem. They had come the long way from Caesarea, going first north then south to avoid Samaria, rife as it was with bandits. The Jordan River was snaking its way through the arid landscape below them. As Pilate's eyes adjusted to the bright light he realised the hillside was moving, moving with people.

The captain of the guard drew level with the window of the carriage. "What is it, Felix?" asked Pilate.

"It seems to be some sort of religious ceremony, sir. Down by the river. I've questioned one of the locals and they say it's a holy man. He appears to be pushing people under the water and bringing them up again; 'baptizo' was the word he used. Baptism."

"It sounds like they are following Mithras!" Procula exclaimed, craning to get a good view of the events below.

"It sounds like he's trying to kill them!" observed Pilate.

"Can we have a look?" Procula was gathering her skirts in anticipation.

"I don't think that would be wise, my dear. Would you agree with that, captain?"

"I would, sir. They seem peaceful enough, but –"

"Followers of Mithras are peaceful."

"– but you never know with these Jews."

"I'll ask Caiphas about it tomorrow," said Pilate.

"But Pontius…"

"Tomorrow, Procula, and that's final." His wife huffed and settled back into the upholstery.

To his surprise Claudia appeared indifferent. Normally she would have been backing her mother in this sort of discussion; trying to cajole him to let them have their own way. But she seemed strangely disinterested. Her thoughts were elsewhere and had been since they'd left Caesarea that morning. He'd wanted to talk to her about his plans for her engagement to Marcus, but every time he'd tried to raise the subject she had yawned and said she was too tired to discuss it. He'd let it pass, for now, but they needed to address it sooner rather than later. After all, it was the wedding, or, more correctly, the need to raise money for her over-inflated dowry that had precipitated this sudden trip to Jerusalem in the first place. He hadn't been planning on coming to the capital for at least another three weeks, but he wanted to be certain that he could honour his extremely generous pledge to Marcus before he returned from Samaria and made plans to visit his uncle in Rome.

Five hundred thousand sesterces. The figure gave him a headache just thinking about it. Between him and Procula they could scrape together just under four hundred thousand, but neither of them had budgeted for the extra hundred thousand. As governor of Judea he earned a hundred thousand a year. But that was for the upkeep of his households in Caesarea and Jerusalem. And of course he needed to send some home to his younger brother who was keeping the family estate running back in Pontus. A hundred thousand wasn't all he received, though. There were certain – how should he put it – *gratuities* to be counted upon. The role of Head Priest for instance had to be approved by the governor each year, and Caiphas had many rivals; though none as competent or well-heeled as he. Then there were various civic projects and contracts to be awarded. The most ambitious was a long-mooted aqueduct to carry water from the springs and wadis of central Judea to Jerusalem. The proposed construction would cover nigh on twenty-three stadia and be a marvel of Roman engineering. Ever since Pilate had first seen the plans he had decided that this would be the thing for which history would remember him: Pontius Pilate, architect of the Great Judean Aqueduct, bringer of water, harbinger of life. There were currently four potential contractors – each with their own combination of strengths and weaknesses – now all was left was for Pilate to decide whom to award it to. As soon as he could, he would make it known to the people who knew the right people that one hundred thousand sesterces might just swing the deal. Money alone could not influence him though – he was a man of honour, good at his job and responsible for the prudent management of this corner of the empire – but add a substantial gratuity to good engineering credentials, and a deal could be done.

The carriage started moving again, slowly. Pilate looked out of the window to see the soldiers cajoling the pilgrims off the road so the entourage could pass. The locals did not seem to mind as much as they usually did, perhaps because their minds were focused on the holy man in the valley below. There was the usual mix of cripples and beggars and families on a picnic outing. But there were wealthier people too. This holy man seemed to have a wide appeal. He'd be interested to hear what Caiphas had to say about him in the morning.

Suddenly there was a commotion at the front of the cavalcade. Pilate squinted ahead to see a soldier beating someone and the accompanying screams of the unfortunate victim.

"What is it, father?" asked Claudia.

"Someone not getting out of the way, I suspect."

"But why should they? They have as much right to be on this road as we do. Perhaps more so."

Her parents looked at her incredulously.

"What in the Emperor's name are you talking about?" asked Procula.

"I was just saying we should respect our hosts a little bit more."

"Our *hosts*?" Pilate's shock was turning to anger. "You don't know what you are talking about, girl! I will expect you to keep a civil tongue in future!"

"But father, I was just saying–"

"Enough, I said!" Pilate called out to the driver to get a move on and the carriage rumbled on. By this time the commotion had shifted to the side of the road. As they past, Pilate saw a pile of rags lying on the ground, and a bandaged hand reaching out from it, clutching a leper's bell.

"Father! It's a leper. They've beaten a leper!"

"Then he should have known to stay away," intoned Pilate, but he too felt uncomfortable and made a mental note to speak to the captain about his troops' behaviour.

Soon the tide of pilgrims was left behind and as sunset fell, the tired entourage approached the northern gate of Jerusalem. Pilate sighed in relief as the local guards ushered them into the walled city and locked the gates on the dangers that lay beyond. He was looking forward to a long soak and a goblet of Jerusalem's best wine.

Chapter 21 – The Palace of Herod the Great

Claudia stretched and yawned. It was her first morning in the palace of Herod the Great. The sun pooling on the marble and mosaic floor – some conceit of naked bathing beauties in a forest – told her that it was already well after sunrise. She didn't usually sleep this late but she was exhausted after the long journey from Caesarea. She had prised her aching joints out of the carriage, shuffled through the shimmering bronze doorway as it caught the last rays of the setting sun, and plodded up the sweeping marble staircase towards her bed chamber. She couldn't remember much of the gilded halls, but simply that they seemed to go on forever before the palace slave opened a cedar and bronze door and led her and Nebela into their private quarters.

Nebela had slept in an adjoining room and Claudia could hear her moving about. Any moment now she would be coming in to see if her mistress was awake. Claudia wasn't sure if she should pretend to still be asleep, send her slave away, or be brave and face the day before her. She sighed deeply. What was there to face? No slipping out of the palace before sunrise to meet Judah in the olive grove; no sitting by his side, feeling his every breath as if it were her own, listening to his stories of the Maccabees and the Jewish Messiah while daydreaming of that kiss…

She hadn't even had a chance to say goodbye. She remembered the look of shock on his face when they passed him on the way out of Caesarea. He must have thought she had known about the trip and deliberately stood him up. She couldn't bear to think that he would think so poorly of her. And then that soldier had kicked him! Oh, how she had wanted to leap out of the carriage and hold him, to minister to him, to take away the pain.

She didn't know her family was going to Jerusalem until her mother came into her bed chamber yesterday morning – just as she was getting dressed to meet Judah – and announced that it was just as well she was up because her father had decided on an unscheduled business trip and that he expected the whole family to accompany him. Her father was not usually this spontaneous: he normally planned his trips weeks, if not months in advance, and as far as Claudia knew, he was not scheduled for another trip to Jerusalem for at least another three weeks. Something was up. When she had asked him about it, he said it was to confuse the Zealots in case they were planning anything. He said that he had decided to try and not be so predictable in his movements, to make it harder for them to launch an attack and that now was a good time because Marcus Sejanus had intelligence that they were holed up in the Samarian mountains.

But Claudia suspected there was another motive for the sudden trip and that it had something to do with her. Her father all but confirmed it when he kept trying to talk to her about Marcus in the carriage. Claudia realised with a deep ache in her stomach that the inevitable betrothal to the eligible Roman Tribune was finally going to take place. And if it did, her beautiful friendship with Judah would be over. What was she going to do?

"Ah, mistress, you're awake." Nebela pulled aside the richly embroidered curtain that separated the two sleeping chambers. The slave girl was fully dressed – in a cast-off gown of Claudia's – and her hair was braided into a long, black plait down her back. Her shoulders were bare, and the Herodian mark – a tattoo of a swaying reed – was clearly seen.

"Did you sleep well?" Nebela walked over to the balconied window and drew back the drapes, allowing the Jerusalem sun to blaze into the room.

Claudia flinched and drew the embroidered quilt up to shield her eyes.

"It's late, mistress: much later than you usually wake. Your mother was up earlier, wondering where you were. I told her you were still asleep. She wondered if you were ill; I said I think you are just weary from the journey."

"Yes, I'm weary, Nebela, but not just of the journey. What is the point of waking before dawn in a place like this?"

Nebela looked at her mistress curiously. The Babylonian girl had never asked her where she was going so early in the morning in Caesarea, though Claudia thought she must have had suspicions, particularly when the workman's cloak she washed had suddenly disappeared. But whatever suspicions Nebela might have had were easily silenced with a denarius. What a slave needed with money of her own, Claudia could only surmise. The girl was provided with food, clothing and accommodation; what more could she need? Claudia suspected she was saving up to buy her freedom; she had heard of slaves doing that. But it would take many, many years – unless she came by a particular windfall.

"Come, mistress, you need to get up. Your mother has asked for you to accompany her on an outing."

"I don't want to get up. I never want to get up again."

Claudia turned her back on Nebela and buried her head under the quilt, cutting out the invasive sun. But suddenly, the quilt was thrown off and she lay completely exposed in her shift. Above her stood Nebela, but it was Nebela as Claudia had never seen her: hands on hips, head tossed back and eyes blazing.

"Pull yourself together! If your mother suspects you're lovelorn for someone other than Marcus –"

"Other than Marcus? Who else could there be other than Marcus?"

Nebela let out an exasperated sigh. "I know about Judah."

Claudia sat bolt upright. "Y-you know?"

"I followed you one day to find out who it was you were meeting. You must have been meeting someone forbidden or you would not have bribed me."

Claudia leapt up and grabbed Nebela by the arm and shook her. "How dare you! How dare you spy on me!'

The Babylonian girl did not flinch despite Claudia's nails digging into her flesh. "Your mother told me to."

At this, Claudia let go, all colour draining from her face. "My mother?" she asked in a strangled whisper. "My mother knows about Judah?"

Nebela rubbed the angry red welts on her arm below the Herodian reed. "No, I never told her. I told her you went to the olive grove to write poetry." She pushed passed her mistress and started straightening the bed.

"Why didn't you tell her the truth?" Claudia's voice was still soft, fearful her matriarch would walk in on them.

"Because you are my mistress, not Procula Claudiana."

Claudia doubted this was the real reason. "Is that all?"

"What other reason could there be?" Nebela finished making the bed then flung open the door of the closet. "And what will you wear today, mistress?" She ran her fingers through the waterfall of fabric that she had hung there the previous night while her mistress bathed.

Claudia wasn't sure what game her slave was playing. But she decided to play along, for now... "Oh, I don't know... the green damask."

Nebela took out the sea-green gown and laid it across the bed then poured some water into a bowl so her mistress could wash. As she passed her a sponge, Claudia grabbed Nebela's wrist and looked straight into her amber eyes. "Don't cross me, Nebela. One word from me and my father will send you back to the Herods. I'm grateful that you didn't tell my mother but I cannot accept it is due to loyalty. I have known you now for six months and I think by now I have the measure of you. Your goal is freedom. That's why you have taken the money from me. That's why you have kept quiet about my friendship with Judah – for now. But I have no doubts that if betraying me will bring you closer to your freedom, you will do it. Am I right?"

Nebela met Claudia's gaze and for a moment the Roman girl thought she saw hatred flash in the amber eyes. But then the Babylonian girl lowered her lashes and in a voice as soft as a serpent's said: "We both desire freedom, mistress. You to be with the man you love and I with mine. And for that, I have a plan."

"Who is it that you love?" Claudia was genuinely puzzled but then the truth began to take shape. She remembered the look Nebela had given her when Marcus carried her on his horse from the Zealot camp and the way the slave's eyes were transfixed on him as he played cat and mouse with Mattheus in the arena. She remembered too how sometimes she would call for Nebela at night – needing a drink of water or another cover for the bed – but the girl did not come. When questioned the next day she would say that she had just been to see her mother, Zandra, ignoring the fact that she smelt of military leather and manly sweat. Claudia let go of Nebela's wrist. "It's Marcus Sejanus, isn't it?"

Nebela's silence told Claudia everything she needed to know. And despite her reservations about the girl's loyalty and the undeniable animosity between them she suddenly felt very sorry for her. "Oh, Nebela, he will never marry you. Even if he doesn't marry me he will not marry you. You are a slave. And even if you were free, you still do not stand a chance. Men like Marcus marry to enhance their social position, earn a storehouse full of money or make strategic alliances for their families. All three, if possible. You can provide him with none of those things."

"He loves me," said Nebela simply. "And when a man loves a woman she has power. I will use that power."

"And that is your plan?"

"Part of it. Mark my words, one day I will be free and one day I will have Marcus."

"But first you have to get me out of the way."

Nebela smiled, coldly. "Fortunately for both of us – *mistress* – you will not mind that part of the plan."

The two girls looked at each other over the bowl of water. Claudia thought Nebela was living in a fool's paradise, but then, who was she to judge? If there was a chance – just a chance – that Nebela could help her get Judah, then she was prepared to give her a hearing. "All right then, tell me, how do you propose to make this miracle happen?"

"Well, in a month's time it will be–"

Suddenly the door to the chamber was flung open and Procula swept in. "Hurry up Claudia, I have plans for us today!"

The mother's eyes sparkled with excitement. She clapped and Nebela jumped to attention. Claudia sighed. Another woman with a plan; just what she didn't need.

*

A Dream of Procula Pilate

I am falling backwards, but I'm not out of control. Someone is holding me, supporting me, lowering me into water. My eyes are closed but I am not afraid. The water washes over me: my arms, my shoulders, my chest, my face. "Breathe, Procula, breathe." The voice is soothing. I have heard it before. I do not doubt it. I do not ask, "How can I breathe under water?" I just do. Then, I open my eyes and I see a shadow fall across the pool. It is in the shape of a cross. I stretch out my arms to match it. I float, blissfully, fully supported by the water and the hands. Then they pull me up out of the pool and the arms of the cross begin to flap: like the wings of a bird. I whoosh out of the depths, the air fills my lungs, and I devour it. Above me hovers a dove, its wings stretched out; a bloody stain on its chest in the shape of a heart. The bird speaks: "Come to me."

Chapter 22 – Caiphas

On any other day Procula would have been worried about her daughter. She had hardly said a word since they'd left Caesarea the previous morning. She had loafed around in bed until mid-morning: completely out of character. When she went into the chamber to rouse her she could have sworn the girl looked frightened – no, not frightened, guilty – yes, that was it, guilty. What did she feel guilty about? Since being rescued from the Zealot fiends she had been acting very oddly: sneaking off at unearthly times, giving her slave and guard the slip, refusing to confide in her very own mother... that was the worst of it. Procula felt shut out of her daughter's heart and mind for the first time in her life. She was losing her, just like the dreams foretold... but no, she would not think of that today.

Today she was basking in another dream. A wonderful dream. A dream that had nothing to do with her daughter. Apart from the voice... it was the same voice that had spoken to her before when she was looking for Claudia... but Claudia Lucretia had nothing to do with this, Procula was sure; last night the voice spoke to her heart and her heart alone. And this morning when she woke she knew what to do. "Come to me," the voice had said, and Procula knew exactly where she had to go.

She had spoken to her husband first thing when she woke. "Pontius, wake up. You have business to attend to." Her husband groaned and stretched, tossing an arm and a leg over her. "Pontius," she said again, more gently, seductively. This seemed to do the trick. His hands started wandering over her body and she knew he was awake. On any other morning she would have let him. After nearly twenty years of marriage – despite what her mother had foretold to the contrary – she still enjoyed their love-making. Perhaps knowing that she would not have another child – after her innards were misplaced after the birth of Claudia – she knew she was not likely to fall pregnant again. But rather than saddening her, it liberated her. She had nothing to fear. Her pregnancy with Claudia had been a difficult one and her child's birth had nearly cost her her life. So she was secretly pleased she didn't have to go through it all again. Pontius, on the other hand, was ever hopeful of a son. So he made love to her with relish and sacrificed to Saturn once a year and Minerva, the goddess of fertility, at every full moon. But seventeen years later his prayers had still not been answered. However, he was philosophical about it and continued to try; it was not such an onerous duty after all. He loved his wife and he loved making love to her. But this morning Procula's mind was elsewhere.

"Not now, Pontius, you must meet with Caiphas. He will be here shortly. You know what an early riser he is."

Pilate groaned. "He can wait for another hour, my love." And proceeded to loosen the ties on her nightgown.

She pushed his hands away and sat up, pulling the gown closed over her bosom. "Not today, Pontius. You must ask him about the Baptist. The holy man we saw at the river. I've had a dream…"

Pilate sighed. When Procula had a dream there was no distracting her from getting to the bottom of it. "Can't it wait until we get back to Caesarea? Zandra can help you then. Or if it's that urgent, I can send for her and bring her here. She can be here by tomorrow night."

Pilate tried one more time to woo his wife back to bed but she was having none of it. She threw back the covers and stood up. "It is not an interpretation I need, Pontius. I know what it means. I must go and see the Baptist. Today." She stood over him, hands on hips. "Well?"

Pilate let out a long sigh of resignation and got up. "All right, I'll speak to Caiphas. But we have a lot of business to attend to and we may not discuss the Baptist until the end."

"No, Pontius, that will not do. First thing. You must speak to him first thing."

"I am the Governor of Judea, madam. I will conduct my business as I see fit!" Now it was Pilate's turn to have his hands on his hips. But Procula knew how to handle her man. She knelt on the bed and wrapped her arms around her husband's waist, resting her cheek on the soft paunch of his belly.

"I'm sorry, my lord, I do not mean to tell you how to conduct your business. But I want to see the Baptist today. And the sooner I go, the sooner I can lay this to rest. Then tonight…" she started planting butterfly kisses in a downwards line from his belly button. Pilate sucked in his breath. She stopped and looked up at him. "Well, my love?"

"Yes, yes, anything you ask!" He pushed her down onto the bed. "But Caiphas can wait a few minutes at least." Procula looked up at him and knew that it would not take long for him to reach his peak. And besides, she too was suddenly feeling aroused. She reached up and grabbed him by the waist, pulling him towards her. At the window she heard a flutter. She looked and saw a dove sitting on the windowsill watching them. *I'll be there soon, my Lord*, she whispered inside her mind, and the dove settled down to wait.

*

Finally, Procula was on her way. As promised, Pontius had spoken to Caiphas as soon as it was polite to do so and by mid-morning he had gained the assurance that it was safe to send his wife and daughter to see the holy man. Caiphas even offered to send some of the Temple Guard with them. So with Procula and Claudia out of the palace, the men could finally get down to business.

Joseph Caiphas was a Sadducee. Pilate had been briefed by his predecessor on the various Jewish sects before he took up his post. The Sadducees were the ruling class, the aristocrats of Jewish society. They were the people, Pilate was told, who could be trusted – as far as you could trust any Jew – to help support the status quo. They were a pragmatic group who saw the benefits Rome brought to their country and were assured of remaining the ruling class as long as they remained on good terms with the Emperor and his representative.

Then there were the Pharisees: a political group who were more overtly 'religious' than the Sadducees and although they shared Pilate's views on good moral values, did it in such a way that made everyone else feel like a degenerate. Some of the Pharisees, it was rumoured, were supporters of the Zealot cause. Pilate had not yet met a Pharisee he liked but he realised he was going to have to start making overtures to some of their more moderate leaders on the Sanhedrin Council if he was going to get a handle on the Zealot problem. That was one of the things he was going to speak to Caiphas about today.

Pilate liked Caiphas: he was urbane and good-humoured, pragmatic and shrewd. He was exceptionally well bred, but didn't lord his aristocratic bloodline. Pilate was grateful for that. He'd had enough of it with his in-laws.

When Pilate had got off the boat in Caesarea and was told that his first job in Judea would be to meet the High Priest, he was dreading it. He was expecting a grim-faced and hand-wringing Pharisee – a religious man for a religious position – and was pleasantly surprised to find out that the top job was in fact held by a Sadducee. Although priests could be drawn from either the Pharisee or Sadducee class, the role of High Priest as leader of the nation was far more political than spiritual. A religious nut would be dangerous in the job. The Jews had had the good sense to realise this and since the Maccabean reconstruction of Jewish society nigh on two hundred years ago, the Sadducees had become entrenched in the role. When the old Temple of Solomon – that had been razed and raised like a child's sandcastle for half a millennium – was again rebuilt under Herod the Great, the Sadducees were ready to take up their role as keepers of the Temple. Not that the Sadducees didn't believe in God – they did – but He was a God who kept a polite distance, didn't interfere much in human affairs and, beyond the festivals and sacrifices prescribed in the Law of Moses, didn't require much in return. On this they differed vastly from the Pharisees who believed God was a busybody, micromanaging everything from how to comb your hair to what and how you could eat. The other major difference was in their view of eternal life. Simply put: the Pharisees believed in a resurrection after death; the Sadducees didn't. This life, they believed, was all you got. And they were determined to live it well. No religious nut would be permitted to interfere with that. On this, Pilate and Caiphas were in complete agreement.

Chapter 23 – Corban

Caiphas and Pilate were taking morning tea. The Sadducee reached out a tastefully bejewelled hand and plucked a sugared almond from the silver platter. He popped it into his mouth and sucked, smiling at the sweet pleasure. Pilate, on strict instructions from Procula Claudiana to watch his weight, was sticking to the Judean dates. But Caiphas had no such qualms. Now in his fiftieth year, he could easily fit into the high priestly robes that his predecessor had to have let out year after year. He was so fat his attendants truly feared he would collapse in the Holy of Holies and they would have to haul him out by the traditional rope around the ankle. Caiphas would never suffer such an indignity. And when death eventually claimed him, Pilate mused, he would approach it with style. It was a pity the Jews did not approve of statues; Caiphas would have made a perfect subject for an artist: his long, glossy curls and pristinely trimmed beard, his splendid robes and scrupulously clean nails, his dark intelligent eyes and strong, hooked nose, were a marvel to behold.

Pilate shook his head, surprised at the direction his thoughts had taken him. Time to get back to business.

"So, what do you think of my funding proposal for the aqueduct?"

Caiphas paused, mid suck, and contemplated the question for a while. He crunched the almond between his molars, swallowed and delicately dabbed at his lips with the corner of a linen napkin. "Interesting," he finally said.

"Interesting 'yes' or interesting 'no'?".

"Yes and no."

Pilate gave him a sardonic stare. Caiphas chuckled.

"Yes – I think some of the contractors would be prepared to consider the gratuity you proposed. But…" he reached for another almond, "…I think you need to reconsider your source of funding for the overall project."

"The Corban? Surely it is acceptable to use Temple money to fund a civic project. It's going to bring water. You need water."

"We have water."

"But not enough. Admit it."

Caiphas smiled. "True."

"And you have more than enough gold stashed away."

"Now that is not true, Pontius. I don't know what rumours you've been hearing–"

"Rumours? They're not rumours, Joseph."

"And you have seen this gold for yourself? You, a gentile, who has not been beyond the outer courts..."

"I have it on good authority."

"From whom?"

It was Pilate's turn to smile. "Ah, my dear Caiphas, you do not expect me to reveal my sources, do you? We do not have Roman soldiers stationed in the Temple to protect an empty room."

"And for their protection we are grateful," Caiphas acceded. "But this rumour of gold... if it gets out..."

"It's out already, Joseph. You know it is. So will you or will you not persuade the Sanhedrin to release Corban funds for the aqueduct?"

"There must be an alternative, Pontius. Antipas, for instance..."

"Antipas! I do not want that toad to have any more influence in Judea than he already has," snapped Pilate, forgetting himself for a moment and whipping an almond off the platter.

Caiphas laughed at this and motioned to the luxuriant chamber in which they sat: "Pity we are meeting in his palace, then."

"It is not his. It was his father's. His dead father's. And now it belongs to Rome. I know my history, Joseph."

"And so you should, my dear governor. But you should also know that he has never given up his hope of reclaiming the Judean throne."

"There is no Judean throne."

"He will not accept that. He wishes to be king of the whole of Palestine, not just Galilee. And he will pay his way if he has to."

"Are you saying I should sell him the promise of a tinsel crown in order to get money from him for the aqueduct?"

"It would be one way of funding it."

"And what will I say to him when the crown never comes? You and I both know Tiberius does not want a royal line reinstated in Jerusalem. It's caused too many problems in the past."

"Quite," observed Caiphas. "The last thing we want is anyone claiming to be King of the Jews."

"And yet the people wait for one."

"Ah, you've been listening to more rumours."

"Rumours it seems that your own scriptures encourage."

"That depends on how you interpret them."

"And how do you interpret them, oh High Priest of Judea?"

Caiphas stood up, walked to the window and out onto the balcony. Pilate joined him. The two men looked out over the paved, mosaic, piazza – known locally as the Gabbatha – past the fortress of Antonia, to the magnificent white marble Temple of Herod beyond. The Temple was built on a mound in concentric squares or 'courts'. Caiphas was right: Pilate had never been beyond the outer Court of the Gentiles, which was a noisy, smelly place, dominated by market stalls. The next court in was reserved for Jewish women and then the one inside that, for circumcised Jewish men only. As Pilate was a complete man – and he intended to remain that way – he would not be permitted to enter. Not that he would want to. Pilate saw no need to make sacrifice for his sins. The gods he followed didn't seem to mind them and he did not understand why anyone would follow a god that thought otherwise.

However, there was one thing he did envy about the Jewish religion: he wished he could enter the marble cube at the centre of the Temple. In the first chamber there were apparently golden accoutrements of worship. Then there was a richly embroidered curtain that led to an apparently empty room called the Holy of Holies. Only the High Priest was allowed in there once a year to perform some kind of ritual, and although he had asked Caiphas to tell him what happened there, the Jew had refused to answer. Politely, of course, but it was still a refusal. Pilate did not like to be refused. And it just fuelled his belief that the empty room was a cover for something: more likely than not, the entrance to a great treasure trove, heralding back to the time of Solomon. Yes, the Assyrians, Babylonians, Macedonians and even the Romans had plundered their way in search of it – only to be disappointed – but Pilate, like many others, was convinced there was a secret entrance that simply had not yet been found.

Pilate sighed. No use pondering what he could not do. He was under strict orders from Tiberius to co-operate with the Jewish leaders in the protection of their Temple and not to interfere with their strange religious practices.

Nothing special was going on at the Temple today. Likewise, the Gabbatha, which was sometimes used for public meetings, was today just a thoroughfare for soldiers and ordinary folk, some going to the Temple to offer small, daily sacrifices, some simply bypassing it on the way to other business. There were market stalls around the perimeter – an overflow from the market in the outer Temple court – a few beggars, some children playing a game with pebbles, a gaggle of women off to do some shopping, a couple of scribes selling their transcription services and a money changer or two, accepting coinage from across the Empire.

Pilate was still surprised at how cosmopolitan the city was. He saw Phrygians and Greeks, Ethiopians, Egyptians and Persians, rubbing shoulders with Hebrews, Idumeans and Samarians. Although 'foreign', most of them, Pilate knew, were followers of the Jewish faith. Some were just visitors, staying on for a while after the Feast of Atonement; others were permanent residents of the city. Rich and poor, educated and illiterate, slave and free, Jew and gentile: Jerusalem was a microcosm of the Roman world as Pilate knew it. What were they looking for in this city? What did they hope to find here that they did not find elsewhere?

Caiphas seemed to be sharing his thoughts. "They are sheep without a shepherd, Pontius. And we must protect them or they will follow anyone who claims he can save them from the wolves and wild dogs."

"And who are the wolves?"

A cohort of Roman soldiers marched past. The centurion spotted Pilate and Caiphas on the balcony and saluted. Pilate saluted back.

Caiphas chuckled. "That is not for me to say, Lord Governor."

"And the Baptist? Are the sheep following him?"

"They're watching him to see where he will lead. As is Antipas."

"Antipas?"

"Like your wife, he has a strange fascination for the holy man."

Pontius laughed and Caiphas joined in. A pair of Pharisees, crossing the Gabbatha on the way to the Temple, looked up. They frowned in disapproval at the levity of the two leaders. Pilate looked down on them imperiously and they quickly hurried away.

"I wouldn't have put Antipas down as a religious man," Pilate observed.

"Let's just say he's a man who covers all bases. The Herods have always realised that the way to the hearts and minds of the people is through enabling them to worship. Why else do you think the old fox rebuilt the Temple?"

"And just as well he did, or you wouldn't have a job," quipped Pilate.

"And you would have nothing to protect," countered Caiphas.

"Which brings me back to the Corban…"

Caiphas sighed. "Let me talk to Antipas first. I think we could use his interest in the Baptist to our advantage. But not before lunch, eh Pontius?"

"How long will that take?"

"Lunch?"

"No, your negotiations with Antipas."

"A few weeks perhaps. Or a few months. There's plenty of time before the building starts in spring."

Pilate sighed. He was hoping to have had this aqueduct business – and the accompanying payment of the gratuity – wrapped up before Marcus Sejanus returned from his Samarian campaign. But he couldn't tell Caiphas that. So instead he said: "Lunch it is, then." And the two men withdrew from the sun-lit balcony into the shadow of the palace of Herod the Great.

Chapter 24 – The Baptist

Claudia was not happy to be back in the carriage. Her body was still aching from yesterday's jarring journey and she wished she was still in bed. Or better still, Caesarea. She scowled at her mother. Procula Claudiana didn't respond. Her mind appeared to be elsewhere. Her eyes were lit with some unspoken hope, her cheeks flushed in excitement. Claudia had no idea why. They were only going to see a holy man and the circus show surrounding him. Claudia had seen many of them before: her mother had a strange fascination for them.

Claudia had once asked her why and she had answered: "There is more to this life than what we can feel and touch, Claudia, and these people can see beyond. I want to see what they see." But each time they went on one of these pilgrimages, her mother always came home disappointed. And yet here she was, trying again. Claudia sighed and looked out of the window.

The carriage was winding its way east of Jerusalem, the oxen plodding their way carefully down the Jordan Valley. They were flanked by a cohort of their own guards as well as a further half dozen Temple guards, provided by Joseph Caiphas. Just like yesterday the road was full of other pilgrims heading towards the last reported viewing site of the Baptist.

Oh, well, best make the most of it, thought Claudia. She could at least find out a little bit more about the man they were going to see so she would have something to talk to Judah about when she saw him again. If she saw him again… Claudia pulled herself together and called out to the nearest Temple guard – a captain – who was riding a bay mare, beside the open carriage window. "Excuse me, captain."

"Yes, my lady."

"Do we have far to go?"

"Not far."

"Do you know much about the man we are going to see?"

"Only what I've heard in the Temple market."

"And what is that?"

"His name is John. He comes from somewhere in the north: Galilee, I think. But he's lived in the desert for the last few years. He's a wild man. He eats locusts and wears animal skins. Best not get too close to him, my lady, he's likely to stink!"

"Is he mad?"

"I don't know. He might be. He says he's a messenger of God. He calls himself the Baptist. He washes people in the river."

"And why does he need to do that?"

"Perhaps because our God YHWH wants us to be clean. In our religion we wash before religious ceremonies."

"How can water wash the heart?" asked Procula, joining in the conversation.

"I don't know, my lady, I'm a simple man. I leave these things to the priests."

"Is it true that the people believe he is the Messiah?" asked Claudia.

Both Procula and the guard looked at Claudia, surprised at her question. "You know about Messiah?" asked the guard.

"I've heard it spoken. Well, is he?"

"He couldn't be." Answered the guard.

"Why not?" asked Procula.

"Because Messiah will drive the Romans out of the land," declared Claudia dramatically. "And he hasn't done that, has he? And if the authorities were worried that he would, they would have shut him down by now. And we wouldn't be going to see him, would we? Isn't that right, captain?"

"Claudia!"

The captain adopted a blank expression. "I couldn't say, my lady. But you are safe. I can promise you that." He patted his sword hilt.

"Forgive my daughter, captain. She does not know when to hold her tongue."

"That's all right, my lady," he said, as they approached a bend in the road. "Now if you'll excuse me, I need to check that the road ahead is safe."

"Of course." Procula fixed a smile on her face and waited for the captain to trot away. Then she turned on her daughter: "That sort of talk is unbecoming for a lady, Claudia, particularly a Roman lady. That man is a Jew and you insulted him."

"How did I insult him?"

"By lording our rule over him."

"But it's true. Let's not pretend it isn't."

"It is un-genteel to say so – to his face."

Claudia opened her mouth to speak again, but closed it swiftly as she caught one of her mother's looks.

"This is an important day for me, Claudia Lucretia, and I will not have you spoiling it. Do you hear me?"

"Yes, mother, I hear you."

A few minutes later the carriage ground to a stop. Procula leapt up – in a most un-genteel way – and threw open the carriage door, pre-empting the captain who had come to assist her. "Come, Claudia!" shouted Procula. Claudia rolled her eyes and followed her fervent mother.

The guards cleared a path for them through the excited crowd, too intent on getting a glimpse of the holy man to worry about kow-towing to Roman aristocrats. There must have been over a thousand people there and, like the day before, they were drawn from all echelons of Judean society. The Baptist was holding court at a bend in the river at the bottom of a saucer-shaped depression. A motley collection of transportation jostled for parking space around the rim: regal carriages like that of the Pilates, sturdy carts, litters and even a chariot or two. Horses, donkeys, oxen and slaves were left with the vehicles while their occupants made their way down to the river bank, now on even pegging with the masses that had only their feet to carry them.

Procula hardly needed the guards to clear the way for her: she was like a tornado, sweeping aside everything in her path. Claudia had to almost run to keep up. The matriarch didn't even stop when a group of lavishly dressed people called out to her. "Procula Claudiana! Fancy seeing you here! I didn't know you were in town."

Procula half waved and muttered something as she hurtled past.

"Well I never!"

Embarrassed, Claudia slowed down, intent on making amends. "I'm very sorry; my mother is a bit distracted today."

She looked into the outraged face of Queen Herodias, whose make-up cracked in indignation.

"Well I never!" said the queen again and turned for support to Salome and Herod. But the latter was too busy conversing with a gaggle of priests to pay her any heed. This only stoked Herodias' ire further. "I have never been so insulted in my life! I am appalled! Outraged! I would never have expected it from a woman of your mother's breeding. And she calls herself a Claudian!"

"I'm sure she didn't mean it. She didn't realise it was you. I'll go and tell her..." Claudia scampered after her mother who, it appeared, had finally lost her mind in some religious frenzy, leaving Herodias and Salome in a socially snubbed froth.

She caught up with her just as she was entering the water, her skirts hitched up above her ankles, wading towards a wild-looking man whose beard and scraggly hair hung wet and limp over his skinny shoulders.

"Mother! What are you doing? Mother!" But Procula ignored her. Claudia turned to the captain of the Temple Guard who had accompanied them on their journey. "Do something!"

"What do you want me to do, my lady?"

"Stop her!"

"Why? She will come to no harm."

"But – but –" but Claudia did not know what else to say. So, like the thousand other people on the hillside, she watched her mother and the Baptist as they met in the shallows of the river. She stood before him, her honey-coloured hair which that morning had been piled high and kept in place by a dozen pins, was falling loose. Her blue cloak was slipping from her shoulders. Her soaked, hitched skirt was moulding itself to her wet calves. Claudia had never seen her in such disarray. But she didn't seem to care.

The Baptist reached out his rough hands and took her milky soft ones. "What do you want, woman?" he asked.

"I'm looking for my Lord. He's come to me in a dream."

"Who is your Lord?" asked the Baptist.

"I don't know. But I will know Him when I see Him. I will know Him when I hear Him."

Someone from the shore shouted out: "Are you the one we have been waiting for?"

John did not take his eyes from Procula. "Do you think I am the one?"

"You're not. But you know who He is, I think. I dreamt I was being baptised and then I saw Him in the form of a dove. You are the Baptist. Can you baptise me so I can see Him?"

"I can't." His voice was rough but not unkind. "I have been called to baptise the people of Israel – not the gentiles – to bring them to repentance, to prepare the way for the one we are all waiting for."

"Are you the one?" someone again asked from the shore and then laughed, mockingly. It was one of the Pharisees who had been talking to Herod.

John dropped Procula's hands and turned towards the voice. He pointed his finger at each of the men in the group of clerics, one at a time: "Are you really here to confess your sins with the rest of Israel? You brood of vipers!" he bellowed. "Who warned you to flee from the coming wrath? You had better prove your repentance by bearing the right sort of fruit! And you needn't start thinking to yourselves: 'We have Abraham as our father.' I tell you, God is quite capable of raising up children for Abraham from these stones! The axe is already taking aim at the root of the tree. Every tree that doesn't produce good fruit is to be cut down and thrown into the fire!"

The clerics flapped their arms and tore at their clothes, squawking like outraged geese. But Herod silenced them. He stepped forward, warily, as if approaching a vicious dog.

"Do you know who I am?"

"You are the one who has stolen your brother's wife. Are you here to repent?"

A collective gasp spread across the hillside. A thousand people were craning to hear what the wild man would say to the king.

Herod laughed mirthlessly, his jowls quivering. "I am the one who has the power to forgive or not to forgive."

"Blasphemy!" bellowed John.

"Be careful, holy man. You are here only at my pleasure."

"I am here at the pleasure of Almighty God! I am here to prepare the way for the One who is to come." Then he turned his back on Herod and addressed the multitude on the opposite hill. "I baptise you with water for repentance, but the one who is coming is more powerful than me! I'm not even worthy to carry his sandals. He will baptise you with the Holy Spirit and fire. He's got his winnowing fork ready to clear out the barn and gather his corn into the granary." He then turned once more and pointed at Herod and the clerics and this time he included Herodias in his diatribe. "But he'll burn up the chaff with a fire that will never go out."

"Well I never! Arrest this man!" Herodias called to the guards around her.

A collective growl went up from the crowd. Herod reached out his hand and placed it on his wife's shoulder. "Not now, my dear. The crowd will go wild."

"But – but –"

"Not now," he said firmly. Then he gathered his retinue and started heading up the hill.

Procula was still standing in the water, entranced. The Baptist was no longer paying her any attention but she didn't look as if she was about to move. So Claudia decided she would have to retrieve her bewitched mother herself. She waded into the water accompanied by the captain of the Temple Guard and took hold of her mother's arm. Procula did not resist but her eyes were looking to the hillside above.

John's voice boomed out again: "Behold! The lamb of God who takes away the sins of the world!"

Claudia squinted to see who John was talking about but before she could focus, her mother let out a scream and collapsed in a dead faint.

Chapter 25 – The Via Grande

The December air was biting. Claudia pulled her cloak more tightly around her. It had been nearly six weeks since the Pilates had come back from Jerusalem and Claudia had once again got into the habit of rising before dawn and walking in the olive grove. But unlike before she was unable to walk alone and a pair of guards always accompanied her, albeit from a discreet distance. Apparently Marcus' expedition to Samaria had been a mixed bag of success: he had flushed out a nest of Zealots but they were now on the run. The tribune and his men were hot on their heels, criss-crossing Palestine from north to south, and he was confident he would soon have them all in the bag. But until that auspicious eventuality came to pass, he had sent word to Caesarea to be extra vigilant in case some of the escapees tried to attack the port or attempt another kidnapping or assassination.

So despite Claudia's protestations, she was stuck with her double shadow, which put pay to her hope that Judah might once more reveal himself to her. And yet still she came to the olive grove. Like Claudia's heart, the trees were barren now; their stripped boughs clawing at the wintry sky.

Claudia had asked Nebela to make clandestine enquiries about Judah. Apparently no one had seen him since the day the Pilates went to Jerusalem. Some of his neighbours in the labourer's village – the few who over-wintered in Caesarea – believed that he might have gone to rejoin the Zealots in the Samarian mountains. Claudia shuddered at the thought: her fiancé hunting her true love.

Nebela seemed to take it as a personal sleight that Judah had absconded. But Claudia knew better than to think her slave sympathised with her mistress's broken heart. Judah's absence scuppered Nebela's plan to get rid of her so she could have Marcus. Nebela had not spoken of her plan since the family left Jerusalem, but Claudia could see the girl scheming behind her amber eyes. Claudia did not trust the Babylonian as far as she could throw her, but she dared not dismiss her: she knew too much. Keep your friends close and your enemies even closer, Claudia had once heard; it was sage advice.

Yet Claudia felt completely alone. She had no friends in Caesarea, her slave could not be trusted and the man she loved was on the run. Oh how she wished she could talk to someone about it all. Someone like her mother. There had been a time when Claudia could tell Procula anything. But all that changed when she fell in love with Judah. Procula would simply not understand. But even if she did, she was not currently in a position to comfort her daughter.

Since the incident with the Baptist, Procula had sunk into a deep melancholia. She spent all her time in her chambers and barely ate. Once Pilate's fury at the reports of her undignified behaviour had worn off, he had tried to woo her back to her old self. But none of the wiles learnt over eighteen years of marriage could reach his wife. The only person Procula would talk to was Zandra. When pressed, the soothsayer said her mistress had told her that she was waiting to meet her god. This had alarmed both Pilate and Claudia, fearing that Procula was going to try to kill herself. Claudia had suggested that Pilate bring the Baptist to see her. But when Pilate had sent for him he was told that the holy man was now languishing in a prison in Herod's palace in Galilee. Pilate promised to speak to Antipas about it when the Herods came to celebrate Saturnalia with them, to mark the beginning of the winter solstice. And that was today, Claudia reminded herself, so she had better get back.

The Herods were the last people with whom Claudia felt like celebrating. In fact, Claudia didn't feel much like celebrating at all. Despite the presents she was bound to get, and the beautiful candles that would bedeck the palace, symbolising the conquering of darkness by the sun-god Saturn, the mid-winter feast was bound to be full of drink-fuelled frivolity and uppity slaves, taking advantage of the tradition of role reversal. Each year one of the slaves was rewarded for good service by being allowed to be King for the Day. In some families, Claudia had heard, the 'King' was often a criminal or runaway slave who would be mocked and given a robe and crown of thorns then executed at the end of the festival.

But the Pilates were not of that sort. In their home, like all the civilised households across the Empire, the King and the other slaves would be served a banquet by the family. Occasionally, depending on the good will of the *pater familias*, the King could make decrees that would last for seven days; but would be overturned at the end of the festival.

However, some of the decrees could be upheld if the master considered them reasonable.

Claudia turned back towards the palace with her shadows. Soon the olive grove was left behind and the winding road summited a hill overlooking the port. Claudia always stopped at the top of the hill to watch the boats in the harbour swaying on the turquoise sea before turning down the *via grande* towards the town centre. But today, as she came over the hill, she did not see the cross masts of ships, but the cross bars of around two dozen crucifixes lining the road, with some of the victims already nailed in place. Their groans and cries accosted her and she froze to the spot.

"Come, my lady, let's go another way," suggested one of her guards.

"I didn't know my father had approved a mass execution today."

"He probably wanted to do it quickly before the Saturnalia began." The guard took her arm, attempting to guide her in another direction.

"Tribune Sejanus arrived with them last night," added the other guard.

"Who are they?" Claudia already feared the answer.

"Zealots. The great Sejanus finally managed to track them down," answered the guard in a tone that suggested he would far rather have been in on the capture than guarding the governor's daughter. And then: "Come, my lady, let's go the other way."

But Claudia pulled away from him and ran down the hill. Startled, the guards ran after her, their scabbards slapping against their thighs as they struggled to catch up.

But Claudia had a head start and a purpose neither of them could fathom. She slowed down briefly at the foot of each crucifix and looked intently up into the face of each dying man. She did not stop until she got to the end of the avenue of torture and fell to her knees. When the guards finally caught up with her, she was sobbing.

"What is it, my lady?"

"He isn't there! He isn't there!"

The guards looked at each other in puzzlement. Perhaps she was hoping to see one of her kidnappers, they thought, and was disappointed that he was not there. The girl had never quite been the same since her horrific ordeal in the summer.

"Let's get you home," said one of the guards sympathetically and helped her to her feet. And for once Claudia did not complain.

A Dream of Procula Pilate

I am floating, just under the surface. But I am not alone. I am bumped by arms and legs. A woman's hair billows out like a curtain of seaweed. I look around me and there are dozens of swimmers, all heading towards the same place: a light, just above the surface. Suddenly a shadow falls between us and the light. It is in the shape of a boat. Then something is tossed into the water – a net – it floats down towards us. I and my companions stare at it; we are afraid but cannot swim away. Soon my limbs are caught in the tangled mesh. But then we are hauled upwards, we will soon see who has captured us – I am afraid, I am very afraid.

Chapter 26 – Ladies Bathing

Caught in a fisherman's net? Hmm, what could it mean? Zandra was finding it increasingly difficult to interpret Procula's confusing dreams. Her spirits were disturbingly quiet about it all too, not giving any clues in bones, smoke or entrails. So Zandra had to figure it out for herself. The fact that she was feeling trapped was obvious, but trapped by whom? Or what? And what did it have to do with the crucified man or the dove with the bleeding heart? And who was this Lamb of God that the Baptist had spoken of? Zandra wished she could have been with her mistress at the river the day she had fainted and then she would have had a more accurate picture. But the first she had heard of it was when she had been summoned to Jerusalem by Pilate who was worried that his wife had not emerged from her chambers since her faint. The governor had waited a few days to see if Procula would rally, but when no progress was made, he decided to move his entire entourage home.

Zandra was disappointed. She had enjoyed her visit to Jerusalem. When she was not attending her mistress she was free to roam the city. That was a place she could do business. Yes, she would have to be careful of the Jewish priests, but she could see herself setting up shop on the outskirts of the city – perhaps at a boarding house – servicing the non-Jewish population. Or even the occasional Jew who wanted to double his chances of divine favour. But sadly, she was not a free woman and her hopes of buying her freedom with gratuities earned from Procula were diminishing with every day the Roman woman wallowed in her malaise.

And Marcus Sejanus was no help either. She had been so sure a few months ago that he would provide an answer for Procula's questions – to be able to point her to the crucified man – but so far he had not done so. Apparently he had just crucified a couple of dozen Zealots on the Via Grande, but, as far as Zandra could see, there was no connection to Procula's dream. Or perhaps she was missing something…

"There you are, mother!" Nebela flounced into the soothsayer's apartment with a wicked smile on her face. It was the first time in weeks that Zandra had seen her daughter in a good mood; no doubt she had just been reunited with the returning tribune. At least the man was good for something.

Nebela threw herself down on a pile of cushions and helped herself to a sugared almond. But just as she was about to pop it in her mouth she stopped. "This isn't one of the 'special' ones I asked for, is it?"

"Of course not! And I hope you weren't serious when you asked."

"Well…"

"Nebela! I am not going to help you kill Claudia!"

"Bad for business?"

"To say the least!"

Nebela laughed and stretched out on the cushions. "Of course I wasn't serious. I was just a bit frustrated, that's all. Now that Judah has disappeared, my plan is not going to work out the way I thought it would."

Zandra sat down beside her daughter. "So you're not going ahead with it then?" She tried to disguise the relief in her voice but the look on Nebela's face told her she had failed.

"No mother, I am. I just have to change tactics, that's all. My plan will still work."

"How do you know?" Zandra took her hand. "If it fails, I could lose you forever."

Nebela squeezed her mother's hand then let go. "It won't. Now, did you manage to ask Procula?"

"I did."

"And what did she say?"

"I found it hard to keep her focused. All she would talk about was her dreams."

"But you did ask her?"

"I did."

"And will she?"

"I think so. But if she doesn't?"

Nebela laughed and tossed another almond into her mouth. "Then I may be forced to take more drastic measures."

*

Claudia was feeling a little better after the incident on the Via Grande. She'd had a lie down and now wanted a bath. But Nebela was nowhere to be found. Claudia stuck her head out into the corridor and called her slave's name. But instead of Nebela, Judith, the timid Jewess, who looked half-starved even after a full feast, came at her bidding. "Have you seen Nebela?" asked Claudia. The Jewish girl muttered something in broken Greek to the effect that Nebela was on an errand for Tribune Sejanus and then she blushed. Claudia looked at her intently, considering whether or not to press her more, but decided instead to commandeer her for the baths.

Claudia did not give a widow's mite what Marcus did with his spare time, although she knew that her father would. She hoped, for everyone's sake, that Marcus and Nebela were being discreet. Whether or not she would feel the same if this farce of an engagement actually progressed to marriage, she didn't know. She didn't want to think about it. But part of her, the sensible part, told her she had no realistic future with Judah. She knew she had to face up to it sooner or later, and better she do it with dignity. She couldn't have her fiancé, less still her husband, fooling around with her slave. But Saturnalia was not the time for serious conversations and, after what she'd seen on the Via Grande today, she simply did not have the emotional energy to deal with it. So despite her knowing Marcus and Nebela's days were numbered she would let them lie in each other's arms for a while longer.

The baths were decked out for Saturnalia with festive evergreen garlands adorning the lintels and sills. The air was pungent with spruce and balsam and for a moment she thought she was back in Rome. Oh, how she missed the poetry readings and the philosophers' circles. Although generally considered a male domain, there was a small but thriving community of female intelligentsia, inspired by the likes of the Greek poetess Sappho and the Roman, Sulpicia. Her parents disapproved of them, fearing she would be tarred with the brush of spinsterhood and would not allow her to follow the moveable feast around the philosophers' quarter. But they could not stop her attending the symposia hosted by the mother of her best friend Viola, whose widowhood had brought on some very bizarre ideas that a woman could become a professional scholar. If it were not for Viola's mother's impeccable patrician bloodline, Procula and Pontius would have been more forthright in their protests. So it was with relief – from her parent's perspective – that the Pilates were compelled to leave Rome for Judea, putting a not too premature end to the unhealthy friendship.

Oh, but Claudia missed Viola! What the girl lacked in looks she made up for in good humour and intelligent conversation, something sorely lacking in what passed for polite society in Caesarea. Claudia nodded to a gaggle of women relaxing on the side of the cold pool, none of them over-eager to start their ablutions. Instead they were snacking on *libuma* cheesecake and gossiping; and to judge from the sidelong glances and tittering behind manicured hands, she was the object of their mockery. But Claudia cared even less for their opinion than she did for Marcus' dalliances, so she stripped off, tossed her robe to Judith and plunged into the depths of the pool.

She did a few lengths, her body gradually growing accustomed to the icy water as her muscles warmed to the exercise. She knew she would have the pool to herself for a while as the other female bathers rarely tarried in the cold, hurrying as quickly as they could to the warmer waters of the hypocaust and then wilting in the sauna. But Claudia enjoyed stretching her body as much as she enjoyed stretching her mind. Other women played ball games in the bath house courtyard during the hours reserved for the fairer sex, but Claudia was not a team player and preferred the more solitary pursuit of swimming. So it was most unwelcome when someone called out her name.

"Claudia Lucretia! Is that you?"

Claudia slowed her pace and treaded water, slicking back her hair and blinking through wet lashes. On the side of the pool – with a retinue of slaves to rival the late Empress – was Salome. The Idumean girl was wearing a garish orange and purple bathrobe of shot silk that clung seductively to her ample curves. She teetered precariously on the highest *carlatina* sandals Claudia had ever seen with at least six *polices* of cork separating Salome's not-so-dainty feet from the bathhouse tiles.

"You're early," said Claudia, flatly.

"For what?"

"Saturnalia."

"Well, forgive me, I did not realise there was a time limit on our arrival."

"There isn't." Claudia swam towards the edge of the pool. Judith approached, ready to cover her mistress's athletic frame with a simple muslin robe. But Claudia stayed in the water.

"Is your mother here?"

147

"Yes. She's trying to coax yours to come with her to the baths."

"She'll have a hard job of it."

"So I hear. It's all to do with the Baptist, isn't it?"

"I heard he's a prisoner in your dungeons."

"We like to think of him as our guest."

"I'm sure you do."

Salome's eyes narrowed. "If you don't believe me you can come and see for yourself. After all, we did have such a lovely time together the last time you came to visit, didn't we?"

"Apart from being abducted, you mean?"

"And from being rescued by Marcus Gaius Sejanus. Now how convenient was that?"

"Convenient?"

"Yes, convenient. Quite a stroke of fortune that he was available to leave at a moment's notice and to know exactly where to find you, wasn't it?"

Claudia was getting cold. It was time to draw this conversation to a close. "Say what you mean, Salome, I haven't got all day."

"Well, Claudia, I just think that it was very convenient, that's all. No wonder people have been suggesting your father arranged it to set you up with Marcus."

"Set me up? Why would he need to do that?"

"To make the noble tribune think he was protecting you. Everyone knows that certain kinds of men like their women weak and helpless. It makes them appear more feminine. And Juno knows you need help with that."

"Oh really? And you think Marcus is one of those men?"

"I do."

Claudia sighed. This was becoming very, very boring. "Tell me, Salome, why is this any of your business?"

Salome twirled a raven curl around her little finger beguilingly. "I don't like seeing a man trapped into marriage, that's all."

Claudia laughed. "I don't think Marcus would do anything he didn't want to do."

Salome's eyes widened. "So it's true, then. Marcus is about to be taken off the market."

Suddenly Claudia saw everything very, very clearly. "You're jealous. You want Marcus for yourself."

"Jealous? Don't be ridiculous. I am a princess. I will marry someone of royal blood. Not a mere tribune."

The conversation was going nowhere. Claudia decided to draw it to a close. "Well, I'm glad we cleared that up then. If you'll excuse me, Salome, I need to finish my ablutions." And before waiting for an answer she plunged beneath the water into blissful silence.

Chapter 27 – The Kitchen

Marcus Sejanus whistled a little ditty as he headed down to the palace kitchens. A couple of hours in bed with Nebela were enough to rouse any man's appetite. She had offered to bring him food, but he declined. It would be too much like playing 'house'. It was one thing to make love to the girl, but if she started considering his apartment their communal home, that would complicate things. Marcus lived his life in separate compartments. Nebela was for sex and general relaxation, Judith served his domestic needs such as food and clean clothing. For bathing at the public baths he had two male slaves, one of whom doubled as his scribe. In his military guise he had two legionaries who fed him and looked after his armour. All his needs were capably met, he thought, as he trotted down the stairs. So what need did he have for Claudia Lucretia?

The answer was simple: social and financial. Marcus knew that even though his uncle was currently the most powerful man in Rome, powerful men had a habit of tripping on Roman cobbles. Uncle Lucius had stepped on a lot of equally powerful men on his way to the top, and those men, or their families if they had not survived, had long, bitter memories. History was littered with the likes of his uncle: blazing lights that burnt brightly but briefly. Although Uncle Lucius spoke of founding a dynasty, his own children had not produced any heirs, which meant he was dependent on his adoptive son, Marcus. Marcus knew that the best families in Rome did not want to link themselves to Lucius Sejanus in the long term; although a short-term alliance might be sought. The Pilates were the perfect solution: provincial enough to not know the true precariousness of his illustrious uncle's position, but with sufficient patrician connections to make them more than a cut above respectable. Added to that, Pilate's loyalty to Tiberius and his solid work ethic that would help him make even an appointment to Palestine a success. Marcus could not deny that Claudia would make a good match. And of course there was the question of the dowry: a substantial amount not to be sniffed at. Definitely not to be sniffed at. And although he did not find Claudia attractive in the same way as Nebela, she was not a bad-looking girl. He could cope with doing his duty in that department. At least until the first child came along. And after that? Well, that's what he needed to work out.

The obvious thing to do was to buy Nebela from the Herods and formally give her to Claudia as a wedding present. But Nebela, he knew, would not be happy. The girl had notions of being free and the two of them living together as man and wife. She was nothing but trouble and he feared what she might do if her jealousy reached its full height. But that's what he loved about her: her passion, her fire, her refusal to think of herself as a slave. Nebela was as intoxicating as opium and he needed to wean himself off her before it was too late.

Marcus sighed as he entered the kitchen. Judith normally fetched food for him when he wasn't formally eating with the Pilates or the officers. He occasionally hosted dinner parties in his own quarters too, but the food always came from the same palace kitchens. But today Judith could not be found. When he emerged from his lovemaking with Nebela, the Jewish girl was not waiting for him in the hall. He could have summoned one of the other palace slaves, but firstly, they did not know his tastes as Judith did, and secondly, it was a good opportunity for him to cast his shadow over the cooks and scullery slaves. One of the prisoners crucified that morning had mentioned under interrogation that he had heard a rumour that there may be a plot to poison one or all of the Pilates. Marcus did not put much confidence in the man's testimony though as he looked like he would say anything to save himself from the cross. Like a typical Jew, he had blubbered and cried and begged to be spared. Marcus might have considered sparing him if he had given him some definite, verifiable information, but he hadn't. It was just rumours and suggestions: a desperate ploy of a condemned man.

Still, it would do no harm to make the occasional unannounced visit to the kitchen, just to keep them on their toes. If a poison plot was afoot, the kitchen would be the best place to enact it. If the traitor was indeed part of the palace staff he or she might be put off by the presence of the tribune. He had already made it known that someone in the household was under observation; let them think he knew exactly who it was and he was sure they would eventually slip up and reveal themselves. And if there was no traitor, then there was no harm keeping them on their toes anyway.

The kitchen was running at full hilt. The chief cook, a large Bithynian woman who, Pilate had told him, had been with the family since he was a lad in Pontus, was belting out orders like a decurion on the battlefield. Two young lads were running to and fro carrying wood to feed the furnaces while a crop of filthy urchins manned the bellows. Scullery maids washed and chopped baskets of fresh vegetables while the three assistant cooks supervised the preparation of the Saturnalia party favourites: a sideboard of dormice skinned and ready for roasting, a giant pot of jellyfish bubbling on the range and a platter of sows' udders, washed and ready for stuffing. The Bithynian cook held the neck of a recently strangled flamingo destined to be boiled and sautéed with dates; its long, pink legs reinforced with metal rods so it could stand, post-mortem, with its feathers dried, as the centrepiece of the banquet. She spotted Marcus.

"Tribune Sejanus! What brings you to the kitchen?"

"Greetings, Cook. It looks like you're feeding an army."

"Sixty-five guests. The best that Palestine can offer." She had a thick Bithynian accent and Marcus could not tell if she was being sarcastic. She stood there, clutching the ringed neck of the flamingo, its legs dangling against her starched, white apron. She was impatient to have him gone, he could see, but too polite – or too politic, perhaps – to attempt to hurry her betters.

"Why I am here, my good woman, is to procure some food. That useless slave Judith seems to have disappeared."

The cook did well to hide her impatience. Finding a light lunch for a hungry soldier, no matter what his rank, was not part of her carefully planned strategy to produce a Saturnalia feast that would be talked about for years to come. He took pity on her.

"Just point me in the direction of the bread and cheese and I shall help myself."

"Over there, sir," she said, relieved, pointing to a mound under a cheesecloth. Marcus pulled back the cloth to discover bread, cheese, olives and shaved ham.

"Give the tribune a platter," the cook instructed one of the scullery maids, who obeyed with shaking hands. She was a pretty lass and Marcus was tempted to hold her small hands until they stilled. But he contained himself. He took the platter without thanks and then helped himself.

"Have you had to bring in more staff for the banquet?" he asked the cook, ladling some olives onto his plate.

"Yes. We've got some of the farm hands from the olive grove."

"Point them out to me."

If the cook was surprised by his request she did not show it. "Him and him." She gestured to two young Jewish men, barely more than boys. They were carrying some wood for the furnace. "And there's another one. But I sent him off on an errand."

Marcus carried his platter and nonchalantly blocked the boys' path. They stopped, uncertain what to do.

"Do you know who I am?" Neither of them answered or met his eye.

"Answer the tribune," ordered the cook. And then, with barely disguised impatience: "I'm sure he must have good reason to interrupt preparations for the most important banquet of the year."

"Y-y-yes, sir," said the older of the boys. "You're the soldier who crucified those men."

"That's right. Then you know what I do to traitors. Do you know any traitors?"

"N-no sir," said the older boy again and the younger lad shook his head vehemently.

"But if you did you would report them to me, wouldn't you?" This he addressed to the whole kitchen staff which had stopped work the moment the mass crucifixion was mentioned.

"Y-yes, sir," said the older lad again. And everyone else nodded in agreement.

Good, thought Marcus, they've got the fear of Hades in them. "Because if something happens tonight at the banquet, I'll know where to look and I'll know who to blame. Do you understand me?" He was met with silence. "Do you understand me?" he bellowed. This time there was a chorus of "Yes, sir!"

By now the cook's patience had come to an end. "If that's all, Tribune, I would like my kitchen back."

"By all means, dear lady," he conceded with a mock bow and took his lunch back upstairs. Mission accomplished.

Chapter 28 – Saturnalia

Frankly, Pontius Pilate was just not in the mood for Saturnalia this year. He usually enjoyed the festivities and tolerated the gentle subversion of the slaves with good humour, but this year there was just too much to worry about. If it hadn't been for the need to make amends for Procula Claudiana's bizarre snub of the Herods at the Jordan, he would have cancelled the whole thing.

Pilate adjusted the pleats of his toga and pinned them firmly at the shoulder. The gold and ivory ram's head pin had been a gift from Procula; oh, how he wished he could rouse her out of her melancholy. He'd spoken to the priests and they'd suggested daily sacrifices to Apollo in conjunction with regular bleedings of the patient to suck out the black bile. The first part of the prescription was easy enough, but the second was proving more problematic. The more blood that was taken, the more melancholic she became. She lay on her pillows like an alabaster sarcophagus, muttering about the blood of a crucified man. Her once beautiful eyes stared fixedly on the open window. When he had asked her what she hoped to see, she answered: "My Lord sometimes appears in the form of a dove. Perhaps he will fly to me." Whenever he attempted to close the window – and Apollo knew it needed closing to keep out the bite of winter – she would cry out as if in pain. So instead he ordered a fire to remain constantly kindled and her couch to be brought near it whenever she started shivering. He did not want her to die, but she seemed intent upon it. He breathed hard, holding back the tears. Life without Procula would be intolerable. There had to be a way to reach her.

*

As Pilate entered the dining hall, the entire retinue rose to greet him, as was befitting the evening's host. He seated himself on the couch between Antipas and Marcus Sejanus. He noticed with approval that Claudia Lucretia was seated to the left of Marcus. Her alleged threat to Salome that she was planning on boycotting proceedings in protest against her 'forced' engagement thankfully appeared to be an unfounded, jealous rumour.

However, Pilate simply could not understand why Claudia did not welcome the imminent engagement to Marcus with more enthusiasm. Perhaps she was just waiting for it to be formalised. Well she wouldn't have to wait long. He had had a brief meeting with Antipas earlier in the day and received the king's assurance that he would get the funds he needed to go ahead with the aqueduct, so he could start calling in his gratuities from the contractors. At least that was one load off his mind: the dowry was finally secured. The engagement would formally be announced tonight. It was just a pity Procula would not be there to see it.

*

Claudia was trying her hardest to sound interested in Marcus' anecdotes. She laughed at the right times and feigned admiration as he regaled the dinner guests with tales of his recent exploits while hunting down the Zealots. One would swear he'd taken on an entire rebel army single-handedly, the way he went on. Still, he wasn't that bad. She suspected that much of the pomposity was an act and behind it was a fairly decent – if slightly vain – man.

She had done a good deal of thinking while swimming her lengths at the baths earlier in the day. After Salome had finally left her in peace, she had come to the conclusion that Judah was not coming back and that she'd better start taking care of her future; or Salome might just try to usurp her.

She'd cried herself to sleep for three solid months over her Jewish lover, but it was time to move on. Her fear that Marcus had killed him with the Zealots had finally been laid to rest today as she knelt in front of the line of crucified men. Now that she knew he was very likely still alive, she allowed her anger to take control. How dare he put her through all of this? How dare he let her think he might be dead without sending word to the contrary? How dare he leave Caesarea without so much as a word? How dare he treat the daughter of Pontius Pilate this way?

She laughed again at one of Marcus' jokes, making sure she outdid Salome in fawning while putting a flirtatious hand on his forearm. Marcus raised an eyebrow and smiled; oh, the look on Salome's face was priceless!

Her father had been wise in his seating arrangements, keeping the eligible tribune out of arm's reach of the Idumean princess. Her poor father, he had so much to deal with at the moment without having to think about such trivial things as seating arrangements. She watched him talking to Antipas, feigning interest as much as she had with Marcus. Like father like daughter. A surge of love and admiration rose in her. The poor man was heartbroken by her mother's malady, which he insisted on calling melancholia. However, after seeing her mother at the Jordan and witnessing first-hand her hysterical display, Claudia feared it was much more.

Procula Claudiana had always been embarrassingly earnest about religion and Claudia sensed that she had finally crossed the line between devotion and fanaticism and was in danger of sinking into madness. Her father deserved better than that. And she was not going to add to his worries by being difficult about the engagement to Marcus. Of course, if Judah had not abandoned her things might have been different, but they weren't. Her chance of love was gone. Now all that was left was to be a dutiful daughter and – she tried not to cringe at the thought – wife.

The room was filled with a thousand candles; many of them displayed on an elaborate candelabra, hanging from the ceiling. The lights twinkled off the assorted jewels of Palestine's finest leading ladies. Salome had competition tonight, thought Claudia, as she looked around at the wives and daughters of the invited guests. How many of them wanted to marry Marcus? Claudia had never thought about that before and was surprised to find a twinge of jealousy rising up in her. Could she actually have feelings for him? Well, perhaps not yet, but she was beginning to at least entertain the possibility.

Her father was whispering something to the eligible tribune who seemed to nod in assent. Then Pilate stood up and tapped his knife against his goblet. The convivial dinner hubbub gradually subsided. Some of the guests shifted their positions so they could see their host who was partially masked by the flamingo centrepiece, straddling the table like a pink Colossus.

"*Io Saturnalia!*"

"*Io Saturnalia!*" chorused the guests.

"Welcome to our Saturnalia celebrations in honour of the divine Saturn, lord of light, and of the august Tiberius Caesar, lord of the world. We will shortly be entertaining you with the finest acts in the Near East. But first, I have two announcements to make. The first is who has the honour of being this year's *Saturnalicus Princepas*: the King for the

Day." There was an excited murmur from one corner of the hall where, as was customary, the household slaves had gathered to hear the announcement. They would be looking forward to the following evening when the tables were turned, the family would serve them and the 'King' would be able to give orders and issue decrees that could not be overturned for the duration of the holiday. But for now, some of them still had jobs to do. Claudia noticed Nebela circulating with a tray of sugared almonds. She had offered one to her earlier, but, not wanting to spoil her appetite for the stuffed dormice and flamingo, she had declined.

With all eyes on him, her father continued: "After consulting with my wife – who, unfortunately, is not well enough to join us this evening – we have decided that the King of Saturnalia, or in this case the Queen, is to be Nebela. Come here, girl."

Accompanied by a round of applause, Nebela put down her tray of almonds and knelt before Pilate. "You have served us well this year. Helping firstly to save our precious daughter from the Zealot brigands and then becoming a most helpful member of the household staff. My wife tells me you have become invaluable to my daughter. Is that not so, my dear?"

This last was directed at Claudia who nearly choked on her wine. "Y-yes, invaluable. She has been most helpful in – in – helping me – with certain – things." She started coughing again and Marcus patted her gently on the back. Claudia recovered enough to see Nebela's eyes narrow as the tribune allowed his hand to linger on her shoulders.

"Excellent! Then she is a worthy appointment." Then to Nebela: "Well, *Princepessa*, what is to be your first decree?"

Nebela, though kneeling, held herself with a regalness the likes of which Salome could only dream. For a moment Claudia wondered who this Babylonian girl really was. She'd heard that she had not been born a slave. Perhaps she was descended from some Eastern royal family. Or perhaps it was all an act. Claudia would not put it past her.

"Well, my lord," purred Nebela, "my first decree will require the co-operation of your guest and my true master, King Herod Antipas."

The guests who had shifted to the right to see past the flamingo, now shifted to the left. Antipas, his cheeks flushed with wine, nodded good-humouredly. It was well known that the Herods were more Roman than the Romans in observing Roman traditions. Claudia was sure that whatever Nebela asked, he would give it.

"Yes, girl, speak."

"My lord," she bowed deeply. "My lord King Antipas. I command you to give me, as a slave, to Tribune Marcus Gaius Sejanus." The gasps of shock were so intense the thousand candles were nearly extinguished. This was not the usual decree of the King for the Day; they had expected something along the lines of emptying the wine cellar in favour of the slaves, insisting everyone wear their clothes inside-out or making the lord of the house perform a silly task. A decree of this magnitude was unprecedented. Everyone held their breath to see how Pilate and Antipas would react.

Pilate was the first to recover. "Well, *Princepessa*, that is a bold decree."

"It is what I desire."

"And is it what you desire, King Antipas?"

Antipas was just on the right side of sober and considered this more carefully than he would have after a few more drinks. "A girl of her beauty is very valuable. She would fetch a good price on the open market."

"Then name your price," declared Marcus, standing up and reaching out his hand to Nebela. More gasps rose from the crowd and Salome smirked at Claudia across the table. Claudia wished the ground would open up and swallow her. Oh, the humiliation! How could Marcus do this to her? How could her father let him? But Pilate seemed too stunned to speak for a moment, watching in shock as Nebela reached out and took Marcus' hand.

"No!" cried Claudia. "No! This cannot be. Tell him father, tell *them*!"

"Tell me what?" asked Marcus. "That I cannot buy a slave for my bride to be?"

Claudia opened her mouth to speak then closed it again. As she was directly behind the flamingo, some guests actually stood up to see her reaction.

"You are giving me to *her*?" spat Nebela, trying to pull away her hand; but Marcus held her fast.

"Er, yes," said Pilate, finally recovering. "That was to be my second announcement of the evening. I am very happy to tell you all that the honourable Marcus Gaius Sejanus has agreed to marry my daughter, the beloved and beautiful Claudia Lucretia."

Sighs of relief were followed by enthusiastic applause and vigorous backslapping of both Pilate and Marcus. But neither Claudia nor Nebela joined in. Their eyes were locked in a pact of mutual hatred. So neither of them saw the candle overturn in the melee to congratulate the two men; neither of them saw first the table cloth then the feathers of the flamingo catch alight; neither of them saw the frenetic efforts of the guests to douse the flames as they roared up the silk drapes and spewed foul fumes into the hall; but then one of them *did* see the cloaked stranger slip into the hall and clasp a hand over Claudia's mouth and carry her away.

*

A Dream of Procula Pilate

My Lord is a dove. His wings brush my face as he passes by. His wings beat faster and faster. His wings become fire. The flames brush my hair. My hair is aflame. My Lord is ablaze. Burn me, Lord, burn me! Ignite me, consume me, may my hair, my flesh, my bones be turned to ash. And then may I arise. Like a Phoenix from the flame. May I receive a new body, a new mind! May I live again! I see a shadow in the flame. It is no longer a dove. It is no longer a man. It is a child. She is crying. She is calling to me. Her arms outstretched. It is Claudia! Oh Lord, do not destroy my child! Fan your wings Lord, extinguish the flames. Save her, Lord, save her. Save me.

Chapter 29 – The Abduction

Claudia felt sick. Her chest was tight, her head throbbed; she felt like she had been ridden over by a span of oxen. She had been emerging from consciousness for the last few minutes or so, but it took her a little longer than that to realise that she was not simply waking up after a particularly bad night's sleep. Her shoulders ached and as she tried to readjust her position, she realised that her hands were tied together. Why were they tied together? She tried to stretch her legs and discovered that her feet were similarly bound. There was something in her mouth, something that soaked up all her saliva. Was she gagged? She tried to speak, but only a muffled sound came out. Yes, she was gagged.

Where was she? And why did she feel like she was moving? She felt something hard beneath her. Wood? Planks? Above her was some kind of rough, dusty fabric. Sack cloth? She strained to see something and out of the corner of her eye she made out a watery light, seeping through the edge of the fabric. It was then that she realised where she was. She was on the back of a cart: a moving cart. And she was trussed up like a hog for slaughter.

She tried to recall her last conscious moments. She was at the Saturnalia banquet; she had just been publicly humiliated by Marcus Gaius and that slut Nebela. How could they do that to her? How could they play her like a fool? Well, if Marcus thought she was going to marry him now, he had another thing coming! As soon as she got out of here she would march right into her father's quarters and tell him to call the engagement off. And then she would have Nebela flogged and sent back to the Herods. That would show the stupid girl not to have ideas above her station. And if she decided to divulge the information she had about Judah – which was always the implicit threat and why Claudia had let her get away with so much for so long – then let her! She would deny it all and say it was simply the jealous fantasy of a slave. Without any physical proof or other witnesses – witnesses that were not slaves – then who would believe her? There, that was easily sorted.

The cart lurched as it hit a pot hole in the road, bashing her aching body painfully against the side. She cursed, and so too did a male voice.

She strained her ears to hear if he would speak again, but he didn't. All she could hear was the creak of the cart and the snort of an animal: a donkey? Possibly.

Who was he? Claudia strained again to remember the events at the banquet. She and Nebela had been staring daggers at one another while everyone else seemed to think it was a splendid joke. There were people everywhere and she could hear her father and Marcus laughing and joking along with them. Men! Did the feelings of two women ... two? What was she thinking? For a moment there she had almost seen Nebela as a fellow victim! No, did *her* feelings mean nothing to them? Apparently not. Then, somehow, in all the chaos, she remembered seeing something behind Nebela – something on the table – a giant – a giant – *flaming bird*. A phoenix? No, it was the flamingo. The giant outstretched wings of the flamingo had been on fire! A fire! There had been a fire! Then – then – the smoke. Her chest wheezed. She must have inhaled the smoke. She remembered the room spinning and the flames – and the screams – and Nebela's face – then falling into someone's arms – then being lifted up – then – then – that was the last thing she remembered; until now.

The cart clattered to a stop. Her heart started racing. What was happening?

She strained at her bonds, trying to loosen the knots; they were unyielding. She felt something sharp against her ankle. Gingerly she scraped her foot along the side of the cart, tracing the outline of what she thought might be a broken, metal strut. If she could reposition herself she might be able to lift her feet and use the strut as a saw. She rolled her body back and forth until she picked up enough momentum to shift herself towards the sharp metal.

"Be quiet in there!" a male voice growled in Aramaic. Claudia froze. After a while she heard the man talking soothingly, to the donkey she supposed, asking if it was hungry; then a muffled chomping as the beast munched contentedly on its meal. She started rocking again, renewing her efforts to sever her bonds. Suddenly a corner of the sackcloth was flung back and a large, dark shadow loomed over her. His face was only a hand's-breadth away from hers. She smelt his breath and it was as acrid as the smoke that clung to her clothes and hair. "I said be quiet! They'll hear us!" – this time in thickly accented Greek.

Who'll hear us? Who was this man? She didn't recognise his voice or his face; although it was hard to tell because of the shadow cast by his hood.

She suddenly heard the clatter of hooves and the jingle of bridles then the laughter of a group of men sharing a ribald joke. They were speaking common Latin: Roman soldiers! Claudia bashed her heels up and down against the floor of the cart and squealed as best she could through the gag. The sound of the hooves slowed.

"Did you hear that?" asked one of the soldiers.

A hand came down and covered Claudia's nose and mouth and she felt the prick of a blade at her throat. "Try that again and I'll kill you," whispered her abductor.

"You mean you farting?" replied one of the soldiers. Whatever the first soldier said in retort was drowned by the guffawing of his companions. Claudia's heart sank as the hooves and bridles started to clatter again. Her abductor kept the blade at her throat until the sound of the Roman patrol faded into the night.

When all she could hear was the chomping of the donkey and the screech of a night owl, he bundled her up and heaved her over his shoulder. Her instinct was to kick at him, but she controlled it. He carried her a short distance and put her down with her back against a tree, then knelt down and peered into her face.

"I'm going to take off your gag so you can eat and drink. But if you scream I will kill you. Do you understand?"

Claudia nodded. He removed the gag and held a flagon of water to her lips. She drank furiously. When she had finished he took his hand and wiped away the wetness from her chin. It was a surprisingly gentle move and his thumb lingered for a moment on her bottom lip. Claudia cringed with memories of Matthias at the Zealot camp flooding back. There was no Judah to save her now. But the man withdrew his hand without intervention.

"Who are you?" Her voice was hoarse. She coughed to clear her throat.

"You don't recognise me?" He pulled down his hood so that his face was bathed in moonlight. Claudia looked at him intently. He was a young man in his early to mid twenties. His hair was dark brown and hung to his shoulders. He had a full, neatly trimmed beard. His eyes were dark and intense. He looked Jewish, which wasn't much of a surprise, but no, Claudia could not place him.

"Have we met before?"

A look of anger flashed in his dark eyes. "I've brought wood to your chamber every day for the last three months."

"Wood?" Claudia was confused and her head hurt. "You deliver wood? You're a slave at the palace?"

"A slave? I am not a slave! I am a freeborn son of Israel. And you, Roman, are not welcome in our land!" Claudia thought for a moment that he was going to strike her, but with obvious restraint he stalked away and busied himself retrieving some things from the back of the cart.

"You're a Zealot," concluded Claudia, her worst fears confirmed. They had come to finish off what they had started. Judah had been right; her life had been in danger. Her life *was* in danger. But why had he not just killed her at the palace during all the confusion of the fire?

"Are you going to kill me?" She did not really want to know the answer.

He placed wood in a pile and busied himself lighting a fire.

She tried again. "Are you going to kill me?"

He stopped, flint in hand, and looked at her. "That is not my job."

"And what is your job? Apart from delivering wood."

She thought she saw his mouth twitch into a slight smile. "It's not so different. I'm still making a delivery."

"What are you delivering?"

"I thought that was obvious, *princess*, I'm delivering you." Suddenly there was a rustle of undergrowth and the sound of footsteps on gravel behind her. The donkey looked up from its dinner, its eyes mild and curious. Claudia tried to look around too but her bonds would not let her. Her abductor stood up, wiped his hands on his cloak, and greeted the newcomer brusquely in Aramaic: "Better late than never, cousin."

Chapter 30 – The Assassin's Plot

"What have you done to her?" A man dropped to his knees and started untying her bonds. "Are you all right, my love? Has he hurt you?"

Claudia was too stunned to speak. It was Judah. He untied her hands and feet and threw the ropes at the other man. "What the hell do you think you're doing?" Then he turned back to Claudia and cupped her face in his hands and repeated: "Has he hurt you?"

Claudia shook her head, still unable to vocalise her torrent of thoughts while trying to translate the rapid volley of Aramaic between the two men.

"No, I haven't hurt the bitch," said the other man and tossed the ropes back at Judah. "And if that's the thanks I get for risking my life then don't bother asking for any more help. I owed you one, and now we're even." He went to the cart and lifted out some supplies and left them by the fireside. Then he took the reins of the donkey and climbed on board.

"Where are you going?"

"What's it to you?"

"Don't be like that, Simeon. I just didn't expect her to be tied up, that's all."

"It was the best way. She wouldn't have come quietly otherwise."

"I suppose not."

Claudia finally found her voice. "You know this man?"

"He's my cousin, Simeon. It wasn't safe for me to come to the palace. I would have been recognised. But no one knew Simeon. He's been keeping an eye on you since you returned from Jerusalem."

"The woodcutter!" said Claudia, suddenly placing the man.

"Not any more." Simeon geed the donkey forward.

Judah cupped her face in his hands once more – "I'll be back in a moment" – and caught up with the donkey. He spoke quietly to Simeon, with his back to her, and Claudia caught only snatches of conversation: "Fire"; "Sejanus"; "Barabbas"; "Uncle Hillel"; "Jairus"; "East". Then the two men embraced and Simeon and the donkey clopped their way into the night.

Claudia tried to get up, but the circulation to her limbs had been restricted for too long. She stumbled and fell back down. Judah rushed to her, taking her calves in his hands and rubbing them until the pain subsided. "Better?" She nodded then started shivering uncontrollably. He took off his cloak and put it over her, then helped her move closer to the fire. He sat down and put his arm around her, pulling her close. She sank into his side, resting her cheek on his chest. She inhaled him and the sweet memories of the hours they had spent together in the olive grove came flooding back. As he rubbed her arms in a rhythmic motion, all thoughts of giving him a piece of her mind and berating him for abandoning her without an explanation were washed away.

After a while he spoke. "Simeon told me there was a fire and he had to rescue you. Are you all right?"

She nodded against his chest.

"Thank YHWH for that. I would have no reason to live if you died."

"Did he set the fire?" she asked quietly.

"Simeon? No."

"Then who did?"

"It might have been an accident – or –"

"Or?"

"It might have been the assassin Barabbas sent to kill you and Nebela. Simeon didn't know, so he decided not to take any chances. The killer could still be in the palace."

Claudia sat up. "There's a killer in the palace?"

"That's what I've heard."

"Is he still there?"

"I don't know. But it doesn't matter; you're safe here with me."

"But my parents aren't! I need to warn them, Judah." She started to get up but he pulled her back down. She was too weak to resist.

"Your Marcus Sejanus will be on high alert after the fire –"

"If any of them survived it!"

"Simeon said they were getting it under control as he was leaving."

"Even so, there's a killer on the loose."

"As much as I despise your tribune, he's good at his job. Simeon said he was already asking questions in the kitchen. That's where the assassin was hiding out, apparently."

"How does he know?"

"Because he recognised one of the kitchen staff as one of his father's men."

"His father?"

"Barabbas is Simeon's father. And my uncle by marriage."

"Your uncle? Barabbas is your uncle? And – and – Simeon is your – your – he can't be trusted!"

"Don't worry, Simeon and his father have parted ways. They don't share the same – how do you say it in Greek – the same vision."

"They don't both want to get rid of the Romans?"

"They do, but Simeon doesn't agree with Barabbas' methods; and neither do I."

"What methods?"

"Kidnapping and killing Roman women and children. Neither of us were prepared to do it and so we've fallen out with him."

"And he's let you go? Just like that?"

"No, not just like that. But right now I'm hungry. I'm sure you are too."

Claudia was about to object when a loud rumbling from her stomach told them both he was right. He unfolded himself from Claudia and got up. She pulled the cloak more tightly around her and hugged her knees to her chest. It was the same cloak he had worn the first time they had met in the olive grove; the cloak that was singed when she threw it on the fire. Judah scratched around in the sack of supplies that Simeon had left for them and came out with some bread, olives and dried fish. Then he flattened out the sack like a picnic blanket and laid out the wares before them. He tore off a chunk of bread and gave it to Claudia. She devoured it.

Their appetites sated, Judah stoked the fire and settled down again beside her. "What are we going to do?" she asked him.

"I have a plan."

"And are you going to share this plan with me?" Now that her hunger had subsided she was feeling a lot more like her usual self: her usual combative self.

"We're going to spend the rest of the night here then in the morning we're going to my Uncle Hillel's house to pick up some more supplies."

"We're going to stay with your uncle?"

"Not for long. Your Tribune Sejanus will be on our scent as soon as the ash at the palace settles."

"He is not *my* tribune."

"Not according to Simeon."

Claudia looked at him suspiciously. "Why? What did he say?"

"He said the two of you had just announced your engagement." He stoked the fire more vigorously than necessary.

"Are you jealous, Judah?"

"Of course I'm jealous!"

"Well, you have no right to be. And come to think of it, you are being a bit presumptuous, assuming I would want to go with you in the first place. You haven't even asked if I want to!" She stood up then – finally having enough strength to stand on her own two feet – and glared down at him. "I'm sick of men making decisions for me as if I do not have a mind to think for myself!"

She whipped around and stomped off.

"Where are you going?"

She stopped. Where was she going? She didn't even know where she was: somewhere in the wilderness; surrounded by rocks and shrubs and some scraggly trees. She looked up to see if there were any stars to help her, but a canopy of cloud stood between her and their guidance. "I'm going right here," she said and sat down huffily on the opposite side of the fire.

He laughed, which just infuriated her more. But then, after a moment, she saw the ridiculousness of the situation and laughed too. He rushed over and pulled her up and into his arms. "That's the Claudia I've missed!" He kissed her furiously. She returned his passion and the two of them fell to the ground in a tumble of limbs. His hands were everywhere, but she didn't mind. It was madness, yes, but she didn't want to stop and think about it. All she wanted was Judah – all of him – and she wanted it with every fibre of her being.

"Sorry to interrupt," said a voice in Aramaic.

Judah leapt to his feet, pulling Claudia with him. Simeon stood in front of them holding the donkey's reins.

"That Roman patrol is camped a couple of stadia from here, right on the side of the road. I couldn't get passed with the cart. Mind if I sleep here tonight?"

"Of course not!" Judah stepped in front of Claudia while she straightened her clothes, mortified with embarrassment. "Do you mind if the lady sleeps in the back of the cart?"

"Alone?" asked Simeon, busy unhitching the donkey.

"Yes, alone!" declared Claudia, strutting over to the cart with all the haughtiness she could muster.

"Be my guest," Simeon muttered in Greek. Then in Aramaic: "I don't know what you see in her, cousin, I really don't."

Chapter 31 – Meanwhile, Back at the Palace...

Marcus Gaius Sejanus came out of the dungeon, wiping blood from his hands. Once the fire had been doused and the dead and injured dealt with, he had wasted no time rounding up the prime suspects in the tragedy: the kitchen staff. Despite most of the guests insisting that the fire had been a terrible accident, Marcus did not agree. Perhaps it was his rage that Nebela was one of the half dozen injured (but thankfully not one of the two dead) that drove him to torture the three kitchen lads. Whatever his motivation, his suspicions turned out to be well founded. With only the most cursory pain endured, the two boys he had spoken to that afternoon were quick to point the finger at their colleague: the third lad who had not been there during the tribune's visit.

Not so much a lad as a man in his early twenties; he proved a much harder nut to crack. But Marcus and his men were experts at applying the maximum amount of pain for the minimum amount of effort, and after an hour of it, the traitor told him everything he needed to know – and more.

As Marcus suspected, he had been sent by the Zealot leader Barabbas to infiltrate the Pilate household, waiting for an opportune moment to kill the governor and his family. The young man, though, was ambitious, and decided that wiping out the entire Judean aristocracy at the same time was also in his grasp. That did not surprise Marcus, but what did, was that Nebela was on the assassin's list too, sharing top spot with Claudia. Thank Juno he had failed to kill either of them.

But all was not well. It was only after the second head count and a frantic search of the palace by every able-bodied slave not attending to the dead and injured, that they realised Claudia Lucretia was gone. Marcus had immediately sent out patrols to scour the city and set up roadblocks on every road out of Caesarea. The harbour was shut down so no one could escape by sea. Pilate insisted that he lead one of the patrols and was vexed that Marcus did not join him. Marcus, however, realised he would be better deployed at the palace extracting information from the kitchen staff. If Claudia was not found in the city within the next hour he would lead a patrol out into the countryside and call on his network of spies positioned in every village and town from Caesarea to

Galilee to Jerusalem. He doubted Claudia and her captor – if that's what he was – would manage to move beyond the security triangle and he was confident he would have her back, dead or alive.

But before he headed out on any rescue mission he first needed to verify some information. The traitor had told him something that had shocked him to the core, and, if true, might jeopardise his entire future. There was only one person who could tell him what he needed to know and she was lying injured in her mother's chambers. He had taken her there himself.

*

In the chaos of the fire, with the silk sashes and drapes fuelling the blaze, the rope to the giant chandelier burnt through and the massive wrought-iron construction plummeted to the floor below. Two people were crushed – fortunately only slaves – and a handful trampled as the guests tried to flee the blaze. Marcus and Pilate had managed to rally enough level-headed slaves to fight the fire until a contingent of soldiers arrived from the barracks, bringing the fire under control.

After the worst was over, Marcus plunged his face into the ornamental fountain to clear his head. It was then that he heard the whimper. "Marcus! Marcus!" He looked down and saw a giant tureen with the innards of a jellyfish spilling out of it. But under the glutinous mush something moved. A hand reached out and clutched at his foot. Then an arm emerged. On the shoulder was a reed tattoo: the mark of the House of Herod.

His heart lurched. "Nebela!" He heaved the tureen off her and fell to his knees to examine the damage. He cleared away the gloop until he saw a bone piercing her thigh. "Oh, Nebela!" He looked around and found a broken piece of furniture that could serve as a splint and did as much remedial triage as he could. She was barely conscious, mumbling his name over and over. He brushed back her hair from her face and tried to get her to focus on him. "I'm here, Nebela, I'm here." The sound of his voice seemed to calm her and he kept on talking to her as he lifted her into his arms and carried her out of the hall. He did not care how many tongues were left wagging in his wake.

Her mother, Zandra, hurriedly joined him and she led the way to her chambers where he placed Nebela as gently as he could on a bed. Zandra immediately got to work tending to her wounds. Nebela was in good hands but it was with the utmost reluctance that he left her to go look for Claudia.

*

Now, two hours later, he stood on the threshold of Zandra's chambers, wondering how to approach the interrogation when Nebela was in such a fragile state. But it couldn't wait. It was imperative that he find out if what the traitor had told him was true.

He opened the door and swept aside the thick velveteen curtain. He was struck by the usual pungent odours of incense and perfume that hung like a thick mist over the soothsayer's apartment, but tonight it was tinged with something else: the smell of blood. Marcus was used to the smell; but on the battlefield, not here in the palace and particularly not emanating from the woman he loved. Marcus shook his head to dismiss the sentimental thoughts. There was no time to indulge in such saccharine fantasies.

Zandra was mumbling and muttering over her daughter, wafting a smouldering bouquet of myrtle over her body. Nebela lay as still as a corpse. If it weren't for the almost imperceptible rise and fall of her chest, he would think she had left this world to join the shades.

"How is she?" he asked, gruffly, clearing his throat of unmanly emotion.

"She has settled. She seems to be in a little less pain." Zandra nodded to an empty vial on the bedside table.

"Has she woken?"

"No."

"Then she must." Marcus sat down and took Nebela's hand, squeezing it gently.

"Nebela, Nebela, wake up."

"Leave her to sleep."

"I can't. Claudia Lucretia's life depends on it."

Marcus ignored the angry flash in Zandra's eyes and persisted in rousing his lover from her near-comatose state. After a few minutes of persistent calling and gentle shaking, Nebela started to open her eyes. She saw Marcus and her mother hovering over her.

"Marcus," she whispered.

He leaned in closer to her and spoke as gently as he could. "Nebela, I need to ask you something. It's very important. Claudia has been kidnapped."

"Again?" asked Zandra.

"Yes, again. We believe it's the Zealots. One of the boys in the kitchen has been working with them. It was he who set the fire. He told me that Claudia and Nebela were the main targets."

"Nebela? What has she got to do with it?"

"The boy said it was because she could identify some of the Zealots. She knew who they were. Did you know this boy, Nebela, the one called Aaron?"

Nebela shook her head.

"All right," said Marcus, wanting to believe her, but needing to press on, "And did you know someone called Judah?"

Nebela's hand flinched involuntarily in his.

"You do, don't you?"

"O – o – ol..."

He leaned in closer, but couldn't make it out. "What's she trying to say?" he asked Zandra.

"I don't know. Ol-something. Olive? Are you trying to say olive?" Nebela nodded.

"Olive," said Marcus, not quite understanding.

"Perhaps she means the olive grove. Maybe that's where she has seen this Judah. She used to go there sometimes with Claudia."

Nebela's eyes flitted to her mother. Her eyebrows came together in a frown. Marcus wondered if she was trying to warn Zandra not to say anything or was simply grimacing with pain.

"I think that's enough," said Zandra. "You can talk to her more when she is better."

"No, I must talk to her now. There is one final thing I must know." He leant in closely again. "Nebela, did Claudia know this Judah?" Nebela's eyes flitted again to her mother. Her mother nodded, encouragingly. Nebela opened her mouth and tried to speak. But whatever she said was drowned out by a commotion in the hall. Someone was shouting, loudly. "Where is he? I'll kill the bastard myself!"

Suddenly the door flew open and Pontius Pilate stormed into the room, grabbed Marcus by his tunic and thrust him against the wall. Marcus could have fought back against the older man, but he didn't.

"What in Juno's name are you doing with your slave whore when my daughter's life is hanging in the balance?"

It took every fibre of Marcus' willpower to keep his voice calm. "That's what I'm doing here, my lord. I'm trying to find out some information as to her whereabouts."

Pilate looked at Zandra and Nebela. "Do you know anything? If you do and you don't tell the tribune, you will be flayed alive. Do you understand?"

"Yes, my lord. But I don't know anything," said Zandra.

"And her?" Pilate nodded to Nebela who appeared to have slipped back into unconsciousness.

"That's what we're trying to find out," said Marcus.

"Well, whatever it is, we can find out later." Pilate released his grip on Marcus. "Some of your scouts have returned. Claudia Lucretia was spotted with the woodcutter who used to work for us. The one they called Simeon. The fishmonger's wife saw them. She thought at first he was just saving her from the fire, but when she heard Claudia was missing, she came forward."

"Simeon? Are you sure the name was Simeon? Not Judah?"

"What difference does it make what his name is!" bellowed Pilate. "We need to rescue her!" And he turned on his heel and strode out of Zandra's apartment. He did not look back to see if Marcus was following him. He knew, and the tribune knew, his career and his social progression depended on his obedience.

But as he left, he allowed himself one more glance at Nebela. Perhaps the kitchen boy was wrong. Perhaps Nebela and Claudia didn't know the abductor. He hoped with all his heart that that was true.

Chapter 32 – East of Eden

Claudia awoke to the sound of a donkey braying, then a man scolding it, not unkindly, in Aramaic. "You have already had your breakfast, Bobo, you silly ass."

"You're the silly ass for talking to a donkey," said a voice that Claudia recognised immediately. It was Judah. Suddenly the memories of last night came flooding back: the banquet, the fire, the abduction by the woodcutter, the close encounter with the Roman patrol, the surprise arrival of Judah and then... oh then... what might have happened if Simeon had not returned?

Claudia allowed herself to luxuriate in the fantasy for a while. She felt again Judah's hands on her body, his lips, his tongue... but then, just like last night, the woodcutter interrupted. She was really beginning to dislike the man.

"Time to get up princess," he said as he threw back the canvas tarpaulin covering the cart. Claudia instinctively pulled her flimsy and revealing Saturnalia gown more tightly around her, retreating further into the cart.

Simeon laughed, coarsely. "Don't flatter yourself. Unlike your boyfriend I'm not attracted to spoilt Roman brats."

"Leave her alone, Simeon, she's been through a lot." It was Judah. He pushed passed his cousin, reached out his hand and helped Claudia up.

"Good morning, my love," he whispered. It was intended only for Claudia's ears, but an ass-like snort from Simeon suggested he had heard it too.

My love? Claudia's heart was beating as fast as a sparrow's. She had hoped Judah felt the same about her as she did about him, but she had never been completely certain of his intentions. Part of her feared that it was all a ploy and that he was still working for Barabbas. Even the kisses they had shared could simply be interpreted on a physical level. He was a man, she was a woman; it was the nature of things. But another part of her – the bigger part – did not accept that. She believed Judah when he said he did not approve of Barabbas' methods. Judah was a Zealot, yes, but he was not a cruel man. Claudia was convinced of that. Yes, she was safe with him. He would not hurt her... physically. Emotionally though, Claudia had no real idea of the state of Judah's heart. If he didn't love her, it would devastate her. But what if he did? How did he really feel about her? Why had he authorised her abduction (or as he phrased it, her *rescue*)? Was it to simply protect her as he claimed, or was it more? And if it was more, what was going to happen to them? Could they really have a future together? She, the daughter of a Roman governor and he, a wanted revolutionary? But before Claudia could ponder this further, Simeon interrupted again.

"Get some food down her, Judah; we need to get to Uncle Hillel's house before noon."

*

"Where are we going?" Claudia asked, as she and Judah walked behind Simeon's cart. Although Claudia's party sandals were finding it difficult going on the rocky Galilean roads, she wanted to keep as far away from the gruff woodcutter as possible. And by walking behind the cart she was also able to talk to Judah. He had given her his hooded cloak – the singed one – to keep her warm and to cover her inappropriate travelling attire. Only her painted toenails and beaded sandals belied that she was not a Jewish maiden walking with her brothers. And those trivial details would only be seen on close inspection. Judah and Simeon did not intend to get close enough to any fellow travellers to allow that.

"We're going to our Uncle Hillel's house. He's the leader of the synagogue in Capernaum. Well, at least he was. He had a stroke a few years back and my brother, Jairus, took over the day-to-day running of the place."

"What are we going to do there?"

"Get some food and supplies," Judah gave her a sideways glance, "and find you some clothes. My sister-in-law Hannah may have something for you."

"Do they know we're coming?"

"No. The fewer people who know about you the better."

"Then how do you know they will help us?"

Judah shrugged. "They're family."

Claudia wondered what Judah's family would think of her; or she of them. She doubted they would approve of her any more than her family

175

would approve of him. She didn't hold out much hope for a warm welcome.

"But we won't be staying there," she observed.

"No. It wouldn't be safe; for them or us. We will stay the night and then move on in the morning."

"Move on to where?"

Judah lowered his voice and looked around, as if worried the rocks and shrubs on either side of the deserted road had ears. It was early, just after sun-up, and there were no other travellers. "We're going east. Beyond the Jordan. Beyond the land of the Syrians. We're going to where Rome has no hold... to Parthia."

Parthia! The Parthian Empire stretched from the border of Syria in the west to the fabled land of the Sinae in the east. Everything Claudia knew about the Parthians was summed up in one word: "barbarian". Roman children were raised to believe the nomadic warriors were monstrous louts who beat their wives and children, abused their subjects, cannibalised their enemies and lacked any culture whatsoever.

Claudia shivered. "Why do you want to go there?"

"Because there there is no Rome."

"But I'm Roman. I don't want to go."

"You have no choice."

Claudia stopped and placed her hands on her hips. "So, this is an abduction."

"Of course it isn't." Judah put his hand on her shoulder to hurry her along.

She shook him off. "Come to think of it, you have never even asked me if I want to come with you at all."

"It's for your own protection. Barabbas will not stop until he captures or kills you. It's become a matter of honour with him. An obsession."

Claudia felt her heart sink. "Is that the only reason you have taken me?"

"I have not 'taken' you. I have rescued you."

"Then why don't you simply return me to the Romans with a warning that they will need to increase their vigilance?"

"Because they will want to know where I received my information. And although I want to protect you, I don't want to betray Barabbas. He is my uncle and his men are my countrymen. We share the same cause, if not the same methods."

So that was it then. There was no other reason. And there was no further reason to go with him. She turned around and started heading back down the road.

"Where are you going?" Judah ran after her and grabbed her arm. This time he didn't let go when she tried to shrug him off.

"I'm going to the nearest town and I'm going to find the local centurion and tell him I have escaped from my abductors. I will claim I did not know who they were. You will not be implicated and I will be returned to my family."

"But I don't want you to return to your family!"

Claudia looked at him curiously.

"Well, I do – or I would – if it were possible –"

"It is possible. I've just told you."

"Will you let me finish, woman!"

By now Simeon had realised they were not following him, stopped the cart and sat himself down with his back against a rock; his body language implying he was heartily sick of the drama his cousin had roped him into. The donkey didn't seem to care.

"I would be happy to return you to your family, if – if – if it were possible –" Judah ran his hands through his hair in agitation, gripping his scalp as if trying to pull the courage to say what he needed to say from the roots of his hair. "– if it were possible to still marry you."

"Marry me? You want to marry me?"

"Of course! Haven't I made that obvious?"

Claudia laughed incredulously. "No, Judah, you have made it anything but obvious."

"So will you? Will you marry me?"

Claudia did not miss a beat. It may not have been maidenly and it certainly did not befit the daughter of a governor, but time for circumspection was long gone. "If you can convince me that we can genuinely have a life together, then yes," she declared, as if agreeing to a mere party invitation.

Judah let out a whoop and swung Claudia around. "Steady!" she scolded, but didn't really mean it. He was standing in front of her as eager as a puppy, his brown eyes dancing with pent-up dreams. Claudia's heart was doing somersaults and she laughed at his enthusiasm.

"Of course we can have a life together! We will go to Parthia. My father used to work for a silk merchant. The old codger was as rich as King Solomon! He used to import silks and fine linens from the East. I could set up my own business somewhere on the Silk Road. Seleucia, perhaps."

"You want to become a shopkeeper?"

"A merchant! And when I'm wealthy enough your father will no longer object to you being married to a poor Jew!"

"Oh Judah, money is not the issue."

"But it's part of it. I know it is. Money can buy you a lot of prestige. How do you think Herod the Great did so well for himself? He part-financed Augustus' military campaigns."

"True…" said Claudia, warming to Judah's line of thinking despite her better judgment. "But Judah…"

"But Judah, nothing." It was Simeon; he'd had enough. "Listen, cousin, I'm going. I don't know what fantasy world you're living in, but I don't want to be a part of it. I've helped you as much as I can. I saved the girl's life, but what you do with her now is up to you. If you finally come to your senses and want to get back to fighting the Romans instead of wooing their daughters, you know where to find me."

Judah came back down to earth and turned to his cousin. He took a few calming breaths then said: "Thank you, Simeon. You've been a faithful comrade, but I need to do this. I have not forgotten our cause. The Parthians share our goals to drive the Romans back into the sea. And when Claudia and I are settled in Seleucia…"

Simeon shook his head in despair. "No, Judah, you will not. You always have the best intentions, but you don't see things as they really are. You're a dreamer. You will always be a dreamer." Then he tugged on the donkey's reins and led the beast away.

*

Claudia and Judah walked on in silence. Simeon's accusations had cut Judah to the core and he needed to think about what had been said. Claudia let him. She was worried that he would change his mind but she knew she needed to let him work through it himself. The hand that held hers reassured her that the man she loved was still connected to her.

But as they rounded a bend Judah thrust her behind him. The road ahead was scattered with bodies: dead Roman bodies. It was the platoon from the previous night. Judah drew his sword from his belt and backed him and Claudia away, scouring the road from left to right and squinting to see movement through the shrubbery. He pulled her behind a boulder and whispered: "We have to go another route. They'll be waiting for us."

"Who?" whispered Claudia, but before Judah could answer, three men rounded the boulder and blocked their exit. Their Jewish looks and bloodied swords suggested they were the Zealots who were responsible for the butchery on the road.

"Hello, Judah," said one of the men.

"Hello, Avram," said Judah, his hand clutching Claudia's so hard it hurt. "I thought I recognised your handiwork."

Avram grinned. He only had two rotting teeth left in his mouth. Claudia shivered.

"Can't take all the credit for it. The lads did their bit."

"Just the three of you?"

"Nah, Bart and the boys helped too. They've gone ahead to catch up with your uncle."

"And he left you behind to wait for us."

Avram grinned again.

"Funny how you knew we were coming."

"Blood's thicker than water," said Avram and used the point of his sword to push aside the lapels of Claudia's cloak. Judah's hand tightened even further.

"We've got to take her. You know that."

"I know," said Judah as he simultaneously pushed Claudia away and swung his sword in a wide arc in front of the three zealots. "Run, Claudia, run!"

One of the men reached out to grab her, but Judah's sword came down on his forearm, lacerating him from elbow to wrist. The man screamed, clutching his arm, his hand ineffectual in quenching the arterial bleeding. The other two men rounded on Judah. "Run!" he cried again.

So she ran. But she didn't run into the wilderness as Judah expected. As he battled the two men she ran around the boulder to find a tethered horse. It was one of the Roman steeds, by the look of its livery. She unleashed the horse and leapt on its back, pulling its head so it turned towards the boulder. She could hear the clash of swords and the grunts of fighting men; Judah was still holding his own. But how long could he hold off two armed men? She squeezed her knees and lashed the reins, whipping the horse into a canter. She rounded the boulder and rode the horse straight into the fighting men. They scattered to left and right.

"Jump on!" screamed Claudia.

Judah had fallen to the ground but leapt to his feet before the other two had time to recover. He clutched Claudia's outstretched arm and jumped on the horse behind her. Avram tried to grab the reins but Judah kicked him in the chest. Then with a "Yah-hah!" Claudia, Judah and the horse made their getaway.

Chapter 33 – Jairus' Daughter

It was nearly nightfall before Claudia, Judah and the half-lame horse plodded into Capernaum. When they had finally slowed from their hell-for-leather gallop, Judah said they needed to stay off the road in case Barabbas and his men were planning another ambush. He also did not want to arrive at Uncle Hillel's house at midday – the time he and Simeon agreed – just in case the woodcutter had betrayed them. Claudia was convinced that he had, but Judah thought it was either a coincidence or Simeon had been discovered by Avram and his men and compelled to give up the information. Claudia did not argue with him, but she thought he was blinded by familial loyalty. Whether by accident or intent, Barabbas seemed to know their movements; so they decided to take the most circuitous route possible to Capernaum.

Capernaum was a thriving little town on the north-west shore of Lake Galilee. Around fifteen hundred people lived there, most of them involved in some way with the fishing industry. The northern part of the town abutted fertile cornfields, providing a viable alternative to those who didn't want to fish. The town was full of small businesses related in one way or other to fish and corn, and prosperous enough to boast a substantial synagogue, supported by generous donations from local entrepreneurs.

The synagogue was not just the centre of religious teaching in the community but the seat of local government. The leader of the synagogue was to all extents and purposes the town mayor, magistrate and purveyor of religious instruction, all rolled into one. The synagogue leader was not by default a priest, but in Uncle Hillel's case, he was. Judah told Claudia that his Uncle Hillel, brother to Judah and Jairus' poor, abused, mother, had taken the boys in when she was killed by her good-for-nothing husband. The boys were raised with strict, but kind, religious instruction. Uncle Hillel had never married and he considered the boys his own sons, formally adopting them. As synagogue leader he was an important man and Claudia suspected fairly well-to-do. So Judah was not quite the poor peasant she had first assumed him to be.

Although, it appeared, the older brother Jairus was set to inherit the family "business" rather than he.

The role of synagogue leader was technically an elected one, drawn from the elders in the community, but it was generally accepted that the eldest son – or in this case, nephew – of the old leader would be given preference for election if he was of sufficient good standing. And Jairus, it seemed, was. At thirty-two he was married with three children, and although young to be an elder, had all but taken over his uncle's position and was much respected for it. So it was just a matter of time until Jairus' de facto role was formalised when it was polite to admit to what everyone already knew: Uncle Hillel would not recover.

Claudia was unsure of the wisdom of going to Capernaum, convinced that Barabbas would simply be waiting for them. But Judah thought that when they did not arrive at midday as scheduled, Barabbas would lurk for a few hours then be gone. He would not be welcome at his brother Hillel's house; one was a man of peace, the other a man of war. And it was imperative that the leader of the synagogue was not to be seen consorting with known revolutionaries. The Romans and the Herodians tolerated the synagogue system, recognising it as a stabilising influence in the community, so no sensible synagogue leader would want to rock the boat. And that is where Judah and Jairus differed: Judah was most definitely a boat rocker.

"If they won't take in your Uncle Barabbas, why will they help you?" asked Claudia.

"They still think I can be redeemed."

"And can you?"

"You are my redemption," said Judah, and kissed the top of her head.

Not wanting to attract undue attention, they left the horse on the outskirts of the town. They took off its saddle and tack and stowed it under a bush, then let the horse roam freely by the lake, munching on the lush grass on the banks. It would be found sooner or later; probably by the men attached to the local Roman garrison, which, Judah told her, was located on the far side of Capernaum. With lights already being lit in windows across the town, he doubted that would be much before the morning.

So Claudia and Judah approached the house of the leader of the synagogue on foot, like any other pilgrim or supplicant. Judah knocked on the door and waited. After a few moments, the door swung open and they were met by a young girl of about twelve. Claudia thought her dark brown eyes and mane of curly black hair familiar: she looked a lot like Judah. Her thick brows arched curiously as she took in the travel-weary couple on the doorstep.

"Hello?"

"Hello, Eliza," said Judah. "Do you remember me?"

The girl shook her head.

"I am your Uncle Judah, your father's brother. The last time I saw you, you were playing with dolls. I gave you one. Do you remember?"

Realisation dawned on the girl and she looked over her shoulder, nervously. "I don't think Daddy wants to see you, Uncle Judah," she whispered.

"Who is it?" asked a deep voice from behind her.

"No one," said Eliza, sounding guilty.

A man, about five years older than Judah, appeared. He wore the embroidered robes of a synagogue leader and unlike Judah, sported a long, luscious beard. But the eyes were unmistakably the same as his brother's. And they flashed with anger.

"Go to your room, Eliza."

"But Daddy!"

"Now!"

The girl scurried off.

"Judah."

"Jairus."

"Who's this?" Jairus nodded towards Claudia. He was speaking in Aramaic.

"This is Sylvia," said Judah, the lie they had agreed to tripping easily from his tongue.

Jairus assessed 'Sylvia', his eyes dwelling for a moment on her painted toenails and expensively beaded sandals.

"And where are you from, my dear?" he asked, switching to perfect Greek.

"She's from –"

"A-ah, Judah, let the girl answer for herself."

"I'm from Caesarea," said Claudia, truthfully.

"And your family, are they also from Caesarea?"

Claudia swallowed hard and Judah squeezed her hand. "No, they are from Pontus on the Black Sea. I went first with the Pilate family to Rome and then came with them to Caesarea."

"Are you a slave? A runaway?"

"Of course not!" said Judah. "She's a –"

Claudia squeezed his hand back. "I'm a freedwoman; a hairdresser. The lady Procula invited me to accompany them. I'm the only one she trusts with her hair."

Jairus smiled. "My wife will be pleased to meet you then. She's been saying for a while she needs a new hairstyle."

"I'd be glad to help her," said Claudia, relaxing.

Jairus' smile disappeared. "I don't know what Judah has told you about me, but I am no fool. You are Claudia Lucretia Pilate. You are on the run from my Uncle Barabbas who is trying to kill you, and –" he looked askance at Judah – "you seem to be eloping with my brother."

"Jairus…"

"Shut up, Judah. Then come in. You're welcome to stay the night but in the morning you will be gone. Agreed?"

Judah sighed. "Agreed."

*

It was completely dark outside by the time the family were finished with their evening meal. Uncle Hillel, a shadow of a man, was propped up at the table, supported by a barricade of cushions. His head lolled and his hands picked repeatedly at the fabric of his robe. Hannah, Jairus' plump and pretty wife, had fed him efficiently with one hand, while attending to the needs of her children with the other. Judah asked at one point if he could take over; Hannah let him.

"Hello, Uncle. It's me, Judah. I'm home."

The side of Uncle Hillel's mouth quivered on the brink of either a smile or a grimace; Claudia couldn't tell which. But his eyes fixed intently on his nephew. He saw him, she was convinced of that. Judah whispered quietly to his uncle, telling him of all he had been up to since he had last seen him. Well, not all, Claudia assumed, but it was difficult to hear over the hubbub of the family dinner.

Eliza had been let back down under strict instructions to keep her five-year-old twin brothers under control. The little boys were beside themselves with excitement. They warmed instantly to their uncle Judah, particularly when he got down on all fours and they took turns riding him like a horse. They were a little shyer with Claudia – or 'Sylvia' as Jairus introduced her to the children while giving his wife a knowing look above their heads. Claudia realised that it was safer for everyone if their charade continued, just in case the children let it slip with their playmates that the daughter of Pontius Pilate had spent the night under their roof.

So for the night she was Sylvia the hairdresser, Uncle Judah's fiancé. Eliza, a quiet but shrewd girl, commented that it was unusual for a betrothed woman to be travelling alone without a chaperone. It was explained that Sylvia's aunt had accompanied them for the first part of the journey but she took ill and was left in Maggido. Eliza also commented that Sylvia's dress looked like it belonged to a princess.

"Are you a princess?" asked one of the little boys.

"No, I'm not," said Claudia, relieved that she could at least tell the truth about that.

"I think we can help you with something more suitable to wear." Hannah dried her hands on her apron. Claudia realised then that she should probably have offered to help with the dishes – Sylvia the hairdresser would have – but Claudia had never washed a dish in her life. She wondered if she would have to start doing so if she were to marry Judah. The thought did not fill her with relish.

"Come," said Hannah, when the table was cleared and the dishes washed. "Eliza, show Sylvia to your room. When I've put the boys to bed I'll bring you some dresses to try on." She looked pointedly at her husband. "The men have important business to discuss, I think."

Claudia looked panicked as she glanced at Judah, not sure how long she could manage the role-play on her own. But Judah just smiled at her. He seemed to be relaxing into the family environment even though Claudia knew he would be expecting a lecture from Jairus the moment she left the room.

"Good night, then, husband. Uncle Hillel. Judah."

"Good night, Hannah, it's been good to see you again. And thank you for taking us in."

"It was Jairus' decision, not mine," said Hannah, with a less than submissive look at her spouse.

"Good night," said Jairus before it could get out of hand.

*

Eliza sat quietly on the bed. Claudia sat beside her. They both waited for Hannah. Claudia could hear the older woman in the room next door, telling a bed-time story to the twins. She seemed to be doing a whole cast of voices, cheered on by her sons.

Eventually Eliza spoke: "I also have a secret."

The girl's voice startled Claudia. It was filled with passion. Not excitement, like her brothers, but an intense fervour.

"I don't have a secret," said Claudia.

"Yes, you do. I'm not stupid."

Claudia did not know what to say to that so she said nothing. After a while, the girl spoke again.

"Do you want to know my secret?"

As long as you don't expect me to tell you mine in return, thought Claudia. But said instead: "It's your secret; you may do with it as you please."

"Then I will tell you." Eliza patted the bed beside her. "Do you see this bed?"

Claudia nodded.

"Three months ago this was my death bed."

"You were ill?"

"I was dead," said Eliza, but the look she gave Claudia was filled with more life than Claudia had ever seen. The child glowed.

"Your father thinks he's an important man."

Claudia was about to challenge that, but the girl continued before she could formulate her denial.

"King Herod thinks he's an important man. The Emperor thinks he's an important man. But these men are not important. I have met the most important man in the world."

"And who is that?" asked Claudia.

"The man who brought me back to life in this very room."

"Is that your secret?"

"Yes. I have met the Son of God. Is your secret better than that?"

"No, my secret is not better than that."

"Then I will not ask you to tell me," said Eliza, the daughter of Jairus, the girl who claimed to have met the Son of God.

Claudia felt her skin crawl. Was the girl mad? Probably. But that was not what disturbed her. On the windowsill was a dove; it cocked its head to left and right as if listening to them. It reminded Claudia of the day her mother had collapsed at the Jordan. The day the Baptist had announced the coming of the man he called the Lamb of God. The Son of God? The Lamb of God? Was this the same person? Claudia did not know but she feared he would bring nothing but tragedy to her life.

That night, as she lay beside the sleeping Eliza, she prayed to every god she could think of to keep her and Judah and the rest of her family safe from this mysterious man and the curse she sensed had already come.

*

A Dream of Procula Pilate

I am walking by the lake. A dove flies down and lands on my shoulder. He whispers to me: "Come, come, I have something to show you." I follow him as he flies low to the ground, up the hill and into a town. Night has fallen. He leads the way to a house, then up the outside staircase onto a flat roof. I look out and see the lights of the town flickering below me between the palm trees, reflected in the lake. They look like the candles of Saturnalia. "Look," says the dove, and he alights on a windowsill. I look in the window and see two girls sitting together on a bed: the younger one with long, wild, curly black hair; the older one, with tamer chestnut tresses. The dove raises its wings and begins to beat them, and as it does, a wind arises and blows into the room. The girls' hair is swept up in the wind and begins to mingle until my whole vision is filled with a curtain of chestnut and black. The wings slow down; the wind settles and on the bed, under a blanket of hair, lies a girl. The dove beckons me forward until I am standing over the girl, looking down. It is Claudia Lucretia. She is dead. "I can raise her to life if she will let me," says the dove. "But she will not let me.".

Chapter 34 – The Prophet of Galilee

The next morning Claudia was rudely awakened by two little boys jumping up and down on her bed. "Wake up, Princess! Wake up! You're going to miss breakfast!" Before she could object, she was dragged out of bed, shoved towards the ablution facilities and given a mere five minutes to get herself ready before the boys barged in again and hustled her downstairs.

"Boys! Boys! What did I tell you about leaving Sylvia to come down in her own time?" said Hannah who was frying fish.

"Is it ready?" the boys asked in unison.

"As soon as I get the bread out of the oven."

"Oh, I can do that," said Claudia.

Hannah looked at her doubtfully, but passed her some thick wadding and nodded in the direction of a clay oven. Claudia hovered over it, unsure how to open it. Hannah tutted and took the wadding from her. "I don't suppose hairdressers do much baking."

She opened the hatch, then took a wooden spatula and flipped out the bread. It smelt delicious. Claudia couldn't wait for the men to arrive so they could start eating.

"Where are Judah and Jairus?"

"They had breakfast early. It's just you and the boys who are going to eat now."

"But where are they?"

"They've gone to the other side of the lake to see the prophet."

"What prophet?"

"Oh, just a prophet. They've taken Eliza with them because she wants to see him again."

"Again?"

"Yes, again. He came to the house a few months ago when Eliza was ill."

"And raised her from the dead," said Claudia as a chill ran down her spine.

Hannah put down the bread on the table and wiped her hands on her apron. Her pretty, plump face looked stern, softened only by a halo of black curls so similar to her daughter's.

"She shouldn't have told you."

"Do you think he is the Son of God too?"

"I don't know. But he can do amazing things. He brought my daughter back to life."

"Surely she was just in a swoon."

"No, she was dead."

"How do you know?"

"A mother knows."

Then Hannah called the boys to join them for breakfast and they waited for their men to come home.

*

Judah had been reluctant to go with Jairus. He had been keen to continue his journey east as soon as Claudia awoke. But the girl had slept and slept: Claudia obviously needed the rest after the last traumatic days. In addition, he felt he owed his brother something for taking them in, with all the incumbent risk to his reputation – and even his liberty – if it were found out he had aided and abetted the abduction of Claudia Lucretia Pilate.

For some reason, Jairus thought it would be good for Judah to meet the prophet. He had told him a story – which Judah had not believed for a moment – about this holy man using his power to bring Eliza back from the dead. Jairus was usually far too shrewd to be duped by party tricks. The girl had clearly been ill – very ill – but dead? Judah had been involved in enough fatal skirmishes in his time with the Zealots to know what death looked like, and what it didn't. Jairus, in his cloistered position as leader of the synagogue, had not.

Uncle Hillel, as chief priest of Capernaum, would have attended enough bereavements; but Jairus was not a priest. Apparently a novice from Bethsaida was filling in until a more permanent replacement could be found. *A novice? No wonder he thought Eliza deceased. A novice indeed!* As well as the novice priest, the synagogue also employed a teacher of the law of the Pharisee sect. But fortunately for Judah, both he and the priest were at a meeting in Tiberias with Herod Antipas discussing the implications of the arrest of John the Baptist.

Coincidentally, the prophet they were going to see was a cousin of John from Nazareth. Judah had followed John for a while when he first came onto the scene. It was partly to gather intelligence for Barabbas but also out of genuine curiosity. Judah, like most other Israelites, was waiting for the coming of YHWH's long-promised Messiah. The one who would raise an army on earth reinforced by angels from heaven and drive the enemies of God into the sea. Uncle Hillel had taught Judah well. He knew the scriptures. He knew the ancient prophecies that declared that YHWH would release a deliverer like in the time of Moses, who would shatter the yoke of oppression and use it as a rod to beat their enemies. And some had even declared that the deliverer would come from Galilee. This man, known as Messiah, would be the true king of Israel, of the line of the great David and Solomon. The pretenders like Herod Antipas and Pontius Pilate would have to bow to him; even the old Emperor in Rome. A Jewish king who would rule the world? There was a time when that's all Judah would have hoped for. But things had changed. Judah was beginning to feel that the destiny of his people lay in their own hands, not that of a much-hoped-for saviour who never seemed to come.

John had declared that he was not Messiah. Apparently the nation should still expect him though, any time. Judah was reluctant to believe him. It meant too much to him to be duped again. Before John, Judah had followed a man called Theudas but he had also proven to be false and had died on a Roman cross charged with rabble rousing. Judah had half-hoped Theudas would leap off the cross and fell the Roman guards with the cross-bar of the crucifix. It was said that Messiah would have the strength of Samson. So it was certainly possible; possible, but not probable. And frankly, Judah was weary of hoping.

So today, as he accompanied his brother and niece to a hillside about an hour's walk from Capernaum, he did not go with the expectation of meeting someone special. He hoped he could convince his family of that before he left. The last thing they needed was to be taken in by a charlatan; particularly a charlatan from Nazareth.

*

The hill was covered with thousands of excited people. Some of them Judah recognised from his youth in Capernaum. There were the brothers Andrew and James who ran a little fishing business. And there was their friend, the burly Simon, also a fisherman. Judah and Simon had not got on as children, so Judah avoided catching his eye. It wasn't difficult. There were children everywhere; running around like it was the last day of Purim. Eliza spotted some friends and ran off to join them pressing in to get close to the man at the centre of the crowd. He could hardly be seen under a pile of children, hanging onto his robes, all hoping for a chance to be swung around. The man, in his mid thirties, seemed as delighted as the children in this high-spirited game and shooed off some men, including Simon, who were trying to restrain the little ones. "Let them come! Let them come!" he shouted. "The kingdom of God belongs to them!" Then he laughed and picked up another child.

"Is that him? He doesn't look like a proper prophet to me."

"There's nothing 'proper' about Jesus of Nazareth."

"Oh?"

Jairus did not need much cajoling; he had clearly been waiting to tell his brother everything there was to know about the Prophet of Galilee.

"He came onto the scene about a year ago. At the beginning it was fairly low key; you know, the usual. Preaching in his local synagogue; claiming he was some kind of fulfilment of prophecy. Ruffled some feathers and was driven out of town. Then he came down to Capernaum and started gathering disciples around him. Andrew and James over there, and Simon. They have practically abandoned their business. Their dad's not happy, I can tell you that. He came to see me to ask if I could talk some sense into them. I tried, but they didn't listen."

"Simon's not the listening type," observed Judah.

"To say the least! Well, then I started hearing of some strange goings on in Cana. Seems like there was a wedding and they hadn't planned for the number of guests who would arrive. They ran out of wine…"

"Disaster!"

"It would have been, but apparently Jesus' mother – a widow of a carpenter from Nazareth – was one of the guests and she had taken her whole family along with her, uninvited; including Jesus."

"That would account for the shortage of wine."

"Quite. But he made up for it. Apparently – and I didn't believe it at first; thought it was a drunken tale – he turned some urns of water into wine."

"Don't believe it."

"They all swear by it. There were about hundred and fifty people there."

"They just brought it out from the cellar when the guests wouldn't leave."

"Possibly…"

By now the prophet had fallen to the ground, exhausted, and the grown-ups had gathered their offspring and settled down on the grass. They sat in ring after ring, looking to him expectantly, like baby birds waiting to be fed by their parent. Eliza was close to the front and Judah noticed the prophet smile at her. And he could have sworn she started to glow.

"So, what happened after that?"

Jairus' eyes lit up at the invitation. "Well, after that he moved on to Magdala. Do you remember that old whore?"

Judah laughed. "The one who cornered you at that Succoth festival and Uncle Hillel had to save you?"

Jairus laughed too, despite himself. "Hannah must never know about that. Never!"

"My lips are sealed."

"Well, seems like she got her sights on Jesus too."

Judah chuckled. "How did he get out of that one?"

"He cast seven demons out of her."

"What?" He hadn't expected that.

"Apparently she had seven demons in her and when they were gone, well – you wouldn't believe the difference." Jairus nodded to a woman a few rows in front of them. She was about thirty and very beautiful. She was dressed respectably but not conservatively. She, like Eliza, seemed to have an inner glow. And the people around her were drawn to it. Not, as in the past, in a lustful way, but just that they enjoyed her company. Men and women alike laughed at her jokes and clearly no longer thought of her as "that old whore from Magdala".

Judah was astounded. "She looks at least ten years younger!"

"At least!"

"And who thought she was such a beauty?"

"Not me, for one! But now… what? Oh, stop it!"

Judah was laughing on the outside but something inside him was troubled. He looked again at the young prophet talking and laughing so easily with the people around him. And the old whore – what was her name again? Mary? – seemed connected to him as if by an invisible umbilical cord. And so was Eliza.

"And see him?" Jairus indicated a short, tubby, middle-aged man wearing an expensive cloak.

"Isn't that Zachaeus? The tax collector?"

"The very one. Well, he's gone straight. He's stopped taking bribes and gives half of his monthly earnings to the synagogue widow and orphan fund."

"Never!"

"It's true! And he's started throwing the most raucous parties! You wouldn't believe it! I don't think he's had a friend in his life and now he's the most popular guy in town!"

"Well, he would be, if he's giving away all his money."

"True. But he's not giving away money to his friends. Just to the widow and orphan fund. So it can be properly managed, he said."

"So why does everyone go to his parties?"

"Well," Jairus pulled back his shoulders. "I can't tell you because I've never been."

"Never been invited?"

"I've been invited. I just never thought it was right, that's all, for a man in my position."

"And Jesus?"

"Oh, Jesus never worries about such things. If there's a party going, he's the first man there! Doesn't matter who's on the guest list: prostitutes, tax collectors, Zealots…"

"My kind of prophet."

Jairus looked at Judah thoughtfully. "That's why I brought you here."

Chapter 35 – Food for an Army

It was about four hours later when Judah's stomach began to grumble. He asked Jairus if he had any food with him: he did not. Like other people in the crowd, Jairus had just intended to listen to the prophet for an hour or two and then go home for lunch. But it was now well past midday and lunch-time was over. Everyone had been so enraptured by the words and deeds of the young prophet that they hadn't seemed to notice.

Judah counted at least three healings: a blind man regained his sight, a crippled woman walked and a boy with hysterical seizures had regained his senses. The story Jairus had told him about Eliza being brought back from the dead was becoming more and more plausible.

And then there was his teaching. He told stories about farmers going to look for lost sheep, seed scattered on rocky and fertile land, landowners going away and coming back, debtors being forgiven their debts and banquets where everyone was invited. The stories were simple tales but Judah felt the meaning of them all deep within his soul. The prophet – if that's all he was – was talking about another reality and Judah sensed what he was really talking about was the kingdom of God coming to earth. It's what Judah had most longed for. Perhaps the time had indeed come. Judah's spirit soared within him. He sensed that heaven was very, very near. But it was the story of the pearl that struck him the most. And Jesus seemed to know that.

The young prophet glanced across the rows of people and looked Judah directly in the eye. He fell silent and the people around him craned to see what had caught his attention. Many of them knew Judah was a wanted revolutionary, but in the current atmosphere of forgiveness and acceptance of social outcasts, no one was about to turn him in. Not today, anyway. Judah could not fathom Jesus' expression. There was a gentleness and knowledge and – and – was that sadness? Judah must have imagined it because Jesus shook it off and started speaking again.

"There was once a very rich merchant who had made his fortune buying and selling things. He had everything he could possibly have ever wanted. But then one day, someone showed him a beautiful pearl. The merchant had never seen anything like it before and when he compared all the wealth he had accumulated over the years he realised he was poor indeed. So he decided to sell all that he had to buy that pearl because nothing, absolutely nothing could compare to it." Jesus did not have to explain the parable. When he looked at Judah the young Zealot knew it was meant specifically for him. The Prophet of Galilee was offering him a choice: did Judah want to pursue his plan to become a rich merchant or instead to give everything he had to embrace the kingdom of heaven. What exactly the kingdom of heaven was, Judah was not entirely sure, but he knew that he had glimpsed some of it today. He didn't know what to do. What of Claudia? What would she think when he told her of Jesus? Would she be prepared to help him find the pearl? Would it even be safe for her to stay in Israel? Perhaps he could take her to safety and then return. Perhaps he could...

"We need to start getting home. Eliza's hungry." Jairus interrupted his brother's thoughts. "Come on, Eliza, it's time to go!" He called out to his daughter. But she didn't respond. "Come on!" he called again.

This time she turned around. "No, father, I don't want to miss a word of what he says!"

Other parents seemed to be having similar conversations with their children. Jesus' disciples realised what was going on and suggested to Jesus that he let the people go so they could get food. Jesus looked around and saw the hungry masses surrounding him. "It's too far for some of them to walk. The elderly and the children won't make it home without fainting. You give them something to eat."

"But we don't have anything," said Simon in the gruff way Judah remembered.

Then a little boy, no more than six or seven, tugged at Simon's sleeve. The fisherman looked down to see what he wanted.

"You can have this." The lad was holding a small basket filled with what looked like a couple of loaves and small fish.

"Thank you, lad, but it won't be enough," said Simon, not unkindly.

"Oh Simon, have you no faith?" said Jesus. "Of course it will be enough. Give it to me."

So Simon handed over the little boy's lunch. Jesus took it, closed his eyes and prayed. Then he took out the bread and fish and broke them into pieces. Then he reached into the basket and took out loaf after loaf after loaf and passed them to his disciples. "Give this to them." Then he did the same with the fish. The bread and fish never seemed to end. They were passed up and down the hillside and when everyone had received their portion, they sat down to eat. Neighbours and strangers shared what they had with each other and then started to bring out their own hidden food that they had been trying to hide from those without. Jairus, Judah and Eliza, who genuinely had none, were happy to receive some directly from Simon. Simon and Judah stared at each other for a moment, and Judah thought he would not give him any food, but Simon smiled ruefully and gave him his share. Judah took it gratefully.

When everyone had eaten they started gathering up leftovers. "Here," said a voice behind Judah, "why don't you help?" He turned around and came face to face with Jesus. He held out a basket. "I need your help, Judah ben Hillel."

Judah took the basket from him, then side by side they walked around gathering up the leftovers of the miraculous meal.

*

Back at the synagogue leader's house, Claudia was getting very, very worried. She had helped clean up the breakfast dishes, much to the hilarity of the twins who recognised she was an amateur when she tried to use bath soap to scrub the frying pan. She had then spent some time on the roof-top verandah with Uncle Hillel until she couldn't stand his drooling and staring any longer. At one point, she announced to Hannah that she was going to go looking for Judah. Hannah managed to talk her out of it. She suggested instead Claudia pass the time by reading one of the books from the synagogue's collection. Claudia agreed, and chose a scroll written in Greek about the Maccabean Revolt. It was a story she already knew from her conversations with Judah, but she thought she might as well read it for herself. She went to Eliza's room and lay down on the bed.

She had just got to the part when the Seleucid king Antiochus IV Epiphanes had set up a statue of himself in the Temple in Jerusalem, causing outrage amongst the Jews who claimed it was the "abomination that would cause desolation" as prophesied by the Prophet Daniel, when she heard a commotion outside. She heard the jingling of bridles, shouting and then banging on the door. She looked out of the window and to her horror saw Marcus Gaius Sejanus talking to Hannah. The

196

Jewish woman pointed to the rooftop room. Claudia ran to the door, intending to flee, but couldn't because it was locked. She was just about to clamber out of the window and onto the roof, when the door opened to reveal Hannah and Marcus.

"Here she is, completely unharmed. As I told the local centurion, my husband and I found her on the road last night, all alone. Isn't that right, my dear?" She looked pointedly at Claudia.

All alone? What was Hannah doing? Was she trying to save Judah? She must be!

"Yes, yes, that's right, all alone," stuttered Claudia.

Marcus strode into the room and took her by the shoulders, looking intently into her face. "Claudia Lucretia! Did they harm you? The Zealots? How did you get away?"

"I – I – there was a Roman patrol. They stumbled across us."

"Who? Who took you?"

"The woodcutter from Caesarea."

"Only him?"

"Yes. Only him. Then the patrol found us and arrested him. But just as they were going to take me back to Caesarea they were ambushed by a gang of Zealots. They killed the soldiers and freed the woodcutter. But I managed to get away in all the confusion."

"On a horse," added Marcus.

"How do you know?"

"The local militia found it this morning. They knew we were looking for you and they put two and two together. Then when this good lady reported that she had found a Roman girl last night..."

"She reported it?" Claudia flashed an angry look at Hannah but the Jewish woman would not meet her eye.

"And thank Juno she did! Your father is worried sick!"

At the mention of her father, Claudia remembered the last time she had seen him, fighting the blaze in the banqueting hall. Simeon had told her her family were safe, but after his betrayal, she couldn't trust him.

"Is my father all right? And my mother?"

"Yes, yes, they're all fine. Everyone has temporarily moved to Tiberias. The palace at Caesarea will be uninhabitable for a while and Antipas offered that we all stay with him. They travelled there yesterday while I was out looking for you. But come, you can see them all for yourself. It's only an hour away."

He took her arm and led her down the stairs and out of the house. "Where is the princess going?" shouted one of the twins.

"The princess?" asked Marcus, as he lifted Claudia onto his horse.

"I thought it best I keep my identity a secret just in case Barabbas was still looking for me."

"Good thinking," Marcus nodded his thanks to Hannah and led his squadron away.

*

As Jairus, Judah and Eliza entered the main street in Capernaum, they had to step aside to let a Roman patrol pass. As they did, Judah saw Claudia sitting on the saddle in front of the tribune, Sejanus. He was just about to call out to her when Jairus clamped a hand over his mouth and an arm around his neck and pulled him into a nearby alley. Judah fought back and the two men wrestled. The scuffle caught the attention of the last soldier in the cortège who looked back to see what was going on. Eliza, as quick thinking as her father, knocked over a stack of clay pots, causing an almighty clatter. Satisfied that there was nothing more untoward than a young girl and some broken pottery, the soldier geed his horse and caught up with his squadron as they turned south onto the road to Tiberias.

Chapter 36 – The Prisoner

It had been nearly a month since the Pilate household had arrived in Tiberias and Claudia Lucretia had been rescued… again. The frequency of Claudia's abductions and rescues had become a bit of a joke around the palace. But no one laughed in front of Procula Claudiana, particularly since she had come back to her senses.

The first thing Pilate had done when his carriage arrived in the palace courtyard was to leap out, run to Antipas and Herodias' carriage and demand to be directed to the Baptist. Antipas, who was just waking from a snooze, did not understand what he was being asked so it was up to Herodias to reluctantly summon a guard to take Pilate to the dungeon. Five minutes later, while the Herods were entering the portico along with all their luggage, Pilate ran past them and lifted his wife out of their carriage. He carried her in his arms back into the palace and down the way he had just come.

"Well I never!" said Herodias. "These Pilates need to learn some manners. And here we are offering them our hospitality. We should have left them moping in sack cloth and ashes back in Caesarea."

"Yes dear." Antipas yawned again. "I think I'll finish my nap." Then he sauntered off, leaving his wife to supervise the decampment of the household.

This incensed Herodias even further. "I will not be humiliated in my own home, I will not!" And it was then that she began to formulate her plan to embarrass her husband and put her house guests in their place in one fell swoop.

*

Down in the dungeon Pontius Pilate found John the Baptist just where he had left him: chained to a wall. By all accounts the prophet's hygiene had never been of the highest standard, but two months in the bowels of Herod's dungeon made him smell like a Jerusalem sewer rat. Pilate braced himself against the stench and thanked the gods that Procula was too far gone to notice.

"Procula, darling, I've brought you to the Baptist," he whispered. "Come on, my love, wake up, he's agreed to see you."

Through his matted beard and hair, John smiled. "Yes, I've agreed." He raised his emaciated wrists and jangled his shackles.

"I shall speak to Herod about that. If you help my wife, I shall make sure he lets you go."

"I appreciate that," said John, in a far more gentle voice than Pilate had expected. Despite his desperate circumstances, there was a tranquillity about John that surprised the governor. Was this really the wild man of the desert who terrified the priests and Pharisees with his proclamations of doom?

"Now, Procula Claudiana," chided the prophet. "Enough of this nonsense. I've been told you have been like this since our first meeting. I brought you news of great things and you act as if I had unleashed the plagues of Hades."

Procula did not stir against her husband's shoulder. Pilate raised his eyes to John beseechingly. "Is there anything you can do?"

"I can pray." And he did. Pilate did not understand the prayer – it might have been in ancient Hebrew, he wasn't sure – but as the prophet poured out his petition, Procula Claudiana began to stir and raise her head. She looked around, momentarily confused; then she sat up. And then, to Pilate's utter amazement, she smiled. She smiled at her husband and she smiled at John. It wasn't the wild-eyed grin of a madwoman, but the gentle smile of a woman who was finally at peace with herself.

"I've seen him in my dreams," said Procula.

"I know you have," said John. "Don't worry, Procula, he knows who you are. He knows you've been searching for him. And he will let you find him."

"What must I do when I find him?"

"Believe and follow."

Procula nodded as if she understood exactly what the Baptist was on about; which her husband certainly did not. But he didn't care. He had his wife back and for that he would be eternally grateful.

"Thank you." Pilate felt awkward, not used to thanking dirty prisoners in dungeons. "I shall keep my promise and ask Herod to let you go."

John sighed. "You can ask, but it will make no difference. My time is over. I've done what I've been called to do."

Pilate gave him a sympathetic look then helped Procula to her feet; then together, arm in arm, they left the prophet where they had found him.

*

A week later, a rejuvenated Procula Claudiana Pilate was knocking on the door of her daughter's chambers.

"Come in."

Procula opened the door and found Claudia Lucretia exactly where she had left her two hours before: moping in bed. She had been like this since Marcus Gaius Sejanus had brought her to the palace. No one was surprised – the girl had been through yet another traumatic ordeal – but her mother suspected there was more to it than the shock of the abduction. Procula was beginning to suspect Claudia Lucretia was pining. It couldn't be for Marcus Gaius – he visited her every day – so who could it be? She had every intention of finding out.

That evening the Herods were to hold a banquet of thanksgiving for the lives that had been saved at Caesarea. The Judean, Galilean and Decapolian aristocracy would all attend. If Claudia had met someone at the Saturnalia banquet before the fire began, he was bound to be there. Procula intended to watch her daughter very, very carefully and when she had a good idea of who it might be, she would confront her. The girl had to come to her senses. Marcus Gaius was due to leave for Rome in the morning to finalise the betrothal arrangements with his uncle and he needed to go knowing Claudia was eager for his return.

The next few months would also be an opportunity for him to get over his infatuation with that slave Nebela. Procula's staff had filled her in on the scandalous way she behaved at Saturnalia, and if it hadn't been for the fact that the girl had been unconscious ever since, she would have had her sent away.

But first things first: Claudia Lucretia needed to be roused for the banquet.

"I'm not going, mother," said Claudia with her head under the blanket.

"Yes you are, dear. It will be good for you."

"Why will it be good for me?"

"You've had a terrible ordeal and a social occasion is just what you need to stir your spirits."

"Herodian banquets stir nothing but my wrath."

Procula sighed. It was time to bring out her trump card. She pulled back the covers, took her daughter's hands and looked directly into her violet eyes. "I understand, my sweet, but please, do it for me. I have been away from you for so long. There is nothing more I want than to show the whole of Palestine that the Pilates cannot be defeated. Neither illness, nor accident, nor insurrection, nor abductions will defeat us. Can you do this for me? Please?"

Claudia let out an exasperated sigh. "All right, mother, I'll do it for you. But I intend to leave early. I don't think I could stomach another performance from Salome."

Her mother laughed. "I don't blame you."

*

Herodias was in a marvellous mood. Normally she found banqueting preparations extremely stressful: particularly when she was juggling the petty political ambitions of her guests. The sooner her husband was king of *all* of Palestine, the better. She was sure it was just a matter of time before Tiberius could be convinced that a divided Palestine was not the safest Palestine. Yes, there should be one king – and one queen. Royalty suited her. Royal palaces suited her. And the palace that suited her the most was that of her late grandfather cum father-in-law, Herod the Great in Jerusalem. Jerusalem, not Galilee, was the centre of power. Well, Rome was, but first things first.

And first on Herodias' agenda today was adjusting the power relations between the Pilates and the Herods. Procula Claudiana might have patrician blood – just – but her husband was a mere provincial. And what made Pontus better than Palestine? Absolutely nothing. It didn't even have a king!

Herodias hummed to herself – a ditty she'd heard at a recital in Rome when she lived there with her previous husband – and put the finishing touches on the evening's banquet. She whisked through the menu, nodding approval here, insisting on changes there, with such good humour that the cook began to worry that her job – at the very least – was on the line. As everyone knew, bipolar moods ran in the Herod family and the bloody legacy of the tyrannical Herod Agrippa was never far from their minds. Nervous servants were doubly quick to do her bidding, sensing a sinister sub-text to the evening's script. The gardener trimmed the topiary peacocks to the last quivering leaf, the maid scrubbed the chamber pots in the guest rooms until she could see her pock-marked reflection and the butler made sure the candlesticks were positioned well out of the way of any diaphanous swags. Even Salome came without protest when summoned – despite being on her way to Uncle Philip's apartment – to receive detailed instructions about her role in the evening's festivities. "It will be a triumph!" declared her mother. But after hearing what Herodias had planned, Salome wished she'd never come at all.

Chapter 37 – Seeking the Healer

Marcus Gaius Sejanus left the dungeon in a thoughtful mood. He was not normally a religious man, nor even a superstitious man – which was unusual for a Roman soldier – but there was something about the dirty prophet that compelled him to pay attention. He had been stunned by the transformation in Procula Claudiana after she had visited him. Marcus, like most in the Pilate entourage, had given up hope that the governor's wife would regain her health: physically or mentally. She was too far gone. If being carried from a burning palace and told that her daughter had been abducted – again – had not roused her, then, it was the general consensus, nothing would. But they were all wrong. And that got Marcus thinking. If the Baptist had the power to bring Procula back then maybe, just maybe, he could heal Nebela.

The girl had not gained consciousness since the day of the fire. Her mother sat with her day and night, keeping the dreadful wound on her leg clean. But she had a fever and both Marcus and Zandra feared she was no longer strong enough to fight it. She was just a slave, yes, but Marcus had never felt love for anyone like this before.

So he had come to the Baptist. Herod, the old toad, had arrested the prophet soon after he had publicly denounced the king's marriage to his brother's ex-wife as adulterous. Ordinarily that would not have bothered Antipas or anyone with Roman sensibilities – a divorce was a divorce – but the Jews were more sensitive about that sort of thing: at least, the more pious of them were. Everyone knew Antipas' ambition was to be king of all Palestine and for that he needed Jewish support. Hence his lavish building work at the Temple and his attempts to prove his lineage went all the way back to the esteemed King David (through his son, Solomon's, foreign wives). Marcus knew that the nation was at fever pitch, expecting the apotheosis of Israel's 'true king' at any moment. That's why he and his men were there: to keep order and to suppress any possible signs of revolt in support of an unapproved king. Antipas wanted the Jews to see him as the true king, but accusations of adultery did not endear him to the populace. Hence the Baptist needed to be taken out of circulation.

Nonetheless, Herod visited him daily, intrigued by the man's teaching about the Messiah who was to come. Like his father before him, Antipas intended to identify and dispose of any pretenders before they came to the public's attention. And who better to point him in the right direction than the Messiah's own herald.

According to Marcus' spies in the Herodian guard, John had been very vague in identifying the so-called Messiah, speaking in riddles and quoting from the Jewish scriptures, as prophets were wont to do. Antipas' patience was wearing thin; the Baptist had better cough up the information soon or his time on this earth would be limited.

Knowing all of this, Marcus hoped the holy man could help Nebela before it was too late. And if he could, like Pilate, he promised to put pressure on Antipas to set him free.

However, John did not waste any time in telling Marcus that he could not help the slave girl. He didn't even pretend he could. Marcus was deeply disappointed. But as he turned to leave, the prophet grabbed his wrist. His grip was surprisingly strong for a man who had been half-starved. Marcus turned back to look at him and was held, not so much by the man's hand, but his eyes. They were the colour of bronze and filled with a fire so intense that the tribune felt he would be burnt up if he looked into them any longer. But he could not pull away.

"Come closer, tribune," the prophet whispered.

Marcus did as he was bid. The stench of the man was overpowering, and Marcus felt the rancid breath cloy his neck and ear.

"The one who can heal her is the one they all seek."

"Where is he?" whispered Marcus, understanding that John did not want this information getting to the Herodian guards, and ultimately to Antipas.

John hesitated.

"I will not tell him. I promise."

John sighed deeply, wafting his wretched aroma over Marcus' face. But the tribune did not pull away.

"Go to the house of your fiancée's rescuer, Jairus of Capernaum, and they will tell you where he is. But you must promise not to harm them."

"I promise."

John considered this for a moment, nodded, then released Marcus from his grip.

"And when I return and if Nebela is healed I will have you released," said Marcus, still staring into the strange, strange eyes.

At this the prophet laughed then coughed and spat out a tooth. "Well, you'd better hurry. Soon there will be nothing left of me."

*

Marcus wasted no time before riding north to Capernaum. He went alone, citing 'important imperial business'; and none of his military associates thought anything of it. Tribune Sejanus was a man with access to intelligence from the highest imperial level, everyone knew that, and the peace of the region depended upon their discretion. Only Pilate might have questioned his absence, but fortunately for Marcus, the high priest Joseph Caiphas had come up a day early for the banquet to go over some business with the governor. If all went to plan, Marcus would be back in time for the planned festivities that evening.

Before he left he settled Nebela into an ox cart and gave instructions to Zandra to drive north to Capernaum and he would meet them there. He provided her with the necessary sealed documents to produce if they were questioned by any soldiers en route. As it was still mid-morning and the road was well used by Herodian and Roman soldiers it was highly unlikely they would be accosted by brigands on their journey. Still, he worried for their safety, and gave Zandra a short sword to use as protection. "If anyone tries to lay a hand on us, Tribune, I have far more powerful weapons to use than that." Marcus, not believing in her Eastern mumbo jumbo, simply humoured her with a tight smile. Then he kissed Nebela's fevered brow, leapt on his charger, and rode ahead to Capernaum. He needed to find out exactly where this healer was and be able to ride back and redirect Zandra if necessary. He did not want them wasting time coming all the way to Capernaum if the healer's travelling circus had now moved elsewhere.

*

Marcus arrived at Jairus' house just before noon. He made the final approach at a gentle trot rather than a gallop, so as not to startle the residents. He would be forceful if necessary, but for now he would try using honey to sweeten them. Two little boys were playing with a puppy in the courtyard, watched by a lolling old man in the shade of a fig tree. Hearing the clip-clop of the approaching horse, the boys looked up from their game and waited nervously to see what would happen next. The puppy started barking but was not brave enough to stand between his young masters and the stranger. The old man's demeanour did not change.

Marcus took off his helmet and made an effort to replace his usual commanding expression with a kindly smile. It worked. The children appeared to relax and the puppy stopped yapping. "Hello," he said. "I'm looking for Jairus of Capernaum. Is he here?"

The boys stared at him, overawed by the giant battle steed and the Roman officer. He alighted and holding the reins, crouched down to the children's level, "Is your daddy here?"

Wide-eyed, one of the boys nodded. Then the other, now looking more curious than fearful, asked: "Is this to do with Uncle Judah and Sylvia?"

His brother shushed him and poked him in the ribs.

Marcus forced himself to continue smiling. "No, it is not about Uncle Judah and Sylvia."

The lads looked relieved. "Good. Because that's a secret and we shouldn't tell you."

Marcus swallowed tightly. "You shouldn't tell anyone or you shouldn't tell a Roman soldier?"

One of the boys was just about to answer, when a deep male voice called from the house. "Benjamin, Joseph, come inside." The boys and the puppy immediately scampered away.

A distinguished-looking man in his early to mid thirties stood on the threshold. Marcus did not recall seeing him the last time he was here. Only a woman, his wife, he assumed. Still keeping his 'I am not your enemy, I am your friend' expression on his face, Marcus led his horse towards the house. The Jew walked out to meet him halfway.

"Good day, sir, Can I help you?"

"I was here a few weeks ago. To retrieve the governor's daughter whom your wife very kindly assisted."

"Ah yes. And how is the young lady?"

"She received quite a shock, but she is recovering well, thank you."

"Please pass on mine and my wife's regards to her and her parents."

"I will," said Marcus. "Rome is always glad to find it has friends in its provinces."

"And Israel is always glad to help foreigners in its midst when in need. It is what the Law commands us."

Marcus noticed the use of the words 'Israel' and 'foreigners': clearly this man considered Palestine to be a sovereign nation, although his phrasing was very careful. Marcus doubted a charge of sedition would hold. But... Marcus pulled himself up quickly. He had promised the prophet he would not hurt the man and his family. And he intended to keep that promise. For now.

"So," said the Jew, stroking his luxuriant beard, "are you further investigating the abduction of the honourable Claudia Lucretia?"

Marcus paused for a moment, a calculated move to put the Jew off guard; then shook his head.

"Not today. No." Marcus noted with grudging admiration that the Jew's demeanour did not automatically show relief. His expression behind the beard was inscrutable. He would be a tough nut to crack in interrogation. But today, as long as Marcus got the information he needed, there would be no need to interrogate the man. He filed away his suspicions about 'Sylvia' for future reference.

"Jairus, isn't it?"

"Yes, sir. Jairus ben Hillel. The leader of the Synagogue of Capernaum."

Marcus noted there was no pomposity in his reply; it was a mere statement of fact.

"Well, Jairus, I am Tribune Marcus Gaius Sejanus. And one of my slaves is ill. I have been told that there is a healer in these parts and that you would be able to tell me where to find him."

Again, Jairus' expression was inscrutable. "I could."

"Ah good." Marcus was beginning to tire of the pussy-footing pleasantries.

"You will find him a few miles east of here. Carry on round the top of the lake to Genessaret. He was last seen with some gentile pig farmers."

"Gentile pig farmers? I thought he was a Jewish prophet."

"He is," said Jairus. "But he is not what you would expect." And then, as if to himself: "He is not what any of us had been led to expect."

*

As Tribune Marcus Gaius Sejanus galloped away to meet Zandra and the ox cart, Jairus and his wife Hannah watched from their doorway. "Are you sure he's not looking for Judah?"

"I don't think so. If his business was official he would have had a company of soldiers with him. I think he told the truth: this is personal."

"And if it isn't?"

"Then Judah had better not still be there, hadn't he?"

Chapter 38 – Manumission

It was an unseasonably warm day for the middle of January. The eastern shore of the Lake, usually bleak at this stage of winter, almost felt as though spring were in the air. The steeply rising cliffs soon gave way to pale green grasslands where herds of pigs and goats were enjoying the unexpected treat of newly sprung grass, crocuses and desert anemones that had been tricked into making an early appearance. It was as if the normal rhythm of nature had been put on hold in celebration of a very special guest.

Some of the more outlandish rumours Marcus had heard were that the man he was going to see was more than a simple prophet: he was the son of the Jewish Creator God. Now the whole of creation was applauding his arrival. Marcus laughed at such superstition, but secretly hoped that one part of the story at least was true: that he could heal Nebela. Perhaps the man was simply a doctor with a flair for the theatrical. There were doctors in Rome. Some were quacks, some were more empirically minded, using reason and learning to understand the workings of the body; and some were like this man, claiming divine power. Marcus didn't mind which school he fell into, as long as he could do the job.

He had been a little worried that he would not be able to find the prophet in the unfamiliar territory east of the Lake. But he needn't have worried. By mid-afternoon he and Zandra's ox cart started to overtake throngs of pilgrims heading in the direction of the last recorded location of Jesus of Nazareth. When the crowds started veering off the road into a more remote and inaccessible location, Marcus told Zandra to stay where she was and that he would go ahead to find the prophet and bring him to them. Time was of the essence. The bumpy journey had not done much to help Nebela and her temperature was again on the rise. She was beginning to thrash around in a way that would soon sap all of her remaining energy. Marcus feared if the prophet did not come to her soon, she would pass into the next world without him. The thought of her leaving him so soon when their life together had barely begun, was too much for him to bear. Wiping away tears and pretending they were sweat, he urged his horse forward, forcing the pilgrims to leap out of his way.

It was not long later that he came across the man he was looking for. He was sitting in a natural amphitheatre; surrounded on three sides by sandstone rocks. The rocks were packed with the lucky few who had managed to get close enough to hear him. A group of young men – a dozen or more – sat in a circle around him, their body language claiming special status. His disciples, Marcus assumed. The prophet was in close conversation with one of them who had a vaguely familiar face. The man went as pale as a ghost when he looked up and saw a Roman tribune towering over him on a white stallion. Marcus did not have time to ponder this, but filed it at the back of his mind for later reference.

The prophet, on the other hand, was not in the least bit shaken: "Good day to you, Tribune."

"Good day to you, sir." Marcus was suddenly overcome by the strange feeling he should get down from his horse and show the man some respect. And to the surprise of everyone there, not least himself, he did.

"Teacher," he said, calling him by the title he had heard others mention on his way through the crowds. "My slave is sick and I fear she's going to die. Can you heal her?"

"Do you believe that I can?"

Marcus' horse pawed the ground and let out a snort. It had been a while since it had been fed and watered. The prophet nodded to one of his men who instantly got up and poured some water into a bucket and gave it to the horse. Marcus noted with approval that this was a man who, like him, had authority. And although he did not normally believe in such things, he had seen with his own eyes how the Baptist had helped Procula. Did he truly believe that this man, whom the Baptist considered his superior, had the power to heal? Marcus finally allowed himself to admit that he did. What this meant to his usually cynical outlook on life he would contemplate later, but for now he would allow himself to be carried by his new-found faith in this strange man.

Once the horse had drunk its fill, the tribune and the prophet's eyes met under the beast's proud head, each of them holding onto the bridle.

"So, Tribune, I ask again: do you believe that I can?"

"Yes, Teacher, I do."

"Then I'll come with you," said Jesus and got ready to leave. His disciples jumped up, too, ready to follow their master wherever he would lead.

But the Roman stayed them with his hand. "There's no need. You are a man of authority, Teacher. Just say the word and she'll be healed."

Jesus' warm brown eyes embraced Marcus. "Then that's what will happen." At that, he sat down and continued to teach his disciples.

*

Marcus rode as fast as he could back to the ox cart. Did he really believe Jesus could heal her from a distance? For a moment he had, and he had spoken before he had time to think, but now he wasn't so sure. If she was not healed he would ride back and take the prophet forcefully. And if he still couldn't heal her, Jupiter help him, but he would not be responsible for what he would do. No Jewish prophet would make a fool of Tribune Marcus Gaius Sejanus!

As soon as he reached the cart he leapt off his horse and thrust back the tarpaulin covering his lover's bed. And incredibly, there she was, sitting up while her mother embraced her. He grabbed the soothsayer's shoulder – none too gently – and pulled her back. Then he drew Nebela to him, laughing and weeping into her sweat-soaked hair.

"Marcus! I cannot breathe!"

He immediately released his grip on her and looked anxiously into her almond-shaped eyes. They were a little bloodshot, but the fevered look had gone. Then he checked her leg, pulling back the dressing and was relieved to see a clean wound, free of infection and on the mend. It was too good to be true. "Are you all right, my love?"

"Oh yes," she said, holding his hands with a healthy grip. "But I've had the strangest dream…"

*

Almost completely restored, Nebela rode with Marcus on his horse while Zandra, still in an astounded daze, drove the ox cart behind them. It was late afternoon before they reached the southern shore of the Lake and crossed the ford to where the road forked. To the right was the path which would lead them back up the west bank to Tiberias. To the left, the road continued south to Jericho and then Jerusalem. Marcus reined his horse to a halt. Zandra, now only slightly recovered, pulled the lumbering ox to a standstill. Both animals snuffled the ground to see what grass they could find.

"This is where we must part, my love. For now."

Zandra who had not been privy to the conversation between Nebela and Marcus was confused. "Why must we part, Tribune? Surely you are coming back with us to the palace at Tiberias."

"*He* is going to Tiberias, mother; it is we who are not."

"I have to return for the banquet tonight and then tomorrow I'm travelling back to Caesarea to get on a boat to Rome."

"But surely…"

"Marcus must do what Marcus must do, mother," said Nebela coolly.

Marcus sighed. "Come with me." He got down from the horse, lifting Nebela after him. Then to Zandra, "I must speak to your daughter alone. In the meantime, I want you to open the sealed papers I gave you in Tiberias. There is something there you must see."

Marcus took Nebela's hand and led her down to the estuary, out of sight of her mother and the cart. They came to a copse of trees and he laid down his cloak in the shade. He helped Nebela to sit. She said her leg, though much, much better, still ached a little. He put his arm around her and drew her close. She rested her head against him and cried softly into his chest.

"Don't you love me, Marcus?" she snuffled.

"Oh Nebela, you know that I love you. I have risked the ire of Pilate by seeing you every day. I have flouted the hospitality of the Herods by sneaking away to bring you to the healer. This is not the way an engaged man should behave; particularly when his fiancée is in the same house."

"So she is still your fiancée then?"

"Yes Nebela, she is still my fiancée."

Nebela picked up a pebble and threw it into the shallows. It plopped to the bottom, startling a heron that had been standing in the reeds. The bird spread its wings and took flight, heading south, following the flow of the river down the Jordan valley.

"But why must you still marry her?"

"Because of business and politics."

"Not because of love?"

"Never because of love. You're not a child, Nebela, you know how these things are. My uncle as *pater familias* must approve my match. In

213

my last correspondence with Rome – accompanied by letters from Pilate – he agreed to the terms of the dowry."

"Which are?"

"A lot of money. Some is to be paid on our wedding day, some on the birth of our first child –"

"I can give you a child!"

Marcus was trying not to lose his patience. He knew that Nebela knew what she was asking was impossible. She was just taking advantage of his sympathy towards her because she had recently been near death. He kissed the top of her head.

"And one day maybe you will. But you cannot give me and my uncle what Claudia Lucretia can: blood links to a Roman patrician family and enough money to pay off substantial debts."

Nebela threw another stone into the river; this time far more forcefully.

"Then why did you bother taking me to the healer?"

Marcus lifted her chin with his finger, and looked into her tear-stained face. "You should not have to ask that. I love you and if I were free to marry you, I would. But that does not mean we can't have some kind of life together."

"As your mistress?"

"Yes, as my mistress." His old impatience was beginning to creep back. "Surely for a slave that is far more than you could have ever hoped for."

She pulled away from him, hunching her shoulders. She had hardly eaten for the last three weeks and her frame was pitifully thin. Marcus could see her shoulder blades poking through her dress. He was reminded of how close he had been to losing her. In order to save her life he had been prepared to offend Pilate to the point that the governor might cancel the engagement. So now that she had been returned to him, why was he not willing to do the same? He sighed and rested his hand on her back, slowly stroking back and forth with his thumb.

"There may be a way…"

She sniffed and turned her head towards him, peering through her lank hair. "How?"

"I will only know for sure when I speak to my uncle in Rome."

"You cannot guarantee it?"

"I cannot guarantee it. But it's the best I can do."

She smiled then and he caught a glimpse of the beauty he remembered. His heart lurched.

"That, Marcus, is all I ask." She licked her chapped lips, softening them as best she could. Then she reached out and pulled his head towards her.

As gently as possible he kissed her. Life seemed to surge through her body and she pressed herself against him. He needed no further invitation.

*

When Marcus and Nebela returned to the cart, Zandra was beaming from ear to ear, the opened papers strewn around her.

"Oh Tribune, I don't know how to thank you!"

"By looking after your daughter," he said as he helped Nebela up onto the cart.

"Has he told you what he's done?" Zandra asked Nebela.

"He has," said the girl, her voice still tinged with sadness. She and her mother were now free. Marcus had bought them both from Herod then arranged for their manumission. They had been given enough money to set themselves up in business in Jerusalem and there she must wait for Marcus to return to her: either to make her his wife, but more probably his mistress. Her mother might be happy, but she had hoped for much, much more.

Chapter 39 – A Party Surprise

Claudia Lucretia stifled a yawn. The Herodian banquet was much like the other Herodian banquets she had attended: lavish food, sycophantic guests and the promise of spectacularly crass entertainment to round off the evening. The only unexpected thing had been a blazing argument between her father and Marcus Gaius when the tribune joined proceedings over an hour late and still wearing his travelling cloak.

Pilate had accused him of insulting his daughter by flaunting his affair with a mere slave and demanded that Herod sell the girl off to the next slave train passing through. Antipas had coughed politely and told Pilate he had already sold the girl and her mother to Tribune Sejanus. This enraged Pilate even further. "But you did not ask me!" he bellowed. "You said we could have the use of the soothsayer for as long as we needed her!"

"I did ask your wife. And she said she no longer needed the services of the witch since the Baptist had healed her of her affliction."

"That's right, dear," said Procula Claudiana, placing a soothing hand on his arm. "I would have asked you but you were in discussions with Caiphas," she nodded to the High Priest who sat opposite and nodded politely in return. "I know better than to disturb you with trivial domestic affairs when you are in talks of imperial importance, dear. Besides, I have not been troubled with dreams since the Baptist prayed for me. So when Antipas suggested it I thought it a good way to get rid of the girl, which we all agree is imperative."

"By selling her to her lover?"

"With the promise that he would send her away and then sell her on as soon as she had recovered from her wounds. Isn't that right, Marcus Gaius?"

"It is, my lady," said Marcus.

"You mean *if* she recovers from her wounds," Herodias chipped in. "She wasn't looking good the last time I saw her. Isn't that right, Salome?"

"What's that, mother?" answered the girl who was pushing a pea from one side of her plate to the other. In fact, Claudia noticed, she had hardly eaten or spoken all evening.

"Are you all right?" asked Antipas.

"Yes, uncle, I'm just a bit distracted. You see –"

"Don't interrupt, Salome. It's exceptionally rude," said her mother. "Now, where were we? Ah yes, damaged, I was saying. No one will pay much for damaged goods."

"I got a fair price from Sejanus!" chortled Antipas.

"More like extortionate," muttered Marcus.

"Business is business!"

"Indeed it is," said Marcus and chinked goblets with the king.

But Pilate was not placated. "That does not change the fact that no one asked me! I am the governor of Judea! The Emperor's representative!"

"And none of that has anything to do with the sale of a slave," said Herodias tartly. "I think it is time we established some boundaries about what falls under the governor's hegemony and what does not,"

"Now, now," said Caiphas, sensing the need for an intermediary, "tonight is not the night for discussions about jurisdiction. Surely we are here to give thanks for God's intervention at the Saturnalia banquet?"

"I don't think your God had anything to do with it," grumbled Pilate, but the combined efforts of Procula and Caiphas as well as Marcus' insistence that Nebela had already been sent away and would never again live under the same roof as his daughter, finally calmed him down.

"So you will be leaving for Rome in the morning, then?"

"I will," said Marcus. "Be assured I have nothing but the greatest respect for you and your daughter, sir. What man has not dallied on occasion with a slave? It's meant nothing to me, I swear. As soon as my uncle and I have worked out the finer details of the arrangement I'll be back to marry the noble Claudia Lucretia."

He caught Claudia's eye and smiled at her, Claudia smiled back. She knew how to play the game. And she knew too that her mother was watching her like a hawk. Procula Claudiana suspected something. But as she had not seen Judah for nearly a month, Claudia feared there was no longer anything to suspect.

She reminded herself that before the Saturnalia banquet began, she had finally come to terms with the fact that she and Judah would never be together and she had agreed to the engagement with Marcus Gaius. If the Zealot kitchen boy had not lit that fire and Simeon not rescued her, her love for Judah would never have been rekindled. She would have been just where she was now: saying goodbye to her fiancé before he returned to Rome and insisting that the slut Nebela was removed from their lives forever. This was what would have happened and this is what was happening. Obviously, this was what the fates decreed.

Claudia Lucretia looked across the table at the tribune. He was very, very good-looking with his grey eyes and light brown hair that stood on end charmingly when he took his helmet off. Then there was his spectacular physique that no woman could fail to notice. And, when he wanted to be, he was kind and solicitous. He was wealthy too, and well placed in Roman society to give her the life she was used to. Unlike Judah. Despite his dreams of becoming a wealthy merchant she feared they would spend the rest of their lives running from her father's search parties. Her father, she knew, would never give up. He loved her too much. And did she really have it in her heart to disappoint him that way? She smiled at the older man and he smiled back, patting her hand fondly. Yes, that was the one thing she was sure of: her father's love. Could she say the same for Judah? Where had he been the last month? Why had he not come to her? Would this be the pattern of their lives? Was she to wait around forever for the man of her dreams to return? Claudia did not like being the plaything of fate. She was a woman who wanted to be able to make her own choices. So, imagining for a moment she did have a choice, who would she choose? Marcus or Judah? Her head or her heart? She knew who she would want to choose – if circumstances were different – but they were not; and perhaps it was time she finally accepted it.

Out of the corner of her eye she spotted some jugglers taking their positions on the dais. The evening's entertainment was about to start; it was time she took her leave.

*

No one had been surprised when Claudia Lucretia declared she had a headache and would be going to bed early. Marcus, no doubt eager to put on a good show for her father, had insisted he escort her to her chamber. And she, knowing how to play the game, agreed. On the way through the lavishly decorated corridors, they had made polite chit-chat. Marcus spoke of his trip to Rome and what he hoped to achieve with his uncle. She spoke of her hope that the palace at Caesarea would be restored in time for his return so they could hold their wedding there. He asked her where she would like to honeymoon. She said she had always wanted to see the pyramids. Then Egypt it would be, he agreed. At the door to her chamber she allowed him to kiss her. She closed her eyes and tried not to think of Judah. But she did not have to endure it long. Marcus Gaius soon pulled away and declared that he needed to get back to the banquet; Claudia Lucretia needed her rest. She opened the door and bid him good night. However, just as he was turning to leave, he stopped. "Claudia…"

"Yes, Marcus?"

"Who are Uncle Judah and Sylvia?"

Claudia felt her heart pound against her chest wall. "I don't know; why do you ask?"

"No reason," said Marcus, his handsome face inscrutable. "Good night, then."

"Good night. And travel safely. May Mercury protect you."

"And may Juno protect you."

*

Claudia closed the door, her heart still pounding. What did Marcus know? Was this a warning? A threat? He had no right to threaten her! She had already chosen to marry him. She had…

"Claudia."

It was Judah. He stood in a pool of moonlight, his curly black hair tousled by the breeze from the open window. She ran to him and threw herself into his arms. He caught her and together they fell onto the bed, their mouths hungrily seeking the other. Claudia should have asked him where he had been, why it had taken him so long to come to her; she should have told him she had decided to marry Marcus and not elope with him. She should have said no, she did not want him to make love to her, as he pulled her gown from her shoulders and laid her bare on the silk sheets. She should have stayed his hand as he took off his own tunic and lowered his lean, brown torso onto her soft white chest. She should have, but she didn't; that would have been her head talking. And Judah, she knew, belonged not to her head, but her heart. He always would.

*

Claudia and Judah lay entwined in each others' arms, their bodies and emotions finally in unison. He lifted tendrils of her hair and allowed them to flow through his fingers like a chestnut waterfall. She sketched delicate patterns on his chest with her fingertips.

"I'm sorry I didn't come sooner," he said.

"It probably wasn't safe."

"It never will be."

She agreed, but said nothing.

"But when I saw Sejanus today with Jesus –"

She pulled herself up on the heels of her hands, her hair falling like a curtain around them. "You saw Marcus Gaius? With Jesus?"

"Yes, he was asking for healing for his slave. Nebela, I assume."

"Oh really? And did he get it? Did the prophet heal her?"

"I don't know. But that's not the point. When I saw him it reminded me of you. It woke me up, I suppose. I think I've been in some kind of dream."

"A dream? About what?"

"The Messiah. I think that Jesus really could be the one we've all been waiting for."

Claudia went cold. It was the same feeling she'd had when she'd spoken to Jairus' daughter. "*We*? I haven't been waiting for him, Judah. I've been waiting for you."

"I know you have, and I'm sorry. It's just that –"

Suddenly there was a commotion in the corridor: men shouting and a woman screaming. It sounded like Procula. Claudia and Judah leapt up. Judah grabbed his clothes and sprinted towards the window. Claudia snatched her robe and headed for the door. Before she could reach it it was flung open to reveal Marcus and her father, carrying a hysterical Procula between them.

"Pack your things, Claudia. Call Judith to help you. We're leaving immediately," Pilate ordered.

"What is it? What's happened?"

"They're animals! Monsters!" cried Procula, her eyes wild with terror.

"By Juno, tell me!"

"They have taken the head of John the Baptist," said Marcus grimly. "And served it to us on a platter."

*

A Dream of Procula Pilate

I am walking through the streets of Jerusalem; the cobbles are bruising my feet. I am walking in circles: round and round and round. I am circling a building in the middle of the city. I look up and see the Jewish Temple, gleaming white in the blinding sunlight. On each corner of the Temple someone is standing: on the first is my beloved Pontius. On the second is Antipas, like a giant toad. On the third is Joseph Caiphas the High Priest and on the fourth is a man I can't identify. I cannot see his face clearly because a giant shadow, in the shape of a cross, has fallen across it. I hear the creak of wood and iron, like a door opening on its hinges. The gates to the temple are opening and Salome, completely naked and unashamed, is dancing through them and down the steps towards me. She is carrying a covered platter. When she reaches me I know that I must lift the lid. I am too scared to do so. So she does it for me. And there, floating in a soup of blood, is a face-down head. She picks it up by the hair and turns it towards me – it is Claudia Lucretia, her mouth open in an eternal scream.

Chapter 40 – The Clearing of the Temple

Zandra woke from a fevered dream. The sun streaming through the slats in the shutters told her she had over-slept. It had been happening more often than it should lately, and it was not good for business. She heard the cry of the oyster-monger down the road announcing his fresh stock had arrived and the scolding of the spice merchant that his apprentice had left the lid off one of his amphora again. She knew that shoppers would already be filling the street outside their two-storey premises, waiting for the shutters to be flung back to announce that the dressmaker was open for business.

Nebela's creative designs, drawn from what she'd seen at the palaces of Caesarea and Tiberias, were, within a few short months, on the 'must-have' lists of the more fashionable ladies of Jerusalem. She sourced her fabrics in the market around the Temple and would simply have had a stall there, except they needed a backroom for Zandra's business too. So they used some of the money given to them by Marcus to buy an attractive premises in the commercial quarter with a downstairs shop front, a back room for Zandra and an upstairs living area, accessed, as most Judean buildings were, by an outside staircase. An open-plan roof patio accentuated with brightly coloured flowerpots served as an outdoor living area with a collection of tastefully decorated bedrooms and salons en suite.

Zandra completed her ablutions, got dressed and went downstairs. The shutters were already open. Inside the shop there was a gaggle of ladies looking at some pre-made samples. They looked mainly Syrian and Greek although there were also some Hebrew women who aspired to the more cosmopolitan looks of the Empire. Nebela had cleverly seen that that would be their niche market, in this the most Jewish city of Judea. They would, of course, have fitted in better in multicultural Caesarea, but there they would have been one of many; and of course would have had more chance of running into the Pilates whom, Marcus insisted, they avoid. So Jerusalem it was; for now.

Zandra had a hankering to go back east at some stage, to return to her country of birth from which she and Nebela had been taken ten years ago. Ten years of slavery. It still left a bitter taste in Zandra's mouth. And if she ever caught up with her good-for-nothing husband who had allowed them to be taken in the first place... Zandra shook her head, not allowing herself to dwell on thoughts of what might have been. Here in this Jerusalem shop she and her daughter were starting a new life. She watched Nebela holding up fabrics against her clients, draping them this way or that and flattering the matrons with comparisons to the governor's wife or the queen in Tiberias or even the empress-apparent Livia – whom Nebela had never laid eyes on! The girl was proving to have good business sense, thought her mother approvingly. And just as well, seeing the soothsayer's business was not going well at all.

Zandra wasn't sure why, but ever since they arrived in Jerusalem she was having a great deal of trouble hearing the spirits. Oh, she could con her clients into believing she had – her 'gift' after all was two-thirds theatre – but she knew, the genuine part, the true prophetic insight, was gone. Or at least suppressed. Every time she closed her eyes and allowed her mind to sink into her heart and open her being to communication from beyond, she saw only one thing: the face of the prophet of Galilee. At least she assumed it was he. The visions had started the moment her daughter was healed in the ox cart. Zandra 'saw' him, there in the cart with them, touching Nebela's brow and leg. Embracing her with his warm brown eyes and breathing life into the near-dead girl. Then he had turned to Zandra and smiled.

And that was the vision Zandra saw day after day when she tried to reach the spirits for a word for a jealous husband or a worried parent or a desperate widow. She told them what they wanted to hear, but she knew it was all a sham. And her heart was no longer in it. She knew the power she had once had was a mere shadow of what she had glimpsed in that cart in Galilee. So what was she to do? Give up her business as a soothsayer? It was all she had known for all of her adult life.

She was glad to see there were no clients sitting in the small waiting area outside her booth. For now, she would not have to pretend. Instead she picked up a needle and thread and started hemming a gown that her daughter – her fully healed daughter – had created, and thought she must thank the prophet if ever she saw him again.

*

Nebela was worried about her mother. The much-dreamed chance to set up her own business as a soothsayer, not at the beck and call of their so-called masters, had finally been given to her; but she had not embraced it. Nebela did not know why. She was happy for her mother's help – there were too many dresses to make all by herself – but the woman whom she had looked up to all her life seemed to have slipped into the shadows.

Zandra stumbled beside her, her heel catching one of the cobbles of the Gabbatha pavement. Nebela steadied her mother and patted her arm. They were on the way to the market. Nebela needed to see if the cloth merchant had finally got the new fabric he had said was coming on a camel train from the East. The man was proving limited in his ability to supply her with what she needed. Oh, his workaday fabrics were good enough for the average dressmaker, but Nebela was not your average dressmaker. What set her apart was quality and innovation and for that she needed access to better merchandise. She was beginning to think she may have to venture east herself to establish her own supply chain, but she couldn't do that until Marcus returned.

She sighed and looked across the marketplace, past the Palace of Herod the Great, beyond the Jewish temple on the rise to their right and to the fortress of Antonia that housed the Roman garrison at the end of the main thoroughfare. When Marcus returned that is where he would go. It had been three months since they had parted at the ford in the river. Three months of hoping and yearning and longing. Oh, she had kept herself busy setting up her business – and worrying about her mother – but her real worry was that Marcus would not return. Or if he did, it would still be to marry Claudia. She looked towards the Palace overlooking the Gabbatha, wondering when the Pilates would be coming to town. The Jewish festival of Passover was only a few days away and the governor would be expected to be in attendance. Whether Claudia and her mother would accompany him did not really matter. And frankly, Nebela didn't care.

She heard the jingle of a bridle and looked up to see a centurion scanning the market from his elevated height, on the look-out for thieves and troublemakers. She recognised him as one of the men who had ridden with Marcus on that day last summer when they had rescued Claudia for the first time from the Zealots. Oh how she wished she'd just left the girl to her fate! But then, perhaps, she might never have met Marcus…

She stepped in front of the centurion and smiled up at him. He looked down at her and squinted through the April sunshine to see who she was. If he did recognise her he didn't let on.

She smiled again, knowing the effect she normally had on men. A slight smile teased the corners of his mouth. It was working.

"Hello, soldier. Are you expecting trouble?"

"No more than usual."

"Must be a hard job being in charge of so many men," said Nebela, feigning admiration.

"It is," he said, preening. "But when you're as experienced as I am…"

"A tribune, aren't you?" asked Nebela innocently.

The centurion paused for a moment, no doubt wondering whether or not he should lie to impress the pretty girl, then decided against it. "No, I'm a centurion. I'm in charge of over a hundred men!"

"Over a hundred men! Or course! Sorry, I got it mixed up. I don't understand all the ins and outs of the military. I had heard that a man called Marcus Gaius Sejanus was the tribune and I thought you were he."

"No, the tribune is away."

"Oh. Is he coming back soon?"

"He should be. We're expecting him any time now."

Suddenly there was a commotion in the crowd and shouting could be heard from the Temple. The centurion and Nebela looked up to the white building on the hill and saw people running out carrying cages, pots and sacks, tripping up on goats and sheep trying to make their escape. Then in the gateway appeared an incredible sight: a man dressed in the rough-weave of a Galilean fisherman thrashing a whip from side to side and bellowing at the top of his voice: "Get out! Get out! Get out of my father's house! It's supposed to be a place of prayer for all nations and you – you – you've made it into a den of thieves!"

A well-dressed merchant stumbled in front of him and dropped a sack of coins. The cloth split and the coins scattered everywhere. The Galilean reached down, picked up a handful and threw them with all his might down the Temple steps and onto the pavement below. There was chaos as shoppers and shopkeepers alike scrambled to snatch some coins and the merchants from the Temple tried to outrun the madman with the whip.

The centurion geed his horse, unsheathed his sword and charged into the crowd, calling for reinforcements who were running to join him from the Antonia fortress.

There was going to be a riot. Nebela and her mother needed to get out of there. She turned to grab her mother's hand, but she was gone. Panic-stricken she scoured the crowd and finally saw her: heading up the Temple steps!

"Mother! Mother!" screamed Nebela. But her voice could not carry over the roar of the brewing riot. Suddenly she was knocked from behind and she fell to the ground, scuffing her knees on the cobbles. Then someone lifted her back onto her feet. She looked first to her mother, but saw that she and the Galilean had both disappeared into the crowd. She whipped her head from left to right, desperate to locate them. Then, she stopped in her tracks. There in front of her stood Marcus.

"Hello, my love," he said.

Chapter 41 – The Roof Garden

Marcus and Nebela reclined on a pile of cushions as the last of the sun's rays warmed their naked limbs. Soothed by the sound of cicadas, the smell of magnolia blossom sweetened the scent of love. They were on the patio of the roof garden; a balustrade and potted palms ensured privacy from the prying eyes of neighbours. Since Zandra had not yet come home, they had the place all to themselves.

Marcus, at Nebela's insistence, had sent one of his men to look for her mother. He had reported back that she was with the Prophet of Galilee in the house of Simon, a Pharisee. She had been invited to stay for dinner. Nebela was surprised at this strange turn of events and planned to interrogate her mother ruthlessly when she returned, but for now she was content that Zandra was safe and she and Marcus free to reunite.

They sipped wine from matching goblets and snacked on olives and goat's cheese canapés. It was hard to imagine that only four months before she had been a slave at the palace of Caesarea cleaning up the slops of Claudia Lucretia Pilate.

Marcus pinched the plumpness of her cheek "You look so much better than the last time I saw you."

"My gaunt looks didn't seem to stop you desiring me."

"Nothing would stop me desiring you," he said, his eyes ranging over the length of her beautiful body; her skin the colour of the bronze pelt of a mountain gazelle.

"Is that what you told your uncle?"

"It is."

A warm glow filled Nebela's chest but then subsided as her natural pessimism – the product of a decade of slavery – blocked its path. She raised her full lips to his and kissed him until her fear was under control. Then she asked, as casually as she could: "So what did he say?"

"He said I was a fool."

She pulled away from him and threw herself back on the cushions, covering her eyes with her forearm. He leaned up on one elbow and looked down on her, shaking his head. "Don't give up so easily, little cat, I haven't finished yet."

She peeked at him over her arm.

"He said I was a fool… but… he could tell I would not be dissuaded."

She lowered her arm fully this time, waiting for him to continue.

"And he's right. I won't be. I love you, Nebela, and I plan to be with you."

"And he agreed?" her voice catching on hope.

"He agreed to my plan, yes."

"Which is?"

"That I will marry Claudia Lucretia, as agreed, but then divorce her after a respectable amount of time; preferably after the first child has been born."

Nebela stood up, not caring whether the neighbours could see her and stood over him, hands on hips, her hair a tangled, black mane.

"Respectable? You call that respectable? That is neither respectable of me nor Claudia!"

"I didn't think you cared about Claudia!"

"I don't! But I don't want her to be used. I don't want you to father her child. And I don't want to have to wait for you! Why can't you just let her go now?"

"You know why."

"Out of respect? And you think she will respect you after that? Do you think her father will? Or the stuck-up Roman prigs you're so keen to impress?"

"People get divorced all the time."

"But they usually don't plan to when they first get married!" She kicked at the pile of cushions, sending one of them over the balustrade; then she grabbed her robe, threw it over her shoulders and tossed Marcus his tunic.

"Nebela…"

She glared down at him. "I wasn't going to tell you this but now you leave me no choice. I know you don't think I care for Claudia, but that's not entirely true. She treated me with far more respect than the Herods ever did and she turned a blind eye to allow us to be together."

"Yes, she did, which is why I think –"

"You know nothing! You think she did it because she didn't mind you sowing your wild oats before you married her?"

"Well, yes…"

228

"Well, no! She did it because she knew I would tell her secret if she told ours."

"Ours was never much of a secret, Nebela," he said, his impatience vying with his amusement.

"But hers was!"

This caught his attention. He sat up and grabbed her wrist, pulling her down onto the cushions beside him.

"What secret?" he said quietly, all pretence that he was amused by Nebela's little tantrum gone.

But Nebela was too angry to care. This was her last chance to have Marcus on her own terms: as a free woman and a free man. If he went off and married Claudia what guarantee did she have that he would come back to her? Absolutely none.

"She has been having an affair with Judah ben Hillel."

Judah. Uncle Judah. "And who is Judah ben Hillel?"

"He is a Zealot. He was undercover as a guard at the Palace of Tiberias. He was the one who led us into the ambush near Nazareth."

"The one who tried to rape Claudia?"

"No. Apparently he saved her from being raped. Then later he came to Caesarea to spy on the Pilates. He worked in the olive grove –"

"The olive grove…"

"She used to meet him there. And I think it was him who took her away the second time too."

"She went willingly?"

"Yes."

Marcus' jaw clenched dangerously. "Then she has played me for a fool." In one harsh, swift move, he pushed Nebela down and stood up. He towered over her, his muscular chest rising and falling like the bellows of a furnace. He pointed a finger at her as his other hand clenched into a fist. "You have both played me for a fool."

Nebela feared he was going to hit her. But he didn't. He turned on his heel, picked up his sword and stormed down the stairs, leaving her as the last rays of sun finally slipped away.

*

Nebela ran through the streets, her dark hair flying behind her and tears streaming down her face. She knew better than to follow Marcus. She was searching for her mother. She needed her mother like she'd never needed her before. She had made frantic enquiries of her neighbours as to the location of Simon the Pharisee's house, and she was heading there as fast as her legs could carry her.

It was dark as she arrived but the house was ablaze with light and bubbling with loud conversation. The luxury townhouse was packed with guests spilling out of the doorways and sitting in open windows. Nebela managed to worm her way through, scanning the crowd for her mother. She asked some of the guests if they had seen Zandra the Soothsayer and she was eventually pointed in the right direction. Zandra it seemed had managed to wheedle an invitation to the top table with the most important guests at the party. Nebela saw an older bearded man who looked like he might be Simon the Pharisee, a well-dressed woman, she assumed to be his wife, several other well-to-dos and the man she had seen on the Temple steps, all reclining on dining couches. Her mother, bizarrely, was seated on the floor at the prophet's feet.

Jesus, Nebela remembered. *Jesus of Nazareth, the Prophet of Galilee: the healer.* Nebela had not thought much about her miraculous recovery since she had been in Jerusalem, as she was too busy setting up her business. Also, for her, it was as if she had fallen asleep during the fire into a fitful dream and then woken in Marcus' arms. She had not been the one worrying whether she would live or die. But her mother had told her what had happened and she was curious to finally meet the man whom both Zandra and Marcus believed had brought her back to them. She should thank him; it would be the polite thing to do.

But before she could say anything her mother suddenly produced an alabaster jar. Nebela knew that it contained very expensive perfume that Procula had given Zandra in gratitude for helping her interpret her dreams. Zandra had been keeping it to sell one day so she could buy back her old house in Babylon. Nebela knew how much that meant to Zandra so she was stunned when her mother stood up and poured the entire contents over Jesus' head. Then she knelt down and kissed his feet, wetting them with her tears. And as if that wasn't enough, she then loosened her hair and used it to dry the prophet's feet. Nebela was not the only one who was stunned. A young man stood up and pointed at Zandra.

"How could you let her do that, Master? Do you know how much that perfume cost? I thought we were supposed to be helping the poor and freeing the oppressed, not wasting the little we have on party favours!"

It was Judah. Nebela didn't know if he recognised Zandra – she was usually veiled when she went out, trying to maintain the mystique of a fortune-teller – but he was clearly incensed by what she was doing.

Jesus tried to calm him. "Judas, Judas, why are you so upset? She's done a beautiful thing for me. She's anointed me for my burial."

"Why are you talking about your burial?" asked Judah. "It's as if you're planning on dying! If you are who you say you are, you should be planning your campaign!" Then he threw down his napkin and stormed out of the house.

Nebela followed him and caught up with him as he was heading down the street. She clutched at his sleeve and he tried to shake her off. But she persisted.

"Judah! Judah! It's me, Nebela!"

He turned to look more closely at her, his eyes wild with rage. Then suddenly he recognised her.

"Nebela! He looked at her curiously. "So he did heal you."

"Yes. And that was my mother. The one who poured the perfume. I think she was saying thank you."

Judah flung his hands in the air in exasperation. "That's what I don't understand! He has all this – this – *power* and he wastes his time at parties and talking about loving our enemies and forgiving them and hobnobbing with foreigners. And he talks in such riddles. You can't get a straight word out of him!"

"Then why are you with him?"

"Because I thought he might be the one. Our Messiah."

"And that's why you left Claudia? To follow a pretend Messiah?"

"I have not left Claudia."

"Then why aren't you with her?"

"It's difficult. I tried. But she was taken back."

"Then you haven't tried hard enough!" Nebela was thinking on the hop. If she could get Judah to finally follow through with his plan and take Claudia away…

"I don't know where she is."

"She's coming to Jerusalem. Marcus Gaius Sejanus told me. She'll be here tomorrow."

"It will be hard to get to her in the palace…"

"I can help you. I can get word to her to come to my dress shop. I can ask Judith to help us. She's kept quiet about everything in the past. I think she'll do the same."

"Do you think you can?"

"Yes. Come to my shop on Oyster Street tomorrow evening at sunset. Can you do that?"

Judah was calming down. He was weighing up his options, looking back at the Pharisees' house and then to Nebela. One of his friends had come out and was calling to him. "Judas! Judas! Come back! The Master wants to talk to you!"

"So will you do it?"

"Yes," said Judah. "I'll do it. The dress shop on Oyster Street at sunset. I'll be there."

"Good," said Nebela.

"Judas!" the man called again.

"Why do they call you Judas?"

Judah shrugged. "Judah ben Hillel is my adopted name. My real name, my birth name, was Judas, Judas Iscariot. It's what the Master now calls me."

Chapter 42 – The Sanhedrin

Pilate was really too tired to deal with business at this time of day. He and his family had barely arrived from Caesarea when a messenger came from Caiphas saying his presence was urgently requested at a special meeting of the Sanhedrin convened at the High Priest's residence. He was sorely tempted to tell the boy to tell his master that the only meeting he had planned to attend that evening was with his masseuse and a carafe of good wine. But the message he received was that the meeting had been called to stop a potential insurrection. This was very serious business.

Claudia Lucretia, it seemed, also had business that evening. She had an appointment with a dressmaker who was making a special gown for her to wear to receive Marcus Gaius on his return from Rome. Why it could not wait until tomorrow he did not know. And neither did Procula Claudiana. She was just as flummoxed as he was, but neither of them wanted to put a damper on their daughter's unusually good mood that had unaccountably dawned on her within an hour of arriving at the palace in Jerusalem. Could it actually be that Claudia Lucretia was looking forward to seeing her fiancé? They could only hope. So Pilate had given his permission for her to go to the dressmaker (who for some reason to do with a last minute delivery of fabric could not come to them). Procula was too tired to accompany her, but they both felt she would be safe enough with Judith and a couple of guards.

So Pilate had had a light meal with his wife and then left her, promising he would return as soon as he could. He hoped that would not be too late.

Pilate could hear raised voices from the moment he walked through the imposing gates of the High Priest's residence. *Not good for my headache*, he thought but comforted himself knowing that Procula's nimble fingers would be able to soothe it away later. It was a delight to have her back. He had thought that terrible business with the Baptist would have pushed her over the edge again, but he was wrong. After a couple of days she rallied and channelled her rage into writing letters to the Emperor demanding that Antipas be removed from his throne – or more technically his *tetrarchy*, as Procula Claudiana emphasised: "It's not as if he's even a proper king!" Procula had declared that she would never be under the same roof as the Herods again: which might prove difficult if they remained in Judea.

A cohort of Temple Guards greeted Pilate and his soldiers as they marched into the courtyard. Caiphas' assistant, Malchus, was waiting for them and immediately ushered the governor into the meeting chamber. It was mayhem. Seventy members of the Jewish ruling council representing both the Pharisee and Sadducee parties were trying to outdo each other with denouncements. Caiphas was trying to bring them to order but even he, the most accomplished of campaigners, was not having much success. The language being spoken was Aramaic. Pilate hoped they would switch to Greek when they realised he was there but he caught snatches of a few words he did understand: 'revolution' and 'insurrection' were two of them. But then there was another word that was being shouted louder than any other. He asked Malchus what it meant. "Blasphemy. Some fool has just declared himself the Son of God."

*

Two hours later and Pilate was still no clearer on why the prophet from Galilee was causing such consternation. As far as he could tell he was not leading a revolution – unless you counted healing people as insurrectionary – and the worst he had done had been to insult the priests by saying they were self-righteous. Well, they were! The rest of the so-called evidence related to some finer points of religious interpretation: was he or was he not the prophesied Messiah; did he or did he not represent a visitation of the Jewish god to earth; could he or could he not undermine the centrality of the Temple in the Jewish faith? Pilate didn't know and didn't care. As far as he could tell this was an internal matter for the religious nuts to sort out for themselves. Granted, what had happened at the Temple yesterday – barging in and driving out the stallholders – had nearly caused a riot and that needed to be monitored; but that was all. He might just ask some of his soldiers to go and have a quiet word with this Jesus to tell him to take his circus out into the desert like the Baptist did. *Though he'd better watch his head*!

Pilate chuckled at his own joke. No, there were far more important things to worry about. Like the latest Zealot raids on Roman outposts.

Although the last six months had seen some significant progress in hunting down those outlaws, there were still enough of them to give Pilate indigestion whenever he thought about them. In fact, before he went back to the palace, he might just check in at the Antonia to see if the latest search party had come up with anything. Just before leaving Caesarea that morning he had been informed that Marcus Gaius Sejanus, newly returned from Rome, had received some intelligence that the leader, Barabbas, had disguised himself as a pilgrim heading up to Jerusalem for the Passover. He had last been seen in Jericho and Sejanus was leading a crack team to intercept him.

Pilate waved away the litter bearers waiting for him outside the High Priest's palace, opting instead to walk to the Antonia. It was a lovely evening and he needed the fresh air to clear his head of all the hysteria of the last couple of hours before meeting with some eminently sensible military types. Being an ex-tribune himself, Pilate admired the calm and simplicity of the army. There would be no hysteria at the Antonia, he could be sure of that.

The streets were filled with pilgrims trying to get in some last-minute shopping before the start of Passover the following evening. The population of Jerusalem almost doubled at Passover as devout Jews from all over Judea, Palestine and beyond made a pilgrimage to this, their most holy of cities. The whole point, according to Caiphas who played a starring role in the event, was that once a year the Jewish god expected a sacrifice on behalf of all the people to wipe away their sins. And then the year after that, and the year after that, and the year after that … Why they couldn't just do it at any time and in any temple like the rest of the civilised world, Pilate did not know. *Oh hang on, wasn't that the day of Atonement, not Passover?* Pilate tried to remember exactly what Caiphas had told him about Passover: *A remembrance of Israel's rescue from slavery? When their god had slaughtered the Egyptians, not them? Something about the blood of a lamb being used to fend off the spirit of Death?* Oh, it was all so confusing!

But it brought business to the city that they would not normally have. And business that was good for Jerusalem would be good for Rome. A thriving economy meant a happier populace and higher taxes. And that, as Pilate reminded himself, was the main reason he was there: to keep peace and to ensure the flow of tax revenue from this troublesome province to the Emperor's coffers.

Pilate looked around him and saw lights in every building. The hospitality industry was flourishing with formal guest houses and inns full to the rafters and even private homes renting out spare rooms and rooftops. The market – inside and outside the Temple walls – was chockablock with people buying food and souvenirs of their special holiday.

But all seemed calm. Those who had not already bought their Passover Lamb and stocked up on the rest of the ingredients for the festive meal – the bitter herbs, the unleavened bread, the wine – were getting them now. Whatever had happened here yesterday had caused barely a ripple. No, there was no insurrection in the air, Pilate was sure of it. His mood began to lift as he thought of getting through the Passover and then going back to Caesarea where one could almost imagine one was not in Judea at all.

Suddenly there was a call of "Io Lord Pilate!" and a troupe of cavalry – about a dozen men – reined in their horses as they arrived simultaneously with the governor at the gates of the Antonia Fortress. They had come from the other direction, avoiding the busy commercial district of the city. Pilate looked up and returned the salute of the leader of the group. It was Marcus Gaius Sejanus.

"Io, Tribune!" said Pilate. "Just the man I was hoping to see."

"We've got him, sir!" said Marcus triumphantly. "After all this time hunting him through mountains and deserts we finally found him in a backroom of a tavern in Jericho."

"Did someone turn him in?"

"Someone always does if the price is right."

Pilate looked around and then leaned in close to whisper: "Where is he?"

Marcus nodded to his left and Pilate noticed a pack horse with a body-shaped sack trussed up on it.

"Is he…"

"He's very much alive, sir. We just wanted to bring him in quietly."

"Rightly so. There's been enough of a hullabaloo already with the Sanhedrin."

"Oh?"

"I'll tell you about it later." Pilate rubbed his temples. "Actually, I'll tell you about it tomorrow. Come and see me first thing. I want to hear what happened in Rome. I assume your discussions with your uncle were a success?"

"Oh yes, sir. They were a success."

Pilate patted Marcus' horse on the rump. "Good man. Claudia can't wait to see you. She's currently at a dressmaker's shop having a new gown fitted. Why it couldn't wait until tomorrow, I'll never know. Young love, eh?"

Chapter 43 – The Shop on Oyster Street

It was sunset and Judah was on his way to the dress shop on Oyster Street. It was in a part of town known as the New City. The streets were wider here and less convoluted than the Upper and Lower City and lacked the blood-soaked history of the even older City of David. The architecture, although still Judean, had more of a Hellenistic influence. This was the new Israel: adapting to change; assimilating foreign cultures; living and letting live. It was everything Judah had once stood against. But that had all started to change the day he first met Claudia.

He could not wait to see her: it had been too long. That blissful night at the Palace of Tiberias had been cut far too short. What might have happened if the wretched tribune had not interrupted them? Would he have had the courage to whisk her away? He had gone to the palace with that half in mind, but had not quite figured out how he would actually achieve it. His first priority had simply been to see her.

He was still furious with Hannah – and he suspected his brother – for turning them in to the Romans. By now they would have been safe in Seleucia and he would have made a start with his silk import and export business. Who knows, perhaps he would have been shipping fabric to Nebela! Hah! She had certainly landed in the butter: a dress shop on Oyster Street in the most prosperous part of Jerusalem. No doubt paid for by Tribune Sejanus. Judah ground his teeth thinking of his rival. Why the man could not leave Claudia alone, he did not know. He obviously didn't love her, not like Judah did, so what was it that kept him interested? Pride? Loyalty to her father? Greed? Well, he wouldn't have to worry about it for long. He had made his mind up: he was finally taking Claudia away. There was nothing keeping him in Israel any more.

Well, there was one thing. But that would be dealt with later tonight and then tomorrow he and Claudia would be free to leave. He just needed to sort out the final details and to attend one last meal with the man he had once hoped was the Messiah.

Last night at Simon the Pharisee's house had been the final straw. As he'd said to Nebela, Jesus had all this power and yet did nothing with it. He had seen him heal lepers and cripples, give sight to the blind and hearing to the deaf. He had seen him feed five thousand people and calm a storm with a single word. He had even seen him walk on water and raise a man called Lazarus from the dead. If he hadn't seen it all with his own eyes he would not have believed it. Oh yes, Jesus of Nazareth had all the credentials of the Messiah and yet obtusely refused to do the job.

He had failed to turn his ever increasing band of followers into an army. He encouraged them to lay down whatever weapons they had and forgive their enemies instead. What kind of Messiah did that? He was supposed to lead an uprising against the Romans and drive them out of Israel once and for all. And then, when that was done, to be enthroned the true King of Israel in Jerusalem and deal decisively with puppet kings like Herod Antipas. If national pride was not enough motivation to do that then surely Herod's murder of his cousin should spur him on to revenge. But revenge seemed to be the last thing on Jesus' agenda. And Judah could simply not understand it.

He still had hope up to a few days ago. Jesus, Judah and the other disciples had come into Jerusalem leading a procession. Jesus had gone out of his way to procure a young donkey, just like was prophesied by the prophet Zechariah. When the Passover pilgrims saw it they immediately made the connection and greeted him with the psalm of welcome for Israel's true King:

Hosanna! Blessed is the one who comes in the name of the Lord. Hosanna to the Son of David the true King of Israel!

Judah could not believe it was finally happening! And he danced and sang with the crowds as they laid down their cloaks and lined the streets with palm branches. And there he was, one of the twelve chosen, ready to re-establish the twelve tribes of Israel! But then, instead of proclaiming his Kingdom at the Temple as he should have, Jesus made a fool of himself and everyone with him by taking a whip to the stallholders in the Temple market. And that was as militant as he got. Why didn't he take the whip to the Romans? Why didn't he head up to the Antonia and use his indisputable power to wipe them all out? He could have called down an army of angels! He could have called down hail and lightning. But he didn't. He just went to dinner at some Pharisee's house and let that foreign woman fawn all over him.

No, whatever Judah had thought about Jesus being the Messiah was wrong. He was just another pretender. Judah had been fooled again.

There was only one thing he wanted now: and she was waiting for him at the dress shop on Oyster Street.

*

By the time Claudia arrived at Oyster Street, accompanied by Judith and two palace guards, her initial euphoria at being contacted by Judah after three-and-a-half long months was beginning to fade. She had been through this too many times before. He flitted in and out of her life like the moon: full and bright and all consuming one moment then nearly invisible behind a cloud the next. He had waxed and waned in her life for nearly a year and it was time to get him to commit to a course of action once and for all.

She understood that he had to flee when Marcus and her parents came to her chamber that night in Tiberias, but why had he not come back again? Why had it taken him until now to make an appearance? Why had he sent no word? Claudia did not enjoy being anyone's plaything and she was beginning to suspect that was all she was. And now that Marcus Gaius was back from Rome it was time to make a decision once and for all. Was she really prepared to throw away a respectable life as an upwardly mobile tribune's wife, with the blessing of her parents and the Emperor, for a life on the run with a fugitive? If Judah had asked her in the afterglow of their lovemaking in Tiberias, she might have said yes, but now, after being abandoned by him yet again, she wasn't so sure.

And yet, here she was. She could have told Judith to decline the invitation from Nebela. It would have been as easy as that. But she could not deny that her heart had lurched when she read the note, written in the hand of her ex-slave and rival for Marcus' affection. She needed to see him one more time. She needed to confront him and ask him to make a choice between her and this puppet Messiah. But even if he did, she knew that she could never fully trust him. Was she really prepared to live like that?

Nebela was waiting for her in the doorway. She greeted her with a false smile which Claudia matched with a fake one of her own. They both knew how to play the game. The guards waited outside while Claudia, Judith and Nebela went into the shop. Despite herself, Claudia was impressed with what Nebela had built up in such a short space of time. *The girl always had impeccable taste*, Claudia thought begrudgingly. But she was under no illusions. Nebela had arranged all this in order to rid Marcus of her once and for all.

Keeping the fake smile for the sake of the guards who were watching through the shop window, Nebela draped some swatches of fabric over Claudia's shoulder.

"You always looked good in sage."

Claudia noted the absence of 'my lady'.

"I need to take your measurements and for that you will have to disrobe," she said loudly enough for the guards to hear her. "Come into the back room."

Claudia nodded to the guards to assure them that this was a perfectly normal request, and followed the Babylonian girl into the back of the shop, leaving Judith behind.

Nebela closed the doors behind them and slid a bolt across with a quiet click. "I'll wait outside the back door. When you're ready, call me; and I can distract the guards while you escape. There are horses waiting in the alley. It's all been arranged."

Claudia raised her eyebrows at the girl's presumptuousness, but said nothing.

Taking this as assent, Nebela slipped out the back leaving Claudia in the exotically decorated soothsayer's booth that doubled as a storeroom for Nebela's fabric. Swatches and bales of silk and damask were piled into a multi-coloured pyramid in the corner and a pair of headless dressmaker's dummies stood guard.

The door closed behind Nebela with a clunk; then Judah stepped out from behind a curtain. Claudia's heart lurched.

Without a moment's hesitation they were in each other's arms, kissing one another until their mutual pent-up desire was satisfied. But Claudia knew time was of the essence and the guards would not wait outside indefinitely. She pulled away and held him at arm's-length.

"Where have you been?"

"With Jesus. But –"

"Why didn't you come for me?"

"I've come for you now."

"And when will you leave?"

"I won't leave. Never again. Not without you. I love you, Claudia, and I want to start a new life with you. Just like we agreed. After tomorrow –"

"Tomorrow?"

"I have some final business to attend to."

"Ah," said Claudia, and stepped away.

"But once that's done –"

"It will never be done, Judah. There will always be one more thing. Does it involve the fake Messiah?"

"It does. But this will be the final thing. I promise!"

Claudia's heart still yearned for him but she forced herself to finally listen to her head. "I can't do it any more, Judah. It's over. It's time to say goodbye."

"No!" cried Judah and reached for her again.

She stepped back and held up her hands. "Don't touch me. Please don't touch me."

"Please, Claudia. Give me one more day. Meet me tomorrow at the Potter's Field at noon. You can say you're going there to read poetry like you used to in the olive grove. By then I'll have finished my business once and for all and we'll be free to leave."

He looked at her so beseechingly that despite her better judgement she crumbled. "One more day. But if you're not there and ready to leave, it's over between us. Do you understand that?"

Judah nodded his assent. Then he opened the back door to call Nebela – only to reveal Tribune Marcus Gaius Sejanus. In one hand he held his sword; the other was over Nebela's mouth.

He strode into the room and dragged Nebela after him. He thrust the sword at Judah who leapt back, his arms raised, his legs sprung wide ready for action.

"Marcus!" cried Claudia.

"All this time and you've been philandering with this peasant behind my back!"

He shoved Nebela towards her. "And she's been helping you!"

The two women clutched each other without thinking. Marcus ranged his sword in a waist-height arc encompassing the three of them. Judah thrust his arm under his cloak and pulled out a sword. Claudia and Nebela gasped as one.

The two men started circling one another, their blades almost touching in the middle of the small room. Claudia and Nebela edged into a corner.

"I recognise you," said Marcus. "You were with that prophet, Jesus. And your face is familiar from Caesarea too."

"Not very observant then, are you?" said Judah. "I've been around your fiancée for nearly a year and you haven't even noticed. Now what does that tell you about your true feelings for her?"

"My true feelings? Hah! This is not about love, Jew, it's about you as an insurrectionist and me as a representative of the Emperor. We've got your leader Barabbas and now we've got you. This so-called revolt is over." He thrust his sword, Judah parried, Marcus thrust again. Then they launched at each other like two dogs in a pit.

Claudia could see that Marcus was the better swordsman, but Judah was holding his own. Like that morning when they were ambushed by Barabbas' men, Judah was fighting manfully. But Claudia did not know how long he could hold out. She had seen Marcus at work in the arena when he killed Matthias; it was just a matter of time. She acted quickly: she grabbed an armful of silk and threw it in the air over Marcus' head. He cursed as the fabric billowed out and fell on him like a crimson cloud, tangling his sword arm for a moment. It was just a reprieve, but it was enough.

Someone was shouting and banging on the bolted door between them and the shop. "Run, Judah! Run!" shouted Claudia and she lurched at Marcus's legs, tripping him up so they fell together into a pile on the floor. Marcus tried to get up but his ankles were caught on a silk swatch. It gave Judah just the time he needed to run for the back door. He stopped for a moment and looked beseechingly at Claudia.

"Go! Go!" she screamed. And he went.

Then the guards burst in, Judith cowering behind them. Marcus was slashing at the silk with his sword. He pointed to the door. "After him!" The guards obeyed.

Marcus got up and towered over Claudia, his sword pointed at her throat.

Nebela ran forward and grabbed his arm. "No, Marcus!"

He threw her off him and she cannoned into the headless dummies. Marcus' voice dripped with malice: "Oh no, Nebela. I'm not going to hurt her. This is my fiancée: Claudia Lucretia Pilate, the daughter of the Governor of Judea. And as soon as Passover is over, we will be married."

He grabbed Claudia's wrist, pulled her up and then dragged her, sobbing, out of the shop, leaving Nebela and the dummies huddled in a corner on the floor.

Chapter 44 – The Judas Kiss

Judah ran down the alley as fast as he could, thrusting his sword back into his belt so he would not attract undue attention. He bypassed the whinnying horses for the same reason. It would be far easier to hide in the back streets of Jerusalem if he was on foot. If he had been planning on fleeing the city he might have been tempted to take one of the horses, but he knew he was not an experienced horseman and did not rate his chances outrunning a cavalry officer and his mount.

He had enough of a head start on the two guards to lose them after five minutes of twisting, turning and doubling back. By the time he got to the edge of the New City and crossed over into the Upper City he knew he was no longer being pursued. He slowed down to a walk but his heart was still racing. He had never been so angry in his life! Not since the day his mother was killed and the Roman soldiers failed to help her had he felt such rage overwhelm him. He swore that the next time he had a chance to do so he would slit Marcus Gaius Sejanus' throat from ear to ear and spit on him as he bled to death in the gutter.

The thought calmed him enough for him to remember that he had some other business to attend to that evening; after he had done that he would give some thought to what was to be done about Claudia.

He patted his money bag, strapped under his arm. Yes, it was still there. The thirty pieces of silver he had collected from the High Priest Caiphas before he came to see Claudia. It was a fortune: more than enough to get him and Claudia to Seleucia and set them up in business. He had not even had a chance to tell her about it. If she knew that he finally had the financial wherewithal to give her a semblance of the life she was accustomed to, she might not be so doubtful. But first he had a job to do. He turned into Vine Street, stopped outside a house and knocked on the door. After a few moments the door opened. Simon, whom the Master now called Peter, was standing there.

"So you've finally decided to grace us with your presence," he said.

"Shut up, Simon," said Judah and pushed past him. "Where is everyone?"

Simon nodded to the ceiling. "They're in the upper room."

Claudia snivelled all the way back to the palace. Marcus never said a word. When they arrived at the stables, Marcus lifted her down, called over some guards and instructed them to take the Lady Claudia to her quarters and to stay with her until further notice. "There has been another attempt to abduct her," said Marcus. "I'll speak to her father about it now. Is the Lord Pilate in?"

"He's not," said one of the guards. "He's at the High Priest's house on some urgent business."

"Then I shall see him when he returns." Then to Claudia: "I'm going to suggest you leave Judea after the wedding. You could stay at the villa in Pontus until I arrange for a transfer to another legion."

If he expected an answer from Claudia, he didn't get one. His voice was fading as nausea was rising in her. Claudia felt a hot wave engulf her then shooting pains in her abdomen. She staggered and reached out to steady herself. There was nothing there to hold her and she fell to the cobbles in a dead faint.

Cursing, Marcus picked her up and carried her into the palace, calling to a slave to fetch Procula Claudiana to her daughter's quarters.

"Pregnant? Your daughter's pregnant?" Marcus Gaius Sejanus was pacing up and down in an ante-chamber outside Claudia's bedroom. Procula Claudiana stood, hands on hips, staring daggers at the tribune.

"Yes, she's pregnant. How could you let this happen?"

Marcus stopped pacing. "You think it was me?"

"Of course! Who else?" But as Procula said it, realisation dawned. "Oh," she said and sat down heavily on a damask day bed.

"You didn't know?"

"I suspected that she was infatuated with someone – someone other than you – but I never thought anything had come of it. When did you find out?"

"Only tonight," Marcus lied. For some reason he could not fathom, he did not want to implicate Nebela. "I followed her to the dressmaker's shop – for her own safety – and discovered that she was not going there for a dress fitting at all."

"The dressmaker arranged it?"

"No. I don't think so. She looked just as surprised as I was when he arrived."

"And who is he?"

"His name is Judah ben Hillel. He's a Zealot. One of Barabbas' men. It seems he seduced her the first time she was abducted. And he was responsible for the so-called abduction on the night of the Saturnalia fire. Only it wasn't an abduction: Claudia went willingly."

Procula went pale. "In the name of Juno!" She threw her head back onto the arm of the day bed and breathed deeply, trying to compose herself. After a few moments she did. She sat up, her hands primly on her lap and asked: "Have you told my husband?"

"No. The Lord Pilate is dealing with urgent business at the High Priest's house."

"So he is," said Procula, her eyes flitting from side to side as she conceived a plan. "Can I ask you not to tell him?"

"Well, I don't know how long –"

"He cannot know!"

"He has a right!"

"He has a right to kill her! As *pater familias* he has the right of life and death over his daughter. And if she has brought shame to his name…"

"Pontius Pilate would never do that!"

"He might, Marcus, he might. I don't want to take the chance. Please. Just until I can figure out what to do…"

Marcus ran his hand through his hair and then sat down beside Procula. She did not comment on his familiarity. The two of them sat side by side in silence, each of them contemplating the enormity of the problem before them. Eventually Marcus spoke.

"I will still marry her. I will say the child is mine."

"Why would you do that?"

"It would be what my uncle would want me to do."

"You would raise the child as your own?"

"I would give it my name, yes. Then after a decent amount of time I will divorce her but still continue to support her and the child."

"You will divorce her? But –"

"It's my best offer. It's the best offer she will ever have." He rose then and stood over his future mother-in-law. "Think about it, Procula Claudiana."

The beautiful blonde woman looked up at him, her face awash with confusion. "Give me until the end of the Passover weekend. I need to talk to Claudia Lucretia. Agreed?"

"Agreed."

"And you won't say a word to Pontius?"

"No, I won't say a word."

"Thank you."

Claudia called out from the next room. Marcus nodded to Procula that she should respond and then left as the mother went to tend to her daughter.

*

The moon rose above the Mount of Olives. Judah had led the High Priest's assistant and his men through the Valley of Jehosophat, past the Garden of Gethsemane and beyond the tombs of the prophets onto the ridge of Olivet. The High Priest Caiphas had asked him to lead them to Jesus when he was outside the city. He feared that a public arrest on the streets of Jerusalem might have led to a riot. And that was to be avoided at all costs.

Judah knew this was Jesus' usual route. Since coming to the city, Jesus had followed it every night. He had friends in Bethany on the other side of the ridge who were supposedly putting him up over the Passover. However, Jesus frequently didn't sleep in the bed Mary, Martha and Lazarus had prepared for him but spent the night on the mountain in prayer. They were approaching his usual spot.

After the way he had been going on during the Passover meal, Judah reckoned he was intending to pray through the night. He seemed to be troubled about something and perhaps suspected that his bluff was finally going to be called. And he might also know that Judah was going to turn him in. Now that had disturbed him: that business with him and Jesus dipping the bread at the same time. Judah almost changed his mind at that point; knowing that Jesus knew he was going to betray him was almost too much to bear. Almost. But Judah's anger at the Romans and Jesus' refusal to do anything about it was too great.

Perhaps tonight Jesus would finally be provoked into unleashing the power Judah knew he had. Judah hoped so. The last thing he wanted to do was betray the prophet – he was a kind and gentle man – but that was the problem. Jesus was a lamb. Israel needed a lion. And if Judah's plan

248

came to fruition, the Lion would finally roar. And if it didn't… well, he'd work something out. He always did.

"Are you sure he's going to be here?" whispered Malchus.

There must have been around fifty priests, guards and hangers-on in the search party, all of them carrying torches, swords and cudgels, and none of them, other than Malchus, tried to be quiet. So Judah had no idea why the High Priest's assistant was whispering. Judah began to wonder if Jesus and his friends had heard them and decided to hide. It would have been out of character for Jesus, but the other lads were cowards.

"He's *probably* going to be here, I said. If he isn't, I'll take you to where he's been staying in Bethany: the house of Lazarus."

"Lazarus who supposedly rose from the dead?" asked Malchus.

"Lazarus who did rise from the dead. I saw it with my own eyes."

"I don't understand. If you're a believer, why are you turning him over to us?"

"I have my reasons."

"And you have your money," said Malchus dryly.

"Yes, I do, so let's get the job done. If he is here, it should be just around the next bend. He'll probably have some men with him. It's dark, so you might not know which one he is. I'll go up to him and kiss him so you'll know."

"All right," said Malchus.

They rounded the bend and there they were: Jesus, Simon, John and Andrew. Judah's immediate response was dismay – he had half-hoped they would have made a run for it – but then he forced himself to stick to his plan. He fixed a smile on his face and walked forward to greet them. In the torchlight Judah could see Jesus' face register deep sadness and disappointment.

"Do what you have to do and do it quickly, Judas," said Jesus quietly.

So Judah reached out and embraced him, kissing his cheek and holding him close for a moment longer than he needed to. "I'm sorry, but it's for the best," whispered Judah. "You'll see."

Then he was thrust aside as Malchus and the Temple Guards rushed forward to arrest Jesus. Suddenly there was a scream and Malchus clutched the side of his head, blood seeping through his fingers. Simon stood there with a manic look on his face, his sword drawn, ready for a fight. *Good lad*, thought Judah, ready to draw his own sword and join

Jesus' army if the insurrection was starting here and now. But he was disappointed, yet again. Jesus chastised Simon and told him to put his sword away. "Those who live by the sword will die by the sword," he said and reached out his hand and healed Malchus' ear. The posse let out a collective gasp. Malchus stood for a moment, feeling his ear and looking at the blood on his hand. But then his eyes hardened and he gave the order to lay hands on Jesus. And this time, no one came to their master's aid.

*

The Dreams of Procula Pilate

I

What's that? Over there: down that alley? A procession? A hunt? It matters not. He means nothing to me. The one who does, where is she? I still feel her, filling my belly, stretching my flesh. I'm going to burst if she doesn't leave me. I will lose myself if she does. But I still feel her, screaming her way out into the world. Flesh of my flesh, bone of my bone. We are one. The hunt has moved on. I'm running in the opposite direction. I've forgotten my sandals. The cobbles are cutting me; curses on these Jewish stones. Why can't they smooth them off like they do in Rome?

*

II

I must forget about the pain in my feet. There are more important things to think about. My child is in trouble. Why won't she come to me? Why must I chase her through these Jerusalem streets? Have I not been a good mother? Have I not loved her as I have loved my very soul? But she has gone. No, she hasn't: she's still here, running around in the same maze that I'm trapped in. I can still hear the sounds of the hunt, cutting through the night like a sacrificial knife. Who is it they are looking for? Whose blood are they trying to shed? Ah yes, now I remember, it is the one who has caused all the trouble. It is the one who has caused my child to run from the mother who gave her birth.

*

III

Bang. Bang. Bang. I am drawn by the sound. Bang. Bang. Bang. I have lost my child. She is somewhere in these Jerusalem streets; perhaps I will find her, perhaps I will not, but for now she has gone. I have found

250

something else. I cannot yet see it, but I can hear: bang, bang, bang. It is not the sound of iron on iron. Or iron on wood: although there is both iron and wood. It is the sound I hear when I pass the kitchens in the palace: the sound of iron, cutting through flesh and into the board below. Bang. Bang. Bang. It is getting closer, or am I closer to it? If I just go a little further up this street perhaps I will see it.

*

IV

The banging is inside my head. Nails are being driven into my skull. I must make it stop. Only when it stops will I find my daughter again. Where should I go? What should I do? I will ask this soldier: an officer, a tribune, I think. He is talking to a girl – a slave – I cannot see her face. I ask: "Sir, where can I go to stop the banging? Who can I ask to make it go away?" He points to a hill above the city: a rubbish dump with three crosses on it. I thank him. He turns his face to me. It is Marcus Gaius Sejanus, but he does not recognise me. He does not smile. I wonder why. Am I not properly dressed? Perhaps it is my bleeding feet; it does not matter. I pass a tree with a corpse hanging from it: it is a young man, his contorted face strangely familiar. But I do not stop to stare. I climb the hill until I am at the foot of the centre-most cross. A man is nailed to it: a Jewish man. His blood drips upon my head. "What do you want, Procula?" he asks. "I want this banging to stop?" I say. "Is that all?" he asks again. "No, I want my daughter to return to me." His smile touches me without hands. "Then find me, follow me, have faith in me." "But where will I find you?" I ask, as his blood runs down my face, obscuring my vision. When the blood clears he is gone, but the question still remains.

Chapter 45 – The Passover Lamb

Pontius Pilate woke at the third cock crow. Was it morning already? It was only a few hours ago that he had fallen exhausted into bed next to his sleeping wife. Procula still slept next to him. She was twitching and mumbling; no doubt having another of her dreams. They had started again the night after John the Baptist was killed. He was beginning to think he needed to send her away from Judea – there was something here that disturbed her; and his daughter too. He resolved to write to the Emperor after Passover and request a transfer to another province.

But first he had to get through Passover. Pilate felt sick to his stomach thinking about it. After what he had been through last night he did not want to deal with the ceremonial release of the Passover Lamb. How in Jupiter's name had it become the job of the Roman governor to participate in the Jews' religious pantomime? If he wasn't able to get a transfer next year he was damned sure he would not be doing this again.

On the other hand, it might be an opportunity to release the so-called King of the Jews. This Jesus might have delusions of grandeur, but he was harmless, of that Pilate was sure. He certainly wasn't guilty of all the things the priests would have him believe. Pilate could simply not understand the vitriol with which they had presented the prophet to him last night demanding he pass a sentence of death.

But there was something about Jesus; something immensely compelling… Pilate could see why people followed him. But followed him towards what? A revolution of healing, peace and love? For that, as far as Pilate could see, was all the man had done.

But the Sanhedrin would have none of it. When he was told that Antipas had come to town – Jupiter help him when Procula heard that! – he decided to pass the buck and hand him over to the tetrarch. He was, after all, a Galilean, and so technically came under Antipas' jurisdiction. Pilate hoped he would do the right thing; although his track record with holy men was not very encouraging. The important thing was that it was no longer his decision. He could not be blamed one way or another for what happened to Jesus. But Pilate suspected that Antipas would simply pass the buck back.

Procula was waking up. Pilate wrapped his arms around her and kissed her. "Good morning, my darling."

"Is it a good morning? I hope so. I had that terrible dream again: about the crucified man. But this time I think I know who it is: it's that holy man from Galilee. The one everyone is talking about."

"It might be," said Pilate, intrigued and wanting to know more, but not wanting to encourage his wife to dwell on her nightmares.

"You are the only one who can order crucifixions, aren't you?"

"Yes."

"Then that's all right then. It's simple: don't order it, Pontius. He's someone special."

"The King of the Jews?"

"Oh, far more special than that," said Procula and yawned, snuggling up to him. "Promise me you won't allow him to be crucified."

"I promise I will try," he said; but felt a dark cloud of foreboding edge towards the morning sun.

*

The crowd had been gathering on the Gabattha since first light. Judah found a spot on the Temple steps with a good view of proceedings. He had not slept at all last night, desperately worried that his plan to provoke Jesus to action would fail. He had had so many chances already and the healing of Malchus' ear did not bode well.

However, the rage that he had felt for the last week seemed to have dissipated overnight; as if some demon that had been haunting him had decided to leave. Now all that was left was a dark sense of foreboding and unbearable sadness.

If Jesus wasn't going to save himself then there was only one thing to hope for: that Claudia's father would release him as the symbolic Passover Lamb. As was the custom, once a year the Roman governor was asked to release a condemned prisoner as a symbolic gesture representing the way YHWH had ameliorated the death sentence on the first born of the Israelites in Egypt. Why a Roman was given this power of life and death Judah could not fathom. But on previous days when the thought would have provoked him to rage, it just added to his deep sadness. If he had had a chance he would have asked Claudia to petition her father. But he doubted he would ever see her again.

As he had walked the streets last night he had come to terms with a number of things: firstly, that he had been wrong to turn Jesus over; secondly, that even if Jesus had misled him into believing he was the Messiah, he did not deserve to die; and thirdly, that he and Claudia Lucretia Pilate were destined to never be together. Well, never with her parents' blessing. He could not do that to her. He loved her too much. So he had attempted to return the money to Caiphas last night. He had not been able to get into the High Priest's house while Jesus' trial was underway, but he had managed to speak to Malchus. The man had just laughed at him and sent him away. *Blood money.* That's what it was. Judah had been mad to take it in the first place.

Judah watched as Pilate took his seat on the Gabattha on an ornately carved ceremonial stool. He was joined, on his left, by his wife, Procula Claudiana. But the stool on his right – reserved for Claudia Lucretia – remained empty. *No doubt they have locked her up in case she runs off again with a dirty Jew*, thought Judah with resignation.

"Hoping to see your girlfriend again?" asked a voice behind him. Judah turned to see his cousin Simeon. The bearded woodcutter took a seat on the steps beside him.

"No. I'm hoping to see Jesus of Nazareth. And you?"

"My father," said Simeon; the anger in his voice barely restrained.

"Barabbas? He's here?" Judah looked around for his uncle.

"They captured him two days ago. Some bastard turned him in. What people will do for money," he said and spat on the marble steps.

There was a festival atmosphere in the crowd; it sickened Judah. But in between he spotted some of Jesus' followers, mainly the women, but a few men too. There was John, supporting Jesus' mother Mary, and alongside him James, the Master's younger brother. And there was that woman Zandra – Nebela's mother – with the old whore from Magdala. They were both crying quietly. But most of the so-called disciples were absent, no doubt fearing they too would be arrested and condemned.

Judah did not fear arrest. His betrayal of Jesus had ensured that. Nonetheless, he wore a cloak and kept the hood up as he feared being turned on by the Master's friends and followers. For now they were focused on Pilate and the judgment seat.

Pilate, who had been joined on the platform by Caiphas and some of the other members of the Sanhedrin, stood up and gave a short speech about the benefits of Roman rule and the value of the 'partnership' between him and the Jewish leaders. He declared that they all wanted the same thing: peace. Nothing should be allowed to disturb it. He then announced that two men had recently been accused of that very thing: Jesus and Barabbas. He asked for them to be led forward.

The crowd let out a mutual gasp as Barabbas entered, as it were, from stage left and Jesus from stage right. Both men looked like they had been tortured. Both men had to be supported. Then Pilate asked Tribune Sejanus to read out the list of charges against Barabbas. It was long and they included murder, rape, abduction, brigandry, attacking Roman outposts, stirring up insurrection and finally: disturbing the peace. The crowd booed. Judah wasn't sure whether they were booing Barabbas or the charges.

Then Sejanus was asked to read out the charges against Jesus. They included threats to destroy the Temple, pretending to be a king, refusal to worship the Emperor as a god, and finally: claiming to be the Son of God. The crowd booed again.

Judah was now standing, his hood dropped and all efforts to disguise his identity gone. His heart was racing. There before him stood his life: his past life and his present; there was no future. One man was his uncle, the other his Master and friend. He had followed both of them in the hope of freeing Israel, avenging his mother and saving himself. Neither of them had delivered.

Pilate raised his hands for silence. The crowd's roar subsided to a mumble. He reminded them – as if they needed reminding – of the custom of the release of a condemned prisoner as a symbol of the Passover Lamb. He declared that only Barabbas had been condemned both by the Sanhedrin and the Roman court. Then he said:

"But Jesus has done nothing worthy of death."

The crowd let out a gasp. His wife nodded beside him. But Caiphas and the priests quickly surrounded him and whispered. Judah could not hear what they were saying but by their body language it was a heated discussion. This time Caiphas stepped forward, raised his arms and declared in a booming voice:

"This man is guilty of blasphemy against the most High God! Let his blood be on us and our children!"

The crowd roared.

Pilate, shaking his head, again stepped forward. "So, people of Jerusalem, you have a choice. Do I release an innocent man who has done nothing deserving of death, or a rebel and murderer who has terrorised this land for years." He reached out his hands as if to pass the decision to them. "The choice is yours."

Beside Judah, Simeon began to chant: "Ba-ra-bbas! Ba-ra-bbas!" Then those near him took up the chant and it began to ripple through the crowd, gaining momentum, until it crashed onto the podium at the front. Caiphas shrugged at Pilate as if to say: "Sorry, the people have spoken. Are you going to ignore it?"

Procula, now standing, was tugging on the sleeve of her husband's toga. He shook her off and stepped forward again. The crowd quietened to hear what he was going to say. "Bring me a basin of water."

A slave was hurriedly dispatched and returned with some water and a towel. The crowd held their breath as the drama unfolded. Even Barabbas raised his head to see what was happening. But Jesus did not. His chin was on his chest and he was muttering to himself: *praying to his Father,* thought Judah. *A Father who will not help him.*

Pilate washed his hands and then dried them. He passed the towel to Caiphas. The High Priest took it.

"This man has done nothing wrong," said Pilate. "But, as has been pointed out to me, the people have made their choice. And this is a Jewish custom that should be decided by Jews. Indeed, let his blood be on you and your children. Crucify him."

Then all Hades broke out. Simeon ran forward to get to his father, fighting his way through the crowd. Jesus was taken off by some soldiers. Judah stood rooted to the spot, tears streaming down his face. His last hope was gone and there was only one thing that was now certain: he was beyond redemption. He had killed an innocent man. He reached under his cloak and took out his money bag. He opened it and held the thirty pieces of silver in his hands. Then he turned, slowly, and as a man condemned, walked up the Temple steps. When he reached the top he turned once more to see if he could catch a glimpse of Jesus. But he was gone. He took the coins in both fists and threw them into the Temple then he turned and ran as fast as he could away from the madness to the place where he knew it would end.

Chapter 46 – The Potter's Field

Claudia Lucretia Pilate had been watching proceedings on the Gabattha from her bedroom window. It was compelling viewing, and even Judith and the guards tasked with protecting her, had slipped away to watch. Claudia was all alone. She watched enough of the drama to know who was who and what was at stake and wondered whether Judah was in the crowd. Would he be there to watch the puppet Messiah be condemned or released? Claudia hoped he would be released, not because she believed in him, but that his release would mean Barabbas' conviction. She hated the man for how he had brutalised Judah and caused her and her family to live in terror. Jesus, on the other hand, had done nothing to her: apart from being a rival for her lover's affections. But that was not his fault.

She so desperately wanted to tell Judah about the baby. Their baby. She had been feeling unwell for the last couple of months and had suspected something might be amiss, but she had not had her suspicions confirmed until yesterday when her mother assessed her symptoms and declared that she was indeed pregnant. She had not mentioned her suspicions to Judah because she wanted to test his loyalty to her first. If he could not be loyal to her without a baby, what difference would a child make? She wanted him to choose her out of love, not guilt.

But was any of that possible any more? Had their discovery by Marcus Gaius scuppered their chances of being together once and for all? She feared so. No, she knew so. Her future was now with Marcus. He had told her mother that he would still marry her. It was more than she could ask.

But then, as she watched the trial on the pavement below her, she spotted something at the back of the crowd, on the Temple steps. It was a good distance away, but there was something in the way the man moved that was familiar. Then, as the whole crowd surged forward after her father announced that Jesus was to be crucified, she saw the man turn and walk up the Temple steps. That walk… that build… that cloak… it could only be Judah. She looked to the sky and saw that it was nearly midday. *Meet me at the Potter's Field at noon…* Claudia picked up her cloak and slipped out of the palace by a back door.

Procula was furious with Pilate. She refused to talk to him and stormed off the platform as soon as Jesus was sentenced to be crucified. She tried to catch the prophet's eye, to communicate to him that she had no part in it, but his back was turned. Perhaps she would see him again in a dream... her dream... was this all inevitable? If Jesus was indeed to be crucified, what did that mean for her forebodings of Claudia's death? Her heart lurched as she looked up to her daughter's bedroom window. She must check on her. She signalled to Marcus to follow her. He asked Pilate's permission who gave it absent-mindedly.

Together, Procula and Marcus entered the palace. They did not speak of Jesus, they did not have to; they both knew he was an innocent man and that a great travesty had just taken place. Procula would consider the implications of that later, but first she needed to see if Claudia was safe.

Procula shared her concerns about Claudia, telling Marcus that she had seen today's events in a dream. She also told him that in her dream he had been the one to point her to her missing daughter.

Marcus was not convinced but played along to humour her. It was also a welcome distraction from what was going on outside. He did not want to have any further personal involvement with carrying out Jesus' sentence.

When they arrived outside Claudia's quarters and saw the door was wide open and the room empty, Procula clasped her hand to her mouth. "It's happening, Marcus, just like in my dream. Where will she be? You're supposed to know."

"She could be anywhere! I haven't seen her today. I have no idea... I..."

"What?"

"I just remembered something... when I was eavesdropping on Claudia and the Zealot at the dressmaker's shop, before I attempted to arrest him, I heard him ask her to meet him at the Potter's Field at noon today."

"The Potter's Field? Do you think that's where she is?"

"I don't know. But it's all I can think of. Can you ride, Lady Procula?"

"I can."

"Then let's get to the stables."

*

258

Claudia arrived at the Potter's Field and dismounted. She had managed to procure a horse while the stable slaves and guards were busy gawping at Jesus being taken away. The field was on the outskirts of the City of David. It was more of an open-cast clay pit than a field. It was where the potters of the city collected material for their pots and was very close to the southern Huldah Gate. Claudia could see why Judah had chosen this as their meeting place. It would be very easy to slip out of the gate unnoticed and soon be on the road to Qumran.

The earth was claggy underfoot and recent rains had created blood-red pools of sediment. Claudia picked up her skirts and picked her way through the pit, looking for her lover. If he wasn't there she would know once and for all that it was over. But if he was…

Something caught her eye. She looked up and saw a shadow hanging from a tree whose roots were clutching the edge of the clay pit like the cold hand that clutched her heart. She ran towards it, fearing what she would find, but knowing she had to see for herself. Behind her, someone was calling her name.

*

Procula and Marcus were having difficulty getting their mounts through the city streets. At every turn there was a crowd streaming towards the execution site of Golgotha like flies swarming towards a dead dog. A couple of times they intersected the head of the procession: Jesus was carrying his crossbar, barely able to stand. Procula and Marcus could not save him, but they could save Claudia if they hurried. They pulled their horses around, and rode in another direction. Finally, as the gruesome procession advanced, the roads in the City of David cleared, and they found a way through. As they arrived at the Potter's Field they saw a saddled horse, grazing on the sparse grass on the edge of the pit. Marcus jumped down and helped Procula do the same.

And there, across the field, picking her way through bloody pools of clay was Claudia. Procula called out to her, but she did not turn back.

*

Claudia moved closer and closer to the hanging shadow. By now the sun was at its zenith. She squinted and looked up into the face of Judah, grotesquely distorted in death. She screamed and threw her arms around his legs trying to lift him. He was too heavy. And then she saw his sword, lying on the ground next to his cloak; the singed cloak. She clutched it to her and inhaled him. Then falling to her knees she picked up his sword and pointed it at her heart.

"Don't my darling, don't!" It was Procula. She knelt down beside her daughter and clasped her hand over Claudia's on the hilt of the sword.

"He's gone, mother. He didn't even wait for me."

"I know, I know. I saw it in my dream. Oh, I wish you'd told me about it. I could have helped you. Please, Claudia Lucretia, don't leave me. I need you to stay with me. Think about me and your father. Think about the baby."

The baby. Judah's baby. It was now all that was left of him. Claudia collapsed into her mother's arms and sobbed. Procula wrested the sword from her and passed it to Marcus. He took it and as the two women wept at his feet he cut down the corpse of Judah ben Hillel, who would become known to the world as Judas Iscariot.

Chapter 47 – The Third Day

Tribune Marcus Gaius Sejanus decided to call it a day. There were search parties all over the city and beyond. If the body of Jesus had been stolen, as had been reported to the Antonia that morning, Marcus was sure they would find it. As sunset settled over Jerusalem and its sandstone and marble warmed to a golden glow, he stopped by the market on the edge of the New City. He paused at a stall and selected half a dozen apples, sniffing each one to ascertain its freshness and sweetness. He had always loved the smell of apples.

Munching on one of them, he found his way to Oyster Street. The spice merchant called to him, announcing some new exotic stock from the East; the oyster merchant told him the fresh catch would only be in tomorrow, but if the tribune paid now he would personally ensure they were delivered to his barracks… Marcus waved them both away.

At the dressmaker's shop, Zandra was sweeping the front patio to clear the fallen magnolia petals that drifted down from the rooftop garden. She was singing quietly to herself. It sounded like a lament.

"Hello, Zandra."

She looked up, her eyes filled with sadness.

"She's inside. But don't go in unless you plan to stay."

"That's for me to decide."

She inhaled sharply and took to her sweeping with more vigour.

"I heard you spent some time with Jesus," said Marcus.

"I did. I wanted to thank him for bringing Nebela back to us. To me."

"You did a good thing. I never had the chance. It was a sad thing that happened to him."

"Yes."

"And now some fool has gone and stolen the body."

Zandra stopped sweeping and stared at him, her veil falling from her head onto her shoulders. Marcus had never noticed before how much alike Zandra and Nebela were. Before him, he realised, was what Nebela would look like in fifteen or twenty years. She was beautiful.

"How do you know?" asked Zandra. "How do you know the body has been stolen?"

"I've been looking for it all day. It was reported to the Antonia early this morning. Apparently some women went to the tomb in Gethsemane to finish dressing the body and discovered that the stone had been rolled away and the body was gone." He laughed. "They claimed to have seen an angel which told them Jesus had been raised from the dead and was alive... but..." He laughed again.

But Zandra wasn't laughing. She put her broom in the corner and pulled up her scarf. "Tell Nebela where I've gone." Then she rushed off down the street, not acknowledging the greetings of the oyster and spice merchants.

"Mother!" a voice called from inside the shop.

"She's gone," said Marcus and stepped over the threshold.

Nebela stood in a pool of late afternoon sunshine, her raven black hair cascading down her back. Marcus would never forget the saffron dress she wore – the colour worn by Roman brides – with magnolia blossoms embroidered on the bodice. She was pinning the shoulder of a blue silk gown onto a mannequin in the centre of the shop.

"Marcus!" she said, then winced as she pricked herself. She sucked the bead of blood from her finger and looked at him suspiciously. "What do you want?"

"I needed to see you."

"A final farewell before you get married? I don't think so."

She picked up the mannequin with the heel of her hands, careful not to get any blood on the fabric, and placed it in a corner of the room. Then she turned to face Marcus. "I will not be your second port of call after Claudia Lucretia Pilate."

"I know."

"Then why are you here?"

He unhooked his sword belt, took off his helmet and cloak, and sank onto one of the couches usually occupied by well-to-do ladies of Jerusalem. He patted the seat beside him. Nebela did not move.

"Claudia is pregnant."

Nebela's eyes widened but she didn't say anything.

"The Zealot is the father. But he's dead. He killed himself."

Nebela still said nothing, but Marcus thought he saw a shadow pass over her face.

"I have offered to still marry her. On the terms I discussed with my uncle. But Procula Claudiana is not happy that I'm proposing a divorce in advance even though I've promised to still support Claudia and the child who will bear my name."

This time Nebela smirked.

"So, she's spoken to Pilate. She's very angry with him about passing the death sentence on Jesus. Apparently he promised her he wouldn't and now needs to make it up to her. She's told him Claudia was raped when she was abducted at Saturnalia and has been too ashamed to tell them of the pregnancy. She said the father is one of the Zealots; she doesn't know which one. She hasn't told him about the affair. As Claudia Lucretia is being cast as the victim rather than the willing participant, Pilate is sympathetic. He understands that I can't be expected to marry a ruined girl but was greatly appreciative that I had offered to do so."

"How noble of you, Marcus."

Marcus ignored the sarcasm and continued. "But now a counter offer has been made. Claudia and Procula will leave Judea immediately. No one other than her parents, you and I know about the pregnancy. They will go to a secret location until Claudia gives birth. Then they will return. But –" he looked to see if Nebela was really interested to hear what he was going to say next. She appeared to be, so he continued, "– they will say the child is Procula's. Pilate has always wanted a second child. Procula is not too old – she's still in her late thirties, I think – and they will say that the child was conceived in the joy of having her restored to health by the Baptist. They have of course sworn me to secrecy."

"Of course," said Nebela, and sat down beside him, on the very edge of the couch, her body facing forwards. "And you are here to ensure that I will keep the secret too."

"Yes." He reached out to take her hand, but she withdrew it. He sighed and continued.

"Pilate and I had a man to man talk and he told me that in return for my silence he would release me from the terms of our engagement. Unless of course I still wanted to marry Claudia –"

"And do you?" Nebela had turned her body towards him, her eyes showing a glimmer of hope for the first time.

"It's what my uncle wants. He still needs the money and he still needs the blood connections."

"Ah," said Nebela, the hope fading from her amber eyes.

Marcus reached out and took her hand firmly in his, not letting her pull away this time.

"But I think it's time I made a decision for myself. And my decision, Nebela, is that I don't want to marry Claudia Lucretia. I want to marry you."

Nebela gasped and threw herself at him. He wrapped his arms around her and held her close. He felt her heart beating as fast as a sparrow's against his.

"But – but – what about your uncle?"

He sighed into her hair, breathing in the smell of apples. "I will still need to go to Rome to speak to him. Pilate has offered me a hundred and twenty five thousand sesterces – that's a quarter of the proposed dowry – for my trouble. I'll see if that will keep him happy."

"And if it doesn't?"

"Then I'll come up with the money another way. I can't spend my life being dictated to by him, Nebela."

"No, Marcus, you can't." Then she reached out and pulled his mouth to hers. All the words had been spoken. There was nothing more she needed to hear.

*

A Dream of Procula Pilate

The waves are lapping against the side of the boat. I am standing in the stern, looking out over the sea. Behind me is Caesarea, before me is Pontus or Ephesus or Rome. I do not know where this journey will end. But beside me is Claudia, my beautiful daughter, finally returned to me by the crucified man. I must still thank him. I hope I will see him again. But for now my belly is swelling. Inside me a child grows.

AUTHOR'S NOTE

Every year around Easter I read the gospel story of the run-up to the death of Jesus. As a person of faith, it's a story both personal and familiar to me. However, as I am also a historical novelist and trained journalist I started looking at the story from a different perspective. I began to notice 'walk-on' characters, such as Pilate's wife, and allowed my mind to wander into her motives and back story. What particularly struck me was the dream she said she had had and how she tried to warn her husband not to condemn Jesus. Why was she having these dreams? Had she had any others? And more importantly for me, who was she? Who was her husband? Did they have any children? Did they have a 'life' outside of their role in the Jesus story?

I started reading novels set against the same backdrop – or the same period – that were not necessarily written from the traditional Christian perspective. I began to consider what it might have been like for people who were not 'followers of Jesus' but lived at the same time.

Then I began to conceive of writing my own novel and wondered what I could do that was fresh and unique to me. As I am a huge fan of Roman historical novels I wanted to write something in that tradition – a Roman book that intersected with the Jesus story – but in the end remained a Roman not a 'Christian' novel. It was then I came across a fantastic book by Ann Wroe on the life of Pontius Pilate (Wroe, Ann *Pilate: the biography of an invented man*, Vintage, London, 2000). It was there I discovered that Pilate's wife's name was not recorded in any historical records but that the early church traditionally referred to her as Procula, Claudia or Claudia Procula. The apocryphal *Gospel of Nicodemus* (alternatively known as *The Acts of Pilate*, circa 4th Century AD) names her as Claudia Procula (which is where I derive my name for her, Procula Claudiana). The Eastern Orthodox Church lists St Procula as one of their saints, with her feast day on 27 October. No children are mentioned in historical sources; but nor is it mentioned that they did not have any… Hence I felt free to invent Claudia Lucretia, the fictional protagonist of this story.

The character of Judah ben Hillel is completely made up and is my attempt to explore a possible back story for the man known in the Gospels as Judas Iscariot. Some historians believe that Judas might have been a Zealot and/or an assassin before he met Jesus, as the name Iscariot may come from the word *Iscarii*. The Iscarii or Sicarii were a group of assassins in the first century renowned for carrying small daggers in their cloaks to be used in close-quarter assassinations.

As with my other historical novels I blend fact and fiction and, to the best of my ability, have endeavoured to get the facts right. Rather than listing what is 'true' and what is 'made up' here, I would suggest readers interested in the period do their own research – I'm sure you'll find it as fascinating as I did.

And finally a note on the dating: this story starts in 28AD. According to the few historical records available, Pontius Pilate is believed to have started his prefectureship in 26 or 27AD. However, as I needed my story to intersect with the timeline of Jesus of Nazareth, I have the family arriving in 28AD. (Pilate may very well have arrived in advance of his family, and brought them over later.) Regarding the timeline of Jesus, there is no historical consensus on exactly when he was crucified, but it is believed to be between 30 and 33AD. However, some theorists suggest it might have been closer to the beginning of Pilate's prefectureship, as early, perhaps, as 27AD. This lack of a fixed date for the crucifixion has allowed me some flexibility. So, with creative licence, I have placed it in the spring of 29AD; but readers should not take this as historical 'fact'. In addition, the more eagle-eyed of you may note that Lake Tiberias is spelt with an 'a' but the Emperor Tiberius with a 'u'. This is the correct spelling, not an editorial error.

My thanks, as always, go to my wonderfully supportive husband and daughter. And a huge thanks, too, to my publishers, Endeavour Press, who have breathed new life into *Pilate's Daughter*.

Printed in Great Britain
by Amazon